I0647543

The
Himmler
Stratagem

Cordell Cross

REVISED ISBN 978-0-9696248-8-2

The Himmler Stratagem ©
By Cordell Cross
© Revised Copyright 2011
Vanbrugh Management Ltd.

All rights reserved. No part of this publication may be reproduced or transmitted in any form or by any means without the prior consent of:

Vanbrugh Publishing
A Division of Vanbrugh Management Ltd.
PO Box 73038
Evergreen RO
Surrey, B.C., Canada V3R 0J2

E-mail vanbrugh@telus.net

Cover Design – Jana Siller – japla2003@yahoo.ca

Website – Mark Siller – f2marksiller@gmail.com

"There aren't enough tears to shed for those who died in the camps, and history must continue to remind us of that. Then when I asked a high school student if he had learned of Hitler's atrocities, he replied, 'Who's Hitler?' So much for history."

G. Samuel Kare (1924–2000)

DEDICATION

For Mary, William, and Norman.

Also for Sparkie, a grand old swaybacked horse no one wanted but me. I really miss you pal. While we slowly walked everywhere with Mr. Chips, a Bassett Hound buddy, old Sparkie always listened while I discussed my books. There were times he would give me weird looks as if to say we covered that yesterday. Please, not again. Move on my friend move on. In the meantime, I'm gonna munch on some grass.

And Gordon Cassie Cunningham, a boyhood chum, who added laughter, and stock market hope to the lives of thousands. He wanted to buy the first copy of The Himmler Stratagem. We all miss you, Gord.

Cordell Cross

ACKNOWLEDGMENTS

My thanks to Kenneth D. Gourley for his excellent research and advice.

Thanks also to Jana Siller for her exceptional cover design, and Mark Siller, the ultimate creator of websites.

Special thanks to Brian Harwood, and to Edward Asner, one of the world's finest actors. Ed, I think you are undoubtedly the best of the best.

PRELUDE

BERLIN, GERMANY - 1943

"What is it, Bormann?"

"Mein Fuehrer, SS Reichsfuehrer Himmler is here as you ordered."

Adolf Hitler signed a letter and without looking up casually handed it to the officer standing to his left. "Have this distributed immediately, and send in the Reichsfuehrer."

Clicking his heels, Hitler's adjutant asked, "Will there be anything else, Mein Fuehrer?"

"Yes, bring in some tea and cakes."

Moments later, Martin Bormann held the door open for an anxious-looking black-uniformed SS officer of medium height and weight stiffly marching into the huge opulent room. After halting, Heinrich Himmler presented the German leader with the Nazi salute. "You sent for me, Mein Fuehrer?"

Hitler's face lit up seeing his old comrade. Standing and stepping out from behind his mammoth desk he picked up a black-leather dossier embossed with the SS insignia. Shaking the Reichsfuehrer's hand and guiding him to a particular table, the German leader asked, "How have you been? Come and sit down, Heinrich, my friend."

Blinking nervously, Himmler sat on a comfortable chair at a square polished oak table near a window. Adolf Hitler sat opposite him then laid the folder down.

"You look tired, Heinrich. Perhaps you need a holiday."

"I am a little weary," the bespectacled officer said, trying hard to control his eye movements. "But I have no time for such things. There is too much to do, Mein Fuehrer; we are transporting over…"

The German Chancellor's amiable facial expression immediately turned wickedly remote and all signs of civility disappeared as he shouted, "I don't want to hear that! You do what we have agreed to do!"

Himmler flinched and his eyes stopped blinking. Tensely moving his neck around the inside of his collar, he timidly murmured, "Yes, Mein Fuehrer!"

Only the adjutant's knuckles tapping on the immense door defused Hitler's fierce frozen stare. As Bormann placed a silver tray in the centre of the table, the German leader's *sociable* side returned.

"Help yourself, Heinrich," Hitler said holding a pastry to his nose.

"I am rather good at guessing whether or not these are made with butter. You may leave us, Bormann."

"Thank you Mein Fuehrer," Bormann replied, clicking his heels and turning around. As he marched away only the chafing sounds of his taut grey uniform cut the room's silence.

"Where was I? Oh yes, I remember. Heinrich, we've been together for a long time. There are *matters* of which only you and I are aware. Are you still seeing that masseur? Oh what is his name ... Felix Kersten?"

The SS leader's eyes began blinking again. "Er, yes, he is also my doctor. His touch relieves my..."

"I didn't ask for an explanation, my friend," Hitler said, cautiously sipping his hot tea. "I know you too well. How you get your needs taken care of is your business. I do of course trust his visits are ... discreet?"

"Totally, Mein Fuehrer."

"Good, good. The ethical principles of our party must always be foremost in the minds of the German people. You're not drinking your tea, Heinrich?"

Upon hearing, "Tea keeps me awake, Mein Fuehrer," Hitler chortled while selecting another cake. "Everything seems to keep you awake, Heinrich. Nevertheless, in 1928, when I agreed to your fund-raising plans, you carried your robberies off just as cleverly as your blackmailing techniques. Even today, Germany's sexual deviates pay dearly, not knowing we are involved. Are many left?"

A faint grin crept over Himmler's neurotic face as his lips formed the words, "The pink ones?"

"Of course, homosexuals, paedophiles, prostitutes, and ... *the others*."

"The ones we *need* still remain with us, Mein Fuehrer. We provide them with suitable, er, *partners*. You would be surprised to learn who takes pleasure in..."

The Fuehrer became passionless and irritable again. Flicking a crumb off his tunic, he uncrossed his legs and raised his voice. "Don't bother me with your ever incessant lists of names, Heinrich. Are the appropriate participants Jews?"

Himmler's body tightened again. "Jews, Slavs, inferior races, Mein Fuehrer. And it isn't just limited to them, it is quite…"

The German leader did not allow his SS chief to finish. "Good, good. And how much money are we raising?"

"Millions, Mein Fuehrer. Of all our enterprises, it's our most lucrative endeavour."

The chancellor's eyes gleamed as he eagerly slapped his right thigh. "And who is responsible for the organized network throughout Germany and our conquered lands? As well placed as he is, can he be eliminated quickly if need be?"

Himmler nodded and his eyes shared the impassiveness of his sly grin. "Gustaf Schtaff, Mein Fuehrer. Schtaff is a fine young officer, extremely intelligent, and takes pride in his work. The administrative cells of his organization will last a thousand years. Our plan is foolproof, and our Swiss bank accounts grow daily. As we speak, Schtaff is in New York planning the network with our American overseer who was born in Germany."

"Yes, I see that such matters have been initiated," Hitler murmured guardedly. "How can this happen without my final approval?"

The Reichsfuehrer swallowed rapidly before clearing his throat. "Er, perhaps I was too hasty in presuming you would...?"

A slow spreading grin turned into a loud laugh as Adolf Hitler stood up quickly and grabbed the black leather dossier. Slapping his right thigh with the folder again before handing it to the SS leader, he said, "I've read this thoroughly, Heinrich; it's brilliant, exactly what we need, and I congratulate you. Has work started in Paraguay, and at the bunker tunnel?"

"Yes, Mein Fuehrer."

"Good. I'm glad those *matters* are in hand ... not that we'll need them."

Himmler had already jumped to his feet when his idol stood. Puffing out his chest, he said, "Then you approve expanding the second phase of the project into England and North and South America, Mein Fuehrer? You have authorized the Werwulfe Project?"

The German leader put his right arm around Himmler's shoulders. "I'd be a fool not to, wouldn't I, my friend? Destroy that document, Heinrich. It will never be read again, or found for that matter. You can use the code word *Werwulfe*, but I'll refer to it as *The Himmler Stratagem*." Sharply turning away, he added, "Thank you, you're dismissed. Give my regards to your family."

As the Nazi dictator walked back to his desk, the SS Reichsfuehrer presented his leader with the Nazi salute before turning and marching towards the door. His hand had barely touched the doorknob when Hitler casually asked, "Heinrich, is it true what I'm hearing about you and blond blue-eyed boys at the Russian Front?"

Himmler did not turn around so the Fuehrer did not see his Reichsfuehrer's lips and throat dry up when he winced. Quickly licking his lips and clearing his parched throat, Himmler said, "Not one word of it is true, Mein Fuehrer."

"Good. So when are you arranging to initiate the second phase of The Himmler Stratagem?"

The black-uniformed man spun around sharply. Standing at attention, he proudly stated, "At once, Mein Fuehrer."

"Do you really believe your plans will last a thousand years, like the Third Reich?"

Saluting again, Heinrich Himmler replied, "No, the World Reich will last much longer. Heil Hitler!"

"And what is the name of our American *administrator*."

"He was christened Dieter Krueger, but of course his identity has changed. Do you wish to know his current name?"

"No, that will not be necessary. Goodbye."

Adolf Hitler sat thinking for a moment before pressing an intercom button.

"Bormann, find out what information we have on a young SS officer by the name of Gustaf Schtaff, and an ex German national named Dieter Krueger?"

Twenty-five minutes later, Martin Bormann entered the Chancellor's office. After closing the door behind him, he said, "We have absolutely nothing on either man, Mein Fuehrer. They do not appear to exist."

The German leader's eyes shone while his right hand waved his adjutant away. "Excellent. You may go, Bormann."

Chapter 1

SEATTLE WASHINGTON. A DAY IN THE PAST.

Detective Sergeant Joe Stacy did not mind the rain, but he hated not being dressed for it, and not being picked up on time. Standing in front of Seattle's SeaTac airport for forty-five minutes was not exactly how his Hawaiian Christmas holiday was supposed to end. His three-week rest was just what he needed, but damn it, his partner Pete Durnell had promised to meet him.

Checking his pocket-watch again, Stacy was just about to pick up his bags and head for the phones when he heard a car's horn and saw Pete waving a hand.

"What the hell happened to you?" Joe asked, throwing his luggage into the back seat before joining his grinning co-worker in the front. "Here it is pissing down, and I'm walking around freezing my balls off in a flowered shirt and a pair of shorts. People around here must think I'm nuts."

Pete's smile faded as he drove away. "Hey, is that any way to treat a friend who's been stuck in traffic for two hours? Even for a Sunday night, the roads are like hell. There have been three major accidents between here and Seattle, so I'm taking the secondary route back. Besides, lookin' at your tan, I'm the one who should be complaining. While you've been wining and dining the broads, I've been carryin' our case-loads."

Stacy ignored his co-worker and locked his eyes on the passing festive lights adorning most houses and business establishments. Christmas was not far away, and even in the rain, the illumination created a warm relaxed feeling.

"Well, I know you took third place in the jitterbug contest, but did you get lucky?" asked Pete.

Joe's mouth formed a small grin. For some reason, he could never stay mad at Pete. His partner had the unique knack of changing the subject. A few years back when Pete was assigned to work with him, Joe thought his new partner was far too young. It did not take long for him to realize age didn't count - brains and guts did, and the man sitting next to him had more than an abundant supply of both.

"Classical waltzing isn't jitterbugging, you uncultivated simpleton," Joe said, his expression imitating a tired old school teacher about to answer a stupid question. "I could have taken second, and I would have, had my partner not had two left feet. How did you learn I took third spot?"

"It made the local papers. Someone cut the article out and put it on the bulletin board. Even the captain said, 'Our own Mr. Twinkletoes is becoming famous.'"

Stacy's chin climbed two inches higher. "I can't help it if I'm good. Who was it that suggested I should go to the Big Island at this time of year, anyway?"

Durnell took his eyes off the road for a moment and glanced at the now beaming man sitting next to him. "I did, because you could catch some sun and hone in on your *dancing skills*. Jesus, I hate the sound of those two words. Most police officers take up boxing, golf, tennis, handball, or other manly sports, but not you, not Joe Stacy; you've gotta go one better and take up friggin' ballroom dancing. I'm askin' for a transfer if you start wearin' a tutu."

Stacy paid no attention to his associate's ranting. He had heard it all before. A year back, all employees in the detachment had split their guts when he mentioned his new pastime.

"Jealousy, my boy, will get you nowhere," Joe said, staring straight ahead at the metronome windshield wipers. "I've done all those things. Just look at you, you're thirty pounds overweight and still putting on the tonnage. Dancing got rid of my paunch, didn't it? I've got twenty years on you and I'm in better shape. Say, did you also suggest I stay at the Hilo Majestic?"

"You bet; that's where I met Linda. By the way, did ya get lucky?" Durnell asked, taking two Kleenex tissues out of a box sitting between them and wiping his side window before placing the used tissues in a small clear-plastic garbage bag hanging under the dash.

Stacy reached for a pack of cigarettes in his shirt pocket, and then slid them back. He had been trying to quit for months and every time he lit one up, Pete complained.

"Lucky? Yeah, if you can call it that. I've been playing cards with old-age pensioners for the past twenty nights. At a penny a point I really got lucky."

Turning the car onto the old highway, Pete Durnell headed north. "I find that hard to believe, Joe. When I was there three years ago, I screwed myself to death. What about all those broads at the dancing contest? Surely you got next to a couple of those *beauties*?"

Unconsciously, Stacy brought his smokes came out again and took a deep draw. "Like I've told you Pete, I never mix my social life with my favourite recreation. Didn't you read Fred Astaire's book? He said he..."

Scowling, the driver never allowed his friend to finish. "I wouldn't read Fred Astaire's book if I was marooned on a desert island. Now if I had Arne Palmer's book it would be a different matter. Christ that smoke stinks. Give 'em up, Joe."

Rolling his window down and throwing the cigarette out, the senior of the two decided *he had* better get a dig in. "Pete, I thought you said you met your wife during the second week of your holiday."

The question caught his partner off guard. "Uh, yeah I did. I just, er, screwed myself silly the first week before I met her, that's all. You saw me when I got back. I was skin and bone. Why?"

"Just checking. Christ, is this rain ever going to stop?"

"C'mon, Joe, you're bullshittin' me? You weren't just dancin' all the time. The nightclub at the Majestic is loaded with lonely women, and knowing you the way I do, I'd say you got laid at least sixty-nine times. Er, a little play on words, there. You didn't get your tan sitting in a ... What the hell?"

Durnell's foot slammed hard on the brake pedal and he turned his car sharply off the road. Two empty black and white police cars with their top lights running stood outside a dimly lit convenience store.

After screeching to a halt, both detectives hurried through the downpour to witness a distraught young male counter clerk explaining the situation to a uniformed police officer taking notes.

"I told ya, they had their faces covered. I didn't see nothin'! They shot him when they ran out! Ya got an aspirin? I need an aspirin!"

The officer touched the clerk's arm. "Just relax, sir, and lower your voice."

While Durnell felt the pulse of a man lying in a pool of blood, Stacy approached a police officer standing at the end of the counter. "I'm Sergeant Stacy - what happened here?"

The officer pointed to the wounded man. "This unlucky fella came in as the robbers were leavin'. When he attempted to run out, they nailed him. He's got no identification, and that's his blue van outside. I just turned it off 'cause he'd left it runnin'."

"Who are *they*?" Joe asked, glancing at a nearby middle-aged couple nervously drinking coffee and smoking cigarettes. Another uniformed police officer stood with them asking questions and taking notes.

"The clerk says they were here using the phone. The woman is shook up and wants to leave. The bastards stole their wallets, watches, and rings. I've called for an ambulance, but I don't think this poor guy's gonna make it."

"Did you check out his vehicle?" Joe asked, heading for the door.

The officer followed. "Only the front seat before I launched an APB. The two gunmen are drivin' a grey Chevy pickup. Nobody got the licence and we don't know what model year it is."

As an ambulance arrived, a car with two other detectives and a police photographer pulled in next to the van. Stacy knew them. Victorson and Schmidt had been working the Homicide and Robbery late shift for the past six months. Joe had never liked Schmidt and from all indications, the feeling was mutual. Schmidt sweated too much and wore a constant sneaky grin. His shirts were too tight for his big beer belly, and he did not care where the large end of his tie ended up on his body. On hot days, Joe could smell Schmidt across the squad room. He always knew when Schmidt was around; if he didn't smell him, he would hear the flop of a loose shoe sole or the scrape worn down shoe heels make when naked tacks scratch the floor.

While Schmidt and the photographer headed inside, Victorson put his collar up and came over. "Hey Joe, nice duds. Did you come back from Hawaii just to give us a hand?"

Stacy opened the back doors of the van and asked the uniformed officer for a flashlight. "Nah, I missed the rain, and the smell of Schmidt's garlic breath."

Other than a spare tire in the middle of the floor and a large pile of blankets behind the seats, the rear of the vehicle appeared empty, but it wasn't. Removing the layers of covering, the sergeant let out a whistle.

His partner was now outside. "What have we got, Joe?"

Stacy lowered his arms to pick up a limp form. "Pete, get the doc right away. There's an unconscious kid back here, dressed in pyjamas. He's also in handcuffs."

Joe Stacy felt and looked relaxed entering his office the next morning. His holiday had done him some good because he had jumped out of bed before his alarm had sounded. After twenty pushups, a glimpse at the paper, and a long shower, he had actually enjoyed the drive in, even though the rain still had not let up.

Prior to arriving at the third floor, the elevator's mirrored wall indicated a few more grey hairs were present and that he needed a haircut. Stacy did not like the feel of hair touching his shirt's collar, but decided the haircut would have to wait until after lunch.

"Jesus, who decorated that abortion?" he asked, referring to the sparsely branched Christmas tree sitting in a corner of the busy squad room.

A passing uniformed female officer stopped in front of him. "Your partner did. It took him three hours and he's proud of it, too. We took up a collection and bought the decorations." She paused after giving him a *come-on* look. "I like your tan, Joey. Welcome back."

"You could have been with me, beautiful!" Joe replied, moving his face six inches from hers and exhibiting a come on look.

"I wasn't asked," she sang, moving closer and flapping her eyelashes over her big brown affectionate eyes

Before strolling towards his desk, Joe gently touched the tip of her nose with the forefinger of his right hand. "I know. I've got this thing about jealous husbands carryin' baseball bats lookin' for me."

"Mine's a pussycat; you know that, Joe?"

Stacy turned her around and sent her on her way. "Yeah, a pussycat wearing the department's boxing champion belt. No, thank you, sweetheart."

Durnell was already sitting at his desk. Slowly looking up, he said, "Are you alleging you don't like my work of art?"

Joe laughed while taking off his topcoat and jacket and hanging them on a nearby coat-rack. The feigned seriousness of his friend's voice was more than he could take at times.

"Uh, yeah, I like it. It's... er, different, that's all. I just happen to prefer trees with more than two branches on 'em."

Pete's face duplicated Stacy's mischievous grin. "Joe, other than dancing, you never were the artistic type. By the way, don't forget supper tonight. Linda just phoned to say she's making your favourite dish."

"Did she now? Well, at least she's got her priorities right. I wouldn't miss Linda's roast beef for the world. Er, what time...?"

Durnell's smile departed as he picked up a file. "The usual, around six-thirty. Sit down, there's something you should read."

Still jovial, Stacy sat at the desk facing Pete who handed him a binder. After a few moments reading the single page, the sergeant's faint grin changed to a quizzed expression. "How the hell could this happen?"

Pete shrugged. "Who knows? All the information concerning the robbery is still being typed. Because we arrived on the scene first, the captain's passed it to us."

"How many cases are we working on now?" Joe asked, lighting up a smoke and picking up three portfolios.

"Six, er, make that seven including this one. Hey, where're ya goin'?"

Heading towards the captain's office, Pete's *friend* answered, "Don't ask me why, but I've got a gut feeling about this case. If we take it on, some of the others can take these off our hands."

"Are you Doctor Abraham?" Stacy asked, displaying his badge while standing at the counter of a busy ward on the second floor of Seattle's Memorial Hospital. Both investigators had studied the complete file before heading to the hospital at two-o'clock that same day.

The balding stocky man without a tie and wearing a white doctor's coat with a stethoscope in the left pocket looked up. "Yes, what can I do for you?"

"I'm Detective Sergeant Stacy, and this is Detective Durnell. Is there a place we can talk ... privately?"

Aged about forty, Doctor Abraham appeared preoccupied and apprehensive. "Well, I'm a little busy, but if you make this quick I suppose we can use the head nurse's office. Come this way."

Halfway to the room, Abraham's preoccupied mind caused him to bump into a physically fit well-dressed middle-aged man, who dropped a bouquet of flowers. The unconcerned doctor did not stop, so Durnell picked up the roses and handed them back.

"Sorry about that, sir."

Instead of offering any form of gratitude, the agile man snatched the flowers and hurried away.

Moments later Abraham opened the door to a small sparsely furnished office and after sitting behind a desk and motioning the two police officers to sit down, he abruptly asked, "What's all this about?"

Pete took out his notebook and Joe asked the questions.

"At about ten o'clock last night, an ambulance brought in a tall, blond, heavy-set fella who had been shot in the back, and an unconscious boy about seven years old. I understand after emergency treatment both of them were brought to this ward. Right?"

Other than fidgeting with his fingers, Abraham seemed unconcerned. "Yes, that's right."

"What time was that?" Stacy asked.

The doctor glanced at his watch. "Uh, I'd say about ... one o'clock in the morning."

"We understand you were the only doctor on duty in this ward when the two were brought up from emergency, is that right?"

"Yes, there's only one of us on at night."

Stacy leaned forward, his eyes glued to the doctor's eyes. "Well, Doctor Abraham ... where are they?"

Searching for words, the doctor appeared confused. "Where are who?"

Feigning an exasperated look at his partner, Joe returned his attention to the doctor. "Who? The man and the boy, of course. How's your hearing, doctor?"

Abraham's fidgeting increased. "Sergeant ... er...?"

"The name is, Stacy."

"Sorry. Well, Sergeant Stacy, it would appear the man didn't wish to stay and took his son with him. I don't know where they are. We can't stop our patients from leaving. Is that all?"

An exasperated expression captured Joe's face and his eyes met Pete's for a moment. "No, that's not all, doctor," he said, strumming his fingers on the small desk and noticing a trace of perspiration forming on the doctor's forehead. "Who said he was the boy's father?"

Abraham's eye contact wavered. "I ... er, just assumed he was."

"Doctor, our records show your emergency staff took a nine-millimetre slug from the victim's right lung, and they also spent about two hours stabilizing the kid. Now you tell us the duo just got up and left. What kind of bullshit are you peddling here? We've been around, doc; the man was barely alive. Also, what was wrong with the boy?"

Searching for words, Abraham stood and turned around to face the window. "The boy had suffered some sort of a seizure. We're not certain and ... Listen, I'm not the one who should be answering these questions?"

Joe's impatience showed. "Why not? You were on duty last night. Also, since the two of them weren't identified, isn't this hospital concerned about the bill?"

Nodding to the open Venetian blind, the medical professional muttered, "Er, yes, I was the physician on duty, but only for a moment after they were brought up here."

"Please speak a little louder, doctor," Durnell said. "So who replaced you?"

"I don't know. I had a rush appointment to attend to outside of the hospital, and my relief hadn't arrived. If you check the staff duty book, you'll be able..."

Leaning slightly over the desk, Stacy also jumped to his feet. "You had an appointment at that hour of the morning, and you don't know who replaced you? C'mon Doc, you're holding something back and we'd appreciate a little co-operation. What the hell's going on here? We all know the pair couldn't leave on their own. When I phoned your emergency room staff this morning, they still had the clothes the two were wearing. Are you telling us open hospital gowns are now in fashion on the street?"

Abraham's hands shook slightly and his nervousness grew. After removing a handkerchief from his pocket and wiping his forehead, his manner became fearful. Slowly turning to face the two policemen, he muttered, "How do I know you're police officers?"

The detectives could not believe the question.

"What? You saw our badges; we're Seattle police officers," Stacy voiced.

"Doctor, what's bothering you?" Durnell asked.

Composing himself somewhat but maintaining an anxious facial expression, the medical professional didn't answer. Walking past them and opening the door, he said, "I'm afraid that's about all I can tell you gentlemen. If you want further information, I would suggest you contact our hospital's public information officer. Good day."

Both puzzled detectives had their eyes fixed on the departing doctor's back before Joe yelled, "Hey, doc, we'll do a hellova lot more than that!"

As the sergeant headed for the emergency ward and Pete Durnell went to question the public information officer, Dr. Abraham shakily picked up the receiver of a nearby pay phone located in the corridor by the elevators. Keeping his voice low and wiping his brow, he asked, "Is he there?"

While waiting, the doctor's eyes never wandered from the front of the payphone. "Then where the hell is he? I've just been questioned by two detectives. Yes, they both showed me their identification, but I can't be sure. Listen, you were the one who advised me to trust no one; what the hell was I supposed to tell them? Yes, the three of us were alone. No, I told them to check with the hospital's public information officer. Certainly, I'm upset! I've got every right to be upset! I told you I don't mind helping out, but ... Oh, all right, all right. Where? I'll be there at four."

Quickly walking back to his ward, Doctor Abraham did not notice the same well-dressed man he had bumped into earlier, waiting in line to use the telephone.

At three o'clock that afternoon, the two police officers sat at their desks comparing notes in the busy squad room. Earlier, Joe had picked up the boy's pyjamas and the wounded man's clothing and dropped them off at the crime lab along with the 9mm round taken from the victim's right lung.

"Fill me in one more time on what the hospital's public information officer said," Stacy asked, loosening his tie before standing and strolling over to the nearby coffee machine and pouring two coffees. "And what's his name?"

Pete cringed after he gladly accepted the cup of hot liquid and sipped. "Why we pay for this horse piss I don't know? Also, those cigarettes are going to kill you *and* me. How the hell can you dance when your lungs are rotting away?"

Joe butted the smoke. "Get on with it, *mother*."

"His name's Brickell and I gave him your card as well as mine. I also checked out the staff book and apparently, Doctor Abraham did leave the ward fifteen minutes before his relief arrived. The I.O. says there were only two nurses on duty, and they were both busy moving a heart attack patient to intensive care, one floor below. When Abraham's replacement arrived and made his rounds, er ... a Doctor Prouse, he discovered the man and boy were missing. The two must have flown the coop during that fifteen minute time frame."

"Was the boy in the same room as the man?" Joe asked, re-lighting and taking a long draw on the smoke he had just butted.

Pete continued to flip through his notebook. "Negative, but they were placed across the hall from each other. The boy shared a room with another kid, a teenager who had broken a leg skiing. I questioned him and he told me he woke up then fell asleep just after the emergency staff placed the youngster in bed. He did say one interesting thing though."

"What?"

"Well, the little guy was still partially out of it when they brought him up, but he kept muttering, 'Jam hand oven.'"

The Sergeant also cringed after sampling his coffee. Standing up, he yelled, "Jesus, this isn't coffee, it's turpentine. Who the hell made this crap?"

Tall, plump, limping, and close to retirement, Captain Ray Glover stormed out of his office and barked in a no-nonsense manner, "I did. What's wrong with it? Strong coffee's good for my blood pressure."

Smiles, whistles, and applause from those in the room greeted Stacy's reply. "Er, nothing ... my taste buds must be ... it's great, Captain, just great. Say, how is your blood pressure and your gout this fine morning? Improving, I hope?"

"It's a lousy morning, and it's worse since you got back," Glover grunted before storming back in his office and slamming his door.

Winking at Joe, Pete muttered, "Gotta protect the pension, right?"

Stacy nodded while he chuckled the words, "Damned right." A moment later, the boy's fate made him turn serious again. "Anyway, the kid said, 'Jam hand oven?' *Jam hand oven?* What the hell does that mean?"

After acknowledging his ringing phone in the busy office, a nearby detective said, "Joe, it's for you ... line three."

Upon pressing a button, and answering, "Homicide and robbery, Sergeant Stacy," Joe's face took on a sudden look of amazement."What? What time did this happen? Are you certain? Jesus, yeah, we'll be right there." Slamming the phone down, he said, "Pete, you ain't gonna believe this..."

Pete Durnell knew something was up, that's why he grabbed Joe's jacket and raincoat along with his own. Rushing to the door with his partner, he said, "Try me ... what's happened?"

"Abraham's dead. He died of a heart attack not long after we left the hospital."

"A heart attack?"

"Yeah, a heart attack. They're holding his body at the emergency ward. Shit, I didn't think we were that rough with the guy."

Running his comb through his hair, Durnell asked, "Why are we going back there now?"

Before the elevator's door opened, Joe replied, "Let's call it thirty years of police instinct."

As the elevator descended, Durnell saw his partner frown. He had seen the same look many times before and knew from twelve years experience that Joe's hunches were seldom wrong. Joe was probably right as usual, so what the hell were they into now?

The packed emergency ward at Memorial Hospital was warm and dry as the automatic doors closed behind the two soaked detectives. The rain hadn't stopped and it was almost cold enough to snow.

Rather than going to the reception desk, Stacy spotted an ambulance driver he knew, and motioned him to come over.

"Hi Joe, Pete? What brings you to the real world in this weather?" the attendant asked.

Joe did not waste any time answering the driver's question. "Andy, who the hell's in charge of this place?"

Scanning the room, the driver pointed to a blond nurse in her thirties helping an elderly woman into a wheelchair.

"That's Gail Manning; she can cut through any red tape around here."

After tapping Andy's shoulder and offering his thanks, Durnell quickly followed Stacy behind the counter where the nurse stood filling out a form.

"Is it *Miss.* or *Mrs.* Manning?" Joe asked, standing next to her, realizing all the perfumes in the world could not compete with the fragrance she wore.

"It's *Nurse Manning* to those I don't know, and Gail to my friends. Can I help you...?" she answered, blinking a set of the bluest eyes the sergeant had ever seen.

Displaying his badge, Joe found himself grinning like a kid. The nurse's angelic smile made her eyes more beautiful than ever and a ring wasn't evident on her left hand. He knew he was as least twenty years older, but he hadn't had this feeling in years. To Joe, Gail Manning's sculptured feminine body, beautiful face, crimson lips, and flawlessly delicate skin rivalled the paintings of old world masters he'd seen in museums. No, she exceeded those images of antiquity, he thought.

"I love your smile and I'd like to call you Gail, but I guess that'll have to wait until we get to know each other better. I'll make a personal note of that and we'll take care of it in a day or so. In the meantime, *Nurse* Manning, where's Doctor Abraham's body?"

Gail manning blushed a little before handing a form to a passing nurse. "Connie, would you take Mrs. Iverson up to x-ray please? Thanks Connie." Composing herself, she said, "Now, Detective, er...?"

Another childlike grin appeared before Joe's professional attitude took over.

"Joe Stacy, and this is my partner, Pete Durnell. Is Doctor Abraham's body still here in emergency?"

A sad expression emerged. "Yes, he's in the far wing. His death shocked all of us. Doctor Abraham hasn't been with us very long, and the staff liked him a lot. Are you the two detectives Mr. Brickell called?"

Durnell replied, "That's right. Can we see the body please, and can you ask Mr. Brickell to join us along with the doctor who attended Abraham?"

After complying with the detective's instructions, Nurse Manning escorted both police officers to a small room in a relatively unused lower wing of the hospital. A sheet covered the naked body of the doctor lying on a gurney, and Joe pulled the garment down to the deceased's feet.

"Is that necessary?" the now scowling nurse asked just as the public information officer arrived accompanied by a square jawed, portly middle-aged doctor named Emil Prouse.

"Why? Do naked men bother you?"

Joe's spontaneous reply went unanswered, but not unheard.

After the usual introductions, Stacy examined the body while questioning the two male hospital employees. He was not sure what he was looking for, but instinct told him a coronary blockage was out of the question.

"Doctor Prouse, how can you be certain this man died of a heart attack?" the sergeant asked, turning Abraham's neck from side to side and lifting up the deceased's arms.

Prouse moved in closer, his eyes catching every movement the detective made. "I had just spoken with him about five minutes before I was called. His forehead was still a little moist and there are no marks whatsoever on his body. Initially, I thought he might have hit his head on something in the linen closet, but as I've said, he couldn't have ... there are no marks."

"In the linen closet?" Stacy asked, partially bending the body on its side. "What would he be doing in the linen closet? Who found him?"

"One of our nurses," Brickell said, before thanking and informing Nurse Manning she could return to the emergency ward. "He was slumped, almost in the sitting position, in the far corner."

No one saw Stacy's small grin accompanying his knowing look as he examined the back of Abraham's right leg. While pulling the sheet up, he asked, "Is the closet normally locked, or is it always open?"

"I don't believe the door has a lock on it," Prouse replied.

"Can we see the room, please?"

Upon leaving the elevator, the four individuals proceeded to the small chamber located around the corner from the corridor in front of the ward's desk - the same desk where Joe and Pete had first met Doctor Abraham. Other than shelves of linen and sundry hospital items, the storage room appeared normal. Requesting Prouse and Brickell stay outside, Joe asked, "Who's been in here since the body was found?"

"No one except the nurse who found him, and Doctor Prouse," Brickell answered.

After signing a paper presented to him by an orderly, Prouse added, "He was dead when I first attended him, but there was no room to work in there so a colleague and I dragged him out. We lifted him on a gurney and rushed him to emergency."

"I take it that camera indicates who enters and leaves the ward?" Stacy asked, indicating with a head movement a closed-circuit camera above the ward's desk.

Brickell nodded. "It has a six hour loop."

Joe nodded. "Good, we'll require the tape and Doctor Abraham's personal file. Pete, get on the phone and have the coroner pick up the body. I want a complete autopsy. Oh, yeah, and have someone check this room for prints. Dr. Prouse, no one is to enter this closet until we're finished with it."

Brickell appeared confused. "Uh, surely you don't believe there's been foul play? Er, this hospital has its reputation to consider. Our administrators will be..."

The sergeant took out his notebook to take down Prouse's home address and phone number. To Joe, all public information officers had a familiar air of sneakiness about them. He never knew if they were telling the truth or not. Taking a deep breath and closing his eyes for a few seconds indicated to the I.O. that this police officer did not take kindly to half-truths.

"Mr. Brickell, you should have thought about that before *your* hospital allowed two patients to disappear in the middle of the night. We're not certain what's going on here, but we're going to find out. Now, please get me the tape and Abraham's particulars. I'll be down in emergency."

The aroma of roast beef and soft Christmas music surrounded Pete standing with a beer in his hand after he had opened his front door and saw Joe.

"What took you so long, buddy? Christ, you're coat is soaked - give it to me."

Stacy took off his shoes and passed his coat to his friend. Once fully inside the neat little house, his eyes took in a brightly lit Christmas tree and dining table set for three. "Thanks Buddy. You know, all the way here, I've been asking myself why I didn't spend an extra two weeks in Hawaii. This has got to be the wettest year on record. Never mind flat feet, it's a wonder we haven't got trench feet."

A voice from the old house's kitchen answered Joe's question for him.

"Because you missed us and the rain. That's why you came home," Linda said, appearing and giving Joe a hug. "Welcome back jitterbug legs, did you notice the water bucket on the porch?"

Still grinning, Joe lightly tapped Linda's stomach, wrapped his arms around her, and kissed her cheek. "You're getting bigger every day, sweetheart. Girl or boy, when this baby's born, you're going to have a football player on your hands. Water bucket on the front porch? Hey, when I smelled what you're cooking', I couldn't notice anything. Your roast beef always puts my senses on hold. How ya doin', kid?"

"I'm fine," Linda said, stately straightening her apron over her abundant belly. "And thank you for your compliment, sir. I wish my husband appreciated my cooking as you do. If he had his way, we'd be eating chicken noon and night."

"And for breakfast," chuckled Pete, passing a beer to Joe. "I can't help it if I like chicken ... I grew up on a farm."

"A farm with no cows?" asked Joe, taking a swig and sitting down on a chair next to the couch in front of the crackling fire.

Pete laughed and sat on the couch. "Yeah, we had cows, but they were pets. Who eats their pets?"

"We did," Linda said, heading back into the kitchen. "I was also brought up on a farm, remember? Dinner won't be ready for another fifteen minutes, so you guys go ahead and talk business. No business later though."

Situated on a quiet street on the west side of Seattle, Pete and Linda Durnell's cosy two-level wooden house appeared made for its owners. Stacy knew Pete enjoyed puttering around, and since they had bought the place, all the couple's spare time had gone into its renovation. The front door opened into a small hallway with the family room off to the left and a staircase to the right. Further, down the hall, Pete had added a bathroom that could be accessed from the hallway and their adjoining bedroom. The house's kitchen stood at the end of the passageway with a door leading to the dining room. Two sliding glass doors linked the dining room to the family room. Upstairs, Pete had finished renovating two bedrooms and added another bathroom. Joe thought the house and its furnishings were like its owners - friendly, run of the mill, and modest.

Joe stretched his legs, and the warmth of the fire felt good. These were his two best friends. It had taken Joe ages to accept Pete's initial invitation for dinner. Joe didn't like being obligated to attend dinner invitations. Such an invite meant reciprocating, and he never entertained at home - it just wasn't in him. A home cooked meal to him meant visiting a local restaurant. Years ago, he would putter around the house, and invite friends over for a few drinks, but not anymore. He knew he'd be a rotten host. Hosts had to have the ability to carry on small talk, and nothing in the world bored him more. It was like talking about the weather just to make conversation. Pete and Linda were different. They were always on the same wavelength and that meant challenging conversations about fascinating subjects.

"Pete, when you and Linda bought the place I never dreamt you'd improve it this much. I thought you'd bought a lemon. Whenever I come here you've added something else."

Durnell stood up heading for the fridge. "Thanks, but you know how busy it keeps me? Linda thinks we should raise the house and put in a basement."

"What do you need a basement for?"

"She thinks all boys like to lift barbells. How's your beer?"

Joe rubbed his feet together in front of the fire. He appreciated this warm convenience his apartment lacked. "I'm good for now. On second thought, sure. Say, how does Linda know the baby's going to be a boy?"

Linda answered from the kitchen. "I'd say the odds are pretty good, Joe. I've got four brothers, and he's got five. I don't want a weight coming through the ceiling."

"But you may not have this house when the kid's that age. Besides, the way you're improving the place, a herd of elephants couldn't damage it. What else have you got planned?"

I'm just about finished except for the porch," Pete said, returning and handing Joe a beer. "It needs a new roof. These days we're emptying the bucket every few hours. Say, I forgot to ask you when we drove back to the office, how you made out with Nurse Manning?"

Joe's adolescent-like grin returned. "I asked her out on a date and she reluctantly accepted."

"What do you mean, reluctantly?" Pete asked before cupping his hands around his mouth and yelling, "Hey, Linda, I think Twinkletoes is in love."

"Easy on the Twinkletoes," Stacy advised. "Yeah, I had to push it. I don't know if she's ever gone out with older guys, but the natural charm did it, *and* she likes dancing."

Linda reappeared, and then went back to her kitchen. "So you should be, Joe Stacy. God, you're fifty-one ... give some poor girl a break. Who are you saving yourself for?"

Twinkletoes grinned, yelling, "Linda, you married a cop! Not too many members of the fairer sex can put up with our lifestyle, you know?"

The voice from the kitchen said, "I do."

"Yeah, but you're a sucker for punishment."

"I know, and it's great," she replied, before bringing out bowls filled with mashed potatoes and steamed carrots.

"I've made your favourite horseradish, Joe."

"Linda, my love, everything you prepare is mouth watering. If you could dance like you can cook, we'd be on television making' millions?"

Keeping a straight face and placing her hands on her hips, Linda said, "I thought you told me I did dance like that?"

Pete thoroughly enjoyed watching his friend squirm. "Don't look at me for backup, Joe."

"Well, er, of course you do," Stacy said, nearly coughing up the beer he had swallowed. "I'd forgotten. Er... yeah, another beer would be great, Pete. Don't bother getting up, I'll get it."

"Ya can't get out of this, Joe - I just handed you one."

"Jesus, you are a real buddy, aren't you?" Joe said, grinning wildly.

Over the next few minutes, the merry voices of three loudly laughing friends managed to drown out Bing Crosby's *White Christmas*.

While the three close friends dined reminiscing, a conference of another kind convened in the large plush boardroom of Wulfe Worldwide Industries Corporation on the ninety-eighth floor of a massive New York office tower. Three exquisitely well dressed men and two smartly attired women, all in their early forties sat quietly in padded black leather chairs on one side of a large oval-shaped highly polished black teakwood table. Each person appeared not to know the identities of the others, while a fourth man in his seventies, sitting in a much finer chair placed his calfskin briefcase on the floor and faced the group. Nothing lay on the table except drinking glasses and jugs of ice water. The drapes had been pulled, completely shutting out the normally breathtaking vista of night time New York.

In broken English, the soft-spoken chairman brought the meeting to order. "I am not fond of calling these meetings, but I have my orders. When our company's concerns go wrong in this hemisphere, I am taken to task. I don't like it when that happens. Transportation, you have placed our enterprise in a dangerous position. What do you have to say about your careless method of handling *matters* in Seattle?"

One of the men squirmed in his chair, his expression indicating he had not anticipated being singled out. "Sir, I... I mean my department conducted the transportation in our usual efficient manner. When we attempted to deliver the *cargo*, we found Security hadn't considered the possibility of ... *interference*."

The chairman kept his eyes on the man for a few moments before glowering at one of the women. "Security?"

Security wasn't about to be intimidated. She had always conducted her job thoroughly, and she knew it. Full of confidence, she said, "Mr. Chairman, there are times when all the planning in the world makes no difference whatsoever to the outcome. My people were there, but..."

The chairman's face took on a burning tint and he compressed his lips. Barely audible, he said, "I don't want to hear excuses. In our business, there is no room for error. It is your responsibility to provide the security for cargo transfer. What happened?"

Security's voice faltered as she sat up straight. Running her hand across her brow and playing with her black short-cut hair, she nervously replied, "An armed hold-up was in place during the translocation. There was no way of knowing another vehicle was parked at the rear of the building. The weather should have assisted us, but ... uh, it didn't, and I admit my blunder, Mr. Chairman. It will never happen again."

The administrator's face returned to its normal colour, but his cold firm eyes stared at her for another five seconds. "You're absolutely right, it won't happen again. If it does, you will be *replaced*. Do you understand me?"

Security suddenly found herself perspiring in the air-conditioned room. "Unmistakably, sir."

"Resolution, do you have the matter in hand?"

A self-satisfied man calmly answered, "Completely, Mr. Chairman. Even the intended interference of the *Israeli Set*."

Resolution knew the term 'Israeli Set,' always brought a slight change to his leader's composed demeanour. Now the Chairman's eyes widened before narrowing when he muttered, "The Israeli set? Hmmm, most interesting; how annoying was the ... *obstacle*?"

"Minuscule, sir, it's been dealt with."

The chairman's small reappearing smile departed just as quickly. "Well done, Resolution. Planning, how many *cargo* shipments have we arranged so far this month?"

"One hundred and sixty, sir."

"And the financial institutions?"

"Twenty-seven, sir."

"And matters of race-relations?"

"Sixteen in four states, sir."

"Organ... *donations*?"

"I've sent you that information, sir. They're numerous."

The headman seemed pleased. After filling his glass and sipping, he turned his attention to the second female.

"Government Relations, I hear rumours our political friends are complaining about our donations?"

"Our contributions have been cut back slightly," a heavily made up moonfaced woman said, uncrossing her legs and leaning forward. "We'll be correcting the matter shortly, Mr. Chairman."

"Why have we reduced them?"

"Finance informs me Switzerland has been a little tardy in transferring funds.

Placing his glass down and wiping a small amount of condensation off the gleaming table, the chairman asked, "Is that correct, Finance?"

A man with eyes piercing like lasers, replied, "The problem has been looked after, Mr. Chairman. One bank was having difficulties with our United Kingdom operations, but it's been taken care of sir. As per your instructions, we are increasing our federal, state, and civic *contributions*."

Before pushing his chair back, the chairman stood and placed his briefcase on the table. Unlocking and opening it, he removed six computer disks and slid one to each person.

"These disks are your updates, and all the information you require is Genesis coded. I'm certain I don't have to inform you of the security these disks demand. Destroy the others immediately. Switzerland has changed the means of access, phone, and fax numbers, e-mail, and all addresses. They have also ordered us to increase our profits and I intend to do just that. There will be no further mistakes. Seattle business will be conducted in Vancouver, Canada, for the next year."

If the room's occupants were troubled about the change, they were not about to ask questions until told to do so.

"Are there any questions?"

Planning cleared his throat. "Sir, have you forgotten about the specific *custom* order being filled in Seattle. We don't wish to jeopardize that operation, do we?"

As the chairman finished off his water, he appeared to be counting days. "Ah, yes, that one almost slipped my mind. It's important that we get the job done expeditiously. It's for a special client in the Middle East. Actually, one of our finest. He apparently intends it as a wedding gift to his best friend. Can we find the cargo elsewhere?"

"The transaction is in motion, Mr. Chairman."

The old man toyed with his tie for a moment. "All right, we'll let that proceed and make it the last one for awhile. Planning, since we're shipping one out, we may as well bring one in on the same plane. Take care of it."

"When this is complete, there are a few things I must do to cover our tracks," Security stated.

The chairman nodded slightly, before asking, "Any further questions?"

Noticing there were none, the speaker re-locked his briefcase. "Resolution, because of the Jewish kid, the police will be heavily involved in this. Work around them and tidy up all ends … and I mean all ends. They are to discover nothing. Is that understood?"

Resolution knew exactly what to say. "Definitely, Mr. Chairman."

"Each of you will leave through separate exits. That will be all."

While Joe Stacy drove home, the heavy rain turned to sleet before large flakes of snow stubbornly began accumulating under the push of a strong north wind.

After locking his apartment door, turning on the television, and kicking off his shoes, Joe threw his keys on a coffee table, took off his windbreaker, and flopped into his favourite chair. His evening with Pete and Linda had been delightful even though the wine he had consumed at dinner made him feel a little light-headed.

Paying no attention to the news, Joe lit up a smoke and glanced around his apartment. He always felt a little forlorn after returning from Pete and Linda's home. To him, they were the perfect couple, perpetually exhibiting their warmth and love for each other as well as their friends. Nothing could interfere with their mutual devotion, and to Joe such allegiance was uncommon.

"Maybe I'm too set in my ways," he muttered, viewing a stack of old newspapers lining the floor next to his couch. He also noticed that he had not yet hung up the set of tails he'd worn at the dance contest in Hawaii. He wondered if it mattered. He spent more time in the squad room than here, and besides, he did not enjoy entertaining people anyway.

A grin appeared from nowhere as Stacy got up to close his drapes. He'd left his .32 calibre (Police Positive) pistol on top of the television set. Captain Glover never stopped asking him to exchange the firearm for a more modern weapon. The weapon should have been exchanged long ago, but why bother; he hadn't fired or cleaned it in three years. As a beat cop, he practised weekly and hardly ever hit the target.

Mesmerized for a moment by the swirling wet snowflakes, Joe at least knew his dishes were washed, but the dishwashing machine did that job, not him. If Mrs. White failed to appear twice a week to clean up the place, he knew he would get lost in a heap of piled up clothes, wet towels, newspapers, bills, shoes and everything else he left hanging around.

Joe wondered why he was so sloppy. Pete and Linda kept their house so immaculate, when their cat Miss. Claws sat on his knee then jumped down, she took her hairs with her.

Sitting back and allowing his eyes to observe his smoke rings explore the ceiling, the detective sergeant thought of Dale. He had loved her very much, and even though she had moved in with him, he could never convince her to marry him. Sure, she would consider his many proposals, but when he got wounded responding to a bank robbery, their relationship suddenly changed for the worse.

"Shit, I only forgot to duck," he murmured. "No big deal, yet she blamed me. Why am I thinking of her anyway? It's long over with."

A resigned look came to Joe, knowing before Dale, other ladies like Marie, Barb, Patricia, Helga, Audrey, and Bea had come along. "Jeez, what a live one Audrey was, he recalled. I wouldn't mind her being around right now."

Lighting up another cigarette, he still could not get Dale off his mind, but after he was wounded, she became irksome, wanting him home at set times. That would have meant getting a desk job, and to him sitting behind a desk was not being a cop. Cops had to solve crimes or at the very least stand like idiots directing traffic in the middle of busy intersections. She also wanted him to buy a cellular phone so they could keep in touch, but to Joe, such an item would be a chain around his neck. Cellular phones were for gossipers and idiots who could not stand their own company.

While watching the television announcer's lips move, Joe's mind remained on Dale. Not long after she walked out, she married her boss, a real asshole always flashing his watch, rings, wallet, and vanity. The same guy who always groped at her during office parties, especially the last one four years ago. The night she moved out; the night he broke her boss's nose and threw in a black eye for the hell of it. He recalled the occasion all too well.

"Honey, that phoney Stanlikky bastard had his hand on your ass when you danced with him. That's the second time tonight."

"Joe, you're imagining things again. Rod Stanlikky wouldn't do that; he's married with three kids and fiercely protects his image."

"Yeah, and I think he's trying for four."

"Joe, I'm getting sick and tired of ... Where are you going?"

"I'm going to get a drink, that's where I'm going. And if I happen to meet Stanlikky on the way, I'll make certain his image gets a little tarnished."

Stacy shook his head thinking of it all, but chance more than anything else brought him back into the real world. Something the television news announcer mentioned shot through him like the bank bullet, and he quickly picked up the remote to turn up the set.

"... as yet unidentified, was dressed only in a hospital gown. Harbour police acknowledged the man was shot twice through the head, and appeared to have suffered a recent wound to his right lung. And now, here's Carol with the weather..."

Pushing the television's remote mute button, and quickly reaching for the phone, Joe punched in the number to his office. After two rings, he recognized the voice.

"Homicide and robbery, Sergeant Rumberg."

Running out of cigarettes did not help as he crushed the empty pouch. "Matt, it's Joe Stacy. Where's the guy they fished out of the harbour?"

"He's in the morgue, Joe. Why, what's up?"

"Tell them not to touch the body until I get there in the morning. Okay?"

"Sure, Joe."

Just after he had hung up, the phone rang, and Pete asked, "Joe, did you catch the news?"

"I sure did, old buddy. Let's get in an hour earlier tomorrow. I'll meet you at the *meat plant*."

Chapter 2

"Here we are, number fourteen," the short, bald-headed coroner's assistant said, licking his lips and fingering his pockmarked face. "Do ya want him in or out?" he added, standing on his toes and opening one of the square stainless steel doors that Joe Stacy referred to as *meat lockers*.

Six inches of snow covered the ground at six-thirty that morning, so Pete had picked Joe up rather than both of them having to take their cars to the office. Instead of the usual thirty minutes, the drive had taken them an hour.

Joe hated everything about the morgue, particularly the smell of chemicals, disinfectants, its echoing hallways, and the morose individuals it employed. The senior detective had been here many times and he always felt confined the second he entered the drab old building. He wanted out of this stinking rat hole now, right now, but he knew there was no quick escape. There never was when the dirty part of his job brought him here.

"Let's just see him," Joe Stacy replied, sarcastically.

When the attendant unzipped the body bag, Pete grimaced. "Jesus, Joe, look at his face. Why didn't the killer just cut off the guy's head? The rounds went right through and took out the back of his skull. It's him all right."

The morgue worker zipped up the bag, slid the body back, and cranked the handle shut. "Kinda tough this happenin' to him so close to Christmas, ain't it?"

Though Joe nodded, his mind was elsewhere. "Has anyone else phoned about him being here?"

Completing a form that Pete initialled, the attendant then ripped it off its pad. "Just the news media," he said, placing the paper in a file folder.

"Tell the doc we want a complete post-mortem examination," Joe uttered, his face still revealing his total abhorrence for the room. Removing his scarf and stuffing it into his overcoat's left pocket, he added, "We want to know how long he was in the water ... and anything else that's pertinent."

Returning to his wooden chair and picking up a copy of Playboy, the coroner's assistant turned the magazine around displaying the centrefold. "Gotcha. It'd be nice if we got one like this in here, wouldn't it?"

Both detectives sneered at him before Pete replied, "Why, do you practice necrophilia in this joint?"

Joe grinned impishly, adding, "You like the odd stiff one, do you?"

As the plainclothesmen left, the man exhibited a baffled look. Still *drooling* at the centrefold and placing his feet up on his desk, he said, "There ain't nothin' wrong with my neck. Yeah, I sure wouldn't mind her showin' up."

Walking back to their office, the pair picked up four doughnuts and two *decent* coffees from Choy's Has-beans, a small coffee, and sandwich cafe that used to be called Choy's Choice, Choy's Choosy Diner, Choy's Chow, and Ahoy, it's Choy's.

When they entered, the sole owner, cook, server, and dishwasher quickly hung up one of his phones. "Hah, Joe, Pete, you rike new name?"

Joe also bought a morning paper. "Yeah, it's got a certain used quality to it. Who suggested this one?"

The lone wrinkled faced cashier's front gold tooth shone as he proudly responded, "Your Captain Grubber did. He tell me it good name."

"Perhaps you should ask him to change *his* name," a grinning Pete suggested. "Grubber sounds better than Glover any day. Now, why don't you paint the place to get rid of the grease stains?"

"No money reft for paint. New sign cost too much."

"Then get *Grubber* to pay for it. On second thought, get rid of your three telephones and two cellulars, and the money you save will pay for it. Why the hell do you need all those phones?"

"Hah, I need phones, but you got good idea, Pete. I ask Captain Grubber to pay."

The grin left Pete's mouth. "Er, yeah, but when you do, don't mention my name."

Both detectives were about to walk out, when Choy reached underneath his counter. "Ah, Joe, you forget something."

A smug look came over Joe. "You've got another load?"

Choy passed his friend a packet of five Cuban cigars. "They just come in."

"Has the cost gone up again?" Stacy asked, taking out his wallet.

"No plice this time – it my Chlistmas plesent to you. Pete, you orso want package for Chlistmas?"

"Thanks anyway, Choy; the only vice I've got is my work."

After Joe thanked Choy, the cafe owner said, "Health department say I got no mices. You got mouses in office? I get you mouse's tlap."

Pete snickered while leaving. "Not mice … vice. Thanks, Choy."

Choy's words followed them out. "I loll dice too, but not at work."

Outside, their breath lanced the cold air as the two headed to their office and as usual, the squad room was a madhouse. The second they took off their coats, Captain *Grubber* joined them, asking, "Is the stiff the same person who drove the van?"

Stacy sat down, opened up his newspaper, and then closed it, deciding he would read it later when his boss was not around.

"Yeah, it's him. He's been given an eye job, a nose job, and the back of his head's been blown off."

The captain placed a clear plastic bag on Joe's desk. "Here's what was found in his vehicle ... before ... are you ready for this?"

A frown crinkled Joe's forehead as the start of a smile appeared. "As Seattle's best, we're always ready, except for cases like this. Now what?"

Glover cocked his head anticipating the response. "Always prepared, eh, Joe? The van's disappeared from our impound lot."

As expected by the official, both police officers sat back wide-eyed and bewildered, shaking their heads in disbelief.

With his surprise declaration over with, Glover headed back to his office, saying, "It happened sometime during the night. Thank God the boys had already gone over it. Get on it, guys."

"How? Where the hell was the night crew?" Joe asked, watching Glover drifting back towards them.

"Oh, yeah, I forgot to mention the prints. They think they've got the driver's prints, the kid's prints, and one other person's thumbprint was found just above where the key fits into the ignition."

Stacy picked up the plastic container. "But how the hell was it snatched?"

"Don't ask *me* how it happened, Joe," Glover barked. "Both the chain and gate locks must have been picked. Even the goddamned vehicle tracks were swept clean."

Before leaving, the captain gave *two of Seattle's finest* a sympathetic grin. "You can read your paper now, Joe. On second thought, you won't have time because I want this thing cleared up. I've transferred your other caseloads, so now you've got plenty of time to work on this one and keep me posted. By the way, Pete, your exams are coming up. If you want to make sergeant, start hitting the books."

After Glover departed, Stacy emptied the contents of the plastic pouch out on his desk. "I've always said he could read minds, have I not?"

Pete rolled his chair around to sit next to his friend. "Yeah, but he's not as good as you. That's all we've got, eh ... a piece of a Europe-American airfreight invoice, a Paris Match magazine and a ballpoint pen? Where are his personal identification and vehicle insurance papers?" Going page by page through the publication, he added, "I'd say this guy travelled light, real light."

"We've also got these," Joe said, standing up and throwing a pair of handcuffs in front of Pete. "They're foreign, so let's find out where they're made, and inquire with Europe-American about that air freight stub."

"Where are you going?" Pete asked.

"I'm gonna look at both the hospital and store's closed circuit videos. Also, Pete, check the phone book and see if there's a corporation around called, Protocol Customs Assurance Company."

"Why, where'd you see that name?" the junior of the two asked.

"It's nearly worn out, but it's in small print on the pen. You should have caught that, Eagle Eyes." A small grin appeared when the sergeant, looking down at his desk, added, "Oh, I forgot, you're only Eagles Eyes on the range, aren't you?"

The grin remained with Stacy as he walked over to a small room at the back of the office and heard Pete muttering, "At least I can shoot."

Making notes while reviewing the hospital tape, it didn't take Joe long to discover a half-hour had been removed. He was still rewinding and fast-forwarding the tape when Pete joined him three hours later carrying sandwiches and two coffees.

"Linda made these for us. Anything there?"

Grabbing and unwrapping a sandwich, Joe loosened his tie before pushing the play button. Biting into the snack, he said, "Thank the good lady for me. There's nothing of interest on the store's tape, and other than a section missing from of the hospital tape, not too much. I've transferred the pertinent scenes onto another videotape. Take a look at this. Okay, there's where we approached the desk. Now, we head away with the doc. When he walked out on us, we both used the stairs, so we don't reappear, but look at this ... Abraham went to the pay phone in the corridor, and after finishing the call, he went back to the desk. Now, check this out. Abraham approaches Prouse behind the desk. They argue, Prouse pushes him, and then a nurse steps in between them. Did you notice something else?"

Pete had caught it. "Yeah, the guy with the flowers is the same one who bumped into the doc. He was using the pay phone when we arrived, but hung up and moved away while we were at the desk. When Abraham was on the phone after he left us, the flower man was standing in line behind him."

Joe finished his sandwich and missed the basket with the empty crumpled up wax paper. "You got it. That's about all there is. Can you believe it, a half hour's missing? The linen closet's in plain view, but there's nothin' except nurses going in and out. Did you get a good look at him?"

"Who? Dapper Dan with the flowers?" Pete asked.

"Yeah."

"You bet! Right down to the birthmark on his neck."

After taking a swallow of his coffee, Stacy said, "Okay, I want our artist to do his thing, and anything he misses you can add. Now, how'd you make out?"

Pete flipped through some pages of his well-worn notebook. "The prints have been sent to the FBI and they'll be getting back to us sometime this afternoon. They ran the artist's conception of the kid and drew a blank. Initially, Chicago police thought the picture resembled a missing child in their area, but that kid's thirteen. Oh, yeah, the van's been found. It was left in the Space Needle's parking lot, and it's being towed back. It belongs to Systems Truck Rentals, and you're gonna love this..."

Joe had been staring at the floor while his partner spoke. Glancing up after shrugging, he gave Pete a frustrated look. "Don't tell me there's more surprises? What now?"

"It's one of twenty some-odd vehicles the company keeps aside for use by Protocol Customs Assurance Company. That firm's known throughout the world for transferring goods in bond. In other words, jewellery, currency, stock certificates, bonds, or anything of value can be locked inside a container by company officials at one international location and conveyed until opened by the company's representatives at the port of entry."

Lighting up a smoke, Joe asked, "You mean the container doesn't have to go through customs?"

"Not all the time. It depends on the manifests and the availability of customs officials."

"Okay, but who signed the van out?"

Pete ran his hand through his hair. "That's the weird part. It wasn't signed out, but it was used that day to pick up a container that came in on a Europe-American flight from Berlin."

"How do you know that?"

"When I phoned Europe-American giving them the number on that piece of air freight invoice found in the van, the airline's people told me it was a bill of lading covering Microsoft mouse hardware. I checked with Microsoft and that's exactly what it was. It must have stuck to the carjacker's shoe, so just for the hell of it I checked with the gate at the freight compound and gave the guard the licence number of the Systems Truck Rentals van. The guy was the same person who was on duty, but when he checked the access log, the page had been ripped out."

"What?"

Pete continued. "The guy remembered the licence number anyway. It's EAT-283. He said if he could eat till he's eighty-three, he'd be happy. That's why he'd remembered it. He jotted the licence down when the vehicle arrived and when it left. The van was there for twenty minutes. Ya know something, Joe, someone is trying to stay one step ahead of us."

Joe's heartfelt chuckle started Pete laughing.

"Pete, when I was a kid, I hated crossword puzzles, jigsaws, and chess. Even as an adult, I've never had the patience it takes to play bridge, and let me tell you why. If I'd mastered them, we would have solved this mess by now, and we wouldn't know what to do with ourselves. Nice piece of work. Finally we've got a break. Also, thanks for reminding me about Microsoft. I've still got five hundred of their cheap shares."

"Christ Joe, they're worth a fortune. When are you going to sell 'em?"

Stacy got up and stretched before tidying up the room. "When Bill Gates gives me the go ahead. Microsoft shares are for buying, not selling."

"Bill Gates? You know Bill Gates, Microsoft's chairman?"

"Do I know Willie Gates? Is that what you're asking me?"

"Yeah."

"Sure, we went to different schools together. "

Etched grins remained when they arrived at their desks and Pete said, "I forgot to mention the handcuffs. They're the type used by German police."

"That doesn't surprise me," Joe replied, putting on his jacket and coat, and throwing two garments to Pete. "The way things are going, I'm amazed they're not Martian. Let's go visit Europe-American."

That afternoon, two men strolled talking to each other in the vehicle parking lot of Systems Truck Rentals. Lightly falling rain had washed away most of the snow, but dark clouds were rolling in from the northwest.

"Where was it?" an impeccably dressed dark haired man in his forties asked, placing his left hand around the other man's shoulders before allowing it to roam and massage the guy's buttocks.

Scratching himself and revealing a mouthful of rotten teeth when he bashfully grinned, the shaven-headed pockmarked man gently crossed his arm over his friend's buttocks, replicating his *pal's* action. "Taped under the seat, where you said it would be. The motherfuckers missed it when they dusted the thing for prints. Erik, that feels so good, can we meet later?"

Stopping and loosening their arms Erik kissed the other's left cheek. "I'd like to, but not tonight. Give it to me."

A small slip of paper changed hands and Erik placed it in the inside pocket of his suede jacket, before asking, "Where did you leave the truck?"

"Next to the fuckin' Space Needle. Don't worry, I wore gloves and left everythin' the same. They'll just think some fuckin' teenagers stole it for a joyride."

Eric's alarmed expression started him biting his upper lip. "Then they got Norbert's prints? Maybe the kid's prints as well?"

"Hey, what the fuck could I do about it? The fuckers must have been on it right away. I needed Smitty's help to get the thing out; it was behind a locked gate with a fuckin' chain. Gimmee the two C-notes you promised me."

Grabbing a fistful of the skinhead's clothes that could have walked away by themselves, Erik abruptly murmured, "Don't ever mention his name again, you fuckin' idiot. Also, shit for brains, how could teenagers steal a fuckin' vehicle from a police compound?"

A second after releasing the man, Erik threw two bills on the ground. "Here, fuck off, and go clean yourself up. You smell like a shithouse."

Distressed, the skinhead picked up the money. "You don't talk that way when we're in bed? You said you loved me, you lyin' fucker?"

Erik didn't respond. Offering his *friend* a contemptuous glance he walked away.

After reviewing the logbook and noting where a page had been torn out, Pete Durnell thanked the airport's cargo-entrance guard before he and Joe headed for the Europe-American freight office. As they entered, a black man dressed in coveralls and about the same age as Joe, whistled while weighing a parcel. Noting the number of pounds, the attendant removed the package from the scale before approaching them.

"Yes, gentlemen?"

Stacy displayed his badge. "I'm Sergeant Stacy, and this is Detective Durnell. We're interested in how your company handles bonded goods that don't have to clear customs? Are they locked when they're sent, or...?"

"It's a special process, Sergeant," the attendant said, taking a brochure out from underneath the counter and handing it to Joe. "All goods leaving and entering the United States must be checked by customs at the port of entry, however, there are specific companies that can bypass that procedure."

"How?"

"Well, if the companies are big enough in the business of transporting valuables, customs personnel are assigned to those corporations to check the goods and the weigh-bills. Nice if you can afford it, eh?"

"Do they use special containers of some sort?" Pete asked.

"Yes, sir," the attendant replied, before lifting up a door in the counter. "I was just going to pour myself a coffee, would you officers like to join me?"

Both detectives accepted. Following the man to a coffee machine, Joe asked, "What do these containers look like?"

The airline employee poured three coffees, gesturing that they could add their own cream and sugar if they wanted."They vary. Some look like ... have you ever seen airline food containers ... the ones that hold all the food trays?"

Joe had seen them. "Yeah."

"Well, some look like that, er, others are smaller. But they've each got separate compartments. For example, one section could hold currency, while another division in the same container could carry valuable paintings."

"Did you have a flight come in from Europe on Saturday?" Pete asked, adding sugar to his coffee.

Walking back to the counter, the attendant replied, "Yes, sir, Saturday's flight 2104 from Berlin."

Grimacing, after sipping his coffee for the first time, Stacy glanced at Pete. "This tastes just like the same leopard piss we have in our office, don't it partner?"

A sour look captured Pete's face. "The same," he said before asking, "Any special containers consigned to, or picked up by Protocol Customs Assurance Company, that day? The truck was probably owned by Systems Truck Rentals."

The clerk took a book off a shelf and browsed through a few pages. "Last Saturday?"

"Yeah, last Saturday," Pete said, glancing at the list.

"Yep, there were three shipments for Protocol. Two were taken away, and one was emptied here. If the shipments aren't too valuable, they'll unload them here and send the container back on the next flight. Sometimes someone from that company travels on the same plane. Ah, here we are ... a Mr. Jan VanVliet was on that flight and signed for the container at this end. VanVliet's a really nice fella, he comes here often, makes certain his cargo is unloaded, then heads back on the same flight. Would you like to see it?"

Durnell grimaced placing his coffee spoon down. Running his tongue over his teeth, he said, "See what? The actual container?"

"Sure. It's sealed, but it don't have a customs seal on it yet. They only have customs seals on 'em when they arrive. I can open it for you and secure it afterwards."

Two minutes later when the clerk opened the container in the rear of an adjacent warehouse, a shiver of utter disgust shot down Joe Stacy's spine. Like Joe, Pete could not say anything either, and the attendant stood speechless for a moment before muttering, "Sergeant, I ... I ... don't understand. Oxygen bottles aren't allowed to be transported ... Uh, animals are supposed to enter the port through..." The airline employee's voice trailed off.

The empty aluminium and fibreglass storage vessel resembled a travel trunk with grip handles. White liquid foam rubber that had softly solidified after being poured had left an impression resembling a small human form lying on its side with its knees bent. Twelve rubber straps attached to both sides of the trunk obviously kept the *body* in place. At the top, in a separate compartment, feed lines from four oxygen bottles with gauges lead to a facemask.

"Sir, what's your name?" Joe asked the counter man.

Plainly confused, the clerk replied, "Wilfred Young."

"Well, Wilfred, I'm informing you now to say absolutely nothing about this, do you understand? Not a word to anyone! There's no one here with us, so if this gets out, you've opened your mouth. Do we understand each other?"

The clerk swallowed heavily. "Yes, sir."

"Did a custom's agent clear this when it arrived?"

"Yes, sir, it had to be cleared. I'll find out the name of the person and phone you tomorrow. Is that all right?"

"That's fine. When is this due to leave?"

"On tomorrow night's flight 2105 to Berlin. It leaves at eight."

Joe handed his calling card to Wilfred, and then thought for a moment. "We're going to take it with us, and we'll have it back to you by around four o'clock. Are you on duty at that time tomorrow?"

"Yes, sir, I'll be here."

"Is your supervisor on duty now?"

"No, they've all gone for the day. I'm the boss of this section."

"Okay, Wilfred, is there a secluded doorway where we can move that thing into the trunk of our car without being seen?"

Although the rain had stopped, darkness filled the roads as the two detectives drove back to Seattle on the old highway. With Interstate-5 full of commuter traffic, the duo took the same route Pete had used after picking up his partner on Sunday night. This time the driver didn't complain when Stacy lit up a cigarette. Instead, Pete kept glancing in his rear-view mirror, before saying, "I think I need a drink. The kid was actually transported in that trunk. Joe, what the hell have we got here? Is it possible that...?"

Stacy also had not said a word since leaving the airport. Dispirited, his tone was nearly inaudible as he cut his partner off. "It's not only possible, it's happening, and the thought of it makes my blood boil. Goddamnit, someone's transporting kids for sexual utilization or body parts." His voice intensified, "We know it's happening in South America, the Far East, and India, but how long has it been happening here in the United States? The filthy rotten bastards are..."

This time Pete interrupted, declaring, "We're being tailed. It's the same car that left the airport with us," he said, attempting to keep his eyes glued to both the mirror and the road.

Stacy turned his head, but the car's lights made it impossible for him to see how many occupants it held. "Take the next right and slow down."

The dark-blue Chevrolet Corvette also turned right, staying back about sixty yards.

"The sons-a -bitches! Okay, Pete, there's no one else on this road, pour on the coals and pull a 180. Now! Now!"

After Pete jammed on the breaks and sharply turned the steering wheel, their vehicle careened, nearly sideswiping the Corvette. Swerving wildly, the driver of the oncoming car switched off his headlights and used the entrance of a gravel pit to gain room and speed past them. When the cars passed, two loud shots from a semi-automatic pistol shattered the left and right rear windows of the police auto.

Both police officers had ducked but Pete still managed to turn abruptly around to give chase. He was not fast enough though because the Corvette ran through a flashing railroad signal and disappeared into the night. A second earlier and it would have crashed through two lowering traffic arms.

Amidst the sounds of clanging bells and a fast-moving freight train, both detectives got out of their car.

"Did you get a licence number?" Joe asked, pistol in hand.

Durnell broadly grinned shaking his head. "No, but whoever it was needs his teeth fixed. That's all I saw, how about you?"

The grin was contagious. "Ditto! We've just been shot at; what the hell are you happy about?"

"That's the first time I've ever seen you draw that thing. It's a wonder it didn't fall apart from the pressure of your grip?"

"Screw you!" Joe said, clearing some broken glass off the front seat and making a mental note to take the captain's advice to exchange his revolver. "I can remember when you could turn this car around in one lane, never mind two. C'mon, I'll buy you that drink."

"Where're we goin'?" Pete asked, placing the auto in reverse and turning it around. "Also, I know we weren't followed to the airport, so who the hell knew we'd be there?"

Joe had asked himself the same question, and expanded on it. "Isn't that a bit like asking who took the kid and the deceased out of the hospital? Who knocked off the doc? Who the hell cut a half-hour out of the video? Who allowed the van out of our lock-up? Who drove it to the airport, and who tore out the missing page?"

Turning up his collar, Durnell grinned, saying, "Somethin' like that."

"Pete, what started as a simple robbery is becoming a little complex. Somebody thinks we know more than we do, and we've been one or two steps behind so far. We're obviously missing something here. Who in hell are we talking to that we shouldn't be?"

Pete slowed a little, lifting up his body to remove a fragment of glass lying on the seat under his right thigh. "Ya got me, Joe. If we find 'em, we should thank the thugs who robbed the store. Do you think we've got ourselves a goddamned Judas in the office?"

"No doubt about it," Stacy said, turning on the heater to compensate for the recently installed cold air *vents*. "Pull over where they shot at us, will ya?"

Pete stopped the car just short of the gravel pit and the two got out with their flashlights. Five minutes later Joe found what they were looking for. Although two shots had been fired, one brass casing was enough to go on.

"It looks to me like a .380," he said, picking it up with a pencil and slipping it into a cellophane pouch.

His partner whistled. "Pretty fancy round. Maybe James Bond shot at us? Nah, he drives an Aston Martin."

When their car turned onto the old highway again, Stacy suggested, "Let's go have a beer at Bea Honeywell's - it's not far from here."

"Bea Honeywell's? We haven't been there in years. She's probably still pissed off with you for ditching her."

Lighting up another smoke, the eldest of the two grinned. "Nah, Bea's over it now. I've visited her a few times. She's met some pansy stock broker and it was love at first bite for both of them."

"Is he rich?"

"The phoney bastard's gotta be, just to keep up with her. Her place makes nothing but money. Say, do you remember when we first partnered up, we'd always go to Bea's to compare notes about our cases?"

Pete obviously enjoyed the fond memories. "Yeah, because we could see everyone who came in or went out. Even the captain knew we drank there. It seemed we could figure things out quicker over a few beers."

"Yeah, the good old days before you got married. Them were the days. Well buddy, we've got a hell of a lot of figuring out to do on this one. Somebody don't like us, Pete."

Durnell sighed, "You can say that again."

Deep in thought, Joe rolled his window down and threw his cigarette out. Winding the window back up, he subconsciously repeated, "Somebody don't like us, Pete." When his voice trailed off, he added, "And we're gonna give 'em a reason to dislike us a little more."

Bea Honeywell's Tavern could be seen blocks away because of the number of brightly lit Christmas lights hanging everywhere.

Circular shaped with large spheroid windows, Stacy knew the building was originally built as a new car showroom, but when the recession hit, Bea Honeywell had bought it for fifty percent of its real value. The car company had thought no one would fancy the shape and were going to demolish it, but Bea saw its future and the rest was history. The place was famous for its steaks, chicken, reasonable bar prices, and great entertainment.

"Well, look who the cat dragged in," a tall, stately looking, big boned and well-built blond woman about forty, said sarcastically. "I'm not referring to you, Pete. I'm talking to this haggard lookin' cohort of yours. What brings you around here, Joe? The classy side of the tracks gettin' to ya?"

"I thought you said she'd forgiven you?" Pete whispered.

Smiling and holding his arms out, Joe murmured, "The stock broker can't be giving her what she needs, that's all. Bea, baby, is that any way to talk to the man of your dreams? Come here and give me a hug."

Turning scarlet, the woman always wanting people to notice her large steel claws also had a giant and gentle heart and Joe knew the organ's tolerance of reckless abandon and uncompromising restraint. Bea found it difficult to finish her next statement. When her long lost friend embraced her, lifting her up to swirl her around, his lips got in the way of, "Take a hike, you bas..."

The *perturbed girl* who went up, was a wholly *aroused woman* coming down.

Straightening her clothing and hair, Bea's lustful constraint could not disguise her true feelings. "Oh, Joe, what a waste of talent. I'd almost forgotten what it was like. Get rid of that badge and come give your little baby what she hungers for."

The sergeant gave Bea a smack on her behind. "No time for that Bea, we're here discussing business. What's happened to the stock broker?"

Flushed with excitement but gaining control of herself, Bea led them to a table on the far side from the door. "His shorts caught up to him, so I exchanged him for a banker. Joe, baby, it's like I've always told you - you've ruined my life. How can I settle for vinegar, when I've tasted fine wine?"

Now Stacy's smile turned bigger under Pete's incredulous stare.

"Bea, you're putting the wrong thoughts in this young man's head. Give us a jug o' Budweiser, please, my darlin'."

Seeing more customers entering, Bea cocked her head before turning and smacking her own bottom. "It's always here when you need it, Joe. I'll send Ernie over with your order."

Before Joe could say, "Don't say it!" Pete got the first words out. "Wasted talent? Give baby what she hungers for? Fine wine? It's always here when you need it? Christ, I never realized you were that gifted. Sign me up for the next dance course."

When the jug arrived, Joe filled two glasses, and lit up a smoke. Straight-faced, he said, "Dancing doesn't do it, my boy, personality does. Some of *us* have got it, and some of *us* don't got it. I can't help it if you don't got it?"

After taking out his notebook, Pete rolled his eyes to the ceiling. "In this particular case, I don't got it because I don't want it. Not that it matters ... from what I've just seen and heard, you've got it all anyway."

"I'm studying, I'm studying," a frustrated Pete said, standing and staring at the inquisitive captain. "I don't know if I want to take the exams so soon. What are ya nagging at me for?"

"Yeah, what are you nagging at him for?" Joe asked, also standing while holding on to a file that had grown steadily. Hugging the dossier, he added, "This is gonna take all the manpower we can muster, and then some."

Glover took a thermos out of a side drawer in his desk, but quickly put it back. "Who's nagging? I'm going on medical leave soon, and my replacement..." The devoutly religious captain stopped talking while his right hand displayed the sign of the cross across his body. "... God bless him, might not be as patient as I am, that's why! Get on with it, Pete, that's an order. Now, *gentlemen*, and I use that term loosely ... sit down!"

Both detectives sat after the captain waved away Joe's comment about him hoarding a secret stash of decent coffee in his drawer.

"You don't miss much do you, Stacy? I fill this thermos from the pot outside in the office. Now, quit interrupting me, damn it! If someone shoots at you and misses, you're supposed to arrest them. If you get hit, we arrest them and mop up the mess afterwards. What the hell happened?"

Over the next half-hour, both Joe and Pete explained the shooting incident and how they were progressing on the case. When they were finished, the captain also filled them in on recent developments.

"The first set of prints in the van belong to a Norbert Kroll, who lives at a rooming house at 9567 Cottonwood Street. Kroll's a German citizen and a landed immigrant. Last year, he applied for his American citizenship, but it's been put on hold for two years. He's has never been formally charged, but his name crops up all over the place. He's used phoney identification many times and we've linked him to a minor child sex case in Portland. He's also been mixed up with various white supremacist movements throughout the country."

Joe took his cigarettes out of his shirt pocket but quickly put back again under the captain's scornful gaze.

"How come he's never been convicted?" Joe asked.

Mystery and frustration covered Glover. "That's the sixty-four-thousand dollar question we can't answer. When he gets arrested, someone gets him off. I want you guys to get over to Cottonwood right away and check out his digs."

While Joe and Pete made notes, Glover continued. "Now, Interpol tells us the one thumbprint belongs to another German by the name of Helmut

Bruckman. This guy's wanted in Germany, Belgium, and Holland for speeding, impaired driving, and for distributing illicit racial material. Also, the guy's a certified international securities courier."

Stacy interrupted. "Interesting ... is that all?"

The captain brought his thermos out and refilled his cup. "Not quite. Like Kroll, this guy also appears to have a guardian angel. He was a material witness to a shooting in London two years ago, but when he didn't show up, all charges were dropped."

Glover winced and used both hands to massage his right ankle. "Interpol believes he's involved with race riots, but nothing's been proven. They don't know where Bruckman is, or what he's doing. We've asked them for a photo."

"What about the kid's prints?" Pete asked.

"Well, they are a child's prints, but we've drawn a blank there as well. Your German hunch was wrong Joe. Interpol checked with Hanover police and there are no missing children matching his description. Why did you think of Hanover?"

"Because of what the kid said in the hospital. Something about hand oven."

Glover nodded and was about to say something else when his telephone rang. A moment after picking it up, he said, "Okay, thanks, I'll be right there."

After hanging up the instrument, Glover stood and finished his coffee. "The deputy chief wants me. Check with the crime lab. They've got some information on the clothes the stiff and the kid were wearing, and ballistics has come up with something. Where's the suitcase now?"

"With Sawasy," Joe answered.

Standing up to leave, Pete asked, "What about prints on the Paris Match magazine? Where there any?"

Wincing before tightening his tie and putting on his jacket, Glover shrugged, "None, not even on the cover." Then, following the two of them out and closing his door, he said, "I'll see ya later ... keep me informed."

On the way back to their desks, Joe murmured, "Pete, let's stay tight-lipped on this one, except for those who need to know. Agreed?"

"Need to know basis, right?"

"You got it!"

From the time he was ten years old, Terry Sawasy wanted a chemistry set. His mother started him at the piano when he was three and wanted him to be a concert pianist, but his dad believed Terry should aspire to achieve the pinnacle in any vocation the boy chose. Sawasy's intuitive imaginativeness turned him into the best-trained crime technician in the country. Police forces from New York to London had offered him the world to work for them, but Seattle was his home, and here he had decided to stay. It wasn't the money; it was the Pacific Ocean, the air, the open spaces, and most of all, the people. The people were genuine, Terry thought. They cared about their fellow man, instead of getting lost in the ever-burgeoning labyrinth of selfish indifference.

Both Joe and Pete liked Sawasy, and when they entered "the pigeonhole" as Terry called it, the blond *messiah of the Lilliputian realm* wearing a white laboratory coat had his eyes glued to a microscope. Terry's four assistants were busy doing tasks their boss had assigned.

"What have you got for us, Terry?" Stacy asked, picking up a liquid-filled test tube and holding it to the light.

"Don't touch that!"

When Joe carefully but quickly put the item down, his facial expression portrayed that of a youngster who had been caught going through all the pockets in the class cloakroom. "Jeez ... er, sorry, Terry."

After writing something down in his *black book*, Sawasy grinned and joined them. "That's my new aphrodisiac formula. One sniff of that and you'll want to screw every woman you meet."

Pete reached for it, stopping short of picking it up. "Joe doesn't need it, however I sure as hell do. The captain says you've got something for us."

Sawasy handed each of them a white sheet of paper. "Everything's there, except the container information, which we'll be finished with in half an hour. A firm in France made the kid's pyjamas. I telephoned them and most of the garments they produce are distributed to four European Common Market countries - Italy, Germany, Holland, and Belgium. The boy had peed in them a few times so we've asked for a DNA analysis. As far as the dead fellow is concerned, his clothes were off-the-rack American."

Sawasy paused for a moment straightening his glasses on the bridge of his nose and fumbling with his wedding ring. "Let me ask you guys something ... where's his ring?"

"Whose ring?" Pete asked.

The technician reached for a file folder and took out two photographs. "The deceased's ring. You've already got copies of these. Our photographer took the first picture at the convenience store, and the second one was taken when he was pulled out of the harbour. When the two of you reviewed the body at the morgue, did he have a ring on?"

Pete and Joe's eyes met before Joe answered, "No, he didn't. I would have remembered it. And you're right, at the store, he did wear a ring."

Sawasy took two more photos out of the folder. "These are blow-ups of his left hand. I know they're not very clear, but look at that. What does it look like to you?"

The two detectives squinted at the glossy prints, and Stacy put his glasses on. "It looks like some sort of a dog, or even a..."

"A wolf of some sort," Sawasy said, answering his own question. "There's almost a human countenance to its face. I think it's a howling wolf in the sitting position."

Pete wasn't at the age where he needed glasses. Commonly known as "Eagle Eyes" on the police range, he quickly spotted something else. "Terry, what are those diagonal marks behind it ... there? Are they just scratches?"

"I saw those earlier," Sawasy announced, holding a magnifying glass above the picture. "They're either lightening bolts, or symbols of some kind." Moving the glass back a little, he added, "Yeah, that's what they form - it's the Schutzstaffel emblem."

Joe started thinking out loud. "Bruckman, Kroll, and now Schutzstaffel. Who the hell's Schutzstaffel?"

The crime technician's face took on a grim cast as he placed the photos back in an envelope. "It's not a family name, Joe. The Schutzstaffel was the Third Reich's black-shirt organization, primarily known as the SS. You know, the chicken farmer's dreaded SS and Gestapo mob?"

"I've heard of the SS, but ... chicken farmer?"

"Yeah, Hitler's henchman, Heinrich Himmler. The head case that controlled the horde of SS gangsters and murderers carrying out Hitler's dirty work."

Joe turned to leave, walked a few steps, and then returned. "Goddamnit, I know I've said this before, but what the hell are we on to? Thugs wearing SS rings, and a paedophile circle. Terry, anything you find out comes to us, and us only. Also, do me a favour and let us know immediately if anybody asks you about this matter."

Snow began falling as the detectives drove to Kroll's residence on Cottonwood Street. Earlier, their car's windows had been replaced, allowing the heater to drone on its normal low setting.

After leaving the crime lab, the officers had visited ballistics and learned that only one bullet had completely perforated the dead man's skull. The other had not quite cleared the back of his head and was stuck in his cranium. Both were .380 rounds, fired from a Steyr automatic pistol, the same weapon that had discharged two shots at them on the road. The Steyr, they learned, was an expensive professional European handgun, and whoever used it preferred Ruuko match type high-grade ammunition made in Korea. Ballistics also reported the same weapon had killed two Brink's guards in Spokane, six months earlier. The rare coins stolen in that robbery had a collector's value of two-hundred-and-fifty million. Thirty days later, the collection turned up in Switzerland and an insurance company paid a Swiss bank account ten percent reward recovery fee.

Stacy thought ballistics had done a thorough job. The bullet from the deceased's right lung had been fired from a standard unregistered 9mm Browning pistol; a weapon similar, but larger than the semi-automatic Beretta Joe was issued with when he turned in his old revolver. After firing his new "*piece*," as Pete called it, Joe had found his accuracy had increased substantially. Although heavier than his old revolver, the sergeant admired his new upside-down leather shoulder holster and the fact that each of his two spare magazines held fourteen rounds.

As the two neared Kroll's house, Pete said, "Welcome to the real world, Joe. You'll like the safety features. It's got a magazine safety, a safety strap, and the usual safety lever. Do you find it heavier?"

"Nah, we dancers can handle the weight. Hey, did you see where I hit those targets. Not bad, eh?"

"You've been practising. All along, I've been working with a closet marksman," Durnell said, pulling up in front of 9567 Cottonwood Street, a wooden three level grey paint-peeled run down rooming house that had dispensed at least seventy years of shelter to its occupants.

"Bullshit, it's the first time I've used one of these things," Joe said, eyeing the building. "This joint looks like a dive. Park in the back, Pete."

"Reason?"

"I can't tell you - it's just one of those things."

Pete didn't push the matter. His partner's intuitions were usually right.

Even in snow, the alley behind the Cottonwood address was strewn with litter. Worn-out fences and garages lined both sides of the lane where three scruffy teenagers took turns trying to throw a hunting knife into a telephone pole.

The back of the house the detectives were interested in didn't have a fence or a garage. Instead, a packed dirt driveway displaying fresh vehicle tracks from two cars led to a garage door built into the basement. Bars covered all the windows of the house and smoke came from a red brick chimney looking like it could crumble apart at any moment. Kindling had been stacked on a small back porch atop broken stairs. The yard was strewn with snow-covered garbage, and five cats milled about.

The detectives parked their car at the side of the driveway, making certain not to disturb the visible tread marks of a previously parked vehicle. As they walked towards the house, another two meowing cats came out of the side basement door that was slightly ajar.

Using his right hand to push open the squeaking cellar door, Joe said, "I'll go in here, Pete. You go around to the front and knock on the door."

Stacy could not find a light switch, but enough daylight coming in allowed him to wade slowly through foul smelling garbage and children's clothing scattered and stuck to the damp clay floor. The acrid smell of cat faeces and urine forced him to retch and take out his handkerchief. Holding it over his nose and mouth, he climbed a set of wooden stairs leading to the first floor door. It was locked, but a moment later Pete opened it from the other side.

"Nobody answered when I thumped, so I walked in," Durnell said, wincing at the stench coming up from below. "There're five locks on the front door and they were all unlatched. Oh, and have you noticed all these doors are cushioned to keep in the sound?"

Joe put away his handkerchief but he still wanted to throw up. The smell was so bad he thought it would remain in his nostrils forever. "Yeah. There are also four locks on the basement door. This place is more secure than a prison. You check out this floor, and I'll take the top."

After pushing open a padded door leading to the second floor, the senior investigator had a vague idea what he would find in the five rooms and four attic rooms. From the moment he had entered the house, thirty years of police-work triggered his sixth sense.

Every soundproofed room could be bolted from the outside only, and they all contained iron bunk beds. Bedpans that had not been emptied sat on dingy linoleum floors scattered with dirty rag dolls and other parts of broken plastic toys.

Stacy noticed there were no chests of drawers or closets in the rooms, just iron beds. All the windows were painted black and overlain with heavy black curtains and strong chicken wire. Some bunks had soiled threadbare blankets spread on them, and the mattresses were stained with urine and excrement. Like the *travel case*, strong rubber straps were attached to the sides of the beds.

There were two bathrooms on the second floor, and each held two grimy sinks, baths, and toilets. One bathtub was half-filled with lukewarm water, one flush toilet had overflowed, and two other toilets were *full*. There were no locks on the bathroom doors, and like the rooms, naked bulbs hung at the end of wires attached to the ceilings. When Joe touched one of the bulbs, it felt warm.

Stacy's mind worked a mile a second when he rejoined Pete going through some papers spread out on a desk in the back kitchen. The three rooms on the first floor were quite different from the ones up top. A neat shower room and toilet separated a well-furnished bedroom and living room containing a blazing fireplace. Mounds of burnt paper at the back of the flames indicated a hasty *cleansing* of sorts had recently taken place.

"I've just turned off the burner under the kettle," Pete said, still looking through papers. "Whoever lives here was tipped off we were coming. What's upstairs?"

"People, probably children have been held here against their will. It's a son-of-a-bitchin' body shop. If the sick bastards who ran this place were here, I'd shoot the lot of them."

The unleashed anger in Stacy's voice heightened Pete's scrutiny of the papers. He knew his partner would not conduct such an action, but physically, when Joe was this enraged, Pete knew the guilty party should not be anywhere near him.

"Is there a phone in this rat-hole?" Joe asked, his voice crackling with anger.

Pete found a photograph and held it by a corner edge. Joining Stacy, he said, "It's in the living room, but Joe, take a look at this, first?"

The photo in Durnell's hand portrayed two men sitting on a motorcycle in front of a chain-mesh fence. The grinning driver was blond and the laughing pockmarked shaven-headed passenger had a mouthful of rotten teeth. "There's our morgue resident, and the other's the prick that shot at us."

Stacy put his glasses on but didn't say a word - nor did he touch the photograph. Instead, he memorized every feature of the passenger, even the ring on the left hand clutching the waist of the driver. The driver also wore a ring, and while they appeared similar, Joe could not make out the features with the naked eye.

Hate dominated the team leader's face as he lit up a smoke and left the room. Using his handkerchief to pick up the phone, and the tip of his pen to push the buttons for star sixty-nine, Joe wrote down the last number that had called the house. Afterwards, he pushed three more digits and wrote down the last number called from the house. When he hung up he muttered, "We'll get you bastards, and when we do, I'll volunteer to send the voltage through the chair."

Over the next hour, the two detectives investigated every compartment and cubbyhole in the old dwelling, cautiously ensuring they were not destroying fingerprints. The *residents* who had recently split had done a thorough job of removing most incriminating information the police could use, but in their haste to leave, they had overlooked certain items. These were placed in plastic envelopes for investigation at the lab. As well, a secret nook under the stairs revealed at least a hundred numbered video tapes, with dates going back to 1979.

Grinding his teeth and clenching his right fist, when Joe carefully carried the tapes out into the hallway, he said, "I'm not looking forward to viewing these. Mark my words, Pete, we're going to send these bastards to meet their brother the devil."

Later, Durnell decided to get his brief case from the car. Heading out the back kitchen door, he noticed two of the three teenagers he had seen earlier, sitting in the front seat trying to hot-wire the police auto. The vehicle's right rear door had been left open as a safety haven for the third boy - the designated spotter, standing at the top of the stairs. Fortunately, when Pete came out of the house, the kid never reached the auto's open door. After running down the stairs, the boy had barely approached the vehicle when the ground shook violently. The earth-shattering red-hot blast from the exploding police car blew Durnell back into the kitchen and the badly burned *lookout* into the next yard. If the concussion had not propelled Pete back into the house, a front tire launched with the velocity of a howitzer shell would have struck him.

The car's two young occupants were killed instantly in the eruption that shot flames and black spiralling smoke sixty feet into the air and caused heat so intense Pete and Joe could not get near enough to help.

"Call 911," Joe yelled to the neighbour in the next yard attending the blistered teenager writhing in agony. "We'll look after him."

The ferocious force of the blast had hurled the youth through a wooden fence, spearing a piece of ancient fence-post into the boy's right thigh. Lying, contorted on the ground, his skewered upper leg resembled a red pumpkin with an arrow stuck through it.

Heavy wet snowflakes began falling as Stacy used his belt to tie a tourniquet around the injured leg. Pete took off his topcoat and wrapped it around the mutilated teen's upper body. "You'll be okay, son," he said. "An ambulance is on its way. What's your name?"

Moaning in pain, the disoriented lad murmured, "Malcolm Goodman." Anything else he mumbled was incoherent, other than his telephone number.

It didn't take long for an ambulance, fire trucks, and police to arrive, and the doctor left the *shaft* in the boy's thigh before gently placing him on a gurney. Moments later, the wailing ambulance sped the teen away to the nearest hospital.

Shortly, Captain Glover appeared on the scene with two other detectives that began dispersing the curious crowd.

"What the hell happened here?" Glover grunted, turning up his overcoat's collar and limping over.

"That was meant for us," Joe replied, pointing to the charred smoking vehicle being sprayed by two fire-fighters. "When we were in the house, some kids tried to hot wire it. I'll head over to the hospital later and find out what the injured kid saw. He was a fraction of a second away from being blown away with those other two."

Pete came over, still a little dazed from his ordeal. "The neighbour says he didn't recognize the kid. He might be from around here, but he doesn't know him."

"What about the two others?" Joe asked.

Pete shook his head. "I've asked around. No one saw it happen. I don't know if these people would tell us anyway. With so much crime in this area, they pretty much stick to themselves and keep their mouths shut."

Stacy noticed one of the detectives who had arrived with Glover heading up the porch stairs to the house.

"Hey, Schmidt, stay out, we're not finished in there yet!"

Schmidt nodded, waved, turned, and came down. "Okay, Joe, I just wanted to check out the place. What are you so anxious about? Maybe I can help."

Joe glared wildly at the detective. "If I need your help, I'll ask for it."

Appearing slightly humiliated, Schmidt gave a sheepish grin and shrugged heading back to the crowd of people in the lane. "Suit yourself, Joe."

"What's that all about?" Glover asked. "You've worked with him before."

Lighting up a smoke, Stacy said, "No I haven't! Pete has, but not me. I wouldn't work with him because I don't like him. Listen, Captain, every goddamn move we make is being telegraphed ahead. I'm not blaming Schmidt, or anyone else, but someone knew we were coming here because the place was cleaned out minutes before we arrived. It would have been us in that car instead of the two kids. Until we crack this thing, my trust stays right here," he said, pointing to his own head. "Even if Schmidt were the chief, I wouldn't let him in that house."

A concerned look came over Glover as he searched for words. Rubbing his chin with the thumb and forefinger of his left hand, he kept his voice low. "That's something I want to talk to you two about. I've been *advised* to take you off this case."

With what his partner and he had been through Stacy couldn't believe what he had just heard. "What the hell did you just say? What the hell's going on here?"

Glover was not one for mincing words. "Whoa, hold it there, Joe. Don't take your frustration out on me. The chief was pressured from on high, but I convinced him the two of you should stay with it. I don't know who's influencing him, but whoever it is, it's big time. The chief wants it wrapped up in two weeks."

Gently grabbing Glover by his left arm, Joe mellowed guiding his boss towards the house. "Two weeks? This isn't just a store robbery, Ray; it's much bigger than that. What's going to happen when you're on medical leave?"

"We'll get to that when I'm on sick leave," Glover snorted, finding it difficult to climb the slippery back stairs. "Now, tell me what you've got?"

Joe and Pete gave their boss a complete tour, and with every room they entered, Glover became more incensed. "Guys, I want you to get these pricks, and when you do, give me five minutes alone with them. No, all I'll need is one fucking minute."

By the time they left, one of Sawasy's teams was on the scene detecting what the naked eye could not see, including taking pictures and dusting for prints. When the remains of the two boys were removed from the car, the shattered vehicle was towed away for another contingent of crime-lab professionals to go over it from top to bottom.

Waving to Linda, Joe Stacy declined Pete's offer to come in for supper when he dropped his partner off that same afternoon. Pete usually drove, but Joe had decided to take over the wheel of their newly issued Chevrolet. All Stacy wanted to do was get home and out of the large flakes of snow laying a thick white carpet and making the roads difficult to manoeuvre. The luxury of taking off his clothes, soaking in a hot bathtub, and relaxing, would have to wait though until he returned the *suitcase* to the airport. The crime-lab had gone over it and Sawasy had promised a full report the following day.

Before picking up the item, both detectives had flipped a coin to see who would make the trip, and as usual, Joe had lost. He always lost when he gambled with Pete, but he knew his luck would have to change eventually. "Probably later," he murmured. "With Pete's uncanny luck, it'll be much later."

Earlier, the two had questioned the owners and boarders of the houses in the immediate area of the Kroll house, but had gained no new information. The neighbours had seen car lights at night and the silhouettes of people entering and departing, but nothing else. The building had always remained quiet each day and only once had a nearby resident seen a blond man on the back porch stacking firewood.

"Is, uh ... Mr. Young on duty?" Joe asked an older gent wearing coveralls, a Europe-American Airlines cap, and reading a newspaper at the airline's freight counter. Earlier in the day, the senior detective had expected a message from Wilfred Young concerning the name of the custom's agent, but there was none.

Scratching his left armpit, the man slowly glanced up. "Nope. Can I help you?"

"Where's Mr. Young?"

"He never showed up for work this mornin'. Didn't even phone in sick either. That's not like Wilfred. Do you have a parcel to pick up?"

Stacy displayed his badge. "No, I'm returning an empty Protocol Customs courier case. It's to be on tonight's 8pm flight to Berlin."

The agent returned to his newspaper. "You may as well just leave it 'cause Protocol's cancelled their contract with us. They'll probably pick it up when they get around to it."

"What do you mean they've cancelled their contract?" Stacy asked, sliding the publication out from under the man's eyes. "You had it yesterday?"

"Don't know? We got a rocket from New York this mornin' tellin' us Protocol's buyin' their own planes and doin' their own shippin'. Just leave it here - they'll pick it up."

"Where will their planes be flying out of?"

The agent shook his head. "Dunno, but there's a rumour about Vancouver, Canada. All I know is we ain't handlin' their business anymore. Do ya wanna leave it or not?"

Joe opened the door to leave. Before walking out, he said, "No thanks, I'll drop it off myself."

"Anytime," the airline representative replied, sliding his newspaper back.

As Stacy stopped his vehicle at the gate, the on-duty guard came out of his shack and after cautiously studying Joe's face, whispered, "I didn't recognize the car. Are you one of the detectives that came here yesterday?"

"The same," Joe replied, placing the auto in park then applying the emergency brake. "Why?"

The guard passed a small brown envelope through the car's window. "Last night, one of Willie's buddies came by and asked me to give this to you. He said Willie made it clear it was for no one else but you guys."

The sergeant did not want to read the contents in front of the gatekeeper. Slipping the envelope into his inside jacket pocket and thanking the man, he drove out and pulled over to the side of the road leading to Interstate 5. The note said: *Call me at 567-8709. Important. Wilfred Young.*

On his way home, a public phone booth could have allowed a connection, but when Stacy picked up the device, the mouthpiece had been taken apart.

"Maybe I should get a goddamned cellular," he muttered after turning on his apartment lights, kicking off his shoes and reaching for the phone. He knew Mrs. White had been in because the place had been cleaned.

A woman answered after the first ring, and heavy breathing preceded, "Hello?"

"Yeah, is Wilfred Young there, please?"

Joe heard the phone change hands and some murmuring taking place.

"Is that you, Sergeant?" Wilfred asked, the nervousness in his voice indicating something was seriously amiss.

"Yeah, it's Joe Stacy. What's wrong, Wilfred? Why weren't you at work today?"

"Sergeant, I'm not at home. Just after you left last night, two guys came in asking for the container. I didn't know what to say, so I told them it was locked away. One of them took out a knife, and the other grabbed me by my neck, saying, 'Go get it, Sambo, or we'll cut off your fucking head.'"

"What did they look like?" Joe asked.

"They were skinheads. The bony guy who seized me is about five-ten, or eleven. He's got a pockmarked face and bad teeth. The other was heavyset, about six feet tall. I'd say they're in their late thirties."

"They must have passed the guard at the gate? Did he get their licence number?"

"No, they probably parked at the other side of the building and came in through the front entrance."

Joe picked up a pen and pad. "Where are you calling from?"

"My wife and me are at my daughter's ... 3034 101st Street. I'm using their phone. What's going on, Sergeant?"

"I can't say anything right now, Wilfred. How did you manage to get away from them?"

Wilfred's voice relaxed a little. "The guy released his grip when two fellas from our warehouse came in to have coffee. I told the skinheads to wait a moment. That I'd get the case for them, but they hurried out the same way they came in. The smelly one made a gesture as they passed me. I guess I'm not supposed to say nothin'."

"Smelly? What gesture," Joe asked, doodling with the pen.

"The guy with the bad complexion reeked of body odour. He placed a finger on his lips, then ran it under his chin from ear to ear. You know, like keep quiet, or I'll cut your throat? Oh yeah, I forgot to mention the custom's agent ... his name's Klenz with a K and a Z. I don't know his first name, but he operates between the airport and Protocol."

Joe wrote the name down and before hanging up, he advised Wilfred to phone in sick to Europe-American. He also told him to telephone a police artist's number he gave him, take the next few days off, and not to mention his whereabouts to anyone.

Wilfred nervously licked his lips. "You don't have to worry about that, Sergeant. We're stayin' here. I'm no dummy. I know what that case was used for, and I'm applying for a transfer. Being scared shitless is one thing, but it's better than pushin' up daisies."

After hanging up the phone, Joe sat back, lit up a cigarette, and as usual watched the smoke rise to the ceiling. The mouthful of rotten teeth and the bad body odour had been mentioned again, and now someone new had entered the picture. Could it be the driver of the Corvette? Loosening his tie and throwing his coat and topcoat on a nearby chair, when his coats landed, his jacket parted and he saw the magazine. Earlier on that morning, he had placed the Paris Match in his inside pocket. He didn't know why, but something told him he had better go over it again, for the third time.

While undressing, the noise from the filling bathtub prevented Joe from hearing the first two songs on his favourite compact disk. Once submerged though, with his head and hands out of the water, he turned the magazine's pages and crooned along with Matt Monroe as the music of *Walk Away* softly flowed throughout the apartment.

Page after page of the French magazine revealed the same thing; engaging pictures with tabloid-type headlines and text, but other than that, absolutely nothing, not even a pen marking. He had even read the advertising pages before dropping the magazine on the floor, stretching out and sinking his whole body beneath the relaxing magical liquid stimulant. Though only for a moment. Emerging like a surfacing submarine, Joe reached for the now soaked periodical. There it was. One word, shining out like a beacon in the darkness.

Ecstatic and naked, Stacy ran for the phone. "Pete, the kid didn't say, 'hand oven.' I believe he said 'Eindhoven.' That's a city in Holland. He's Dutch."

Chapter 3

The little girl looked about six years old with the enduring smile of an angel. She had taken off her yellow toque because the wool itched her forehead and ears as she dragged her sled to the edge of the gently sloped hill loaded with other children mainly the same age.

After climbing aboard and giving the snow-covered ground a push with her hands, the sleigh moved slowly at first before picking up speed down the hill. Other kids did the same, and with the wind whipping up her beautiful blond hair, the youngster giggled excitedly while holding on tightly to the sleigh's rope.

Most of the other children had parents or friends with them, but this little girl wearing a red one-piece snowsuit with mittens attached appeared to be alone. That reality had attracted the attention of a stout dark haired man and a thin blond woman sitting eating peanuts on a nearby park bench.

The duo had been watching the child walk home from school for a week, and had checked personal information made available only to them. The girl's mother was a single working parent, therefore quite often she let her daughter go out on her own.

The pair had watched the child play for over an hour on the crowded hillside, staying in her vicinity when she moved around. Their *prey* had not spoken with other kids and it pleased them immensely she did not know anyone in the immediate area. Both thought today was the day they would make their move, and the excitement of reeling in their *catch* was nearly more than they could bear.

Patiently, they knew eventually the girl would fall off her sleigh, and when she finally did, the woman would come to the girl's *rescue* while the man walked to his van parked in a semi-isolated spot nearby.

The tiny mountain climber had eventually progressed to the steeper of two hills and when her sled turned over after hitting a hole, she scratched her face on the ice. Distressed, she totally forgot all her mother's warnings about not talking to strangers.

"Aw, honey, don't cry. Here, let me brush the snow off you. Are you all right? What's your name, sweetheart?"

The girl's crying eased but she remained quiet while a handkerchief tenderly wiped her eyes. Instead, with the woman following, the youngster stomped the few feet to turn her sled upright.

"I'll bet you've got the same name as my daughter, Debbie? Isn't that right, honey?"

After a few more sniffles, a hint of a smile finally appeared. "No, my name's Sarah Goldfarb."

"Sarah? That's right, how could I forget such a lovely name? Would you like some peanuts, Sarah?"

The child took off her mittens and placed her right hand in the offered bag. "Thank you. You look like my Auntie Gimella. She's staying with us over Hanukkah and New Year's Eve."

The woman picked up Sarah's sled in one hand. "I know she is, honey. Your Auntie Gimella told us to come and bring you home, if that's all right with you? Uncle George is heating up the car, so you'll be nice and warm. Give me your hand ... are you still cold, sweetheart?"

Feeling better now, Sarah walked dutifully towards the van. Smiling, she said, "Uh huh, A little. Do I know Uncle George?"

"Sure you do, and you also know me, Auntie Phylis. Your Uncle George and I gave you all those wonderful presents two years ago when you were four, remember?"

The girl thought for a moment walking towards the vehicle. "No, I'm just turning seven ... that would be three years ago, Auntie Phylis."

After opening the side door of the van and placing the sled inside, the woman said, "Are you ever smart, Sarah. How foolish of me not to remember your age. Here, you take this bag of peanuts and jump in. There's a big teddy bear inside who wants to see you. He says he needs a hug."

It only took another five seconds for the doors to close allowing the van to drive away.

"Sarah, this is your Uncle George. Has he changed since you last saw him?"

With his grinning mouth twitching slightly, the peculiar man punching out numbers on a cellular phone turned and winked at the child. "Good to see you again, Sarah."

"I don't think I remember you, Uncle George. Did you come to my birthday party when I was six?"

The woman unscrewed the top of a thermos bottle. "No, Uncle George was away earning lots of money to buy you beautiful presents. Sarah, Auntie Gimella made some nice hot chocolate for the three of us. We've already had some, would you like yours now, sweetheart? It's really good and it will warm you up?"

"Yes, thank you," Sarah said, hugging the bear. Moments later she was so sound asleep, the vehicle's blaring radio did not wake her, nor did the sound of the driver changing licence plates when the van stopped at a secluded two car windowless garage.

"Well, Mr. Grunds, we've done it with lots of time to spare," the woman said, taking off a blond wig, and combing out her own dark brown hair.

Changing his coat and removing a black hairpiece from his bald head, her *associate* wiped his sweating upper lip and chuckled. "It seems to be getting easier, Mrs. Grunds. In addition, the quality has improved. I want to undress this one, she's a real cutie."

Smearing on lipstick, the woman became resolute. "Don't get soft on me, Ernst; she's still a Jew. Since when do you like undressing Jews?"

The man pouted. "But dear, she doesn't look like a Jew. She's got blond hair and ... well, you always undress the boys."

"So do you, but I deserve a few perks. You're not undressing this one - do you understand? Don't get too involved with our merchandise, Ernst, they're just meat."

The brooding man replied, "Yes, dear," then suddenly became cheerful again. "But I want to take some pictures when you've bathed her. All right?"

"Well, you know we're not supposed to, but I guess we can add a few more to our collection. I don't want you touching this one, though, like you did the others. There'll be plenty more, do you understand?"

"Yes, dear."

It was not a coincidence that the couple's Cadillac Eldorado sat with its trunk open in the next stall. After Mr. And Mrs. Grunds transferred Sarah, the bear and the sled inside the trunk, he slammed it shut and then the couple drove away. Five minutes later, a foul smelling man with a pockmarked face and a mouthful of rotten teeth entered the garage, slipped behind the empty van's wheel, and headed to a nearby car wash.

Thirty minutes later, Sarah remained asleep as a garage door opened, allowing the Cadillac to enter a modern house in the Queen Anne Hill area of Seattle. Sarah was still fast asleep when she was undressed, and bathed by the woman. She did moan a bit when her naked body was photographed before being bound with plastic strips and placed lying on her side in a *container*. Liquid foam rubber was pumped around the child, and when the pliable sheet was removed from underneath her, a needle punctured the back of her left hand and an intravenous drip started. Still sleeping soundly, an oxygen mask was placed over Sarah's nose and mouth and rubber straps secured her body before the apparatus was closed and locked.

Approximately two hours later, Mr. Grunds returned the Cadillac to the windowless two-car garage, and transferred the container to the back of a parked orange van marked Systems Truck Rentals. After Mr. Grunds departed, the man with a pockmarked face entered the building and drove the truck away.

As the band played softly, Gail Manning snuggled deeper into Joe Stacy's arms. She knew something was bothering him. From the moment he had picked her up at her house and taken her to The Cat's Meow Cabaret, he had hardly said a word. Even when he asked her to dance, he seemed too preoccupied to notice what he was doing. Still, she enjoyed his company, and the way he held her was different, almost as if he never wanted to let go. While dancing, Gail thought about asking him what was on his mind, but it was none of her business.

Joe did have a lot on his mind, but he didn't think it showed. Earlier that day, Dutch police had responded to his message. Jan Boonstra, a seven-year-old boy from a prominent Eindhoven Jewish family had gone missing while on a stream-fishing trip with his grandfather. Stacy had notified the FBI, and photographs of the boy and all particulars were being forwarded. As for the tapes they had taken from the house, both detectives had spent hours reviewing them before Pete stated, "They're lewd enough to make a maggot want to puke."

Stacy's thoughts were indeed elsewhere as he danced with Gail. The tapes showed children as young as three had been coerced to involve themselves in nearly every sex act possible, and most of the participating *adults* wore masks. There were many more tapes to review, and neither police officer wanted the job.

The relaxing music almost mesmerized Joe as he thought of the teenager in the hospital. The adolescent had seen a blue Corvette drive up behind the police car for a few minutes. The boy knew there were two people inside, but he had not seen their faces. Apparently, one of his friends, a kid named Butch Cooper, suggested it would be a riot to steal a police car, so they made their move after the Corvette left. As for activity around the house itself, although the juvenile only lived a few streets away, he had never seen anything out of place going on. He said, at night when he and his friends hung out in the alley, he had noticed the blond guy driving various Systems rental vans, but that was it.

Joe and Pete had visited Systems Truck Rentals that morning, and the meeting still plagued Joe's mind.

"Is the manager in, please?" Joe had asked.

The cute young receptionist wearing a telephone headset smiled and answered a call before responding, "I believe so; I'll page him for you. Erik, call the front desk, please?" Moments later a red switchboard light popped on. After flipping a switch and saying, "There are two gentlemen here to see you," she looked up, stating, "He'll be right with you. You can help yourself to some coffee, if you'd like?"

The coffee smelled fresh, but both detectives thought it tasted like the diluted fluid known as horse piss in their office. Still, it was hot and any warm liquid was appreciated on this cold morning, Joe thought, noticing the wire-mesh fence outside. A fence similar to the one in the photograph Pete had found in the Cottonwood house.

"Yes, gentlemen, can I help you? I'm Erik Roltz," a smiling, effeminate, well-dressed dark haired man asked, after emerging from a hallway behind the receptionist.

Joe closely watched Roltz's eyes while Pete displayed his badge and made the initial introduction. "We're police officers, Mr. Roltz. Is there a place we can sit down with you for a few minutes?"

The man's eyes did not reveal what Joe was looking for. Instead, he appeared professional and congenial. "Certainly, please come into my office," he said, walking ahead of them in a feminine manner.

The hallway leading to the manager's office was lined with sales representative of the year pictures and engraved plaques listing the best quarterly sales personnel. Roltz had a large well decorated office, and he did not sit behind his desk. Instead, after asking the two detectives to take a seat on a futon couch, he took the nearest chair. "Is this about our stolen van?"

Joe scrutinized Roltz's every move. "It's about that, and some of your other vans, Mr. Roltz."

The manager's permanent smile remained fixed. "Please, call me Erik," he said, passing each investigator a business card. "At Systems, we take pride in our easygoing approach. This business is far too competitive for formalities."

Pete made notes while Joe continued. "Mr. Roltz, how many vans does this company have on consignment to Protocol Customs Assurance Company?"

Stacy's priggishness did not intimidate Roltz one bit.

"Protocol's our largest customer. If I'm not mistaken, they lease ... twenty-seven. Yes, that's right, twenty-seven of our vehicles. Some are vans, trucks, or other large rolling stock."

"What are they used for?"

"Well, Protocol's the nation's largest special customs clearance firm. They use our vehicles to transport international goods requiring distinctive port-to-port customs treatment. It's rare, but sometimes customs personnel travel with the cargo."

"Do you provide drivers?"

"No, sir. Protocol has its own insured drivers. Gentlemen, each year Protocol transports billions of dollars worth of merchandise world wide."

Joe picked up his coffee, took a sip, winced, and placed it down. "But how do you control the use of your vehicles? Don't they have to be signed out?"

"No, they're consigned to that company. Nine of our vehicles are kept at the airport, the rest remain here. All Protocol employees have to do is show their special pass. You see, that way they protect themselves. Our employees, or the public for that matter, have no idea what they're handling, or where the goods are heading."

"What about mileage reports and transport records?"

"It's an all inclusive contract, Sergeant. They pay premium rates, and they do what they want with the vehicles."

Roltz never saw the small grin or the glimmer in Joe's eyes. The man had made his first mistake.

"How do you know I'm a sergeant?" Stacy asked calmly.

"I... er... just assumed... no, I read about you in the paper when you were questioned about our van being stolen from your police lock-up."

Joe did not acknowledge the reply. Instead, he took a paper out of his pocket showing the police artist's conception of the two men who had threatened Wilfred Young. Passing the paper and maintaining eye contact, he asked, "Apparently you know these men, do they work here?"

Joe knew Roltz's confidence was crumbling. When the manager placed his right hand to his face, he tried to hide the fact his forefinger quickly wiped some glimmering perspiration from his forehead.

With more perspiration forming, Roltz asked, "Er ... who said I know them?"

"We're asking the questions. Do you know these men?"

"No! I've never seen them before."

"Are you certain, Mr. Roltz?"

"Look, I said, no! Who told you I know them?"

"Perhaps I was mistaken. Does this inquiry upset you, Mr. Roltz? Roltz ... Roltz ... is that a German name?"

"Yes, I was born in Bavaria. Would you like to know what kind of fucking milk I drank as a baby?"

Both Stacy and Durnell grinned, before Joe said, "No need to get facetious with us, Mr. Roltz. It only makes us wonder what you're trying to hide."

"I'm not hiding anything."

Passing over Kroll's Picture, Joe said, "Perhaps you also recognize ... I mean, do you know this fellow? I feel certain you do."

Stacy saw Roltz's hand shaking as he held the picture. To control the movement, the manager placed both hands against each other.

"Then you're wrong, because I don't know him either."

Standing, Joe asked, "Are you familiar with the penalties for kidnapping, or child pornography, Mr. Roltz?"

Clearly upset, Roltz jumped up. "What's that supposed to mean? Get out of here before I call my lawyer. Get the hell out of my office!"

Stacy's stare punctured the man's eyes. "I think you know exactly what I mean. Thanks for the coffees ... we'll be back."

Leaving the office, the detectives were unaware of the phone call Roltz made seconds later.

"You were wrong, the police know more than we thought ... a lot more. They've got pictures of Lorne and Barry. I've got no idea; a police artist must have drawn them. This asshole isn't going to go away. You will? Good! Make it quick, will you, I don't want him back here."

Yes, Joe had a lot on his mind, and as the dance tune ended, he ground his teeth. "The bastard is as guilty as..."

"What's that?" Gail asked, moving her head to look into his eyes. The music had just stopped and the reflections from the moving mirrored globe smothered all couples heading back to their tables.

Gail's question snapped Joe out of his trance and he livened up. After placing his right hand around her waist and guiding her back to their table, he sat opposite her. "I'm sorry, Gail - I was just talking to myself."

"Do you do that often?" she asked, her cheeks shaping the same dimple he fell in love with at the hospital.

"Not normally, unless I've had a few drinks and I'm sitting home alone feeling sorry for myself. I guess I have been a little quiet tonight. We all have one of those days, and believe me today was one of them."

While he spoke, Joe became engrossed in how exquisite she appeared in her strapless light and tight blue satin dress. Her pearl necklace and earrings were the perfect choice, matching her flawless skin. She had also let her hair down, allowing the glow from their table's candle to cast sprinkles of glittering prancing lights over each golden strand.

Gail's smile never really left, it remained constant in her eyes. "Joe, I can't picture you getting lonely. From where I sit, I see strength, self-assuredness, and determination. Did you ever marry?"

He reached across the table, gently taking hold of her hands. "No. Perhaps you perceive my true image ... egotistical, unmindful, and preoccupied with everything except what matters. That's probably the reason no girl would marry me. I've proposed, but I guess they knew me better than I did at the time."

"And you wouldn't change?"

"It wasn't a matter of changing, Gail. I've always been a nonconformist, and I knew if I changed, I wouldn't be me anymore. Jesus, did they want me, or a stranger? I'm a cop who loves his work, I guess. Until a couple of years ago, I'd say, show me a happily married cop and I'll show you a liar."

Gail chuckled. "And what altered that outlook?"

Joe ran his thumbs over the tops of her fingers. "Pete married Linda. Pete's my partner, the guy you met at the hospital. At one time, he was like me, locked in his ways, unreliable in his personal life, but a hard worker. Linda didn't try to change him because she knew she was marrying a cop. Sometimes when we were out and he invited me home at two in the morning, she'd get up and cook steaks. Even if he brought ten people home, she'd cook ten steaks, before going back to bed. He still does it occasionally, but I think he's outgrown the chauvinistic carefree attitude he had. Pete seems to be thoroughly enjoying married life with its ups and downs. In his case, there doesn't appear to be any downs."

Gail listened intently and Joe loved the patient way she had about her.

"Anyway, I've never rambled on like this before," he said. "What about you? Why are you still single?"

A waiter came by asking if they would like two more drinks, and both nodded.

Searching for words, Gail examined the flickering candle before looking up and trying to smile. "I was married, but my husband was killed in a trucking accident when the children were toddlers."

"Oh, er, I'm sorry Gail, I..." Joe released her hands when the waiter placed the drinks down.

The brightness in her eyes disappeared but only for a moment. "I'm over it now," she said raising her chin. "We weren't getting along anyway. He'd met another woman but I thought we could iron things out. The first year I cried myself to the funny farm, but the thought of my children brought me out of it. They were staying with my mother, and I needed them as much as they needed me. At first, I didn't realize that I'd allowed myself to shut out the world, but I did. I also had to go back to work because our insurance policy was so small. And so ... there you are."

"How many children do you have?" he asked, uncertain if she would object when he lit up a cigarette. She didn't.

"Two. Gordie is eight, and Suzie's nine. They're the light of my life."

When the band started playing again, Joe took a long gulp of his drink and butted his cigarette. "Would you like to dance?"

"I'd love to," she said, standing up and accepting his offered hand.

On the dance floor, Joe wrapped Gail in his arms before delicately kissing her right cheek and whispering, "Can I meet them?"

The dimple reappeared. "I'm really glad you asked me that."

It had been the end of a long shift in the rain for the middle-aged driver of a Dumprite Garbage Disposal truck travelling Seattle's alleys in the early morning hours.

Many business people in the downtown core had stored their trash for a few days, rather than having to trek in the snow to put it out. This doubled the operator's workload and for the past two hours, his stomach kept telling him he needed a coffee and a hamburger.

Normally the driver would have dumped the container and placed it down, but he had seen a street-washing truck approaching his end of the lane. Manoeuvring the vehicle's hydraulic forks, he picked up the fully loaded steel box and tipped it back over the cab of the truck. When it emptied itself, he left the container forward and up in the air. After that, he disembarked and entered the back door of an all night restaurant.

It was quiet for fifteen minutes after the street-cleaning rig washed down the dark alley and two men had taken up different positions. Only one of them used the Dumprite vehicle for cover and he had no idea the other was watching him.

Fully clothed in black and humming to himself, the man in front of the garbage truck took a rifle out of a rifle case, placed a round in the chamber, and slowly closed the bolt. Rolling up his left sleeve and wrapping the weapon's leather sling around his naked oil stained left arm, he focused the cross hairs of the telescopic sight at the entrance to a club called The Cat's Meow Cabaret across the street, and waited.

The rifleman did not have to wait long because he knew the nightclub closed at 2am. Shortly, when Joe and Gail came out, the man's right index finger tightened on the trigger.

Instead of the sudden roar of a rifle shot shattering the night, two insignificant *phut, phut,* sounds went unheard. The gunman aiming the rifle may have heard a portion of the first trivial noise before a soft-nosed bullet accelerated through a silenced barrel and opened up his head. The next projectile, however, went unheard as it dispersed more of the man's brain matter and bone against a nearby brick wall.

Seconds later, after picking up the rifle and removing the bullet from the chamber, a pair of gloved hands threw it and the rifle case into the rear refuse compartment of the truck. The same hands also dislodged the dead man's ring and took some papers from his body before releasing the vehicle's hydraulic mechanism. When the ponderous Dumprite container crashed to the ground, it severed the dead rifleman's left hand, and crushed what remained of his skull.

"My, what was that loud noise?" Gail asked, quickly getting inside Joe's car.

"Somebody's collecting garbage," he replied, placing the car in gear, and applying the accelerator. "Your place or mine?"

Gail quietly chuckled. "Mine of course. Did I give you the impression I always accept invitations to visit strange beds?"

"Uh, who said anything about beds? I thought I'd make you a coffee and we could..."

"We could what?"

Joe shrugged. "Er, talk about our future, that's all."

"Our future? My immediate future is getting up for work tomorrow. For that matter, so is yours."

For the first time in his life, Joe Stacy found himself lost in the extraordinary world of adoration, commitment, and compromise. The stoic battle-scarred coat of impervious armour he had built up and worn over the years had fractured and melted from the moment he had first looked into her eyes. It was gone, and he felt full of life in his new nakedness.

"I've fallen in love with you Gail. God, did I say that? What's happening to me?"

Their eyes met for a moment, and Gail tenderly ran the back of her left hand down the side of Joe's right cheek. *"L'amor che muove il sol e l'altre stelle."*

Stacy delicately took hold of her hand. "That sounds wonderful, what does it mean?"

"The love that moves the sun and the other stars. Joe, let's get to know each other as friends before we travel the universe. I'd like you to meet Suzie and Gordie. Would you like to come over for dinner?"

"On Saturn, Uranus, I'll be there towing the Sun." he replied.

"No, at my place, soon?"

"Hell, that's easier, but I'll move the sun and other stars if I have to."

As he changed gears, a song came on the radio he had not heard before. Turning it up, he asked, "Which group is singing this?"

Gail grinned, turning the radio up a little louder. "A group from our era. It's *Real Love*, a song by the Beatles."

"Wow, are they on my side, or what?" Stacy uttered.

At three o'clock that morning when Joe Stacy locked his apartment door and kicked off his shoes, he didn't know what he was doing. He had not even kissed Gail when he walked her to her door, nor did he remember driving home. When it became time to say goodnight, he had wanted to kiss her and hold her in his arms for eternity, but he hadn't, and he could not understand why.

Sitting back in his favourite chair, he retraced their evening together. The low lights, soft dance music, and wonderful cuisine had created an enchanting evening. The two of them had enjoyed each other's company to the point that the rest of the world just didn't exist. It was as if...

Joe's roving mind did not allow him to hear the first light tap on his door, but it alerted every nerve ending in his body when he heard the second knock.

Quietly jumping up and removing his pistol from its holster lying on top of the table, he crept to the side of the door. "Yes?"

A man's voice whispered, "Sergeant Stacy? Sergeant Joe Stacy?"

"Yes, what is it?"

"I know this is an ungodly hour, but I must come in and speak with you."

Joe's heart picked up the beat. "Who are you and what's this all about? Why are you here?"

The *visitor's* voice remained low. "It's important that I speak with you, Sergeant. It won't take long, I promise. Please, it's important."

Stacy allowed a few seconds to tick away and licked his dry lips. Slowly opening up the door, he said, "Turn around, place your hands in your back pockets and stare at the ceiling."

The man obeyed and when the door was fully open Joe frisked him. He also recognized him, especially the birthmark on his neck.

"Well, if it isn't Dapper Dan, the flower man. I've been looking for you. Come in."

"May I put my hands down?"

"Yes. What do you want?"

"The gun won't be necessary, Sergeant. I'm unarmed."

After re-locking the door, Stacy made certain he kept three paces from the *serious stranger* who had dropped the flowers in the hospital hallway; the same man who had stood in the line-up behind Dr. Abraham when the doctor had used the pay phone.

"I'll decide that. I recognize you from the hospital. What do you want?"

The man appeared quite relaxed and he oozed with sincerity as he held out his hand. "My name's Harvey Cohen."

The detective did not offer his hand. "Good for you. What do you want?"

"I'd like a drink, and I'd appreciate you not pointing that at me. Also, if you do decide to shoot me, it would help if you took off the safety."

Joe had not cocked the weapon he slid back into its holster. Opening the top of a nearby polished cabinet, he poured out two ounces of single malt scotch into each of two glasses. Handing one to the man, he asked, "I repeat, what's this all about, Mr. er ... Cohen?"

Noticing where the ashtrays were, Cohen gently retrieved a silver cigarette case from his suit's inside jacket pocket and sat down. "Would you like one?" he asked, opening the cover and extending the receptacle to Joe.

Joe accepted, and lighting Cohen's before his own, he said, "Well?"

"Sergeant Stacy, I work for a little known international Israeli organization. A foundation … shall we say, funded by private and government donations."

Joe's eyebrows rose inquisitively. "The Mossad?"

Cohen frowned then quickly smiled before sipping his scotch. "Close, Sergeant, very close. Members of that *club* are known all over the world. No, our group is far more surreptitious and professionally superior. At least we feel that way. Unfortunately, I'm not authorized to give you the name. Have you discovered how Doctor Abraham was killed?"

Joe's lips formed a curious grin. "Killed? You obviously know a lot more than I do, Mr. Cohen. He supposedly died of a heart attack?"

"We both know he was murdered, Sergeant. Have you read the autopsy report yet?"

"No, it won't be ready until tomorrow. I assume you also know the cause of his death?"

Cohen finished his drink, stood up, and picked up the half-full bottle of scotch. "Yes, I do, but your people don't. May I...?"

Stacy nodded, indicating his own glass was also empty.

"Murray Abraham died after being injected with a relatively unknown drug called Iodzathene," declared Cohen, pouring scotch into both glasses before sitting down again. "It was developed by Soviet scientists and used by Warsaw bloc intelligence agencies. Iodzathene works extremely quickly and is nearly totally untraceable."

Joe butted his cigarette. "I suspected he was *fixed* with something. Why are you telling me this?"

"Our organization placed Murray Abraham in that hospital. He wasn't one of us, but he kept us informed about certain matters."

"Such as?"

"Are you familiar with the two race riots here in Seattle, and a similar uprising in L.A., last month?"

"Yes."

"Well, Sergeant, they weren't spontaneous. They were meticulously organized and conducted with precise thoroughness. As well, during the past four months, five Jewish cemeteries have been vandalized across the country. One right here in Seattle."

Stacy sat back and crossed his legs. "I know, we've added additional local patrols to ensure it doesn't happen again. But what's this got to do with Abraham?"

Keeping his eyes on Joe, Cohen searched his mind for a moment. "For years, we've known the majority of your country's racial disturbances are contrived. Not just here, all countries, but until recently we couldn't crack the planning *fraternity*. Murray Abraham was our ears and eyes to seven skinheads who were injured in the recent riots. Something must have gone wrong; usually those lowlifes are not around by the time the fur starts flying. When they ended up in hospital, Abraham reported where they lived, their occupations, and most importantly, who visited them."

For some reason, Joe liked the man sitting with him. Cohen's authoritative voice demanded attention, and Stacy's curiosity was secured and fettered from the first second the agent had opened his mouth.

"You said, 'until recently?' That means you've gained information?" Joe asked pouring only one scotch after Cohen declined the gesture of a refill.

Placing his left hand into his jacket pocket, Cohen took out two small objects. Keeping one in the palm of his hand, he tossed the other item to the detective. "I take it, you've been looking for this?"

Joe's eyes widened when he saw the ring. "Kroll's?"

"Yeah, it's Kroll's. I didn't say Abraham was our only insider. That was taken from Kroll ten minutes after he was pulled from the water. Here," he said, tossing over an identical ring. "Now you've got a matching set."

The rings were exactly alike, and as confusion settled over Stacy's face, Cohen didn't mention the scratching inside the rings.

"Where did you get this one?"

The visitor checked his watch. "From a professional hit man who had your head in the centre of his rifle's cross-hairs when you came out of The Cat's Meow one hour and ... seven minutes ago. He won't be practising his trade anymore and you can consider our efforts a favour. Also, you don't have to worry about your partner; we've been keeping an eye on him as well. Somebody really wants you out of the way, Joe. How does it feel to be appreciated?"

The reality of what could have happened sunk in immediately. When it did, Joe finished his booze in one gulp, and poured a heavier shot.

"Absolutely wonderful. Then I owe you my life."

This time Cohen accepted a refill. "You don't owe us anything. We need you and you're doing just fine by staying on this case. To get back to your question of whether or not we've gained information ... Murray Abraham left the hospital that night to pick up a camera from me. He'd phoned us when Kroll and the boy were brought to his ward, and I asked him to take pictures.

Two of the seven skinheads wore identical rings when they were hospitalized, and Murray saw the similarity of Kroll's ring. He didn't know what connection the boy had, and for that matter, we still don't. Abraham didn't want to talk to you because we had warned him not to trust anyone, and I mean anyone. I didn't intend to bump into him at the hospital, I was just trying to find out who the two of you were, and Murray didn't want to tip you off that he knew me."

"Did he know you were standing behind him when he used the payphone?" Joe asked.

"No, I just wanted to see who he was calling. As I said, he called our office."

"Who got Kroll and the boy out?" Joe asked.

"They were moved after Prouse made a phone call."

"Prouse? The doctor who attended Abraham in the linen closet?"

Cohen nodded and checked his watch again. "Is that where he killed him, in a linen closet? Yeah, the same doctor, but I don't believe his real name's Prouse. One hour from now he'll be on an early morning flight to London, connecting to the Middle East."

"How do you know all this?"

"Let's just say we discovered his ticket," Harvey said as the telephone rang.

"Christ, why didn't you stop him? Who the hell is calling me at this hour of the night?"

"Joe, that's your job, not ours."

"Hello?"

"Sergeant Stacy, it's me, Wilfred Young."

"Oh, hello Wilfred, how come you're not tucked away in bed?"

"I was Sergeant, until I received a call from my buddy at the airport. The same one who passed the note to the guard. Sergeant, Protocol's shipping another container like the one we opened. Apparently Klenz the custom's guy, cleared it without even opening it."

"What? On what flight?" Joe asked, glancing at his pocket watch.

"It's on Europe-American's flight 1752 to London, leaving at 5am. I think they were gonna ship it out of Vancouver, but changed their minds."

"How do you know that, Wilfred?"

All the paperwork is another company's, but they've scratched out the name and written Europe-American. Usually, when one container goes out, another comes in, so I asked my friend to check the passenger list. Guess what? VanVliet's on the flight coming in from London."

Joe could not believe his good fortune. "That's a great piece of work, Wilfred. Have you considered changing occupations? We could use you around the department?"

"No thanks, Sergeant, I like the habit I'm into ... waking up every day."

Grinning, the sergeant said, "Wilfred, here's what I want you to do…"

A few moments later after thanking Wilfred and hanging up the phone, Joe put on his shoulder holster and a windbreaker. While punching out Pete's number, he said, "This is too coincidental, Harvey. Prouse is going to London and so is a certain body suitcase. I haven't told you about the boy yet, have I? It'll have to wait until I get back from the airport."

"I'd like to hear all about it."

Joe nodded at his newfound friend. "I'll keep you informed."

"Pete, another container's on the move. Meet me at Europe-American's freight yard right away."

"We can only offer assistance from a distance, Joe," Harvey said, butting his cigarette and standing. "Watch yourselves, there's a hell-of-a lot more to this than you think."

"I guessed as much."

Picking up a newspaper from the floor, the Israeli tore off a portion and wrote on it. "This is my number."

Heading towards the door, Stacy glanced at the paper before pushing it in his right jacket pocket. "Rick Appleton? Who's he?"

"Does it matter?"

Joe followed his visitor out the door and this time shook his hand. "Thanks, Harvey, I enjoyed our chat. I'll be in touch."

There wasn't much traffic at that hour of the cold wet morning, and after placing a red light on top of his car, the detective put his foot to the floor. He figured it would take him a half-hour to reach the airport, and he underestimated his assumption by five minutes. When he arrived, Durnell was already waiting for him.

"How'd you find out about this?" Pete asked, looking like he had grabbed any nearby clothes after his partner had called him.

"Wilfred Young phoned me. His buddy told him."

Pete cupped his hands around his mouth and blew hot air into them. "The plane's not in yet. Christ, it's cold."

"What?"

"It got delayed leaving London, and then hit head winds over the pole. It will be landing shortly though, but the delay means it won't be leaving until 6am."

"Good," Joe said, lightly slapping his associate's back. "Listen, Pete, I asked Wilfred to set up a signal system. I want you to park in the employees' parking lot across the road and stay in your car. When VanVliet clears the container coming off the plane, and loads it in a vehicle, Wilfred's friend will signal the guard shack. When you see the guard shack's lights go on and off, that's the vehicle to follow. Make damned certain you don't get caught. Okay?"

Pete yawned. "Sure, but what are you gonna do?"

I'm going after Prouse."

"What's Doctor Prouse done?"

"I don't believe that's his real name. He may have killed Abraham."

"Nice fella," Pete said, wincing. "How'd you find out?"

"Remember Dapper Dan, the guy with the birthmark on his neck?"

"Yeah."

"He visited me. His name's Cohen and he's with the Israeli Secret Service. I'll fill you in later. Now remember, don't get caught tailing the container."

When Pete left to move his car, Joe entered the airport, talked to an airport security cop, took the indoor train to E.A.'s departure gate, and waited behind a pillar.

It took fifteen minutes for Doctor Prouse to show up, alone. He appeared relaxed, dressed in a light blue sports jacket, white Armani shirt, cream coloured slacks, and light-brown alligator shoes. He also carried a raincoat draped over his left arm.

There were six people in line ahead of the doctor, and Joe thought it would be better if he arrested the man at the x-ray machine. That way, Prouse only had three exits, not four.

Ten minutes later, the sergeant made his move. Prouse had just placed his personal contents in a plastic box and his hands were free when Joe whipped one of them behind the man.

"You're under arrest for the murder of Doctor Murray Abraham. You have the right to remain silent. Anything you say can be held against you in..."

It happened so fast, Stacy ended up on the sliding belt leading to the x-ray machine, and Prouse ran for a nearby escalator.

Scurrying off the belt, Joe and two airport security officers gave chase. At one point the three almost had the doctor cornered on a down escalator, but the man jumped over to another one going up. Joe jumped over as well, and when he reached the top, Prouse had just entered an exit door leading to the stairs. When Stacy tried to open the same door, something on the other side stopped it from opening. Forcing it just enough to enter, Joe found the obstacle – it was Prouse. The man was lying face down, and when Joe turned him over to check his pulse, there was none. A tiny amount of blood coming through the doctor's shirt pocket indicated he'd been shot in the heart with a projectile of some sort.

As Stacy undid the doctor's shirt buttons to look at the wound, he heard feet running down the stairs and the lower door slamming shut.

"There's a small dart stuck in him," he said to one of the airport security officers. "Get it out for me, I'll be back. Also, call the coroner."

Giving chase, when he opened the door, Joe found himself in a silent dimly lit underground car park.

The detective tried to control his heavy breathing as he allowed the door to close quietly behind him. His lips went dry as did his throat and he could feel cold perspiration drying on his forehead and on the small of his back. He could hear his heart pounding as he slowly removed his pistol from its holster. After taking off the safety, he quickly pulled back the weapon's breech block and then released it. The police officer now knew his firearm was cocked.

Cautiously, Joe looked under the rows of cars closest to him. The adverse light did not allow him to see much, but when he stood, he heard a noise on the next level down. Rather than being caught behind a car, he silently made his way to the centre of the driveway, and then it happened. The driver of a speeding vehicle squealing its tires had two intentions; the first was to escape, and if that didn't work, to run over Joe Stacy.

Blinded by the car's lights, Joe used both hands to take firm aim at the driver's form. As the automobile turned upwards, speeding towards him, the detective fired six successive shots before jumping out of the way. All bullets shattered the windshield. That's all it took. When the auto tore past Joe, the driver lay slumped over the steering wheel. Seconds later the car exploded into flames after crashing into two parked cars near the entrance to the floor's up-ramp.

Stacy recognized one of the airport security cops who arrived on the scene almost immediately, unwinding an emergency fire hose.

"Did you get the dart out of him?" Joe asked.

The officer shrugged. "There was nothing stuck in his chest. He must have hit a corner of a concrete stair."

Joe didn't have time to discuss the matter. "I felt it! Go look again and get me the thing. I'll be in the freight area," he said, before running up two levels and stepping out at the side of the main airport terminal.

A few moments later, Joe nodded to the gate guard at shipping and receiving and walked through towards the Europe-American warehouse where Wilfred Young was waiting. On his way, he noticed Pete's car had gone.

"Has it been loaded yet, Wilfred?" he asked, placing a hand on Young's right shoulder.

The warehouseman was visibly nervous. "Yeah, it was loaded by Klenz and some guy I've never seen."

"I have a feeling the devil's handed each of them a shovel. Now, where's VanVliet? Is he heading back to London on this flight?"

"No, Sergeant, VanVliet stayed with the container after it was unloaded. He's driving the van, and that's the first time he's ever done that."

Just the look on Wilfred's face stretched Joe's lips into a sincere smile. "There always a first time for everything, Wilfred. Pete will get the son-of-a-bitch. Okay, guide me to the plane."

Wilfred got behind the wheel of an electric cart, and after ten minutes of driving through large warehouses stacked with luggage, boxes, and wrapped industrial parts, Stacy stood staring at the open cargo hold door of a Lockheed L1011. Before boarding he spotted a spare Europe-American cap hanging on a nail, and after putting it on, he asked Wilfred to telephone for an ambulance and to stay back.

Cargo was still being loaded forward towards the centre of the plane when Joe saw three customs officials going over manifests and filling in forms. Approaching one of them, he said, "I'm Sergeant Stacy with Seattle police. I'm here to remove a small Protocol container. Where would it be?"

The agent's eyes indicated the general location, but he stated, "Sergeant, I'm afraid once it's loaded, it can't be touched or removed until this conveyance arrives at its port of destination. In fact, you should not be in here. Does that help you?"

"It's kind of you to give me a sermon, Joe said, smiling. "Who needs a encyclopaedia when people like you are around? Let me ask you again, where is it?"

Now two agents stood side by side and the *knowledgeable* one placed his right hand on top of his holstered pistol."Like the police department, the U.S. Customs Service also has rules. Please leave this area, Sergeant."

"You mean this doesn't help?" the detective asked, displaying his badge.

"Nope, not at all. Sorry about that, but you're in our territory now."

Checking his pocket watch, Joe said, "Well, I'm also sorry."

"About what?" the leader of the two asked.

"This," Joe replied, flattening the nose area of the *learned* one's face, before kicking the next man in the testicles, and following through with two quick fist-blows to the guy's head.

With both of them out cold, the third one was not about to become brave when Joe beckoned him over. "Where is it?"

"That way. It's, it's, over there."

"Show me!"

The agent guided Joe to a locked storage space holding seven containers.

"Open the door," Joe demanded. "And keep your hand away from your firearm, otherwise I'll have to say you shot yourself."

Once inside, Stacy asked the fellow to open up the smallest container.

"I don't have a key for that, Sergeant. Only Protocol can lock and unlock their containers."

"Have you seen what's inside that thing?"

The agent checked his clipboard. "No, but our records show it was cleared by Archie Klenz, one of our representatives. He's agreed with Protocol's declaration that it contains French bearer bonds."

"Pick it up and walk out. I'll follow you." Joe ordered, grabbing a blanket normally used to protect shiny surfaces of shipped items.

The guard appeared insulted. "Sir, do you realize the trouble I could get into for…?"

"I said, pick it up and walk out!"

The agent did as he was ordered and once inside the giant hanger, Joe took a fire axe off the wall and broke the device's locks. Slowly lifting up the lid, his skin crawled when he discovered the anaesthetised naked little girl. Three of the tight rubber straps had caused white marks on the youngster's body, but colour started returning after Joe unfastened them and took off the oxygen mask. Next, just as the ambulance attendants arrived, the sergeant slowly withdrew the intravenous needle, picked Sara up in his arms, and gently wrapped her in a blanket.

"You'll be okay, Sweetheart. You're going to be just fine," he said, cautiously handing the sleeping girl to an ambulance attendant, before returning his attention to the horrified customs agent now shaking his head.

"Still think Customs has a grip on things? Call this number, ask for Terry Sawasy, and tell him Joe Stacy wants him, a complete crew, and a police photographer here, now."

Wilfred Young turned up as the child was being wheeled away. "Anything else I can do, Sergeant?"

"Yeah, Wilfred, do me a favour. Go with the ambulance and don't leave her side. I don't care what you have to go through at the hospital, don't leave her side under any circumstances until I get there. There are to be no exceptions! Absolutely none … okay?"

Wilfred perked up. "You bet, Sergeant … anytime."

Over an hour later, after Sawasy's crew had finished their inspection, Terry came over to Stacy. "I'm glad you found Sarah, Joe."

"Is that her name?"

Sawasy passed over the morning paper. The headline read: *Girl Disappears While Playing.*

"Do you want to know the name of the guy who tried to run you down?"

Joe sighed. "Yeah, who the hell was it?"

"His name's Archie Klenz and he works for the…"

Stacy cut him off. "Customs, right?"

"Yeah, very good. He was a senior official who was transferred here from New York four years ago. Oh, and you're gonna love this. His ring is in fashion."

"He has one?"

Sawasy grinned. "No, he had one. We've got it now, and it's just like the others. What's going on, Joe?"

A cold expression came over Joe as he shrugged and shook his head. "I don't know, Terry, but it's my guess whatever it is, it's making billions. I just can't seem to..."

An airport security guard yelled, "Telephone Sergeant. You can take the one on the wall over there. Just push line one."

Joe nodded before answering, "Sergeant Stacy."

"Joe, it's me, Pete."

The detective sergeant held his hand around the mouthpiece portion of the phone. Talking softly, he asked, "Pete, where are you?"

"I'm in the lobby of the Leopold Hotel in Bellingham. You better get here right away, Joe."

"Bellingham? What the hell are you doing in Bellingham?" Stacy asked, maintaining an even more subdued voice so he could not be overheard.

"I followed the van here. You've gotta see the size of the joint it drove into. It's a mansion with bars and black-painted windows."

"Have you mentioned anything to the Bellingham police?"

"No, no yet, but we're going to need them. When you see the magnitude of this dive, you might wanna call out the army. There are three other houses on the property and..."

Joe heard his name being called again. Interrupting his partner, he said, "Christ, hold on a second, Pete, somebody wants me. What is it?" he yelled to the same person who informed him of Pete's call.

"There's another call for you, Sergeant. The guy says his name is Captain Glover and it's important. Like, er, he wants you now."

Taking out his notebook and pen, Stacy said, "Glover's on the other phone. What's your number and I'll get back to you?"

After jotting down Pete's number, Joe headed to a nearby support column where the man handing him a red phone mouthed, "How he got this hotline number, I'll never know? It's the president's line and it's hardly ever used."

Joe quipped, "Yeah, I know what ya mean. The chief of police hardly ever uses his either. What's up, Ray?"

Glover's voice was direct and to the point. "I want you in my office at once! That's what's up!"

Startled, Joe asked, "At once? Ray, you've got to be joking? You've heard what's going on here. Pete's onto something and I've got to hightail my ass up to Bellingham, and meet..."

"Did you hear what I said, Sergeant? I want you in my goddamned office, now! Is that clear enough?"

Stacy's facial expression changed from confusion to annoyance. "Yeah, Captain, that's clear enough. I'll jump on my magic carpet and..."

"Don't get smart with me, Sergeant Stacy. Now, where's Durnell?"

Mounting anger made Joe's right hand shake as he lit up a smoke. "He's in Bellingham. Why the hell are you...?"

"Get him back here. I want both of you in my office, immediately! Is that order explicit enough? Well, is it?"

The Captain did not allow Joe to answer because the line went dead.

Clearly upset, the detective got Durnell back on the phone. "Pete, break the speed limit and get back here. I'll meet you at Choy's!"

"What? Jesus, Joe, we can't just..."

"Pete, get in your goddamned car and get back here. The Captain's got a bee up his ass, and he wants the both of us, now."

Before hanging up, Joe suddenly had a second thought. "No, wait. Are you still on the line, Pete?"

"Yeah."

"I'm going to call someone and have him meet you there. Show him the house and get back here in a hurry."

Chapter 4

There were no happy faces or offers of congratulations when Joe and Pete entered the squad room after being ordered to report to Captain Glover. Even the usual office clamour appeared to have been put on hold as the two detectives made the *refrigerated* journey to their desks.

In the many years he had served, Joe had encountered this impassivity only when a member had turned to the other side. Hell, he had even participated in the custom, but now it was happening to him and his partner and he wanted to know why.

Of all people, Schmidt offered a crumb of civility. Exhibiting a diffused look of sympathy, he said, "Fellas, the captain wants you upstairs in the boardroom."

Instead of responding to Sergeant Schmidt's announcement, Joe's irrelevant nonplussed grin banded with his eyes to scan the backs of his co-workers. They were doing their jobs, but not in the normal manner. A few glanced at him displaying friendly looks, but inert ice-block dispositions had replaced the habitual insane jesters' temperament essential for police work. Now Joe wanted to take them one by one out into the alley.

In the elevator, Pete broke the silence. "Is it interesting, or is it interesting?"

Stone-faced, Stacy slapped his buddy's back. "I'd like to know what the hell is going on."

Captain Glover was not sitting alone at the dignified table in the large well-furnished room usually reserved for the head honcho and his cronies. Just after the two detectives knocked and entered, they discovered the chief of police sitting with an assistant to the governor, the mayor, the district attorney, and two FBI agents. Joe also noticed the bigwigs all sat along one side and the ends, leaving only two chairs available on the open side of the table.

Large, balding, and with pot-marked skin, Chief Couling, glanced up through his bifocals, cleared his throat, and brought the meeting to order after informing the two officers the names and titles of the other gentlemen.

"Please be seated. Over the past few days, Captain Glover has been briefing me on what you believe to be a child kidnapping operation. Is that correct, Sergeant Stacy?"

Joe's eyes selected Glover before shifting themselves back to the chief of police. If Chief Couling was choosing precise words, something was being lost in the transliteration.

"What I believe to be a child kidnapping operation?" Have you read the file, Chief?"

"Yes, yes, we've all read the file, Sergeant Stacy. Do both of you know you've humiliated this force to the fullest extent?"

An unbelieving frown accompanied Joe's eyes when they met Pete's eyes. Normally, the two seasoned detectives would have burst out laughing after hearing such an accusation, but silent rage seethed within them as they participated in what had to be a game.

"Oh, have we done that?" Stacy asked, locking on to Couling. "Three murders have been committed, and we know two children have been abducted. As well..."

The top man interrupted him. "The only murder that's taken place is the one you're responsible for, Sergeant Stacy. Today, you killed FBI agent Archie Klenz, who has been working undercover with United States Customs for the past three years."

Joe took his cigarettes out and threw them on the table. "What the hell are you talking about, Chief? We've been shot at, a bomb was placed in our car, a gunman tried to assassinate me on the street, and today if I killed this so-called FBI agent, it's because the son-of-a-bitch was part of an underground organization and he tried to run me down. He killed Prouse, and his cohorts knocked off Norbert Kroll, and Doctor Murray Abraham."

"Kroll was killed for his drug habits, Sergeant Stacy," one of the two FBI agents said, smirking guilefully, and clearing his throat. "He's been a heroin addict for years and the mob finally caught up with him. That's what happens to people when they're in with the wrong crowd and don't pay their debts. As for Doctor Abraham, he died of a heart attack."

Stacey glared disgustingly at the agent. "That's bullshit and you know it."

Paying little attention to Joe's response, the agent simply continued. "Also, both of you know the teenagers were carrying a home-made bomb when they entered your car. Who's Prouse?"

Stacy continued to reveal his contempt and he left the question unanswered for a moment as he glared at the seven men staring at him. Perhaps he had better not say anything else. These assholes were out to get him. Then he had second thoughts. Hell no, they should be put in their place.

"If you're fond of your teeth, fella, don't toy with me," Joe said. "Doctor Prouse is the man who killed Abraham. What the hell's going on here? What are you people attempting to pull off?" Scowling at the captain, he added, "Ray, why haven't you enlightened these idiots?"

Glover remained quiet and glanced down at the table.

Chief Couling's fist slammed the table. "Watch your mouth, Sergeant! Why don't *you* enlighten us?" he said, pointing to both FBI agents and the governor's assistant. "These gentlemen have educated the mayor and me as to what's really going on, not Captain Glover. How could Captain Glover reveal the true facts when he hasn't been properly informed? The two of you have been running around creating a mirage of intrigue so ridiculous this police department looks like a goddamned nut house."

Stacy had had enough and was about to stand. "Fine, is that all?"

"No, it's not!" As of this minute, you're suspended, and I'm going to make damned certain..."

A loud voice outside the door interrupted the department's chief officer. It was his secretary yelling, "I've told you, you can't go in there! You can't go in there!"

The vociferous crowd of media personnel forcing the door open did not intend to listen to the chief's secretary. Before questions were shot from the hip, Stacy and Durnell were surrounded and prodded with microphones, cameras, notebooks, and pencils. The consternation of the chief of police and the mayor didn't matter. Both officials were completely ignored, but for the first time in their careers, they began to understand the pandemonium forming a press feeding frenzy. They also understood they would be the main course if they didn't handle this *properly*.

A female reporter stuck a microphone in front of Joe's face, and other microphones, cameras, yelling voices, and open notebooks followed.

"Sergeant Stacy, is it true you found Sarah in a suitcase?"

"Was the little girl really naked, Sergeant?"

"Did the child say anything?"

"Is the man you shot, a suspect?"

"How did you know she was being shipped out by plane?"

"Sergeant, how many kidnappers are involved?"

"Detective Young says you asked him to guard the girl - is that right?"

Three brightly grinning tight-lipped faces welcomed more reporters piling in, and one of those faces, the one belonging to Captain Glover, made a statement.

"Quiet, please. Quiet Please! I said be quiet! Sergeant Stacy and Detective Durnell have briefed the mayor and chief of police. I think it would be fitting if you received the precise facts from Chief Couling. Chief, would you, er...?"

Chief Couling's expression did not match the mayor's cultivated election-honed smile. Amidst exploding flashbulbs, and television camera lights, he swallowed hard. "Yes, I ... I'm pleased to announce that, er, Mayor Lungley and I have congratulated Sergeant Stacy and Detective Durnell on a job ... uh, extremely well done. I certainly shouldn't be the one to inform you of such an achievement. Joe, perhaps you could explain your triumph much better than I. Thank you, ladies and gentlemen."

Stacy's fierce look disappeared and his stomach turned watching Couling squirm.

"I want you to know with a little luck and Captain Glover's faith in us ... Detective Durnell and I rescued Sarah. Yeah, two of the kidnappers' accomplices are dead, and starting immediately, if I don't quit the force, we'll be doing the best we can to crack this case. I would also like to mention that our investigation has been severely hampered by senior members of this police department and other government agencies. Captain Glover has informed the chief that a press release will be circulated within the hour. Thank you."

Bedlam started again the minute Joe stopped speaking.

"Who hindered your investigation, Sergeant? Was it the chief?"

"No comment."

"Was it the mayor?"

"No comment."

"Has Sarah's mother spoken with you yet?"

"No, not yet."

"Why would you leave the force after such success?"

"Other *individuals* will have to answer that question, not me."

"How was your investigation impeded?"

"Let's just say we are not receiving any support from certain *senior* officials."

"Can you name them?"

"No, not at this time. Perhaps in the future. Ask the chief."

"Chief Couling, have you given the investigating officers your full support?"

Although thoroughly unprepared, Couling immediately stepped to his political front again. "Most certainly. Sergeant Stacy and Detective Durnell have my complete confidence. They are a credit to our proud police department. I've discussed this matter with Mayor Lungley, and I can assure you, no stone will be left unturned."

"Mr. Mayor, will you put a stop to any interference relating to the ongoing investigation?"

"Absolutely, you can count on it! The fine people of our fabulous city fully understand my position on crime. I will thoroughly review this matter with Chief Couling, and I can tell you now, that Sergeant Stacy will have all the co-operation he requires. We're not going to allow a man of his calibre and experience get away from our professional force. We're going all out on this one. Please quote me on that. When I say all out, I mean all out. I'm a mayor of action!"

While the mayor and chief were being *interviewed*, Joe and Pete managed to escape the chamber of evasion. A few moments later after taking the back stairs leading to the alley below, they entered Choy's.

As usual, the place was empty and when the owner hung up one of his many phones, he started singing and washing his walls.

"Hah, Joe, Pete, you back again? I take your advice and get lid of glease stains. My song old Chinese barrad. It mean good times ahead. You want menu or coffee?"

With their minds still reeling from the ordeal, Pete and Joe almost did not hear their friend.

"Just two coffees please, Choy," Durnell said, joining his partner in one of three wooden booths, instead of sitting at the counter. "Well, Joe? What do we do now?"

The uptown Cuban cigar Stacy lit seemed out of place with his whiskers, creased windbreaker, wrinkled pants, messed up hair, and blurry eyes.

"I think you should go home and cuddle up with Linda. I'm going over to the hospital, and after that, it's a scotch, a hot bath and the sack."

Joe paused for a moment, taking a long drag and adding sugar to the coffee Choy delivered. "Can you believe that bullshit? That FBI asshole must be in on the game? Not only him, but…"

Glover entered the restaurant, limped over and without saying a word slumped in next to Pete.

Totally ignored by the two, Glover realized he had better open up the conversation. "I guess the both of you think I owe you an apology, eh?"

Joe's sneer and smoke ring collided with the captain's nose. "Hell no, Captain, why would we think that? We know support when we see it. With you on our team, who needs anyone else?"

Before displaying any sign of atonement, Glover sat back extending an inscrutable smirk for a few seconds. "How long have you served on the force, Joe?"

"By the looks of it, far too long, Captain," the sergeant answered, standing up to leave. "C'mon, Pete, let's get the hell out of here."

Glover didn't move, so Pete was hemmed in. "Hold on a moment, Joe. Please sit down."

Exhibiting his frustration, Joe sat down again before Glover continued. "You've served around thirty years, so I've got about fourteen years on you. I retire next year, you know that?"

Joe's eyes met the ceiling, and he sighed, "Yeah, yeah, yeah."

"I've never been a brilliant cop, Joe. I've always been a grinder, and that's why I never made it any higher up the ladder. The difference between the two of us *now*, is, you don't give a shit about moving up. You skilfully do your job to the best of your ability, and you couldn't care less about police politics. That's the way I once was until I looked around and noticed a million assholes getting promoted because they played the bureaucratic game. One day I examined my reflection in the mirror and said, 'Okay, I'll do the same, but I'll do it my way.' Guess what? After making that decision, I advanced to sergeant, lieutenant, and finally … captain."

The captain's eyes told Joe this dissertation was coming from the heart of a man who usually didn't say much, but knew the ropes better than anyone.

Glover momentarily hesitated, allowing Choy to deliver a coffee, and to move his right leg to ease the discomfort of his gout.

"Whether or not you want to believe me, my department is the most successful department on the force. It prevails because of the way I guide my people. I give them all the latitude possible and I stand behind them, but at what price? I have to listen to meaningless daily lectures from pompous unprofessional officials who only care about one outlook ... image. They don't give one fat fuck about the force, or me, or our personnel, or the protection of our citizens. Now you, with all your know-it-all pomposity actually believe that I could let you down. Give me a break. When you were in diapers, I sat staring out of high school windows dreaming of the day I would become a good cop."

Choy poured two refills while Glover paused to drink half his coffee. After placing his cup down he asked, "Who the hell do you think called the press?"

It took a few seconds before both detectives shook their heads and melted into their seats, and Joe said, "Jesus, I'm sorry Ray. The way you came across on the phone sent me into orbit, and then in the boardroom when you kept your mouth shut, I thought..."

Glover finished the balance of his coffee. "Maybe this is the stuff that's giving me gout. I was ordered to make that call when I was in the chief's office. Fifteen minutes ago, the mayor commanded the chief to give you five assistants of your choosing. You've got carte blanche, Sergeant Stacy, so let me ask you this ... have you ever been in a better position?"

Pete had sat silent throughout Glover's wandering outburst. Now he wanted some answers. "I guess the both of us have got a lot to learn, Captain, but I've got three questions for you. How did you know we had Sarah?"

Glover motioned Choy over for another refill. "Ask me the other two, and then I'll get into it."

"Okay, when you ordered Joe to call me back, you knew it would blow my stakeout of the house in Bellingham, and lastly, how did you know we were here at this moment?"

Glover's lips formed a shrewd grin as he transferred his eyes from detective to detective. "First of all, Sawasy phoned me from the airport. To answer your second question, I think I know Joe Stacy just as well as you. He's a bulldog, and bulldogs don't let go. Joe called Richard Lum, and after obtaining his boss's approval, Richard Lum got William Tong to meet you at the Leopold Hotel, and..."

Joe almost gagged drinking his coffee. "What? Hey, wait a minute," he said, butting in. I phoned Richard Lum, but you don't even know the guy. How the hell...?"

Toying with his juniors, the captain's grin extended into a brimming open-mouthed smile. "I don't know the guy? Is that what you said? I'll get to that. Uh, how long did I say I was on the force? Anyway, Pete, Tong took over your job in Bellingham after you'd filled him in, so everything was fine then. Right?"

"Er, yeah, you bet."

Glover's eyes scanned the small room. "Now, to answer your last question; Christopher, come and join us for a minute, will you please?"

Obviously puzzled, both Pete and Joe glanced around waiting for this mysterious Christopher to enter from the kitchen or the street door. Instead, the low singing stopped and a cheerful but cautious Choy sat down with them.

"Since we're alone, gentlemen, let me introduce you to Christopher Choy, the head of our Asian Gang Squad. Christopher telephoned me ... isn't that right, Chris?"

The gold tooth became visible. "Hah, that's right. I call Ray."

As Glover and Choy nonchalantly relaxed, Joe and Pete gawked at the small unassuming Chinese man sitting with them. Without saying another word, the *restaurant* owner then rose, walked away, and began washing walls again.

"What you've learned today will remain between us alone. Chris isn't even on our payroll. His son receives two cheques, and even the chief doesn't know about Choy. Prior to a few seconds ago, only three people knew. By the way, this is the first time I've ever called him by his first name. I won't use it again and neither will you. Choy is still Choy and he'll never acknowledge today's conversation."

Stacy placed his elbows on the table and cupped his chin in his hands. Sitting up again, Joe cocked his head while his eyes locked on to Glover's. "Boy, were we ever off the mark. Jesus, talk about a lesson in humility; we've been chumps. Then Choy is Lum's boss?"

Glover hobbled to his feet. "He's also his father. I'm not going to bother filling you in on Choy's connections to the various Asian gang squads up and down the West Coast. That's none of your business, but if I were you, I'd utilize Richard's contacts in the different cities. I must leave now, so who's paying for these coffees?"

Pete laughed. I'd toss the both of you but you're getting wise to my methods. I'll pay. Can I ask you two more questions, Captain?"

"Shoot."

"Who called the meeting to make us look like idiots?"

The captain sat down again. "Well, the chief called the meeting but I don't know who fed him the wrong information. It could have come from the mayor's office, the governor, or the FBI. I do know one thing though. A steamroller is in motion trying to shut this case down. Whatever you're onto is massive, and someone doesn't want the truth to be known. Watch yourselves."

"Why did everyone in the office give us the cold shoulder?" Pete asked.

Before leaving, Glover's wholesome gruff disposition returned. "Schmidt passed a rumour around that Joe had killed a cop. I'm going to talk to that son-of-a-bitch."

With a scant smile emerging, Glover stood, adding, "I want you guys in the office tomorrow, and I want this case wrapped up as soon as possible. I'm having the old squad room on the third floor cleared out for your crew. Also, Pete, don't forget your exams."

After the captain left, the dumbfounded detectives observed the short unassuming Chinese restaurant owner humming while filling a bucket with soapy water.

As Joe stroked Sarah Goldfarb's hair, the gratitude of the little girl's mother almost brought on tears. From the moment he had entered Sarah's hospital room, Sophie had extended a mother's indebtedness to him for finding her daughter. The same veneration had already been heaped on Wilfred Young, still standing vigil at the child's bedside.

"Will you come and visit us, Sergeant?" Sophie asked, proudly straightening Sarah's blankets for the umpteenth time. "Wilfred's already accepted. I want to cook both of you a good Jewish meal that will stick to your bones. I can't offer anything else."

Mrs. Goldfarb's genuineness allowed Joe to ponder and appreciate the rarely offered reward of recognition. Normally there were no happy conclusions in the dirty, grimy, daily execution of his job, and he found it difficult to speak. After swallowing, he warmly replied, "Thanks, Mrs. Goldfarb. I'll be around whenever you want. I'm glad everything worked out well. C'mon Wilfred, I'll drive you home."

Before they left, Sophie hugged them, saying, "Thank God, thank God."

With his car's windshield wipers in full motion, Joe quipped, "Well, *Detective Young*, I guess a special medal is in order for you? Thanks pal."

Although Wilfred's eyes had started to close, they came to life. "You don't have to thank me, Sergeant. I've never had this much fun since I joined our school's football team and we raided the cheerleaders' changing room. I've received enough accolades today to last me for the next ten years. Even from Gail."

Hearing the name, 'Gail', Joe's face now showed renewed life."Gail?"

"I think she said that was her name. She saw you on television today and wants you to call her."

"Did she say anything else?" Joe asked, now looking renewed and energetic.

"No, she didn't have to. The look in her eyes said it all. You're a lucky man, Sergeant."

"Wilfred, my friends call me Joe."

"You're a lucky man, Joe."

Mrs. White was just leaving when Stacy entered his apartment.

"Ah, there you are? Are you ever home these days?" the small and stocky grey-haired cleaner asked, straightening out the tam she had put on moments before.

Joe kissed the woman on her forehead, knowing what her reaction would be when he gave her his usual line. "What would I do without you, you gorgeous young thing?"

Slightly blushing as she slipped into her coat, she said, "Joe Stacy, I'm old enough to be your mother."

The sergeant kicked off his shoes, threw his keys on an end table, and picked up the phone. "Ya can't fool me, Madge - you're not a day over forty. I keep tellin' you, sweetheart, if we were on the dance floor together, the rest of the couples would have to stand aside."

Madge White's face now totally burst out in red and her eyes lit up. "Ooh, if I were ten years younger, you'd never get away from me," she pledged, giggling, going out the door.

Joe cracked up. "I'd never want to get away!" he bellowed while punching out a phone number.

A youngster's voice answered, "Manning residence, unless it's you Dwayne Hiscuff ... then it's somebody else's residence, and nobody's home."

"I take it you don't like Dwayne Hiscuff?" Joe asked, grinning at the thought that Dwayne, whoever he was, must have upset someone."

"Oh my God, who is this?" an abashed young girl asked.

"It's Joe Stacy, is your mother there, Suzie?"

Joe heard the phone being put down, before hearing, "Mom, it's some guy by the name of Joe Stacy, and he knows my name. I hope he's not mad because I thought he was that nerd Dwayne Hiscuff."

A moment later Gail's delightful voice came on the line. "Is this the famous detective who's getting more press coverage than the president? How about an autograph Sergeant Stacy?"

Stretching out on the couch and smiling, Joe feigned a television announcer's voice. "I'm sorry, Nurse Manning, I've given out my daily quota of autographs. However, if you're someone special, and I have a feeling you are, then I might make an exception."

Gail laughed before saying, "Why thank you, sir. I hope you're all right, Joe, after what you've been through?"

Hearing her voice was a tonic the doctor ordered. "I'm fine, Gail, but I need some sleep. How are you?"

"Couldn't be better, other than worrying you might have been hurt. Wilfred told me what you were doing. I guess that's the horrible part of the job you spoke to me about?"

"That's part of it, kiddo. It's days like today that make wise ladies keep their distance from police officers."

Gail chuckled, saying, "Well, I'm proud of you, as the whole city is. Would you like to come over for supper tomorrow night?"

Stacy yawned stretching out on the couch. "Tomorrow night? Just give me the time."

"How does seven sound, sleepy head?"

"Great, should I bring anything?"

"Just yourself."

Another yawn appeared. "Sweetheart, I'll be there at seven."

"Wonderful, see you then, Joe. Try and get some sleep."

"I'm already asleep."

After hanging up the phone, Joe rolled on his side, and his last words became reality.

As logging roads go, a winding forest road north of the City of Bellingham in Washington State was in extremely good condition considering the rain. The day's relentless downpour had eroded most of the other trails thirteen-year-old Jimmy Ryerson liked to roam on his dirt bike. As usual, dark creamy mud covered the boy's clothes and any facial skin not covered by his goggles. His dog Boomer now looked more like a black Labrador than a golden retriever.

Jimmy stopped at the top of a grade and lifted his goggles to see if Boomer had come out of the bush. Normally the pooch would disappear for a moment chasing rabbits, but this time he'd been gone for ten minutes causing the boy some concern.

Turning his vehicle around and hitting the 'kill' switch, all Jimmy could hear was the moaning blustering wind catapulting the tops of giant swaying trees, and the sound of rain hammering the leaves and ground. The dominance of the storm had even abolished the shrill of the birds now taking cover from nature's temporary rage.

"Boomer... c'mon boy... Boomer!" the youngster yelled, wiping the rain off his face while listening for his dog's familiar reply. He knew Boomer always barked when he was called after falling behind, but the youth heard nothing.

"Boomer, where are you? C'mon Boomerang!" The boy called again, before recognizing the faint bark of his four-legged companion. The distant response sounded like it came from a hundred yards to his right, probably up the narrow road he'd just passed, the teen thought.

After pulling his goggles down, it took Jimmy only a minute to find his dog digging remorselessly at a soft lump of earth near the road's dead end.

"Boomer, leave the rabbits alone! Boomer, come here! Boomer!"

Panting hard, the dog reluctantly obeyed and returned to the boy's side, but not before Jimmy discovered his friend wasn't burrowing for rabbits. Instead, the dog had been digging around a human foot jutting up from the soil.

"You look like a bag of shit," Pete said, entering the car when Joe picked him up the next day. The rain had stopped, but once again, heavy black clouds darkened the day. "Joe, I thought you were going to get some shut eye?"

"I feel like a bag of shit and I did load up on sleep. Jeez, I'm stiff. It always happens when I doze off on the couch. This time I fell off it during the night and didn't wake up until you called."

"You're not getting any younger, Joe. I can remember when using the couch was your favourite pastime. You never got stiff in those days. Well, not the neck, anyway. You didn't fall off then, either."

Joe turned his neck from side to side, hearing it crack. Grinning, he said, "That's because I had someone with me on the couch, you walking book of knowledge."

Durnell chuckled and patted his friend's right shoulder. "Gee, who would have guessed? Did you listen to the radio this morning?"

Joe massaged his left shoulder but it didn't help matters. "Even if I had turned it on I wouldn't have heard it. Christ, I'm stiff. Why?"

"They found the guy Cohen told you about. A male body was discovered underneath a Dumprite container in an alley close to The Cat's Meow club. Apparently, his face is so badly crushed it's unrecognizable, and one of his hands was found in the middle of the alley. They're taking prints this morning and conducting a dental records check."

Stacy started massaging his other shoulder before leaning on his horn. "Jesus, just look at this idiot trying to turn left. That's a no left turn sign. What the hell's the matter with you?" Joe yelled, before asking, "I wonder if he had anything in his pockets?"

Pete returned the other driver's display of a waving middle finger. "We'll find out shortly. You know, whoever is behind this thing must think we've got something of theirs. Either that or they're convinced we know more than we do. Why else would they try to knock us off?"

"I've considered that, and it's neither, Pete. Someone frantically wants the case closed. We were going to be given the boot yesterday because an individual or individuals with enough power demanded it. If Glover hadn't disrupted the proceedings, the file would have been tightly sealed and placed in the archives. Either that or destroyed."

"Surely not in this day and age?" Durnell asked.

"You bet! There's no doubt influential people are involved. In the shower this morning, I even concluded that the pressure isn't about to stop. Our *fun* is only beginning, and whatever we're on to originates at the top. Now, let's try to determine the top of what?"

A half-hour later when they entered the squad room, Stacy and his partner ignored the *renewed* amiability of the same staff members who had turned their backs on them the day before. At noon after cleaning out their desks, they moved to the office Glover had set up on the third floor. The previous day at Choy's, both detectives had agreed on the names of five officers they wanted to team up with, and Pete had informed the captain.

At one o'clock that afternoon, desks were assigned to Detectives Samir Gebara, Earl Mathieson, Gwen Green, Dave Barker, and Sergeant George Woollam.

Samir, a short, dark-skinned US citizen of Syrian ancestry had served on the force for fifteen years. Both Joe and Pete had worked many times with Samir, and they knew him to be hard working, loyal, and well disciplined.

Mathieson had also served for fifteen years, and like Joe, he never concerned himself with promotion. Both detectives thought Earl's sense of humour and no nonsense professional manner would greatly assist their efforts.

Gwen, an attractive bright-eyed single woman aged 28, had only been a detective for four years, but they thought she knew her stuff and would go places.

Dave Barker was the perfect administrative assistant. His painstaking talent for sorting through reports made him indispensable in any position. Every department wanted Barker, and Joe and Pete were lucky to tear him away from the Juvenile Crime Division.

George Woollam was close to retirement. Originally born in Manchester, England, he'd served with the Manchester Police Department before immigrating to the United States in the seventies. Woollam was well familiar with the intricacies of British and European police departments and had good contacts within Interpol.

Each member of the team knew one another and during the initial briefing and assignment of tasks, Joe omitted any reference to Harvey Cohen or Richard Lum.

"Before we get going, I want you to know there are only seven keys to the lock on this door, and I believe our telephones have been secured. Are there any questions?"

"Why such tight security?" Mathieson asked. "Also, who's staking out the Bellingham house?"

Pete sat on the side of his desk. "There's been an inside leak on this thing from the beginning, and what we do or what we learn, goes no further than these walls. As far as the house is concerned, a friend of mine from Bellingham police is watching the place."

There were no further questions, so after everyone had a bite to eat in the building's basement cafeteria, Joe and Pete made a visit to Protocol Customs Assurance Company's office situated in an immense downtown building. Before leaving, Dave Barker provided them with the local general manager's name, a Mr. Wilhelm Dreischner.

When the duo met the well-dressed, thin, grey-haired and moustached general manager, the man appeared at ease and confident."We've had customs people here all morning," he stated, five minutes into the conversation. "They're still here going through every piece of paper we produce. Gentlemen, the directors of our company find this whole matter most embarrassing. Press coverage across the country is seriously hurting our business."

Joe didn't know why, but he believed the man. For some reason, Dreischner's mannerisms emanated genuineness. The sergeant thought if Dreischner was lying, thirty years of police work couldn't detect it ... yet.

"Mr. Dreischner, just who are the directors of this company?" Stacy asked.

While Pete made notes, the general manager picked up a copy of the company's latest annual report and read off a list of twenty reputable business names, a significant segment of *Who's Who* in American commerce from coast to coast. Handing the report to Joe, he added, "Protocol was formed before the war but reorganized after the war to manage priceless possessions plundered and stored by the Nazis. We still haven't completed sorting through mounds of unclaimed inventory stockpiled in the vaults of Western countries, never mind the liberated Eastern countries. A scandal such as this could devastate our company."

Something Dreischner said intrigued Joe's partner. Looking up from his notebook, Pete asked, "So the company was formed before the war?"

"Yes, sir, before the war. This company originated in Switzerland in the middle 1930s and our international head office remains there. Initially, it was merely an inventory syndicate - then when the Allies won the war, Protocol was expanded to provide information on stolen property. Since then, our company has been engaged in transporting protected valued goods around the world."

"So originally it was a German company?" Joe asked.

"Well, the founders may have been German, but Swiss bank officials occupied the initial directorships," Dreischner said, sipping his coffee. Coffee that Joe and Pete had declined. "You've probably read that the Allies placed their own people in certain directorships of the company just after the war when they were trying to sort the mess out."

Both detectives continued to make notes while Dreischner spoke. Then Joe asked, "Why wouldn't Protocol buy their own vehicles rather than lease them. The cost must be horrendous?"

Dreischner's telephone rang and the general manager answered it stating he didn't wish to be disturbed. "Protocol doesn't own property of any kind. We simply provide a service around the globe. That means we lease everything from vehicles, to computers, to office space. Our head office has always employed that policy, and head office is the boss. I've brought the matter up with our American head office in New York a few times, but the procedure still remains the same."

Joe's eyes snared the other man's eyes. "Mr. Dreischner, we know of two children who have been transported in your so-called *security containers*. What can you tell us about them...?"

Shaking his head, Dreischner cut off the sergeant. "Absolutely nothing, Sergeant. Such a thing is dreadful. This company doesn't provide human transportation. That dead person, uh, Archie Klenz, worked for United States Customs, not us. Don't blame Protocol for his deeds."

"I'm not blaming anyone, sir, but he not only used your containers, Klenz also used your vehicles, as did other people who didn't work for your company."

"Yes, I know and plainly we have a critical procedural flaw. I've already ordered a complete investigation into the matter."

Pete flipped a few pages in his book. "Mr. Dreischner, how well do you know a man named Erik Roltz?"

For a fraction of a second, Joe thought he noticed a minor insecure eye movement before the general manager swallowed asking, "The manager of Systems Truck Rentals?"

"That's him."

"I've only met him once, but our transportation manager Bruce Cooke deals with him quite often. Would you like me to get Bruce up here?"

Stacy smiled. "No, that won't be necessary. We'll be talking with quite a few of your employees. Do you know these men?" he asked, taking two police drawings out of his jacket pocket and passing them over.

Dreischner studied the photograph of Kroll and the artist's conception of the two men who threatened Wilfred Young. Shaking his head he replied, "No, I don't know them."

"Have you ever seen them?" Joe asked.

The general manager handed the sketches back. "No, I'm sorry."

The team of detectives questioned Dreischner for another half-hour before returning to their office. Driving back, one of Joe's statements sent a shiver down Pete's spine. "Pete, that son-of-a-bitch is lying. He's part of the whole thing."

"What the hell's this?" Joe asked, noticing a brand new cellular on his desk that same afternoon. "I swore I'd never use one of these things," he said, spotting another one on Durnell's desk.

Grinning knowledgably, and taking extensive blinks, Dave Barker totally ignored Joe's comments. "I've heard you're an opponent of change, however, the communications age has arrived, Sergeant, and you need one like the rest of us. All our numbers run in sequence. They've been programmed into your phones, and they're taped on the backs as well. Keep them with you and we can remain in touch."

"This is bullshit." Joe said. "Only little old ladies and busybodies use these."

Barker acknowledged Joe's added indignation, but ignored it. "Now, let's move on to those two telephone numbers you got from Cottonwood Street. The first one is the pay phone in our cafeteria, and..."

Stacy's face took on a more shrewd expression. "So someone around here tipped them off using the pay phone down below? Just as I thought ... Pete, we've got a Judas. What about the other number?"

Barker ran a finger down the page in front of him. "The second belongs to the staked-out Bellingham house."

"So the bastards phoned ahead, eh? Whose names are the two phones registered to?"

"The billing name for the Bellingham number and the Cottonwood house is that of a certain Wolfgang Schrems, who lived at 19730 Mountainview Drive here in Seattle."

"Christ, another German name," Joe said, eager to leave. "Good, let's pick him up."

"Joe, I haven't finished yet. Schrems is dead. He's the guy found under the Dumprite container. I obtained a search warrant and Mathieson and Green are on their way there now."

Stacy grabbed his coats. "Nice work, Dave. C'mon Pete, let's join 'em at Cottonwood."

Barker searched through a pile of papers on his desk. "Just before you go. We've received this telephoto from the Eindhoven police in Holland. Is this the kid you took to the hospital?"

Both sets of downcast eyes established each detective's deep emotion as they examined the photograph of the smiling little boy.

"That's him," Joe said, heading to the door and clearing his throat. "Damn it, I had him safe in my arms."

Only small talk occupied the car on the way to Mountainview Drive. The picture Barker had shown them had created a desolated gut-wrenching feeling of compassion normally ignored by professional police officers. Ordinarily, if they let such matters bother them they couldn't get on with each day's activities. This peculiar feeling was different. Innocent children were involved and only heartless human beings could confine such ire.

When Stacy and Durnell drove up, Mathieson and Green had just arrived and were already inside the neatly kept green and white bungalow. They pointed out that Schrems had lived in a run down shack at the back of the house, but used the same address.

"I must have told him a hundred times to use 19730A Mountainview Drive, but it was like talking to the wall," mouthed Arnie Coles, a middle-aged roly-poly man who stated he worked for Boeing Aircraft. "Enid and I knew we'd made a mistake after renting it to him. Schrems and his foul-mouthed biker friends gave this neighbourhood a bad name from the second he moved in."

Green sat with the man's wife. "Why didn't you ask him to move?"

"We were afraid to," Mrs. Coles replied. "You've seen what these skinheads are like."

"Skinheads?" Earl asked.

"Yeah, dirty filthy skinheads. They were here on their motorcycles till all hours drinking, making noise, and fighting. Them and their kids."

To Joe, the couple appeared forthright. The house was impeccably clean, well furnished, and retained the aroma of recently baked bread.

"You mean they had children with them?" Durnell asked Mrs. Coles.

"Yes, sometimes. Young boys around five to seven years of age who always looked like they needed baths. About a month ago one youngster with stains all over his clothes knocked on our back door asking for a drink of water. I was just about to let him in when a friend of Schrems ran over, hit the boy across the side of his head, and yelled at him to go back. I was going to phone the police because the child cried, but my husband said we shouldn't get involved."

"We didn't want any trouble from those people," Arnie said, displaying a piteous expression. "They're tough-looking scoundrels. Here's the key if you want to go in there."

While Mathieson and Green further questioned Mr. and Mrs. Coles, Joe and Pete checked out the fair-sized back shed coated with decomposing shingles. One end of an orange tarpaulin nailed to the flat roof had come loose and it fluttered in the breeze. The only other sound came from across the alley as a woman reeled in her wet laundry.

The squalid two-room *dwelling* reeked of paraffin and other displeasing odours. A kitchen table by the lone window held paper plates loaded with decaying food, and cigarette butts. Empty beer bottles and mouldy pizza containers covered the rest of the table. The top of the small stove at one end of the room bore every cooking stain possible, along with pans coated with encrusted food. The remains of a clothes-littered couch and two old chairs that had been cut open numerous times sat on a defiled crumpled old carpet in the centre of a grimy linoleum butt-burnt floor. Pages torn from child pornography magazines littered the floor and hung from nails and thumbtacks on the grimy cardboard covered walls.

Pete indicated he was very close to throwing up. Holding his handkerchief over his nose, he said, "The dirty bastards. These people aren't human beings, Joe. They're not even animals."

Joe didn't answer his friend as he gently pushed open the door leading to what was supposed to be the bedroom. After turning on the light, the detectives waded through four mattresses dispersed on the dingy dilapidated wooden floor. Each had been discoloured by human waste, and a disgusting smell filled the room. Pictures of naked young boys and girls in every pose possible were taped or pinned to the walls, and nauseous-smelling blankets and uncased pillows full of cigarette burns were mixed with the defiled clothes of children and adults. *Soiled* toilet paper indicated someone had evacuated their bowels in a corner of the room.

The small bathroom off the bedroom was no better. Black towels that were once white scattered the floor, and foul-smelling filthy clothing and boots filled the bathtub and lined the room. The cracked worn out toilet and sink looked like they had not been scoured in years, and the back of the door possessed more pictures of unclothed male and female adolescents.

When Stacy and Durnell returned to the main house, Joe asked Mathieson and Green to give the shed a thorough going over before suggesting to the Coles they should burn it down. Then he phoned Sawasy and asked him to send a crew over.

When the four detectives were outside, Earl said, "Joe, Mrs. Coles described the skinhead who hit the boy. He's most likely your friend with the rotten teeth."

"Then we're getting closer. I can hardly wait till we meet," Joe said, his lips etching a vile leer. "

Suzie shared her mother's nose, lips, and eyes, and her lustrous pony tailed hair mirrored Gail's golden strands.

"Hi, are you Mr. Stacy?" she asked, opening the apartment's door and pushing back her blond younger crew-cut brother who stood behind her trying to get a look.

Joe's grin gave away his reply. "No, I'm Dwayne Hiscuff's dad, and I'm here to arrange a date between the two of you. Dwayne tells me you're madly in love with him. Is that right, Suzie?"

When both children laughed and Suzie said, "Yuck," Stacy found himself chuckling with them.

"Yes, I'm Joe Stacy. Call me Joe," he said, shaking each of their hands. "I hear you guys are offering free meals to famished policemen? Your mom invited me here for dinner."

Gordie pushed himself to the front. "You'll have to take off your shoes. Hey, Sergeant, you're better lookin' than your picture on television."

Suzie took over the lead position. "Gordie, you're not supposed to talk like that. Mom, Gordie's at it again."

Gail came to the door smiling. "What did he say?"

Joe took off his shoes as Suzie closed the door. "Hi, Gail. Your son just paid me a compliment, that's all. Ain't that right, Gordie?"

Gordie's sparsely freckled face beamed even though he was a little bashful. "All I said was he was better lookin' than his picture was on the news."

The boy's mother searched for words and straightened her hair that did not need straightening. "Well, er ... perhaps ... you're right. Yes, I believe you're right, Gordon Manning. Now you two go and wash up for supper. Hurry up, now."

"They're nice kids, Gail," Stacy said, following Gail into the living room.

Gail handed Joe a glass of chilled white wine. "Thanks, but there are times when they get carried away. That's the wine you like, isn't it?"

"It's perfect. Say, this place is large, and you've really got it fixed up nice. It's got that certain home feeling to it, and if I could decorate a tree like that, I might put one up."

Gail's dimple appeared. "Why thank you, Sergeant Stacy. As for the tree, the children decorated it. Better than Pete's job, eh?"

Joe had forgotten he had told Gail about Pete's work of art. "Much better. I'll tell him to come and take lessons. How many rooms do you have?"

Gail sat next to him on the couch. "Six including the den. Suzie and Gordie have their own rooms. I don't think they make apartments like this anymore. Before moving here I searched high and low for a large suite with a reasonable rent, and when a nurse friend told me about it, I jumped. At first, the owner said he wouldn't take children, but when he met them he changed his mind. What's your place like?"

Joe grinned, positioning his cellular phone on the arm of the couch. "You mean when it's tidied up? Pretty good I guess. I've never been one for putting clothes away. Don't get me wrong, I'm not *really* messy, but when you live alone, it just becomes a place to sleep."

Suddenly their eyes met for a few seconds and both adults seemed lost for words. Gail thought it was nice of him to come over, and Joe could not stop admiring her. Her faded red slacks and floppy white sweater made her look cuddly. Softly he said, "I think you're the most beautiful woman I've ever met. To think that I've...”

"Hey, Joe, where's your gun?" Gordie asked, entering the room and sitting in between them. The boy's skin shone, and he had combed his hair.

Gail laughed as she got up to fix dinner. "Well, one thing's for certain, you'll never be alone around here. Suzie's going to help me and we'll eat in a few minutes. Gordie, you be good, now?"

The lad's innocence kept a permanent smile on Joe's lips. Gordie had all the exuberance in the world, and then some.

"My Gun? Uh, I left it at home. Police officers don't always carry their guns with them, Gordie. Guns are pretty dangerous."

"I've got a Daisy B.B. rifle, but my mom says I can't use it until I'm older."

"I think that's wise, Gord. A lot of kids have been hit in the eyes with those pellets. I'm not a fan of guns. Uh, you should only learn about them when you're ready for them. Tell me ... what kind of sports you like?"

Gordie got up and toyed with Joe's cellular phone before placing it down again. "I like football, baseball, hockey, but I really like the Sonics. Do you like basketball, Joe?"

"Well, yeah, I do, but I'm more of a football fan. What do you think of the Seahawks?"

"They're okay, but they'd be a lot better if they had a really super quarterback. Say, did you know we're getting a computer for Christmas?"

"What, from Santa Claus?"

"Nah, mom's gettin' it for us. You don't believe in Santa do you, Joe?"

"Uh, I really don't know if I've made up my mind yet, Gord."

The boy gave Joe's response some thought before changing the subject. "In January, our class is going to tour the Microsoft factory."

"Hey, that will be nice. Maybe they'll give you a..."

The *meeting of the men* was disturbed when Suzie joined them saying, "Dinner's on the table. Gordie, I sit next to Joe, and you sit next to mom."

For the next hour, Joe Stacy felt more relaxed than he had in a long, long time. Dinner conversation centred on sports, the police department, Memorial Hospital, fishing, school, computers, and the space shuttle. With Gail's unhurried touch of contented elegance and the children's genuine innocent inquisitiveness, Joe found himself frivolously floating inside a gracious circle of warmth, and he loved every moment of it. The spick and span apartment oozed with something his life needed ... something he could never put his finger on, something that always lit up his heart when he thought of what he wanted. Gail was delightful, her children were the same, and had there been a dog or cat, Joe knew the pet would mirror the lifestyle of its owners.

Following the fabulous roast chicken dinner, he helped the three with the dishes, and at one point, he ended up on the living room carpet wrestling with Gordie in front of the fireplace.

Later, after the children had had their baths, and both youngsters came over and said goodnight, Joe voiced an aphorism he had not used in years. "Good night, sleep tight and don't let the bedbugs bite."

Out of sight, Gordie's response was, "I ain't got no bedbugs, but I think my hamster's got fleas."

Joe also heard Suzie laugh when she yelled, "Oh yes you have, Gordie. Big fleas and bugs ... all over you, and your bed."

When Gail returned after tucking in the children, she put on a soft tape and handed Joe another glass of wine. Smiling tenderly, she raised her glass and stood before him. "Here's to a happy Christmas, and a successful New Year, Detective Sergeant Stacy."

Joe stood and touched her glass with his. "After another wonderful evening with you ... yes, here's to a happy Christmas and a successful New Year, Mrs. Manning."

A moment later their eyes attached themselves like magnets and Joe took her glass and placed it down with his. Gently, he brought her into his arms and kissed her. Gail's full lips and the warmth of her body felt wonderful to him as their feet shuffled softly to the stereo's romantic melody.

As Gail snuggled closer, nothing in the world could disturb the magical force flowing between them. At this stage of their lives, they found themselves lost in an enchanting hallucinatory dimension only created for young lovers; but now those confines opened up for them and were unmistakably real.

"Oh, baby, I..." The ringing of Joe's cellular interrupted the dawn of Joe's ardent revelation.

Parting slowly, Gail shyly smiled straightening her hair and watching Joe's exasperation. After picking up the device, she passed it to him, saying, "It can't be for me, so it's gotta be for you."

Perplexed, Joe pulled himself together and answered, "Yeah, Pete?"

"How did you know it was me?" Durnell replied, not waiting for an explanation. "Bellingham police have just unearthed VanVliet's body. Guess what?"

Curiosity controlled Joe's face as he picked up his half-finished glass of wine and sat down. "VanVliet as well? What now?"

"Remember the one print by the truck's ignition?"

"Yeah."

"It was his. The name VanVliet was just another alias. He had many, but he mainly used the name Bruckman when he wasn't moving children. With that name, you know the guy's German, not Dutch. Jesus, what a mess. He was shot twice in the back of the head and his right hand ring finger's been cut off."

Grimacing, Joe asked, "Who found him?"

"A kid on a dirt-bike found the nude body yesterday. No clothes, no identification, no rings ... nothing. Woollam and Gebara are on their way there now. It looks as if these bastards are being knocked off before we get to them."

"You got it, Pete. I can't believe this."

"Also, Joe, there's been some movement in the Bellingham house. Two trucks arrived fifteen minutes ago. What do you want to do?"

"It's time to make our move, Pete. Other than the trucks, has anyone visited the house?"

"Two people in separate cars at different times. Tong had them tailed. One's in Vancouver, Canada, and the second person has checked into a motel in the Spokane area. I think they're wise to the phone tap, Joe. No calls have been made in or out."

"They're probably using cellulars. Spokane, eh? Why does Spokane ring a bell?"

"The coin robbery took place in Spokane, remember?"

Stacy finished off his wine. "Yeah. Okay Pete, call Mathieson and Green, and tell them we'll team up at the Bellingham police station. Also, phone Barker and have him liaise with Bellingham police. We're going to need their assistance. Who's got the search warrant?"

"Mathieson."

"Good, thanks buddy. I'll be right over."

When Joe got up, Gail stood in front of him holding his jacket. "Is this the life you were telling me about?" she caringly asked.

"Unfortunately it is," he said, shrugging and wrapping her in his arms for a moment before putting on his coat and shoes. "I'm sorry, Gail, I've got to rush over to Bellingham. Uh, can we all go to the movies, sometime soon?"

Gail's understanding smile spoke before she did. Kissing Joe's left cheek, she said, "I think that would be wonderful. Now, take good care of yourself. I kind of like your style, Joe Stacy."

Going out the door, Joe replied, "The feeling's mutual, Gail."

Slowing for a moment, he turned back for a long last lingering look. "No, not mutual ... it's much more than that. I love you Gail."

Chapter 5

Cold rain mixed with snow welcomed Joe's crew and three Bellingham investigators when they joined Richard Lum and William Tong under the protective branches of a giant maple tree one block from the old house on the large Bellingham estate. In the distance, a train's lonely whistle mingled with the sounds of hammering rain and the huffs of a stubborn wind that insisted on finding every uncovered piece of flesh of those who were foolish enough to be outside.

All cars remained a considerable distance from the house, and Lum issued powerful flashlights to each member along with personal two-way radios and flack jackets. Only two other mansions were in the immediate vicinity of the suspect house and their lights were out.

"What's happening?" Joe asked his friend Richard. It was so cold he found himself pulling up his collar and rubbing his hands together trying to keep them warm.

Richard Lum had drawn a plan of the estate. After introducing William Tong to Joe, he said, "No one has left the main house and I have no idea how many are in there. The house has five doors," he continued, pointing them out on his chart. "There are also two fire escapes, here and here … they lead to bathrooms."

"We've disabled their trucks, Joe," Lum exclaimed while all members scrutinized the plans. "I thought these people were going to make their move tonight, but it looks like they put it off until tomorrow. From what I've observed, only the first and second floors are being used. The basement has remained dark so I think we can exclude that area. Since there are nine of us, I suggest two at the main front door, two at the back, one at each of the other three doors, and one at each fire escape."

Stacy further studied the diagram. "Are there any open doors?"

Tong replied instead. "No, but that won't be a problem, Joe." Producing a palm-sized glasscutter, he added, "We've got two of these, so if it's okay with you, I'll enter from the top floor on the west side, and Richard will enter from the top east side? We'll climb the fire escapes, let ourselves in on the third floor, and open all outside doors."

Joe agreed. "Sounds good, but what about the bars on the windows."

"There are none on the third floor." Lum stated, confidently.

"Any other suggestions?" Joe asked, glancing at the others.

Pete looked at Lum's sketch again. "Considering we've got children to watch out for, it sounds all right to me. We know VanVliet's out of the way, but it would be a hell of a lot easier if we knew what we were up against."

Examining each of their faces and releasing a deep breath, Stacy said, "Okay, let's do it. I just want all of you to know the children are our main concern. Play it safe, understood?"

The question need not have been asked; each officer knew his restraints.

Joe didn't like the way George Woollam looked. Lately the police veteran appeared pale and worn out. If he were sick, or mentally spent, it wouldn't be wise sending him into the upcoming brawl. Also with Linda pregnant, Joe wondered if Pete should be in the middle of the clash. Although most unusual, he made a decision to keep the two out of the fray as best as possible. He knew they wouldn't appreciate his concerns, but it was his call.

"Oh, and George, you won't be going in," Joe said, unemotionally. "Stay at the back of the house. Pete, you'll stay on the front porch." Got it?

Both officers indicated they understood the order, but not the meaning behind the message.

Dressed in black, Lum and Tong had rejected wearing flack jackets. Both pulled dark-coloured woollen hoods over their heads, slipped out of their shoes and put on what appeared to be black ballet slippers.

"How much time will you need?" Joe asked cautiously, itching to get his hands on those inside the house.

Lum checked his watch. "About fifteen minutes. Remember, silence is our best friend. Use your communicators sparingly, if at all."

Stacy concurred. "Yeah, good point. Let's keep this quiet."

Tapping Stacy's shoulder, William Tong said, "We'll get going now, Joe. We suggest you decide what doors you'll be covering. I also think you should leave in pairs, entering the grounds from different routes."

Before the two set off, Stacy assigned entrance paths to his crew. "We'll start making our move in five minutes," he said. "Thanks guys, good luck."

The wind picked up a little as the two Asian Gang Squad members disappeared into the wet black night. Then after five minutes, the remaining officers started departing at one-and-a-half minute intervals.

As Joe and Pete silently climbed the steps at the front of the massive house, two cats jumped off the porch railing and ran past them - their motion accelerating each detective's heartbeat.

Reaching the top, the men parted, singly positioning themselves to each side of the huge door. Once their eyes had become accustomed to the dark, Pete made a motion for Joe to read the message on the doormat - *The Lord Welcomes His Children.*

After examining it, Joe just shook his head.

Ten minutes later two bolts were slowly slipped from their couplings and when the door creaked open, a hooded figure came out. Instead of whispering, Lum closed the door to, lifted up his hood, and spoke quietly. "There's no one on the third floor, and only three rooms on the second floor have children in them."

"Great. Are there any assholes with the kids?" Joe asked.

"No, they're probably all on this first floor. Right about now, William's placing a Bellingham officer in each room where there are children."

"How many rooms are on this floor?" Joe asked.

"About five or six, but we don't know if they hold kids."

Stacy's heart beat like a hammer hitting a cement wall. "Pete, you stay here. Richard, where's the rest of the crew?"

"Behind me. William will be here in a sec."

When William came down and all officers stepped out onto the porch, Joe found his lips and throat so dry he longed for a drink. This was his moment and every nerve ending in his body seem to fuse with his ice-hot skin. After a moment, he arrived at the only conclusion possible. They had to get into those lower rooms.

Withdrawing his pistol from its holster, Joe said, "Okay, we'll each take a room at exactly the same time. When you hear a squawk signal on your radios, move instantly, turn on your lights, enter the rooms, and single out the adults. Make certain you shine your lights in their eyes, and create as much noise as possible. Now remember, these eels are slippery, so watch yourselves. Don't play with these guys and don't give them a chance to think or reach for weapons. If you see a weapon in someone's hand, shoot the son-of-a-bitch."

The quiet ticking of a hall clock split the silence as the police officers took up position in the unlit hallway. Stacy waited an extra fifteen seconds to ensure each was ready before pressing his transceiver button. When he did, the subsequent clash turned paradise into bloody purgatory for the house's adult occupants.

Amidst the fanfare of shock, panic, and total mayhem, a physical outburst of ferocious resistance ensued. When one of two adults in the room Joe burst into reached for a nearby shotgun, two rounds ripped into his chest, catapulting him over his tattooed female bed mate cowering under a blanket.

Concussion from four other shots fractured the screech of severe pain emanating from the other rooms. Tong nearly ripped out the throat of a skinhead who came at him with a butcher knife, and Green defended herself by distributing her flashlight's thick glass with the nose, eyes, and cheekbones of a skinhead intent on splitting her head with a machete. As well, the attacking naked form Mathieson shot, smashed through a front porch window, hitting the security bars and showering Pete and the porch with glass.

If this was conflict, Joe thought it surpassed the limits of Nazi validity. The skinheads put up a strong fight until they realized they were on the losing side. At that point, their rage changed to sobbing appeals for leniency.

While the rooms on the first floor were emptied of "living filth," the name Stacy gave to the skinheads, detectives surveyed individual autographed pictures of Hitler and Himmler, along with other Nazi regalia, memorabilia, and American flags emblazoned with the swastika. Beautifully framed pornographic photos of children and adults adorned all the walls in the house, along with transcribed excerpts of Himmler's speech to the SS at Posen, Poland on October 4th, 1943.

When Pete entered to assist, he found Joe concentrating on one particular extract of the Posen rally. After reading it, Joe looked and felt like Pete had earlier.

"What kind of lowlifes are we dealing with? Pete, get Barker to correlate these written *selections* for us."

The lights in neighbouring houses lit up before the mansion of corruption illuminated brightly. Telephone lines buzzed and it was not necessary for Stacy's crew to call for paddy wagons, they arrived along with ambulances and child welfare personnel to look after the children.

Prior to being whisked away, five girls and six boys ages five to eight were released into the welcoming arms of doctors, nurses, and caring adults.

Paying particular attention to the children, Joe pushed a nude head-shaved handcuffed man in his early twenties at Mathieson. "Load this maggot up. Pete, I see someone we know."

The tired, trembling little blond boy dressed only in underpants did not recognize the beaming sergeant placing a blanket around him. He also didn't understand English, but he smiled as Stacy knelt before him, caressed his face, ran a hand through his hair, and hugged him.

With his eyes getting moist, Joe found it difficult to speak when he gently took hold of the youngster's tiny right hand. Shaking it tenderly before hugging the lad, he whispered, "Hello Jan from Eindhoven. Your mom and dad have missed you very much ... and so have we. This time you're safe, and your granddad is waiting to take you fishing again."

"No more press! That's it, no more," Stacy yelled sitting at his desk the following morning.

Hours prior to Joe's arrival, members from the local and national media had bombarded the Seattle Police Department. They occupied the offices, lobbies, hallways, and the cafeteria, and were spread out like an army on the sidewalk in front of the building.

"If this keeps up, you'll be getting offers from Hollywood," Pete jested, filling in a mound of paperwork with Joe and three others. "I can see it all now. The Sergeant *Joe the Dancer, Stacy Show*, starring the man himself, Sergeant Joe Tiptoes Stacy."

Snickering, the senior detective fanned the remark away. He felt proud of his group's accomplishments the night before. Six adults were in cells, two were dead, and another two were in hospital. With no injuries to his crew, the whole affair had been wrapped up by one o'clock and he was home by two-thirty. Woollam and Gebara had volunteered to remain in Bellingham to clean up loose ends, question the neighbours, and liaise with Sawasy's people. Terry had already teamed up with his Bellingham counterparts going over the house, and trucks.

"It's not Sergeant Stacy, anymore, it's Lieutenant Stacy," Glover voiced, limping into the office during Pete's prophesying. "It's also going to be Acting Sergeant Durnell. The governor's on his way over, the chief's going to promote the two of you, the mayor wants you to pose with him, and the FBI are sending three agents out from Washington. Where the hell's Hollywood when you need it, eh, Joe? Good work, fellas, but watch your back with these FBI types. Something smells because the mouthiest one of the two that visited us has been suspended pending an investigation."

The Captain turned to leave, but as usual remembered something he hadn't mentioned. "Joe, have you ever heard of the National Independent Citizens for Equal and Better Race Relations? It's referred to as NICER for short?"

Joe indicated he had seen something about it in the past. "I think ... Yeah, I have, come to think of it. On television a few years back, ABT covered the group's annual convention. They've got chapters in all states and every two years they donate big money, something like twenty-eight million dollars for the improvement of ethnic relations and religious culture in America."

Glover's wondrous smile got Joe grinning. "Stacy, you continue to amaze me. Even with all your gallivanting, you still manage to keep up on current affairs. What do you do, watch television sitting on the crapper?"

Pete stepped in, "Only after a full belly of beer - right Joe?"

Joe's grin expanded as he lit up a smoke. "Right! As a matter of fact, yeah, I do. Nah, just joking. I caught the article because they present the NICER Humanitarian Prize to ten individuals or groups. It's done every two years and each recipient gets a hundred thousand for his or her contribution to..."

Joe instantly stopped elucidating because the Captain's head didn't stop nodding, and the expression on Glover's face said it all. Something was up, and Joe knew it.

"Yes, go on?" Glover *sang*, displaying a smug facial expression watching the newly promoted and puzzled lieutenant.

If Stacy had not taken the cigarette out of his mouth, it would have fallen out. His mouth remained in the open position as he stared at the captain. "Ray, you've got to be friggin' joking?"

Glover wrapped his right arm around Joe's shoulders. "Someone nominated you and you've made the short list, Charlie Brown. You didn't hear it from me; the mayor's going to make the announcement today after he receives the telegram. Peter Cooper's secretary telephoned this morning. Cooper's one of the country's richest philanthropists and patron of the arts. He's also this year's chairman of NICER. Listen, if you end up winning and have to fly to New York, look up Forbes for me, and tell him I really enjoy his magazine. Also, tell him I think he's honest and he'd make a great president."

"The chance of me winning the NICER Prize could probably be compared to Madonna goin' on a date with Bill Gates," Stacy said getting back to his paperwork.

"I thought you called him, er, your friend, Willie Gates?" Pete asked, sliding on his chair to place some papers in Barker's 'IN' basket.

"Nah, I'm still pissed off with Gates for not inviting me to his wedding."

Glover laughed limping from the office. "Anyway, stay with it, and all the best guys."

A few moments later, Joe stood, stretched, and walked over to a window. "If by chance the prize comes our way, I'll split it eight ways. I don't even know if we can keep it?" Pausing and looking outside, he added, "Dave, what are the rules on keeping it?"

Grinning with a frown, Barker scratched his full head of semi-grey hair. "If it's split eight ways, I'll find us a way to keep it, that's for goddamned certain."

Chuckles spread throughout the office before 'eyes down' time hit each desk.

Scores of bundled-up carefree ice-skaters in New York's Central Park paid no attention to the shadows cast by the monolithic buildings concealing a setting sun rarely showing itself during the icy winter months. Joyful mouths emitting clouds of hot air into the frigid atmosphere differed notably from four tense, irritable faces in a nearby 98th floor conference room.

"You will notice Security and Resolution are not with us this evening," the stern-faced chairman exhorted while examining the fearful faces of the assemblage sitting before him. "They have been *relieved* of their responsibilities and have been terminated. Planning, you have also disappointed us."

As terrified sets of eyes darted around the room, the chairman smirked slyly. He knew his words permeated the worst fears in those attending, and that was his intent.

"Switzerland will not replace them until this matter has been resolved, as I thought it would have been long before now! Our organization has conducted operations in this country for over fifty years, and you allow some insignificant Seattle cop to hamper our progress. If he continues to have free reign then he might learn of the national and international magnitude of our company's operations."

Pausing momentarily, the man conducting the meeting flagrantly displayed his contempt for the faces sitting on one side of the large polished table. "Now, I want answers, and I want them now!"

"Why don't we eliminate him?" Finance suggested, sitting erect in his seat and not looking at the others. "If he's out of the way, it will die down."

The chairman shook his head indicating it would be the wrong thing to do. "Why the hell do you think Security and Resolution are no longer with us? Amongst other blunders, they allowed some idiots at a lower level to attempt an assassination that failed miserably. It's gone beyond that. If this bastard, Stacy, or those around him are interfered with, it will create an unwelcome backlash. Initially, Security convinced me Stacy knew more than we thought, but I don't think so. He has only intruded into a couple of our business affairs in that state and we're closing matters down around him. I just don't want further police interference. Do you hear me? Do you understand me?"

Transportation started licking his lips and scratching areas of his face that didn't need touching. "But look at the press he's getting, Mr. Chairman. He also appears to be manipulating the media. We all know Schrems wasn't a local drunk who died of a heart attack before that garbage container landed on him. That's the way the police reported it. Stacy's watching his back and he seems to have a lot of help."

Government Relations tried to give the impression she was in full control of herself. After pouring a glass of water, she calmly sat back in her seat for a moment before offering, "Let's look at this rationally. Can I elaborate, Mr. Chairman?"

The chairman's eyes kept piercing Transportation's face for a moment before shifting to the exquisitely dressed woman. "Yes, continue. These four floors are empty and the room has been electronically swept."

"Stacy won't have to be stopped - he'll run out of steam, and then..."

Pounding the table with his fist, the chairman yelled, "Have you forgotten we commanded Senator Millington to convince the chief of police that Stacy was a rogue policeman? Not just the senator, we sent senior FBI contacts and the governor's assistant. It didn't do any good, woman. These people benefit from our resources, but we've got nothing to show for it?"

Government Relations knew the chairman would bring that matter up. She was well prepared, and she did not like being referred to as, "woman."

"Resolution should have had them intervene sooner, sir. The press interrupted our plans. Speaking of the FBI, I understand our contact has been suspended, pending an inquiry?"

"That's no concern of yours. The matter's been dealt with."

"May I continue, sir?"

"Yes, get on with it, woman!"

"Stacy believes he's onto a paedophile operation only. He's questioned Systems and Protocol and come up against a brick wall. We've eliminated Kroll, Prouse, and Bruckman, so really the police don't have much to go on. By now, he will have traced Schrems to our two *holding* houses, but Schrems is dead. We mustn't forget Schrems staffed both houses with indoctrinated recruits from our Iowa-training centre and Kravenhall. Those individuals have yet to be cleared to a senior level of intelligence, so the police won't get anything out of them."

Government Relations paused to take some water. "Our weak links are Erik Roltz and Wilhelm Dreischner. Since we're temporarily moving our child operations to Vancouver, Canada, Roltz and Dreischner are expendable. Stacy's looking for the so-called brains, so we set the pair up and eliminate them. It's finished then ... over with. At the very least, it's a dead-end for Stacy. Even if he suspects there is another level, it won't do him any good."

The chairman did not like receiving advice from females. To him, they were only good as bed partners and breeding children, and not that good at the former. This woman was demonstrating initiative normally reserved for males. Unfortunately, she made sense, and he found it disturbing.

Listening to every word before stretching his neck, the chairman replied, "I suppose this is the best we can come up with on short notice, but I don't like it. I really don't like it! Also, hasn't Dreischner got a family?"

Government Relations knew she had whet the chairman's appetite, and she felt extremely pleased with herself.

"He's married, but it's a marriage of convenience, Mr. Chairman. His wife is involved with a girl's swimming team in a destitute part of town, and he assists underprivileged boys. They built a large duplex home for their various pleasures and they entertain on their own sides. As far as Roltz is concerned, he's single, and I've always been troubled with his mental stability."

The chairman's eyes narrowed. "Oh? Why is that?"

"He nurtures relationships with emotionally weak people - not our own kind. Erik took top marks when he was trained in Iowa. He's brilliant, but he insists on keeping company with inferior races. Roltz visits certain leather clubs in Seattle where he enjoys being tied up, whipped, tortured and raped. He relishes pain, Mr. Chairman, and recently one of our informants heard him bragging in a steam room of his net worth and sexual prowess. I know we haven't had any problems up to now, but it's entirely possible he killed Schrems. Erik's always been jealous of Wolfgang and..."

The chairman did not allow her to finish. Strumming the table while she spoke, he said, "All right, enough, thank you. Are there any other suggestions?"

There were none.

"Transportation, you will handle Security's portfolio until Geneva suggests a replacement. Government Relations, you've pleased me with your performance today, therefore you will manage Resolution's duties. As for Roltz and Dreischner, I will make the necessary *arrangements* myself."

"Thank you, Mr. Chairman," Government Relations said, smugly rejecting the covert begrudging looks from the others. To her, men were created only for sperm production. Women were the creatures who could excite and satisfy her when she opened her smooth soft thighs. Members of the opposite sex were dirty hairy animals comparable to monkeys. They had smaller brains than women had, smelled of body odour, tobacco breath, and should be locked up and only let out to have their penises milked. If she were chairman, she would double the establishment's earnings after ridding it of all male participation and influence.

The speaker continued. "Now, let's move on to more important matters. The four hundred million dollar shipment of foreign exchange bank notes from American banks in the Far East is finally arriving. It's presently on the Liberian registered freighter LaHoncha that will enter the Port of Seattle on 30 December. Switzerland has informed me that the shipment's destination is the Denver Colorado mint, and it will be transported the night it arrives."

The chairman removed a disk from his briefcase, and then put it back after realizing Planning already had one.

"Planning, you have a copy of the master disk. I want your operational draft in two days time, and I don't care where we make the interception ... handle it! After it's been approved, if there are any suggested changes, I want to know about them."

Although Planning's palms were moist, and he could feel the sweat building on his forehead, he was gratified the chairman had changed the subject and bestowed such responsibility on him. Swallowing hard, he replied, "Thank you for your confidence, Mr. Chairman. I won't let you down."

The speaker remained seated and checked his watch before adjourning the meeting. "For your sake, Planning, I know you won't! Each of you will leave through separate exits. That will be all."

Two minutes after the room cleared, a side door opened and the administrator stood to shake hands with a tall, blond, blue-eyed, good-looking man about 30 years old.

The chairman's attitude altered considerably. "Sit down Hans, my friend. How was your trip?"

Sitting in a chair at the opposite end of the large table, the impeccably dressed wild-eyed man with every blond hair combed back and in place did not return the chairman's smile. "Adequate," he said, straightening out the sleeves of his Berlin made Bahnhauf Strasse shirt and dark blue suit jacket.

Born in the United States of Germanic parentage, Hans Krupp had moved to Germany after graduating from high school. Before entering Heidelberg University and earning a civil engineering degree, he had attended the University of Munster where he received a degree in political science. An egomaniacal intellectual, the man had attended many courses conducted by Wulfe WorldWide, and he was proud to uphold his family's tradition of being a white supremacist racist and a card-carrying Nazi. Krupp's exemplary records of recruiting, organizing, and motivating skinheads and members of neo-Nazi groups were well noted within the fraternity. The man now sitting with him had heaped praise on Krupp many times for his his ability to promote riots and other demonstrations. He could operate independently without detection, and possessed great skill at casting suspicion elsewhere.

Throughout his life, only one matter tore at Krupp's *heart*. The fact that he wasn't born in the Fatherland bothered him immensely. The United States was an upstart country loaded with liberal-minded uncouth blood mixtures. No golden-haired Germanic warriors should be born in such a country.

Glancing at his Tag-Heuer gold watch and portraying a semblance of boredom, Krupp said, "Let's get on with it, shall we? Why did you call me here?"

Krupp's abrupt mannerism upset the chairman, now thinking who the hell does this impertinent young pup think he is? No one talks to me that way. Extending an angry stare, the chairman stood and calmly offered, "Because I ordered you here, that's why! Keep your mouth shut, and I'll do the talking! Do you understand me, Herr Krupp?"

Although not one shining hair came out of place when Krupp sat to attention, the heels of a highly polished pair of black German Salamander shoes smashed together on the carpet. Chin up with his arms forced downward, he snapped, "Forgive me, Mr. Chairman. I apologize for my display of insolence. It will not happen again."

The chairman did not forgive him. "Do you have the disk?"

"Yes, but my orders are to give it to you only when Dr. Kraven is present. He has the third code."

While the meeting in New York continued, a similar conference was about to take place in Switzerland.

Once the old man sunk into the soft luxury of his fine-grained leather chair, he passed his wet walking cane to his manservant Sigmund; the same well-dressed, burly, stone-faced aide that now stood motionless behind his *master's* chair. Sigmund always remained close, as he had that morning in the back seat of a Mercedes manoeuvring the narrow cobblestone streets of snowy Geneva.

The large, elegant, dark-oak panelled and plush blood-red carpeted office emanated wealth beyond imagination, and the old man felt proud each time he viewed the artefacts and original master portraits he had *collected* during the war.

After lighting up a cigar, the seated patriarch pushed an intercom button and spoke in High German to an outside aide. "Bring me some brandy, and tell Rolf to come in."

Moments later, when a thin man in his early fifties entered after knocking, Sigmund instantly placed his right hand inside the front of his black blazer. The hand returned to its side after the bodyguard recognized the caller, but only for a few seconds – the same hand sheltered his heart again when a domestic male servant entered the room. The servant placed a small crystal tray, two glasses, and an elegant decanter of fine brandy in front of the old man. After pouring the liquor, the attendant departed.

"Rolf, sit down and join me," Gustaf Schtaff ordered, flapping his right hand to clear the cloud of cigar smoke drifting before him. "Have they been keeping you informed of our American problem?"

Thin, balding, and not too tall, Rolf nervously played with his glass before taking in the sweet biting aroma of the spirit. "Most definitely, sir. The coincidence of Krueger asking for Krupp's service assists us immensely. We'd planned on sending Krupp before the request arrived. He has the updates with him."

Schtaff's bushy eyebrows moved when his eyes narrowed and he pointed his cigar at the man sitting in front. "Odd people, these Americans. Once they believe they're God-given constitution is challenged, they become raging lions.

They didn't really win the war you know? Oh no … it was simply a matter of numbers and production. Had our Fuehrer, God bless him, listened to Reichsfuehrer Himmler, we would have won. Like many general officers, Reichsfuehrer Himmler suggested we build up our forces and armaments then start our conquests in 1945. But no, those traitors Göring and Bormann got in the way."

Rolf had heard this speech many times before and it never bored him. "We'll win this time, sir. Betrayers will be exterminated."

"That's what I like about you, Rolf. I'm getting old and mellow, but you retain the pulsating beliefs of our patron, Heinrich Himmler. To Reichsfuehrer Himmler," Schtaff toasted, standing, raising his glass, and downing the balance of his brandy.

Proudly standing up, Rolf joined the homage to his hero. "To Reichsfuehrer Himmler, a man of conviction and a great leader ahead of his time."

When both men took their seats, Schtaff poured two more brandies and reached on his desk to pick up a sterling silver eagle with its talons clenching a globe wrapped in a Nazi swastika.

"Our Fuehrer presented this to Himmler when the Reichsfuehrer married in 1927. Look at its flawlessness, Rolf. The quintessence of infinite enforcement. The sceptre of commitment, subjection, and domination. It epitomizes our meritorious determination. You, and I, and millions of our followers are the Reich, not the Jew-loving puppet impersonators who presently tear Germany and the world apart. We retain the divine guidance our Fuehrer decreed, and the world needs us now more than ever. It's time for world leadership, Rolf. One country, one world, one Fuehrer!"

Schtaff's stiff fingers turned white extending the eagle, and the wideness of Rolf's eyes matched the stern spellbound endorsement of his mentor. Rolf's attention remained even after Schtaff quelled his outburst and placed the object down.

"I'm going to leave this United States matter in your hands, Rolf. It's entirely possible Krueger has become weak. Perhaps he's forgotten we need America for our plans to succeed. Our crusade continues effortlessly elsewhere throughout the world and we cannot allow America to deviate. We didn't spend fifty years planting and nurturing certain world leaders, judges, big businesses, associations, law-enforcement agencies, union bosses, and millions of our kind to allow our cause to fail. This world must be cleansed of wretched human impurity. The Fuehrer dictated it, and we are his sentinels."

Wrapped up in the infectious enthusiasm exploding from the man in front of him, Rolf quickly placed his glass down and jumped to his feet. "The world will be in our hands, Herr Schtaff. The Fuehrer's wishes will be fulfilled."

Gustaf Schtaff's Machiavellian smile waned. "Excellent, you may go."

The strength of Schtaff's profound belief and choice of words still sent shivers of pride through Rolf's body. Clicking his heels while briskly and confidently bowing his head, he said, "Thank you, Herr Schtaff. I will ensure our American priorities are restored."

"Splendid, Rolf. Get it done!"

Joe Stacy didn't enjoy the lights, cameras, and questions. For over an hour he had listened to the governor, mayor, and chief of police drone on and on about their input in solving crime, making Washington State and the City of Seattle a better place to live and to raise families. Pensioners could now walk to the store feeling safe and secure, and young children could play their favourite games on the sidewalks without fear of being abducted or sexually molested.

By the time it ended, both Joe's arms had been raised a hundred times and his shoulders and back were sore from the patting and planting of politicians' arms and hands about his body.

Pete Durnell had stood by his partner's side throughout the ordeal, and many times when their eyes met, mutual body language with Joe intoned the drudgery of the occasion. Even half-an-hour before it ended, Pete had started to leave the pressroom's stage only to be dragged back by a smiling, ebullient mayor who refused to let this *sent from Heaven* press exposure slip by.

Finally, after the last of the speeches, when the cameras were being put away, both detectives slowly walked back to their office, now more aware than ever of the absurdity of the force's pompous and spurious leadership. One minute they were both going to be fired, and the next minute they were national heroes.

"The governor loves garlic," Joe quipped, opening his office door only to have more skin taken off his right hand by Mathieson, Green, and Barker. "Either that, or he's been sharing his tongue with Schmidt."

Presenting a hand to be pumped, Pete roared out laughing. "I think it's the latter," he said before viewing the wall clock. "Christ, look at the time, we've been down there three hours."

Barker turned off the small television on his desk. "And we've watched every minute of it, you 'conquerors of evil.' When the mayor called you that, Gwen suggested if this keeps up, the two of you will eventually replace those animated mannequins."

"Damn right, and do a much better job, too," Gwen cracked, heading to the coffee machine. "I think the titles Governor Stacy and Mayor Durnell have a nice ring to them." A second later she burst out laughing viewing the unbelieving and unsmiling facial casts of the mayor's, "champions of law and order."

Upon handing Joe a message slip, Barker said, "Anyway, getting back to business, a fellow by the name of Harvey called, but didn't leave his number. He said you'd know where to reach him. We've also heard from Woollam and Gebara. George said Sawasy's crew is finished with the house. They're all heading back tonight for tomorrow's debriefing."

"Any news on the two assholes that split up and headed to Vancouver and Spokane?" Joe asked.

Barker straightened his glasses and shuffled more papers trying to find information. "Lum's people have reported the guy in Vancouver spent all day in a skid-road hotel guzzling beer. Our Spokane queen buys Tennessee whisky, copies of Playgirl, and Stud magazines, before going out to watch children in a local mall."

"Queen?"

"Yeah, apparently if this shaven headed motorcycle asshole with double earrings wore a dress, and we viewed him from the rear, we'd all whistle."

Joe cocked his head. "So, he's got a motorcycle has he?"

"Yeah, a new Harley," Barker replied before changing the subject. "Listen Joe, if it's all right with you, can we close up shop for today?"

As far as Joe was concerned, Barker didn't have to ask. "Hey, I'm surprised the three of you are still here. Sure, take off and we'll get together early tomorrow. Before you go, call George and Sam and tell them to make sure they're in by eight tomorrow. I wanna finish the critique by ten. Also, don't forget to sign off at the front desk. They're bitching at us again for not signing out."

As Pete put on his overcoat, he asked, "I'm taking Linda out for dinner before we go Christmas shopping. Would you like to join us, Joe?"

The words "Christmas shopping" jolted Joe's memory. "Er, no thanks," he said, before thinking, Christ, I've got my brother, Mrs. White, Pete and Linda, and Gail and her kids, to shop for. "I'll call you tonight, Pete."

A few minutes later *Lieutenant* Stacy sat alone in his office reading the material in his 'IN' basket. Amongst trivial concerns, there was a note from Sawasy asking if he had made any sense of the turned-down corners on two pages of the Paris Match magazine. After placing the memo aside, Joe thought for a moment. He'd never noticed two turned-down corners.

Upon getting a coffee and turning off the machine, Stacy picked up an internal memo distributed to all departments by Captain Glover. A grey Chevy pickup had been found in an alley on the north side of town. Prints were being taken and the results would be ready tomorrow. Glover had written a note on the bottom of the page. 'Joe, this is probably our hold-up vehicle. Check it out.'

Joe Stacy felt tired driving home, so he turned off his car's heater and opened the driver's window a little more. At one point he thought he spotted Pete and Linda entering J.C. Penny's department store, but a second glance proved otherwise. The couple looked a lot like them, but so did hoards of other happy shoppers with their collars up, wrapped in layers of clothing to keep out the cold wind surging down the coast from Alaska and Canada. When the rain stopped, the same whirling wind parted the fast-moving clouds, revealing the silhouette of a ring around a seldom seen moon, and turning black-iced streets into the type of slides children create at school playgrounds.

Joe Stacy loved this time of year, particularly the lights, the cheerful atmosphere, and the shy giggling children waiting to sit on Santa and Mrs. Claus' knees. Half asleep and chuckling to himself he recalled the time his mother had taken him to sit on Santa's knee and the jolly old elf had burped in his face. To this day he remembered what beer did to a person's breath. To Santa's chagrin, the next kid in line had yelled, "Hey, mom, Santa's been boozin' like granddad."

Joe wanted to drive by Gail's house just to see if he could catch a glimpse of her, but had second thoughts. His mind was a mess, and his bones still ached from pumping human flesh all day.

Daily, more and more strings of coloured lights were added to the balconies and windows of Joe's apartment building, and as he parked his car, the detective noticed just his balcony was bare of the brilliant kaleidoscopic array.

Only after turning his key in the lock, did Stacy know something was amiss. The lock's tumblers didn't move, indicating the door was already open. Slowly, he removed his firearm from its holster, stood to the right side, turned the doorknob, and pushed open the door to the unlit apartment. Straining his ears, all Joe could hear was the hum of the fridge and the whining sound of his clothes dryer, indicating Mrs. White had visited again, recently.

Joe stretched his arm switching on the light before entering and locking the door behind him. No movement occurred as he checked each room with his pistol leading the way. Everything was the same, only neater. Mrs. White had indeed been in and cleaned up, but she had never left the door unlocked before. Replacing his gun back in its holster Joe thought his housekeeper must have been getting like him – forgetful in her old age.

Ten minutes went by before Stacy realized he'd received a *visit* from someone unknown. While making a coffee, the canister's top had fallen off when he'd picked it up. Three other canister tops were loose as well. Even the large bread canister's lid had not been properly closed.

Joe's suspicions where confirmed when he checked out the drawers in his bedroom. Though still neat, changes had been made to the layout of socks, underwear, and the shirts Mrs. White had ironed, folded, and put away. Additionally, two previously closed old briefcases at the bottom of a closet were open, as was the mirrored medicine cabinet door in his bathroom.

After sitting on the couch and lighting up a smoke, Joe glanced around the living room. It appeared normal except for one thing; the magazine rack had been moved. The leg imprints where the object always stood on the carpet were out by an inch. When vacuuming and dusting, Mrs. White always ensured she put the furniture back in exactly the same place.

Placing his coffee and cigarette down, Joe got up and moved the magazine rack's legs back before inspecting its contents. Only the Paris Match was missing. Before he could call Pete, the telephone rang.

"Joe, it's Pete. We received a *visitor* today, how about you?"

"Yeah. He must be a neat son-of-a-bitch; it was hard to tell he was here. Wasn't Linda home?"

"She was out getting her hair done. I'll say he was methodical. The only thing that triggered my suspicion was the firewood."

"What happened to the firewood?"

"He or they even checked out each piece of wood. I know Linda and I don't stack it that way. Also, the mattress had been turned over in the baby's crib." Pete chuckled. "Christ, we don't even have a baby yet, and he's popular already. I guess I shouldn't be making cracks … Linda's really worried. What the hell do you think they were looking for?"

Joe took a slug of his coffee. "Whatever it is, it's important to them. The Paris Match is missing."

"The magazine? There was nothing in the fucking thing."

Stacy heard Linda in the background complaining about Pete's swearing.

"Hold on a sec, Joe. Okay, Linda, okay, I'm sorry. Hi, Joe. She thinks if I swear like this now, I'll do the same when the baby's born, and he'll turn out to be a lawyer, or a politician."

Both detectives laughed, before Joe asked, "Do you remember the magazine's month?"

"Yeah, it was November. Why?"

"We must have missed something, Pete. Also, Sawasy left me a note saying two page corners had been bent back. Knowing Terry, he'll remember the numbers. Do you recall them?"

Durnell paused for a few seconds. "No, but like a stupid fool, I straightened some page corners on that book. Shit, it was an automatic reaction. I never thought for a moment..."

Finishing his coffee, Joe said, "No harm's been done. Anyway, get some sleep and I'll see you in the office at eight."

"Eight it is. See ya tomorrow."

After hanging up, Joe checked his pocket watch and decided against phoning Gail, but he did call Harvey Cohen.

"Hi, Harvey, it's Joe Stacy. What's up?"

The voice on the other end sounded happy. "Joe, good to hear from you. You're sure as hell getting press, aren't ya?"

"It comes with the job. We got the bastards, Harv."

"I know you did, and we're proud of you."

Joe felt like asking who the *we* were, but thought better of it.

"Listen, can we meet sometime tomorrow? Just the two of us?" Cohen asked.

"Sure, but I'm wrapped up until noon. Is it important?"

"Yes, I've got something for you. Do you have a favourite downtown restaurant?"

"Well, there's Choy's Has-beans, but I don't think you'd appreciate Chinese lox. How about twelve-thirty at Honeybea's on the old highway?"

Ten minutes after he hung up the phone, Joe put on a CD and filled his bathtub. Later, when the tub was draining, he set his alarm clock, lay on his back in the middle of his bed, and began snoring. When Woody Herman's big band finished, the lieutenant's stereo turned itself off.

Choy's coffee tasted better than the coffee Barker made, and Joe bought seven cups from the relaxed restaurateur cooking a bacon sandwich for a blurry-eyed motorcycle policeman who acknowledged Stacy's promotion.

"Mornin' Joe - nice work."

"Thanks Grant. We get 'em when we can."

Even Dave Barker appreciated the store-bought liquid. Dumping the balance of his previous cup down a drinking fountain in the hallway, he said, "It's not my coffee-making expertise that's bad; it's this Aunt Hilda's brand of shit the department always buys. I've got a feeling the chief owns a piece of the company."

"Either that or he's getting a piece from Aunt Hilda," Earl cracked, before pouring the dregs of his cup into a shrivelled and deformed potted palm that refused to die.

"Now, now, gentlemen, let's keep it civilized," Gwen suggested, giving Joe dirty looks when he lit up a smoke.

All seven members had arrived before the stroke of eight, and after a few minutes, Joe asked them to get their chairs and form a circle with him, and make notes.

"Let's start at the beginning. I've got a memo from Glover informing us the robbery vehicle has been found. Prints are being checked, and Earl, I want you to get on that right away. We'll nail those two bastards."

Earl Mathieson took hold of Glover's memo. "I'll get on it, Joe."

"Okay, we know that Doctor Abraham was stuck with a needle of some sort. According to the toxicology people in Atlanta, the substance that killed him is called Iodzathene. The autopsy made no mention of the drug, so let's find out who makes it. Gwen, locate the producers of Iodzathene in this country, or the importer. It's probably got a secondary usage, so it might go by another name."

Gwen made notes and was going to say something, but Joe cut her off, saying, "George, I asked you to check out Abraham's apartment and personal file. What did you come up with?"

Again, Joe noticed how tired George Woollam appeared. The situation in Bellingham had obviously taken its toll on the old timer. "How's your health these days, George?"

Woollam grinned wearily. "Why, do I look like I'm at death's door?"

"No, but you look like you need some rest, that's all."

"Thanks, Joe. I'm due for my annual medical next week. Er, Abraham was trained in Israel and allowed to work here temporarily pending a further review by the medical college. There's not much on him. He was a trained anaesthesiologist and he'd received a green card for two years employment. The poor bastard planned on returning to Israel, but never made it. Abraham lived in the doctors' quarters at Memorial and his room was bare except for a few personal effects ... nothing of interest. He had a phone in his room and in the four months he'd worked there, he only made one long distance call. Also, his room was checked for prints and there were only two sets, his and the cleaning lady's."

"Who'd he call?" Pete asked.

"The Israeli embassy in Washington. It lasted ten minutes."

Making notes, Pete nodded. "What about the prints in the linen closet?"

"Too numerous to check. This guy lived a quiet life. Some of the other doctors living in the same building said they hardly ever noticed him. He didn't use the lounge or the pool table, and other than seeing him in the wards or the operating rooms, they saw him always sitting alone in the cafeteria."

Joe stood and wrote certain data on the blackboard behind him before sitting again. "Okay, thanks George. Now, let's move on to Kroll. Dave, what have you got?"

Barker's big writing pad stood out from the other smaller notebooks. Straightening his large brown eyeglasses, he flipped a few pages. "Well, we already know some of the information on this guy, but let's cover it anyway. The guy wasn't married, and he lived at 9567 Cottonwood Street, the first holding house for children.

"He's German, a landed immigrant and his approval for immigration was delayed. We've also confirmed that Kroll didn't work for Systems or Protocol. This guy had no convictions, but his name appears on the police files of five countries, including Canada. Kroll used many false IDs but even those names don't show up in police files. Last year Portland police were going to charge him with molesting a young boy in a public washroom, but the kid retracted his original statement and couldn't or wouldn't identify Kroll in the line-up. As well, the child's parents wanted no part in charging him."

Gebara stood up to pour a Barker *special*. "The guy sounds like he had horseshoes up his ass. Did you ask the kid's parents why they clammed up?"

"They moved two days later. No forwarding address. Even the IRS doesn't know where they are, and schools throughout the country have no record of the boy."

Joe made more notes on the blackboard. "So, the family just disappeared?"

Barker tended to agree. "It seems so."

"Could they have been knocked off?"

"Anything is possible with these bastards, Joe, but I don't know. They were only renting their house, and they sold their car. They've vanished, gone, and flown the coop, with no plane, rail, bus or boat tickets."

"And the weapon?" Joe asked, standing again but this time to stretch.

"We have that information. The weapon that killed Kroll was a Steyr pistol and both rounds were .380 … probably the same firearm that was used on you and Pete. We haven't traced it yet."

Joe sat down again. "If Kroll didn't work, how did he live, and where did he get his money? What about his bank accounts?"

Barker's rarely used know it all smile expanded. "Good point, because this guy wasn't broke. Some of the papers Pete located in the house show Kroll was a member of NAMCA, the North American Man-Child Association based in LA. He also belonged to various skinhead groups, so he could have sold copies of those tapes, or provided porno pictures to underground magazines. But the amounts and dates or the size of the deposits don't make any sense. The guy made a cash deposit of twenty-five thousand nearly every month. You already know the gun used to kill Kroll was the same weapon that fired at you and Pete. It was also used to kill two Spokane armoured car guards on 22 June this year. Here's something else … on 24 June, Kroll deposited twenty-five thousand hard cold cash."

Rain started pounding the windows as Joe rubbed his chin while listening and staring intently at Barker. "Jesus, I wonder if it was...? That was around the date of that rare coin robbery, and the reward paid twenty five million dollars. Dave, check out all the heists pulled in the Pacific Northwest around the same dates Kroll made deposits. Also, check out who claimed the reward money in Switzerland. It's probably a numbered account, but then again, maybe we'll get lucky. Do you have anything else?"

Barker gave Joe a perplexed look. "Do I? They don't call me Elephant Barker for nothing, you know?"

The group of them laughed when Earl Mathieson shot back, "I always thought they called you that because of the size of your jockstrap."

Even Gwen blushed and snickered when Barker quipped, "Yeah, that too, but in high school they called me Dinosaur. I must be gettin' smaller with old age. Anyway, let's talk about Doctor *Prouse's* apartment. This guy Prouse was quite the character. He belonged to the same skinhead organizations Kroll belonged to, but it would appear his sexual preferences were leather-clad women. His apartment was loaded with leather and rubber straps, chains, handcuffs, dildos, and everything under the sun used for sadomasochism."

"My God," Gwen interjected, her face turning bitter. "And he was a doctor? What did he specialize in?"

Dave Barker glanced over his glasses. "Gynaecology."

"I'm sorry I asked," the female officer said, her expression of malevolence altering into an abashed grin. "Also, let me tell you about..."

Barker didn't wait for her to finish. "Prouse was born in Germany and moved to this country as a child. Until now, he lived in Iowa, but also kept a residence in the Spokane area. For some reason, he started working at Memorial around the same time Abraham was taken on staff. Now, here's the interesting part, on 24 June, a deposit of twenty-five thousand was made in his account. Great, eh? We can't prove he knew Kroll, but look at the similarity of the deposits?"

Joe stood up again and walked to the window. The rain had changed to heavy sleet. Waiting for the downpour to abate, the people below took cover under store awnings. He studied their faces. They were everyday people going about their affairs. As far as they were concerned, their country was being well looked after. Not for a minute did they think about sinister organizations vying for ways to control their way of life and liberty.

"He knew Kroll all right," Stacy said, returning his attention back to the room. "The whole damn lot of them knew each other. What about Klenz, the so-called FBI plant? You know, this has been bothering me? Why would the FBI place a known paedophile, and he is known, in the middle of a paedophile ring? To report the goings on? Gimmee a break! This guy didn't report anything - he just partook in the amusement and cleared the body cases through customs. The son of a bitch wasn't a double agent - he was a part of the *establishment*."

George yawned, asking, "How do you know Klenz was a paedophile?"

George Woollam's question even aroused Pete's curiosity. Joe had not mentioned anything about Klenz's background.

Stacy strolled over to Pete's desk and started going through some photos. After picking one out, he handed it to George. "There he is in living colour, standing next to Kroll. Pete, you didn't go over these pictures very well; the ones you collected at the Cottonwood address. It's not that clear, but that's the son-of-a-bitch who tried to run me down."

As the photo made the rounds ending up in Pete's hands, he winced. "How the hell did I miss that?"

"It doesn't matter, Pete. What really matters is how he got into the FBI? Also, why was he assigned to this mob? George, use what contacts you have and find out! I want to know who hired him and assigned him. Get as much background as you can."

After lighting up a cigarette, Joe continued. "Okay, let's move on to Roltz and Dreischner. Gwen, the transportation manager at Systems is a fellow by the name of Bruce Cooke. Check him out."

"Got it. By the way, Joe, I..."

Stacy didn't hear her. "Sam, what did you come up with?"

Gebara turned to the appropriate pages of his notebook. "Both Roltz and Dreischner are clean ... squeaky clean. As a matter of fact, last year Dreischner and his wife received State Governor Awards for their public service to children's causes."

Sam Gebara stopped for a second, his sceptical eyes scanning those around him. Nothing was said, but his statement and gesture were well perceived.

"The Dreischners seem to have a knack for raising donations to help kids' clubs. Maryann Dreischner coaches girls' swimming, and her husband's involved with boys' boxing clubs, football, lacrosse, and hockey clubs. I'm not talking personal donations - I'm talking large corporate contributions. The list of firms is substantial, and..."

"Can you get us a list of those companies?" Joe asked.

"I'm working on that, Joe. I'll have it tomorrow."

"Good, go on?"

"Dreischner was born in Bavaria, and moved to Iowa where he met his wife. They both worked in a large sanatorium owned by, get this, Munich Health Care Inc. They were transferred from the Iowa sanatorium to Munich's Spokane facility four years ago, and then..."

Barker inquisitively interjected. "Munich? Iowa and Spokane? What the hell is it with this German connection? All roads don't lead to Rome, they lead to Spokane, Iowa, and the Third Reich?"

Sam continued, "And then when she was appointed foreign exchange manager at Rhine Shipping, he became manager of Protocol."

"Nice work if you can get it, eh?" Pete said, his face alive with curiosity. They work in sanatoriums then become managers? I guess the prerequisite for being a bigwig is to work in a sanatorium. Where have we gone wrong? In our jobs, we get flat feet before we end up in sanatoriums, or on slabs."

They all laughed when Joe remarked, "Hey when you work for the Seattle Police Department don't think about cosy sanatoriums. All you'll get is a padded cell and a jug of Jack Daniel's. The booze is deducted from your pay, and if you live through the cure and you're straightened out, you're back on duty without a promotion."

Clearing his throat after wiping his eyes, Gebara said, "There's not much on Roltz, but are you all paying attention? Forty thousand dollars were placed in Roltz's bank account and fifty thousand in the Dreischners' account. Both deposits were made on 24 June. Maryann Dreischner doesn't have a bank account, but she's got a safety deposit box. I've asked Dave to get a court order to have it checked out."

"Then we've got the bastards," Joe yelled, jumping to his feet. "Pete, put a *special* tail on Roltz and the Dreischners. Also, get a list of all Systems and Protocol employees. "Christ, just what the hell are we on to?"

Gebara was not finished. "There's more, Joe. George and I sweated it out with each of those skinheads we locked up in Bellingham. They're so goddamned racist, every one of them should be wearing little black moustaches. Not one of them carried identification, and behind each of their confident macho images, they're raving paederasts."

"Can you get a vaccination for that one?" Gwen asked, jesting. "You've obviously been using the dictionary. By the way, Joe, I..."

"No, it seems to be catching," Sam replied. "Especially if one is a white supremacist type. Paederasts practice paederasty; at least that's what the book says. Anyway, such discipline. If we had roughed them up big time they still wouldn't have said anything."

Woollam cut in "You can say that again." "You know, questioning them, I got the feeling they're not from this area. Their prints are being checked out, but for some reason I think these bastards are being rotated through an elaborate underground maze. All their stories are the same. They don't know Kroll, and one by one, each said Schrems offered him a place to stay. As well, they know very little about each other."

"How did you arrive at that?" Joe asked, finally conceding that a cup of Barker's coffee was better than nothing.

"We had them locked up in separate cells. Questioning them individually, I found it totally impossible to intimidate them. If I said, 'Two of your buddies just told us you were the one responsible for kidnapping the kids,' I hit a brick wall. I don't think they don't know each other. No, let me change that. I know goddamned well they don't know one another. Also, they don't seem to give a shit what might happen to them."

"Mention the lawyers," Sam said, passing four business cards to Joe.

Woollam snickered, taking a duplicate set of cards out of his shirt pocket. "Oh yeah, Joe, take a good look at these cards. These attorneys are the best in the business. They're not legal-aid types. Two are from New York, and two are from Washington, DC. The skinheads didn't have to use the phone - these legal beagles just turned up unexpectedly. I'd lay odds bail will be set, and *paid*, today, regardless of what it is."

Stacy passed Gebara's set of cards to Dave Barker. "Dave, see if you can determine who employed these shysters. Also, find out if they've represented similar clients in the past. George, check with missing persons and try to establish how many kids have disappeared off the streets in the western states. Disgruntled parents who have split up take many children away. We don't want those, we only want sudden disappearances. Okay?"

George understood and made notes. "I'll get on it this afternoon."

Addressing Gebara, Joe asked, "What about the giant old estate house? Who owns it?"

"Apparently it's a heritage site owned by the City of Bellingham. It won't be developed for a few years, and the city only leased it out because Schrems paid five-grand a month rent."

"How long did he have it?"

"Two years

"Who owns the other house on Cottonwood? Gwen, you were checking on that. What did you find out?"

Green stood up and curtsied. "I was wondering when you were going to get around to me, Lieutenant Joseph P. Stacy. How come women are always asked last? I've been trying to tell you about this guy, but you've been too busy talking with these creeps."

"Oh Christ, here we go with the women's liberation speech again," Earl cracked. "Joe, make a note to ask her first from now on will ya?"

Tightening her right hand fist and holding it two inches away from Earl's face, Gwen grinned, saying, "You're going to get five in the eye, mister. I'm not a women's libber, but we should be treated equal."

Smiling, Joe stood up in front of the blackboard again. "Gwen, on this team you don't have to be asked. Just speak up and drown out these other bastards. Get on with it ... please?"

"This guy Schrems went through money like Mathieson does," she said, pointing to Earl. "Schrems leased the Cottonwood house for twenty-five hundred a month, and as I was going to say earlier, but was conveniently ignored, he banked a hundred thousand on 24 June. Like everyone else, his monthly bank deposits were quite substantial. The house is owned by a retired couple living in Florida. It was leased by a rental agency. I checked with the rental people and they told me everything was done by mail and they never met Schrems. As far as the trucks are concerned, Schrems had purchased them for cash. I think the trucks were used for transporting kids between houses. Gwen curtsied again. "There, I've finished. Thank you, gentlemen," she said, grinning like a Cheshire cat as she attempted to retake her seat."

Every one of them knew Earl and Gwen were engaged to be married, therefore the room became alive when Mathieson grabbed her, placing her on his knee.

"Well done, Detective Green," Mathieson said, tickling her. "And that's the way I like my morning newspaper read to me when I'm served breakfast in bed."

Red faced, Gwen freed herself and sat down as a knock came to the door, defusing the love bout. "All you'll get in bed is a pitcher of ice water, mister."

"Ooh, I love it when you talk that way."

Pete answered the door and signed for a package.

"The Paris Match magazines are here from the library, Joe. Two whole years of 'em."

"Thanks Pete, just put them on my desk. So, Samir, the Bellingham house was clean?"

Gebara took his chair back to his desk. "Totally, other than smut videos and pictures of naked kids and adults. Bellingham police will be releasing those to us shortly. Oh, and you asked for those extracts from Himmler's speech. Sawasy's team took pictures of them and you'll have them today with anything else they found."

Joe got up and checked his pocket watch. "Good, thanks Sam. My God, is that the time? Is there anything else?"

"Yep, one last thing," Earl said, picking his coffee cup off the floor. "There was a box of .380 rounds in a cupboard at Schrems shack. You know, I don't get it? This guy had enough money to live the life of luxury, yet he lived like a pig. Is it possible he entertained his weird friends at the shack, and lived at another place as well? He might have been leading a double life. I know all bills and invoices were sent to the Mountainview Drive address, but I think he also lived elsewhere. I'm going to check a little deeper into our Mr. Wolfgang Schrems."

Before leaving the office to meet Harvey Cohen, Stacy asked the others to liaise with Pete or Dave Barker if anything came up. He also took his partner aside and asked him to ensure when the *special* tail was placed on Roltz and Dreischner, it should be two more of Tong's people. Pete said he already understood to which Joe was alluding.

"I know you like a book, Joe, therefore I know what the word 'special' meant. I've got brains, you know? You must think I'm just another shapely leg?"

Stacy and Pete both laughed as Joe smacked his friend's back. "Christ, Pete, you're starting to sound like Erik Roltz."

Chapter 6

After opening the room's curtains, the Sheraton Hotel's young bellboy paused before sauntering towards the door. "Will there be anything else, sir? Is there something I can get you?"

Hans Krupp did not acknowledge or tip the dispirited lingering black youth leaving the room. Instead, he slid open the large glass door leading to the decorous room's balcony and stepped out filling his lungs with fresh ocean air.

Krupp knew why he loved Seattle. He had travelled to most cities in the United States, but always looked forward to returning to the Pacific Northwest. In Seattle, he could satisfy his appetite with the progeny of men and women he yearned for; well-built Nordic male and females with blue eyes. He didn't care if they were tainted with the tough temperament of Russian blood. If anything, it added to his pleasure.

At the time of the gold rush, Fins, Swedes, Norwegians, and Danes had unwaveringly left their *mark* to intermix with rugged Russian sailors navigating down the Inside Passage from Alaska. The result, Hans thought, was unparalleled beauty, hanging like rich cherries ready to be picked. Even the women were enticing if he could not find an *appropriate* same sex partner.

Re-entering his room and rubbing his crotch, Krupp was overwhelmed by the thought of lying next to a willing *blue-butterfly*, a sleek-skinned Adonis so aptly named by Venus, the Goddess of love. He knew, however, his obsession for such indulgence would have to wait until he had accomplished his tasks.

Gently removing his clothes and silk underwear, Hans smiled admiringly posing and twisting his tall muscular frame in front of the large mirror. His toned stomach, rock-hard buttocks, and impressive arm and leg muscles stirred him immensely. What body hair he had was short and blond, with the feel of soft goose down. To him, his rugged yet refined Nordic beauty was exquisite - the perfect example of master race stock. Soon, his kind, the conquerors of the planet would rid humankind of the impurities of dark-skinned *primates* and their ilk recklessly breeding and sharing their inferior lineage with half-witted white-skinned weaklings. Yes, when his species reigned, the inevitability of the Fuehrer's wishes would be *settled* conclusively.

After unpacking and showering, Krupp put on a workman's uniform and slipped a Washington Light and Power cap on his head. Sneering at his workman's image of having to wear a blue shirt and black tie, Krupp zipped up his dirty-grey Eisenhower-style journeyman's jacket, removed a small bag from on top of his bed, and left the room. His twelve-story walk down the exit stairs to the alley would allow him to vanish unseen into the throng of engrossed lunch hour office workers.

Once out of the building, Krupp entered a public phone booth and dialled a number the police knew quite well.

"Is Mr. Roltz there?" he asked a chirping switchboard operator.

"Can I tell him who's calling?"

After Krupp said, "Yes, it's Mr Dreischner," it didn't take long for Erik Roltz to take the call.

"Willie, how are you? How nice of you to phone."

"Erik, it's not Willie calling. I just thought I'd see if you were still taking calls from him."

"Who is this?" Roltz asked, sounding irritated that someone would use Dreischner's name.

"It's me, Hans Krupp."

"Hans, you dear sweet boy. Where are you?"

"Here in Seattle. The Chairman sent me up to sort out this mess between you and Wilhelm."

Roltz hesitated for a moment. "What did you say?"

"I'm here to act as a go between you and Dreischner. There's no room for bickering in the family, you know that?"

As planned, Krupp had caught Roltz totally off guard. Roltz hesitated and his voice became cautious. "Hans, I've got no problem with Wilhelm. Who, er ... who told the Chairman there's a problem?"

"Dreischner did. He wants you out of the way. Come now, Erik, it's Hans here; you can level with me. Dreischner thinks you're getting too big headed, and want total control of the coast."

There was another short pause before Erik whistled, saying, "That bastard! And to think I just spoke with him the other day. I'm going to call that mother fucker and give him..."

"No, don't do that, Erik. The Chairman has far too much respect for you to allow Dreischner to start being in charge. I'm here to tell you the whole story, where can we meet?"

"You can come here and..."

"No, you know I don't like being seen around Seattle? How about at the end of Patterson's Pier in half-an-hour? I'll show you Wilhelm's letters, and if you want to sort it out with him after that, it's up to you. Right now, Dreischner wants you out of the way, Erik. The Chairman thinks Dreischner should be the one going on a *trip*."

Erik hesitated again. "Dreischner, that greasy fucker. Okay, I'll see you at the end of Patterson's Pier. How long are you in town for?"

"Not long."

An hour-and-a-half later, Krupp parked his rented Buick on a side street next to a small park and casually walked four blocks to a row of brightly painted duplexes on a crescent-shaped road overlooking a small bay. After ringing both bells of the third unoccupied duplex, he injected a small spiked tool into the left door's lock and entered.

Moments later after putting on surgical gloves, the *visitor* moved a painting aside and placed his ear to a wall-safe. After turning the combination dial a few times, the device opened revealing a bundle of cash, two computer disks, and a small black notebook. Krupp left the currency but replaced the disks and book with similar looking items. He also took a file folder out from under his jacket, placing it inside along with a small .22 handgun and silencer. The gun smelled like it had been fired recently, and had two rounds missing from the magazine. Next to the pistol, he placed two empty casings from those *missing* rounds.

Hans checked his watch before closing the safe and placing the painting back. His actions had taken exactly four minutes, but he wasn't finished. Moving quickly to the laundry room, he bent down and opened up a tiny compartment on the nearby whining gas furnace and put out the pilot light. Before closing the compartment's portal, he adjusted the gas flow valve, the thermal coupling and briskly replaced the control unit.

Krupp felt quite pleased with himself and it showed as he re-entered the front room and turned down the thermostat.

Upon leaving the house, the *repairman* noticed a woman twenty yards away pushing a baby buggy. Not wishing to be seen, he kept his head facing the house's direction and waived as if speaking to the dwelling's occupant. "You're welcome. If you have any further problems, just give Washington Light and Power a call. All the best to you, too."

On the way back to his hotel, Krupp drove up an abandoned dirt road, stopped, and opened his trunk. When he left, Erik Roltz's body rested face down in the mud at the bottom of a small hill.

"Joe Baby, There's someone here waiting for you," Bea Honeywell said, sucking in her stomach to amplify a set of breasts that didn't need enlarging. "I thought you suggested we'd be out dancing some night? Now that you're famous and you've been promoted, we can go to some classy dance hall, right?"

Stacy wrapped his right arm around Bea's waist as she guided him toward Harvey's Cohen's table.

"I think I'm in love, Bea. You know what happens when I fall head over heels ... my memory goes all to hell."

"Joe, you fall in love every week. How about tossing a little bit of it my way once in awhile? My banker's out of town."

Stacy saw Harvey sitting alone and reading a newspaper.

"How long has *he* been here?" he asked, motioning towards Cohen's table.

"Just ten minutes. Did you hear me, Joe? I said, my banker's out of town."

"Mine isn't," he said, winking at her while sitting across from Cohen.

With a knowing smile, Bea placed two menus down before sauntering away wiggling her behind and commenting, "She's a lucky broad, whoever she is. Keep me in mind when this one's over with. All right?"

"You got it, Bea, baby," Joe said, before extending his right hand. "Hi Harv, Sorry I'm a few minutes late."

Cohen's face indicated he wasn't concerned as he placed his newspaper aside and accepting Joe's offered hand. "I'm the one that's usually late. Hey, I hear congratulations are in order, Lieutenant?"

"It's a rags to riches tale, Harvey. One minute I'm fired, the next minute I'm their golden haired boy. All bullshit, same story, different chapter. How's it with you?"

After a waiter came by and both men ordered beer and lunch, Harvey Cohen turned serious. "I'm busy, but not as busy as you. You're busting this thing wide open, aren't you?"

"Thing? I wish I knew what kind of a thing it is?" Joe retorted accepting one of Harvey's cigarettes. "The *organization*, if that's what it is, appears to operate like a slithering snake. Individuals within it keep getting murdered. Also, I don't know if it's local, national, or international? I do know one thing though, there appears to be a hell of a lot of money in the kid trade."

Harvey's eyes brightened. He liked the man sitting with him. For the third time in his life, he knew he could trust this honest, well-trained Seattle cop with a greenhorn understanding of the darker side of human character. Sure, he knew Joe sometimes rolled in the dirt of the city, but was incapable at this point to know that dirt comes in layers, heartless, bloodthirsty human layers of agony.

"Their money isn't limited to the kid trade, Joe. It's much bigger than that."

"Yeah, I figured as much."

"You've unearthed more in a few days than we have in over fifty years. But don't think for a minute you're going to continue. If they can't stop you one way, they'll go another route."

Keeping his voice down, Stacy asked, "Harvey, who the hell are, *they*?"

"Joe, I'm still not in the position to reveal what we believe is going on, but I appeal to you here and now, don't let up."

Stacy curiously studied the man sitting opposite him. Lines displaying the inroads of time and pain united innocently with a cast of determination and faith. What was this man trying to tell him? What did he want? How could he help him when the man wasn't asking for help?

"Harvey, sooner or later you're going to have to open up. You've advised me of certain things, and I want to reciprocate as much as I can, but for God's sake, man, who are *they*?"

Cohen lit up another smoke, gulped down his remaining beer, and allowed his eyes to burn through Joe's. It shouldn't have come to this and he knew it. He had his orders, but damn it, he felt he could trust this man. Keeping his voice lower than a whisper, Cohen asked, "Joe, how much gold do you think there is in Fort Knox?"

Surprised by the question, Stacy inquisitively winced. "Er, I know we're off the gold standard. I have no idea. Why?"

"Suppose America was still on the gold standard, would you know?"

"No. Perhaps hundreds of billions of dollars worth?"

Each indicated to the waiter delivering their food that they wanted two more beers. When the waiter left, Harvey said, "Close enough. You know, it astounds me that people still don't fathom what the Nazi's did during the war. Joe, those goose-stepping gangsters actually conquered Europe. As each country fell, they walked off with its gold, priceless paintings, valued currency, rare coins, and every conceivable precious treasure. Not just government riches, private collections as well. All possessions valuable or otherwise were taken from people transported to the death camps, or rounded up and shot. Whether they were Jews or non-Jews, innocent people paid the ultimate price after being sucked dry. Now you're probably asking yourself what's this got to do with *they*."

Joe nodded. "Go on, I think I now know what you're getting at."

"I don't mean to be long winded, but if I may, let me mention a few scenarios. When Rudolf Hess flew to Britain, he was jailed and imprisoned for life. Shit, they wouldn't even let him be interviewed, or give him notepaper. It was reported he wanted to see the Marquéss of Clydesdale, the future 14th Duke of Hamilton about Britain joining Germany to take on the Soviet Union. Well, Hess may have had such plans, but there is no doubt he told Churchill what Hitler was planning - that the madman had told Hermann Göring to make plans for the so-called *final solution*. I believe some senior Nazis thought Hitler was going too far, and even though Hess was the Nazi Party's deputy leader, he was one of them. He thought a warning from Britain would stop the holocaust, but no such luck. When a guy named Rudy Vrba escaped from Auschwitz, he also passed along the grisly information to Churchill. But what did the politicians do, Joe? Absolutely nothing other than issue small condemning news releases suggesting a few deaths may be taking place. Joe, the Allies knew what was going on from the first death. Not the ordinary person on the street, just the politicians controlled by big business and religious interests. Now you're asking yourself why. It was the money, Joe; more money than you can imagine. At today's value, we're not talking millions we're talking billions upon billions of dollars. Blood-soaked money doesn't bother politicians … it is power. It can literally buy anything, absolutely anything at all."

Stacy studied Harvey's eyes as the man spoke. If truths were cast like spears, then Joe knew he had been pierced a thousand times. Harvey Cohen's heart was screaming frustration and hatred through lips sewn shut by the actions of covetous unfeeling thugs. A despicable batch of elected *humanity* promising hope for the masses, but wearing the invisible cloak of personal ravenousness greed had returned.

"Go on, Harv."

"During the war, England took in a few Jews as a token gesture, but most other countries, particularly the United States and Canada, sent those who managed to get out, back to be murdered. You see the immigrants would tell stories about the Third Reich, and the truth would be known. Understand me?"

Now, Stacy's voice was nearly inaudible. Trying to clear the lump in his throat, he murmured, "Yes, I … I do."

"Do you realize even today, particular war records have been sealed for another hundred to one-hundred-and-fifty years before they become public information? It happened just recently in London and Washington. Certain politicians and government bureaucrats do not want the public to learn what is contained in purported *mysterious* documents. Did you hear me, Joe? I said this is happening today?"

Cohen coughed and cleared his throat again by sipping his beer. "Locked up so fucking tight, a germ couldn't contaminate them. Why? Because the real truth would be known. I don't know the truth, Joe, but I've dedicated my whole life trying to uncover it. Recently, you've heard that the State of Israel and Jewish groups throughout the world are putting the pressure on Swiss banks to, let's say, *check* their records. They want stolen property and money returned to the relatives of holocaust victims and those who survived the genocide. The banks are now paying attention because finally, some international pressure is evident. Now the fun begins, but only a pittance will be returned. The money has been invested, and it's not about to be given up under any circumstances. I'm not referring to the banks, I'm referring to Nazis controlling and utilizing the money. Do you hear me again, Joe? The investment I'm talking about is worth fucking billions."

"Hitler's crew?" Joe asked, naively.

Just the term 'Hitler's crew' forced hate into Harvey's eyes. Almost whispering, he said, "And their successors."

"Successors?"

"Yeah, successors. Does that surprise you? Let me just say this ... my people do not believe Adolf Hitler committed suicide."

While contemplating Harvey's words, Joe had been looking down at the table. Now he suddenly glanced up, puzzled. "Oh, come on, Harvey? I've heard..."

Mindful, Harvey smugly grinned, and cut him off. "I know what you're going to say. You've heard what the world has heard; that the maniac's death has been explained and rationalized a million times. But has it? Hitler told the German people no bombs would fall on Berlin, yet he had the bunker built long before the war began. Joe, I believe Hitler left Germany six months before the Allies and Russians entered Germany. The maniac had at least twelve doubles that looked exactly like him. It's absurd to believe his body was taken out and burned. Convenient as hell, eh? History's most disgusting, deranged, conniving son-of-a-bitch allows his henchmen to escape to all corners of the world while he conveniently commits suicide behind closed doors? Not only that, within minutes, others take it upon themselves to cremate his body? Not on your life. I'm too old of a cat to be fucked by a kitten, Joe. That monster stuck around for a hell of a long time. So did Himmler. He had seven doubles as well."

Joe couldn't believe what he was hearing. "Seven?"

"Now you're getting it! That lily-livered pederast chicken farmer always screamed in pain whenever he cut himself shaving. He was so fucking organized it would be totally impossible for him to be caught. Yet, you and I are taught that he escaped dressed as a common soldier and was caught by British troops whereupon he committed suicide by taking poison. Listen, a fucking kindergarten class wouldn't believe that shit. My God, I may not be a brilliant man, but give me credit for having some common sense. Himmler couldn't commit suicide, he was simply too intent on self-preservation. Himmler's dentist said the fiend had near-perfect teeth without caps or discolouration, yet Himmler's corpse had only twenty seven teeth - five less than normal, and a gold cap."

Harvey paused for a moment to light another smoke and take a sip of his beer. "You've heard of Adolph Eichmann, haven't you?"

"One of Himmler's butchers. Who hasn't?"

"Well, after Israel hanged Eichmann, veiled notations in the bastard's diary indicated Himmler didn't die. Oh, yeah, and there's something else you should know. Himmler's so-called body didn't have an old duelling scar on its left cheek, and it didn't have the scar the fiend supposedly had on his right arm."

"Harvey, you had me convinced with your first sentence. You don't have to put yourself through this."

Harvey didn't respond. "You asked me about '*they*', Joe. Anyway, as you know, even the world's most ruthless killers can do anything they want if they've got billions of dollars ... absolutely anything. For example, Idi Amin should have been hanged and quartered, yet he lived out his days in Saudi Arabia."

Staring blankly but listening intently, Joe nodded slightly, then glancing down at the table again, he said, "Yeah, I know. Many world leaders said they wanted him dead."

"You bet, but they didn't get at him, did they? He took the same route Hitler did, but someday the truth will be known about Hitler and his killers. You can count on it once the innards of elusive bureaucracy are cut open."

"Well, if they did escape, they're in hell now," Joe said, still feeling the emotion from Harvey's dissertation.

The man in front of Stacy let out a loud, "Ha," before lowering his voice again. "They escaped, and their ideology continues, organized by succeeding generations of Nazis, and condoned by certain politicians, international bankers, big business, and specific members of the various intelligence communities. I could never explain to you the enormous power these Nazis wield within and outside government. They literally manipulate the world as we know it. Not only the right and centre ... but also they hold the reins on the left as well. And when I talk about banks, I'm not just talking about Swiss banks, I'm talking about nearly every major bank in the world. It doesn't matter where it comes from, money is money, and they all want to get their share. These banks brandish influence because they've got Nazi funds on deposit, and probably Nazi directors, as do multitudes of large companies. Other board members simply don't know who's sitting with them. That's another thing. Have you noticed how difficult it is to extradite or charge known war criminals?"

Joe nodded knowingly. "You bet. It doesn't happen often."

"Interesting isn't it, Joe? Don't get me wrong, I'm not paranoid. I'm not listening for footsteps that aren't there, I'm hearing goose-steps that are there. We figure these bastards have infiltrated everything from the judiciary, to police departments. Yes, even little old ladies rest homes haven't been ruled out. Another thing, if the Allies supposedly returned all the paintings and artefacts, why are hundreds always being auctioned off from private collections? Also, why are Britain and the United States still hoarding stolen gold that should have been returned years ago?"

Harvey stood up to visit the men's room, but before leaving, he placed his left hand on Joe's left shoulder. "My case rests. And so, Joe Stacy, we harmless, modest, simple-minded people allow the bastards to get away with it again, like they did in Bosnia and that area. And now that you know who *they* are, does it make you feel any better?"

"Feel any better? It scares the living shit out of me," Joe said.

Before leaving, Harvey Cohen chuckled quietly. "I thought it would."

While Harvey was away, Joe glanced around the tables and watched business deals being made, and crossword puzzles completed. Customers played pool for two to five dollars a game. The sports channels blared to some and six couples played darts, while others just sat alone with their beers and newspapers. Even a suave and grinning old veteran stroking back both sides of his bushy tobacco-strained moustache was not concerned with anything except the moment while trying to strike up a conversation with an elderly gal at the next table. Yes, Honeybea's was alive with people doing their own thing. Joe studied the looks on their faces and came to one conclusion; they couldn't care less about Hitler and Himmler. If he went and asked them, he thought the average response would most likely be, "Yeah, sure, probably a new-age group playing here next week?" Or some young person might say, "Who? Hitler and Himmler? Oh yes, I know them. They're that fabulous new team of dancers, aren't they? Cool, man - yeah, cool. My chick really digs their moves."

Joe gently shook his head and a small resigned smile came to his lips. Children are told to look out for the bogeyman by fearless adults too busy getting on with their lives to realize that real murderous phantoms live amongst them. Time had made the world's people complacent again and they had lowered their guard.

Harvey looked a little more relaxed when he returned.

"I get a little worked up when I think of the bastards, Joe. Forgive my tiny exhortation. Some day the world will know the names of the Wall Street companies that financed Adolf Hitler. Not just the companies, but also the individuals. You see, many of those same companies financed the Bolshevik Revolution. Greed fucked up twice. The Bolshevik's weren't supposed to win, and Hitler was to be reigned in."

"Controlled?" asked Stacy.

"You bet. Bastard capitalist industrialists of *all* religions thought that once Hitler got Germany on its feet, he'd go away quietly so democracy could prevail again. If that didn't work, they thought he could be controlled. Actually, the bigwigs within the Nazi Party thought the same. They thought they could manipulate Hitler. I could mention American and British companies and people wrapped in Old Glory and the Union Jack who donated heavily to support Hitler, and thus his friend, *Himmler.*"

An inquiring expression came over Joe, and Harvey immediately recognized it. "You're asking yourself if Jews were involved, aren't you?"

Stacy swallowed heavily when their eyes locked. Almost whispering, he asked, "Were there any?"

"Certainly. Yeah, all greedy pricks were there. At the start when specific concentration camps were built, Himmler received a per diem price for the inmates to produce products. That money came from within, and outside of Germany, Joe."

Harvey paused for a moment, shook his head, and glanced down at his beer. Looking up slowly, he said, "The organized slaughter of animals is so easy because even animals can't conceive other animals being so merciless. The poor things shake and get wild-eyed when prodded or they follow Judas goats up slaughterhouse ramps. Even though they smell death, if they actually knew what was going to happen, the dumbest beasts would revolt. Jewish capitalists like all other capitalists never dreamt for a moment human beings could be so mentally deranged. They simply didn't know Hitler and his gangsters were the epitome of murder and cruelty and all things deranged. Even if the money-men had read his bullshit book Mein Kampf, no human being could believe his psychosis was as real as the sun coming up in the morning. Hitler actually meant what he said, and the majority of Germans went along with him. Can you believe that?"

"Jesus Christ," Joe muttered, staring blankly and sadly at the man in front of him. "I didn't know any of this."

"Few give it any thought, my friend. For some reason Hitler believed Jews cost Germany the First World War. His Nazi Party mentor, Dietrich Eckart probably put that into his head. Even before the war, Hitler issued an ultimatum. If Jews forced Germany into another war, all of Europe's Jews would be exterminated. He blamed everything on the Jews - particularly his own bad judgments and misgivings. That was his nature - always blame someone else."

Lines of deep thought made their way across Joe's forehead. Largely, the knowledge was almost too distressing to comprehend. At that time, Leaders of the Free World had really been asleep at the switch, but when they woke up, they wanted their share at any cost like everyone else.

"Now here's the conundrum of the century, Joe. I have just mentioned that the Allies have again locked up information for another hundred to one-hundred-and-fifty years. Why isn't someone demanding, yes downright demanding it be released? Let's face it - the war has been over for well over half a century; what information could be so dreadfully damaging to countries, industries, churches, or individual families that it has to be smothered for another century?"

Staring at Cohen, Joe gave the question sober thought before his eyes widened. "That the holocaust and Hitler's treatment of Jews could have been stopped. Or, that it wouldn't have begun."

"Exactly, Lieutenant Stacy. Also, who the hell is making these decisions to hide this information? Probably civil servants of some sort acting under orders. What I want to know is how they get away with it? Wouldn't you think at least one politician would step forward and condemn the choking of evidence? No, they've been warned; it won't happen. Even now, all these years later, the information in those files is so dangerous to the reputations of certain past *and present* world politicians. As well, it remains dangerous to many countries, current world banks, current industrial firms, and the Roman Catholic Church, that it can't be released. Tiny Cuba can't escape its mobster past either. After the war, ships from many countries docked at that island to take on portions of divvied up treasure stolen from Europe. Oh, God, I get sick just thinking about it. The systemized killing of human beings didn't mean a thing if the money was at hand."

Stacy couldn't speak. He saw the moisture in Harvey's eyes. Why hadn't he heard all this before? But even if he had, what could he do or say? What could anyone say?

Harvey's voice cracked when he said, "I've told you all I know, and I believe it's only about ten percent of the true facts. We won't know the exact truth until it's released - until someone stirs up the masses to demand its release. It probably won't happen in our lifetime. Even Senator Joe Lieberman hasn't spoken up and asked why that information has been put on hold."

Harvey stopped speaking for a moment, shrugged, and put more thoughts together while slowly glancing around the room.

"A particular power group decides how all money is employed on this planet, Joe. Its few members decide how money should be utilized when it's moved from continent to continent. That same group backed Hitler, and he repaid them through Swiss banks. Those *people* that really shouldn't be called people still pull the strings, and in my opinion, they're mostly ultra right wing criminals disguised as successful businessmen and politicians. If there are Jews amongst them, let each one die unmercifully. Better yet, let all the bastards meet the same end they decree on others."

The waiter came by again and each ordered another beer.

"Here's something you probably need," Harvey said, throwing off his grief and offering the lieutenant a small black book and two computer disks. "Your team did a rotten job of going over Schrems' dump. That disk marked Genesis 'A' was found under a piece of worn floor covering in the bathroom. Genesis 'B' was taken off him after he tried to kill you coming out of the Cat's Meow, as was the book. We've made copies and so far, we've drawn a blank. The rows and rows of numbers don't mean a goddamned thing. They're using a code of some sort, but without the key, we're stymied. Maybe your crime lab can do something with it."

Joe examined the items before placing them in his inside left jacket pocket. "Thanks Harv. I'll let you know if we come up with anything. Harvey, you don't have to worry about me giving up on this. After what you have told me, it won't happen."

"You may not have a choice if you're resting in a pine box six feet under. The guy that checked out your apartment the other day actually duped my people. The bastard dressed himself up as a postman and slipped by our man at Pete's place, too. We only caught on to it after the real postman came along."

Once again, Harvey had tweaked Joe's attention. "Uh, why are your people still watching over us?"

Cohen accepted one of Joe's cigarettes. "Like I said, I need ya, that's why. I don't think our *friends* are going to touch you right now … you're too hot. But, if you don't get out of their way soon, they'll come after you with force equal to a lion going after a mouse. I'll tell ya, they don't fuck around. They'd think nothing of blowing an airliner loaded with people out of the sky just to get one person. They couldn't care less if it's one or millions. They refer to us as the *Israeli Set*, and we've lost fourteen agents.

How many of them have your guys taken out?" Joe asked.

Cohen finally grinned, and after finishing his beer, said, "A few. The score's not in their favour, that's for certain. With these bastards, that can never happen. If it does, they'll get the upper hand."

"Well, this mouse has got sharp teeth," Joe cracked, his eyes lighting up. "And they bite."

Harvey's grin turned into a dead-serious frown. "It's impossible to bite your way out of a mousetrap, Joe."

Harvey Cohen's words continued to drum through Joe's mind when he drove back to his office.

Stacy had seen films of the death camps many times, and afterwards he had always asked himself the same question. How was it possible for human beings to treat other human beings like that? The answer was unmistakably clear - the Nazis were not human, nor were they good enough to be referred to as animals. Even animals possess an understanding of dignified behaviour and respect, but not Hitler's mob of insane butchers. Somewhere at the beginning of time, a wayward gene had taken a route not listed on God's *map*. The result of its actions would create monsters so evil, right-minded human beings would suffer throughout eternity. It will never end, Joe thought. Recently, as Harvey said, these miscreants had reared their ugly heads in Bosnia, and once again, the world turned its eyes and ears the other way while innocent men, women, and children were slaughtered. And who helped supply aid to the Muslims being slaughtered by the Christians? Joe knew full well - the Israelis.

Lighting up a cigarette, the lieutenant asked out loud, "Why? Why? Why?" Then Harvey's words came back to him. *"But what did the politicians do, Joe? Absolutely nothing other than issue small condemning news releases suggesting a few deaths may be taking place. Joe, the Allies knew what was going on from the first death. Not the ordinary person on the street, just the politicians controlled by big business and religious interests. Now you're asking yourself why. It was the money, Joe; more money than you can imagine. At today's value, we're not talking millions we're talking billions upon billions of dollars. Blood-soaked money doesn't bother politicians … it is power. It can literally buy anything, absolutely anything at all."*

Only Pete remained in the office when Joe walked in. "Hi Joe, how did your meeting go?" he asked, instantly recognizing his partner's absorbed look.

Stacy's mind had been so immersed in Harvey's analysis of the existence of the Nazi butchers, he had not remembered what streets he had taken driving back, where he'd parked his car, or the trip up in the elevator.

"Uh, hi Pete. It went well. We had a good talk. Where is everyone?"

"Out following your orders. I got hold of Richard Lum, William Tong's boss. Jesus, he's a hell-of-a nice fella. It's absolutely great not having to hear why things can't be done. The minute I asked him if he could make arrangements to have Roltz and Dreischner tailed and staked out, he said, 'No problem, but it won't be initiated until tomorrow morning.' Apparently it takes him twenty-four hours to organize the details."

Durnell realized Joe's mind was elsewhere. "Hey, are you listening to me?" he asked, slowly waiving his right hand up and down in front of his partner's eyes.

Stacy shook his head and smiled. "Sorry, pal. All the way back from Bea Honeywell's, I've been thinking of what Harvey told me. Sit down and I'll fill you in. It's mind boggling."

For the next half-hour, Joe briefed his partner on the main points Harvey Cohen had covered. Throughout, Durnell's eyes grew wider then narrower as Joe's had during his meeting with Harvey. After the lieutenant finished, both detectives sat back staring at each other. Finally it was Pete who asked the first question. "Jesus, then we're up against a massive international machine?"

"No doubt about it," Joe stated, closing his eyes and rubbing his forehead.

"Then this international machine is going to try to cut off our nuts? That's the plural, Joe, more than one pair."

Stacy thought if Pete and his smile were trying to cheer him up and bring him back to their world, he was doing a good job. "They probably are, and I understand what *plural* means. When I was a kid, I went out with a chick that had it twice. Took two weeks for her to recover."

Pete took the bait. "What? What the hell are you talking about?"

"Pleurisy," Joe replied, winking and leaving the office. "Lock up before you leave, Pete. See you at eight, tomorrow. G'night, Partner?"

"Pleurisy? Smart ass," Pete yelled. "Goodnight, Joe."

Stacy didn't go home. For some reason his car steered itself in the direction of Gail's apartment. Parking outside and trying to convince himself to knock on her door, a tap of another kind took place on the passenger's side window.

"Hi, Uncle Joe," a grinning rosy-cheeked Gordie said, carrying a bag of groceries and peering in. "Whatcha doin'?"

A sincere smile stretched Joe's lips and he feigned surprise. Just seeing Gordie wrapped in a parka with a fur hood cheered him up. Leaning over and rolling the window down, he asked, "Where's your mom?"

"Right next to you," the laughing boy replied, watching Joe quickly turn his head to find Gail peeking in the driver's window. Suzie stood next to her giggling. All three were loaded down with grocery bags that were going to drop any moment.

"Joe Stacy, you're a Godsend," Gail said, gasping while lifting up her right knee to keep a bag from slipping through two others she had in her arms. "If you give us a hand, I'll make supper. How does that sound? Afterwards, the kids are going Christmas shopping. Wanna come with us?"

Gail did not have to ask twice. Seconds later, with four bags under his arms, the lieutenant was in a much improved state of mind as he headed up the stairs.

"I'm sorry I didn't phone," he said placing the groceries on the kitchen table and helping the children unload theirs. "I meant to, but..."

Gail started putting the food away before taking off her jacket. Stopping for a moment, her eyes met his. Tenderly she said, "Joe, I think I know what you're going through. I'm a little the same way. We're both guilty of getting wrapped up in our work to the point of forgetfulness. I'm really delighted you came over, so are the kids. You must be tired. Go take off your coats and sit in front of the fire. I'll put some coffee on in a few minutes. Suzie and Gordie, how about setting the table for four, please?"

"Are you sure there's nothing else I can help with?" he asked.

"No thanks. I've got the impression you need to clear your head."

Stacy took Gail's advice and shortly both children joined him.

"Did I hear you call me Uncle Joe?" he asked Gordie.

Suzie replied instead of her brother. "Yeah, mom thinks it's more polite. You don't mind, do ya?"

"It isn't bad manners, is it?" Gordie asked, opening up a book and sitting next to him.

Joe ran his hand over the front of Gordie's short hair and touched the tip of Suzie's nose. "No, I think it's kind of nice being called Uncle. What have you got there, Gord?"

"It's my book of dinosaurs. Can I ask you a question, Uncle Joe?"

"Sure, I just hope I can answer it."

"Well, this here's a picture of a Tyrannosaurus Rex, see? Why did they give him a dog's name?"

Joe adored the boy's innocent question. Smiling good-naturedly, he said, "I think Rex is Latin for king, but don't quote me on it, Gordie. That guy was king of the dinosaurs. He doesn't look friendly, does he?"

Both *men* stared at the picture for a few moments. The giant animal's jaws and teeth appeared dominant, brazen, and menacing. It looked as if nothing could stop it when it made up its mind to rip into flesh to satisfy its craving voraciousness.

Young Gordie didn't turn the page. To him, the beast was long past, never to return. But to Joe, it represented another form. Harvey Cohen's words kept coming back about the death camps and the brutes conducting the horrors. These were the same fiends he was now up against; brainwashed characters who actually believe if one is not of the Aryan race, he or she was not supposed to exist and would have to be eradicated. No, not what *he* was up against; what the world was up against. Monsters identical to those SS bastards had returned. They had not really gone away at all. They had been rebuilding, and were now ready to taste blood again. Nothing short of total annihilation of non Aryans would stop them, but to do this, the world's younger Aryan generations would have to be educated again. But how could that be done? What about Gail and the kids' safety? If the maniacs come after him, they may get them.

When Gail came into the living room, the children had already gone to wash up and then watch their favourite television programs. Finding Joe staring at the flames, she passed him a coffee and gently asked, "What's the matter?"

Although a small smile came to his lips when he thanked her, a distant restrained look remained on his face.

"When I see the world through Suzie and Gordie's eyes, I love it. It's exhilarating, with a fruitful future to be shared and cherished. But there are those who don't want it shared. They want to dominate the world for their own kind, and their decision is final. Anyone who steps in their way is smashed. They want total control at any cost."

Gail could not hide her concern but remained silent.

"I don't know what happened to me this afternoon, Gail. I went for lunch and received a history lesson I thought I knew ... but I was wrong. Naively, I believed the world was a relatively safe place to live and bring up kids. That the atrocities of the past were over with, finished. But they're not. An associate of mine informed me that I had let my guard down. That the whole world has gone to sleep as well. That history is repeating itself, and we're all sitting back letting it happen."

"Joe, what do you mean by atrocities?"

"I guess the new catchwords are *ethnic cleansing*. The bastards are doing it again, Gail and the whole goddamned world is doing little to stop it. The genocide that happened in Bosnia not too long ago was supposed to have been stopped by the Second World War, a war we thought we'd won. Well, the goose-stepping bastards are back amongst us, Kiddo, and this time they've got all the power money can buy. That means they can bribe the politicians until they don't need them anymore. The new generation won't have a clue when it's being brainwashed. When I sat in front of your place tonight, I heard the laughter of children playing street-hockey, I saw the wind rustling the trees, and I smelled the mist coming from the ocean. I was free, it was free, and I loved it. Then my mind started going back to pictures I'd seen of freight trains carrying millions of kids and adults to the death-camps. Those people were free, but brutes following Hitler's orders snuffed out their lives. Gail, until this afternoon, I never thought a revival of fascism with ultra totalitarianism was possible. Possible? My God, it just happened in what's left of Yugoslavia, and from what I hear, it's spreading like cancer. After the last war, the United Nations was formed to nip this sort of thing in the bud, but that organization has become as bureaucratic as its member countries."

Obviously disturbed, Gail got up to fix dinner. "Joe, are you saying you've discovered some of these people here in America?"

"I shouldn't be saying this, but yes I have, and I don't know where this case is gonna take me. It never dawned on me until now, but even the fact that you know me, places you and the kids in extreme danger."

Without her eyes lighting up, Gail laughed. "Oh phooey," she said, leaving the room. "Joe, your mind's working overtime. Nobody like that cares about a woman with a couple of kids."

When Gail was out of sight, Joe stared at the flames again before murmuring, "Oh yes, they do. And I'll have that matter taken care of tomorrow."

When Joe went to bed that night, he exhibited a satisfied grin while placing his hands behind his head. His evening with Gail and her children had been alive and revitalizing. He had enjoyed it immensely, even fighting the shopping crowds.

After a fabulous dinner, the four had toured the shops and joined some choristers in song. When the *girls* went into women's stores, he and Gordie browsed through electronics stores. At one point the throng was so large he lifted both kids on his shoulders so they could see Santa and Mrs. Claus receiving shopping lists and *shipping instructions.* When he had asked the children if they wanted to sit on Santa's knee, Gordie had said, "Uncle Joe, I'm not seven anymore." Suzie just smiled and rolled her eyes to the ceiling.

That night at about the time Joe rolled over on his right side and went to sleep, Mr. and Mrs. Wilhelm Dreischner's car entered their driveway. After saying goodnight to each other and setting foot in their individual dwellings, Mr. Dreischner found to his chagrin that he must have mistakenly turned down his thermostat. His side of the house was freezing. Quietly singing, "*On a clear day, rise and look around you,"* he turned the thermostat up. Before going to bed, he took a quick pee and changed his choice of songs to, "*Fly me to the moon."*

Joe's dream was perfect. Marty, whoever he was, had given him the tip of the century. "Put a hundred bucks on Ms. 'T' and you'll be able to retire."

The horses were at the post and the starting bell rang and rang along with the announcer's statement: "... And there they go...!"

The bell was loud, too loud, and Ms. 'T' was first out of the gate, but the ringing didn't stop. Finally, Joe realized he was not at the races; his telephone was making all the noise. Licking his lips and trying to clear his eyes, he picked up the phone by his bed.

"Er ... hello?"

Pete sounded cheery. "Good morning, Lieutenant Stacy, did you sleep well?"

"Pete? What ... what time is it?"

"It's five-thirty, the time you should be out jogging."

Joe threw the covers aside and sat up. "Christ, you've disturbed a dream that was gonna make me a bundle. The bookie guaranteed it. What's up?"

"A good question, and the answer is the Dreischners' house. It blew sky high half-an-hour ago."

Stacy quickly sat on the side of his bed. "What?"

"Dreischner and his wife are dead, Joe. An explosion ripped their house apart and shattered most of the windows in the block. Our guys are on the scene along with the fire department. Oh yeah, and more good news. Erik Roltz has gone to never-never land as well."

"He was in the house with 'em?"

"No, his body was discovered at nine-thirty last night by a couple of teenage lovers parked up a dirt road. When the kid got out of the car to take a leak, he looked down a small embankment and saw a pair of occupied yellow pants."

Joe stood up and stretched. "Damn it, they're one step ahead of us again. I'll grab a quick shower and meet you in the office in an hour, okay? Grab a couple of coffees from Choy's."

"Who's paying?"

Stacy grinned. "Who always pays?"

"I do," Pete declared, chortling.

"Shit, then I'll have to reimburse you, won't I?"

"It's about time, but I know you won't," his partner replied, before hanging up."

Half smiling, but with a foreboding chill running up and down his spine, Joe realized these guys, whoever they are, move fast. Getting under the shower, he sputtered, "Harvey was right. These bastards don't screw around."

Only Pete and Dave Barker with his phone to his ear, sat in the office when Joe arrived grabbing the spare coffee.

"Good morning. What do the fire people say about it?"

Dave hung up. "That was them on the phone. They'll have their inspectors on the scene most of the day. It looks like the furnace blew up. It's a real mess. I called Sawasy a few minutes ago, and he's dispatched two of his crew to look around."

"Where's Roltz?" Joe asked.

"In the morgue," Pete said, passing a fax to his boss. "Two shots through his heart, and nothing stolen. He had his wallet on him ... everything."

The morgue's fax verified Pete's statement and he added, "I've asked the coroner's office to rush the details to us."

"Well, there's not much we can do until then," Joe said, checking his pocket watch. "When will the rest of our team be here?"

Barker looked up but only for a moment. "They're on their way."

Finishing his coffee, Joe suggested, "C'mon, I'll buy you guys breakfast."

As Dave and Pete put on their coats, Pete said, "What? It's not my birthday. What's the special occasion? Is it your birthday, Dave?"

"No, I don't celebrate birthdays anymore. Also, I don't know if we should take time out for breakfast."

The senior officer pushed his chortling co-workers through the door, making certain it was locked afterwards. "Let's just say it's because there's three more down, and Lord knows how many more to go. Damn, it's nice of 'em to do our job for us. As I've always said, a good Nazi is a dead Nazi."

Showered and fully dressed, Hans Krupp's eyes followed his right hand stoking the firm bronzed back and smooth white buttocks of the sleeping naked young man lying on his stomach next to him.

It had not taken much to pick up his bed mate the evening before. His offer of two hundred dollars fixed excitement in the blue eyes of the blond-haired, hard bodied Adonis stretched out next to him. And what a night it had been. They had danced, kissed, and held hands throughout the clubs and their bath, before partaking in the ecstasy of bedtime frolic that had worn them out.

"You're beautiful," Hans remembered saying when he had first sat next to him at the bar. "What's your name?"

The young man sipped his drink before slowly turning his head in Hans' direction. "My name's Kurt."

"You're German?"

"My parents were German. I was born here. I'm attending the University of Washington. Where are you from?"

"Deutschland. My name is August. Is the rest of your body like your face, Kurt?"

Kurt swallowed. "I'm not used to this."

Hans snickered and his voice became monotone. "You all say that. This isn't your first time in this type of bar is it?"

"No."

"Have you been with a man before, Kurt?"

"Once. I was broke and badly needed the money."

"Are you broke now?"

Kurt hesitated and kept his eyes away. "Yes."

"Then let me ask you again. Is the rest of your body like your face, Kurt?"

"I work out," the young man said, keeping his eyes elsewhere.

"You're not answering me, Kurt."

Almost inaudibly, the younger of the two said, "Yes, I take care of myself."

"Does two hundred for the night interest you? If you please me, there's plenty more. Will that make you please me, Kurt?"

To Krupp, a pair of the bluest eyes in the world lit up. "Two hundred? Yes, August, I'll do whatever you ask."

Krupp's face firmed. "I don't ask for anything. I demand."

Lying next to Kurt, Hans Krupp smiled paternally when the sleeping young man shivered slightly and murmured something.

Normally, Krupp would have left by now, never to see his *catch* again, but Kurt was different. He was inexperienced, but he gave his all. He could also be directed and the thought of adding another puppet excited Hans more than Kurt's muscular body. Yes, he would introduce his new find to other colleagues, but he wouldn't share him. Kurt would remain his special stock, to sip and savour. The rapture of what Mother Nature indisputably intended when she made *man*, and *man*, would remain his and his alone.

Hans delicately kissed the young man's left cheek and gently shook his left shoulder. "Time to wake up. Get yourself a shower and I'll buy you breakfast."

Kurt's smile revealed a combination of bashfulness and respect for his lover lying next to him. Slowly he reached under his pillow to check if his money was still there ... it was. Palming it, he stood up and walked to the bathroom. "Did I please you, August?"

"More than you'll ever know," Krupp replied, without smiling. Moving to a chair and admiring Kurt's full naked form, he said, "I have a proposition for you. Can you leave school and let me look after you?"

The young man came over, sat on Krupp's knee and wrapped his arms around his benefactor's neck. "The only reason I'm attending university is to suit my parents. If I agree, how much money will I make?"

Hans delighted in rubbing Kurt's firm stomach, legs and back. "Does it matter?"

Kurt ran his fingers through Hans' hair. "No, but ... well, yes it does. I have expensive tastes."

"Then if you say yes, I'll make certain your precious needs are taken care of. If you decline, I may just cut your throat."

Krupp's merciless smirk both intimidated and aroused the young man. "August, I don't have many clothes with me. Can we pick them up?"

"No, leave them. I'll buy you a new wardrobe. Also, tell your family you're going on a trip."

"Where are we going?"

Hans smacked Kurt's backside. "It's none of your business. Now, go take a shower."

Forty minutes later, the two starry-eyed *lovers* sat opposite each other in the Sheraton's coffee bar.

"August, where do you live?" Kurt asked, reaching for a menu, and feeling Krupp's foot rubbing the inside of his thighs.

"I didn't quite tell you the truth last night. My name's not August, it's Hans."

"Why did you lie to me?"

"I have my reasons. Does it matter?"

"No, not really. I just…"

Krupp cut him off. "Good. I travel the world, but right now, we'll be going to Spokane."

While Kurt and Hans gave the waitress their orders, three inconspicuous gentlemen chatting away passed by their table.

"That was the grandest meal I've had in a long time," Pete declared. "Mainly because you paid for it."

"Tasted great," Barker added. "Love these free meals."

Stacy smiled while waving the check in front of their eyes and panning the faces of fellow diners. "Wonderful, because the two of you won't be getting another off me for a long time. Now, let's get back to work."

By the time the three detectives arrived back in their office, Gebara, Woollam, Mathieson, and Green had arrived and were working away. Captain Glover was also there but was just leaving. Connecting his eyes with Joe's, he said, "Interesting about Dreischner and Roltz, eh? Quite a coincidence. Have you seen the house?"

Stacy held the door open. "No, I'm leaving that to the professionals. I expect to hear from Sawasy shortly."

Limping away, Glover paused for a moment. "I visited it on the way to work. There's not much left. Right about now, they're probably still scraping up the Dreischners. Keep me briefed, Joe."

After the lieutenant nodded to the captain and headed to his desk, it was Barker who captured his attention first. "Joe, I was going to show you these pictures before breakfast. Take a gander."

Before removing his coats, Joe sat next to Dave. The photographs were the excerpts of Himmler's Posen speech along with some of the executioner's other views framed and littering the walls of the Bellingham house. Beliefs of other Nazis were mixed with them.

One by one, Barker passed them over. The first one read: *Such good blood of our own kind as there may be among the nations we shall acquire for ourselves, if necessary by taking away the children and bringing them up among us.*

It became obvious Joe was visibly upset. He wanted to strangle monsters who took pleasure in the systemized murder of unarmed innocent human beings. No, strangulation would be too good for them, he thought. A more suitable suffering death would be more appropriate.

Most of you know what it means to see a hundred corpses lying together, five hundred, or a thousand. To have stuck it out and at the same time - apart from exceptions caused by human weakness - to have remained decent fellows, that is what has made us hard. This is a page of glory in our history that has never been written and shall never be written.

Wincing, Stacy took a deep breath as he began reading the rest.

It will be the sublime task of German women and girls of good blood acting not frivolously but from a profound moral seriousness to become mothers to children of soldiers setting off to battle.

We Germans will guide the world's destiny, exterminating any sub-humans in league against us.

These Eastern Jews aid the partisans and help the underground movements; they also fire on us from their ghettos and are the carrier of epidemics such as typhus. In order to control these epidemics, crematoriums were built for the countless corpses of victims. And now, we are threatened with hanging, for that? Where is justice?

Three million Bolsheviks in German captivity were sterilised, so they would be available for work but precluded from propagation. The world needs such far-reaching perspectives.

Jews will not live amongst us. We will create towns for Jews, administered by Jews.

Aryan supremacy will be established by the systematic extermination of Jews and Slavs. Cultivated elite blond blue-eyed heroes will rule the world. Their physiognomy, mental and physical abilities will be matched by their character and spirit.

Only ignoramuses say I have no human feelings. When I witnessed the execution of 100 Eastern Jews (including women) being executed for my benefit on the Russian front, I almost fainted. Afterwards, I commanded that a more merciful means of execution be established. Am I inhumane?

We are the new Teutonic Knights. Honour, Obedience, Courage and Loyalty. Our tentacles will obtain by force all spheres of inferior life in the expanded World Reich.

The value of Aryan blood will be protected by 'creative actions,' and achievement.

Our principle - the SS principle: We must be honest, decent, loyal, and comradely to members of our own blood and to no one else. What matters to others, is a matter of utter indifference.

We shall never be rough or heartless where it is not necessary. We Germans, who are the only people in the world who have a decent attitude to animals, will also adapt a decent attitude to these human animals when we put them out of their misery.

The evacuation and extermination of the Jews will remain with us, and not spoken publicly.

Dave Barker assessed the disgust showing on his boss's face. He had felt the same way when he had first read Himmler's speech excerpts and the mad man's view of the future.

"Joe, do you really want to view the rest?" Barker asked, sensitively.

Stacy didn't answer for a few seconds. His stomach churned and his mind reeled from such barbaric indoctrinate nonsense and hate. He wondered how the so-called *animal loving* population of Germany and many of its conquered lands fell for this abominable load of bullshit. He wondered what was wrong with them. Nearly every person in that country must have been insane, he thought. Yes, that must have been it ... they had all gone mad.

Heading back to his desk, he said, "No, I don't need to see the rest. Pass these and the others around the office and after everyone's satisfied they know what we're up against, do me a big favour - take the pile of shit down to the furnace and burn it."

Barker complied with the lieutenant's request and not long afterwards all the photos were ablaze.

It took Joe a while to settle down, before saying, "Well, let's form a semi-circle up front by the blackboard and compare notes. Earl, what have you got on the stolen Chevy truck?"

Mathieson wheeled his chair around. "Prints galore, and we know who they belong to. I've got an APB out for Clive Corbett and Dave Clark. Both are twenty-eight and have served time for robbery. Their last known whereabouts was Tacoma." Changing the subject, he asked, "Joe, how well did you review the convenience store's closed-circuit video tape?"

Curiously, Stacy's eyes locked with Mathieson's. "I spent a few hours on it, and then discussed it with Pete. Why? Did I miss something?"

Earl had placed some papers on the floor next to his chair. Picking up two pages, he said, "I think so. Maybe it's not important, but it could be. The officer that interviewed the man and woman in the store said they told him they came in to use the phone. I've checked the tape, and they didn't go near the phone. After they came in and looked around, they leafed through a few magazines, went outside again, came in again, and read some newspapers. I'm under the impression they were either looking for someone, or waiting for someone. It looks to me like they were just killing time."

"Did you bring 'em in?" Joe asked, making his own notes.

Earl snickered. "I was going to, but the address they gave is a vacant lot next to a bakery. Remember they didn't have any ID on them because their wallets were stolen? Also, the officer didn't get their licence number."

Pete sat reviewing his notes. Glancing up, he said, "I think there was a new blue Chevy or Pontiac parked outside. Do you remember, Joe?"

Joe did. "Yeah, it was a new Cadillac Eldorado. Shit, why didn't he get their licence number?"

Mathieson displayed a puzzled expression. "I asked Officer Benson and he told me Sergeant Schmidt said he'd do it. Well, I've checked the file, and guess what ... there's no make of car, and no licence number shown."

Suspicious frowns mixed with inquisitive grins slowly mounted the faces of all present, and Stacy found himself rapidly tapping his knee with a pencil. "Hmm, okay, let's leave it at that. You haven't questioned Schmidt have you?"

"No, not yet," Earl replied. "I thought I'd better mention it to you first."

"Fine, leave Schmidt alone, and let me deal with it. What else have you got?"

Earl picked up the balance of his notes. "Our Mr. Schrems did live a double life. He worked in the governor's office as chief policy analyst and he shared a pretty nice house with a certain Mr. Barry Putreds."

Tapping his pencil again, Joe asked, "The governor's office? Christ, what next? All right, what's Putreds' claim to fame if there is any? Hey, great name. I think I'd hide if I had a name like that."

Earl passed a photograph to Stacy. "Take a good look at Putreds' teeth."

Now the group of them stood, looking over Joe's shoulder. There he was in living colour, Mr. Barry (rotten teeth) Putreds.

Pete took hold of the photo. "Let's pick him up, Earl."

"If you want him, you've got a long ride ahead of you," Barker voiced, leaning over Pete's shoulder and peering at the snapshot. "This walking advertisement for a lack of dental hygiene is the queen we're watching in Spokane. He's still buying skin books and drinking Tennessee whiskey."

Joe had written the name Putreds in large letters on a page of his book. Drawing thick lead circles it, he uttered, "So he's the one who took off to Spokane is he? How did you get his description, Dave?"

"A phone call. Our man said when he finally saw Putreds' teeth, he wanted to throw up."

The group relaxed while Joe got himself a coffee.

"Okay, let's move on. Gwen, what's the story on Iodzathene?"

"The story or the motion picture?" Detective Green asked, checking her notes. "No one wants to talk about it, but I managed to track it down. Iodzathene does have a secondary usage. Taken in diminutive dosages, it clears clogged arteries. Anything more and it causes thrombosis, er, massive blood clots. It's called Zatheneal in America and the West, and just one company, Standen Chemical in Wisconsin, produces it worldwide. Only heart specialists can obtain the drug. Soviet scientists developed it, and until the Berlin Wall came down, it was exclusively produced in East Berlin. Here's something interesting, Standen Chemical bought the German firm last year, then closed it down. I think...”

Gebara came to life, rushing to his desk to pick up a piece of foolscap. Interrupting, he said, "Hang on for a second, would you mind, Gwen?"

Upon finding a document, he said, "Yeah, I thought so. Standen Chemical is on my list. That company gave big money to the Dreischners for the kids' clubs. I've got the other names as well."

"Good work, Sam," Joe said, sitting down. "Make a note and we'll get back to that in a few minutes. What else, Gwen?"

"Well, when I phoned Standen Chemical, I nearly hit a brick wall. Their client list is top secret, so I waited until their lunchtime, and a young clerk in the shipping department was obliging. She told me the only customer purchasing it here in Washington is the Kraven Clinic in Spokane. I'm certain you've all heard of Doctor Xavier Kraven, the noted heart specialist?"

"I haven't," Earl stated, smiling.

"You wouldn't," Gwen shot back. "There's a big difference between Dr. *Dawg*, and Dr. Kraven. Earl, how can you stand watching those cartoons?"

Showing no unease, Earl retorted, "Hey, I happen to like Doctor Dawg."

"I know, and it worries me."

"Now, now, you guys can discuss life's finer things after you're married. Carry on, Gwen."

Still giving Earl a perplexed look, Green said, "Thanks Joe. I don't know what the hell the Kraven Clinic is using it for, but it buys Zatheneal by the carton. Oh yes, one other thing, the Kraven Clinic isn't just a clinic. I discovered it's a sanatorium type of health resort on two thousand acres. It also has its own airstrip. Those wishing to stay there have got to be recommended by the man himself, Dr. Xavier Kraven. He's got offices here in Seattle and throughout the Northwest. Treatment at the clinic is not covered by medical plans, and it costs a thousand a day to attend. From what we've found, there have been some powerful people go through the place, including senators, other politicians, heavy business types, and even a previous president or two. All very much on the QT and believe me, I'm going to follow that up."

Distant thunder boomed as Joe asked Gwen to check out Dr. Xavier Kraven.

"Look into his background ... where he was born, and educated, etc. The works, all right?"

Green closed her written note pages but left a blank page open for further data. "I'll get on it as soon as we're through with this," she said.

Stacy was just about to continue when his telephone rang. After answering it and grinning knowingly, he said, "Great, I'll send Mathieson right over."

Placing the phone down, Joe said, "Thank God for beat cops." Joining the others, he placed a hand on Earl's left shoulder. "Our convenience store bandits

Dave Clark and Clive Corbett have been picked up. This is a break for us, Earl. Find out where they dumped the wallets and anything else those bastards stole at the store. Also, grill 'em until they drop."

As Mathieson left the room, ear-splitting overhead thunder rattled the building. The next minute, a blinding hailstorm forced Joe to the windows again along with the rest of his crew. As pedestrians took refuge in stores, and under solid awnings, hailstones the size of marbles bounced off cars and the damp deserted streets. Two minutes later the hail stopped and large raindrops turned the roads and sidewalks into a quagmire of soggy ice.

Stacy appeared captivated by the scene below. He watched cars slide all over the streets, and shoppers slow their pace and go inside stores rather than end up prone on the ice-covered concrete. He knew Mother Nature doesn't let up. When she wants something done, it doesn't matter how much technology is developed, she still reigns supreme, performing her tasks regardless of humanity's interference.

Staring down, Stacy considered the similarity between Mother Nature and the savages he wanted. Both worked on firmly set timetables that couldn't be changed. If someone meddled with mother earth's universal law, she would strike from another direction with all the force necessary and then some to make her subjects yield with respect. These thick-skinned Nazis would attempt to do exactly the same thing. As far as they were concerned nothing could stop them from executing their power to accomplish their world goals. Damn it, Joe thought, the bastards were crushed before, but they're so well organized they came back. Well, let's crush 'em again.

The mirrored image of a far away look met Joe when he saw his reflection in the window. What the hell were their total objectives? Was it really world domination at any cost? Probably, and that meant Harvey was right. These sons-of-bitches would do anything, absolutely anything to stop people getting in the way of their agenda.

Joe became more and more pensive when he realized they would come after him, and everyone he loved. By now they knew exactly who he was, what he was, where he and Gail lived, and what his intentions were. They probably knew his habits better than he did. In this, their second struggle for survival, nothing would be left to chance. Their battle plans must already be formed. If he didn't stop his campaign, every person he loved would be exterminated, including Gail, her kids, and his brother's family.

Mesmerised by his image in the window, Joe had not realized the minutes ticking by. His thoughts had run long and hard and he was stymied. Finally, it was Pete who snapped him out of his trance. "Er, Joe, are you ready to proceed?"

Stern-faced and sighing while walking back to the group, Stacy sat down.

"Yeah, thanks, Pete. Sorry about that guys. Uh, who's next? Dave, what have you got?"

Barker assumed his usual businesslike manner. Forcing his glasses up the bridge of his nose, he said, "Reference those disks you gave me. I passed them on to a computer buddy at the bank and he couldn't come up with anything. He also had a few of his Microsoft friends work on them to no avail. If it's a code of some sort, my pals haven't got a clue what it is."

Joe took the computer disks off Barker. "Well, it was worth a try. What else?"

"Money in the bank accounts. Your hunch was right on the nail. I only went back fifteen months, but every time there's been a major heist around the area, Kroll and the rest made large personal deposits. These pricks have been responsible for all those jobs pulled off around every six to eight weeks."

"When was the last one?" Joe asked.

"The end of October. That diamond heist in Los Angeles when three guards were killed? Los Angeles police have still got thirty officers working on the case."

Stacy nodded. "I saw the funerals on television. Tell LAPD we're on to something and we'll get back to them. Tell them they can pull their guys. What about the reward money on that Spokane job?"

"A numbered account," Barker announced, smiling and stretching his legs before sitting up again.

"And the smug smile means you know something? Right?" asked Pete.

Barker's grin freely stretched. "Yeah, I do," he said proudly. "Don't ask me why, but I conducted an airline computer check. Twenty-eight people from this state flew to Switzerland and returned within three days. Five of them are from this area. Of the five, one lives in Spokane and..."

Note taking stopped as all heads came up, intensely gazing at Barker.

"... Dr. Heinz Krause travels to Switzerland a lot. A further check found that Krause travels every time a job is pulled. Sometimes he flies to New York before he heads over. Other times, he flies direct from here."

Applause began so Barker stood up and bowed.

"Thank you, thank you. Instead of praise, just throw money. I'm just a lowly policeman doing my job. Dr. Heinz Krause is the chief surgeon at the Kraven Clinic. And guess what?"

In order to keep them on the edge of their seats, Dave Barker delayed passing on his information. When he judged he had kept them waiting long enough, he said, "Krause is booked out of SeaTac for Switzerland on January 6th."

"Then there's another fucking *job* coming up," Gebara yelled jumping to his feet. "I knew it."

Gwen's expression was enough to kill. "Watch your language."

Cringing, Sam apologized. "Sorry, Gwen. Then there's another fucking *robbery* coming up."

Green laughed with the others before feigning contriteness.

Writing the details on the blackboard, Joe said, "Once again, a very nice bit of work, Dave. Anything else?"

Dave still was not finished. "Yeah, our skinhead in Vancouver has rented and moved into a large old rooming house in the East End of town. Carpenters arrived this morning and started erecting bars on the windows. Are there any instructions?"

Joe's mind remained preoccupied with Gail's safety, but he managed a self-satisfied smile, and snapped back to the present. "Yeah, Canadian child pornography laws are tougher than ours. Have our contact get hold of the RCMP and the Vancouver City Police and shut the bastard down. We know the trunk of his car is loaded with porno videos and all that other shit; have them make it a routine traffic check. They'll find the material and lock him up. That way we're not involved and the agitation should add grey hairs to the big man's head, wherever he is."

"Doesn't that ruin our chances of catching more of them?" Pete asked.

"Yeah," Joe said, filling his coffee cup and lighting up a smoke. "But this isn't going to stop until we get our hands on the boss, and I think our chances of doing that are one in a million. No, it's another low life out of the way. One by one, they're either getting rid of themselves, or we're doing it for them. They're going to be livid when they find out their Vancouver operation has been shut down before it opened for business. Don't forget, Pete, Protocol is going to be buying its own planes. Dave, when you're on to Vancouver, make certain the RCMP and Canada Customs are aware of the upcoming formation of a new air freight company flying through Vancouver, or other principal airports in British Columbia. I'm certain they'll pass the information on to every major Canadian city. And make certain it's done through secured channels. We don't want the word getting out about this, but I want the name of the new company passed around the world."

Dave knew what was necessary. "You got it, Joe."

Joe checked his watch. "Let's have lunch brought in. I'll buy."

Pete could not believe it. Something was indeed wrong if his partner was buying again. "What? You're buying again? Christ, twice in one day? I think you should fall in love more often."

"Here's a twenty," Stacy mouthed, passing a banknote to his partner. I'm not worried; I'll get it back off you tenfold. What's more, *you're* going down to the restaurant. I'll have a grilled cheese sandwich and a decent coffee. The rest of you, give Pete your orders."

A short time later, small talk filled the office. After Durnell passed out the food, Joe just sat thinking at his desk. Tomorrow was Christmas Eve and he had told Gail he would spend Christmas with them. Reasoning the situation out, he knew it wouldn't be wise. He also knew he couldn't see her again as long as he worked on this case. The bastards almost certainly knew about her. In addition, what about Pete and the others? Their lives were also in danger. Then again, maybe not; if this thing didn't end, he'd be the target. Shit, he shouldn't have gone to Gail's house in the first place. Deep in thought Stacy murmured, "What the hell should I do?"

"Did you say something, Joe?" Pete asked.

Lost in thought, Joe did not answer, so Pete carried on reading a newspaper.

Five minutes later when Pete saw his partner stand up and put on his jacket and topcoat, he said, "Hey Joe, you haven't finished your lunch, yet; where are you going?"

Not turning around, Stacy said, "I'll be back in a few minutes."

After taking the back stairs, Joe entered Choy's. Only one customer sat reading a newspaper, and after a few minutes she paid her bill and departed.

When they were alone, Choy noticed Joe's unease and came over to the booth. "You got plobrem, Joe?"

Half an hour later when the lieutenant left the restaurant, his countenance indicated a weight had been at least partially lifted off his shoulders.

For the next hour, Joe Stacy sat by the blackboard with the others, piecing together the maze of gathered information, and like the others, George Woollam had done a thorough job.

"It's impossible to penetrate the FBI, Joe," Woollam said. "Klenz had worked on many kiddie porn cases but had never brought charges against anyone. This supposedly was a routine assignment for him. Apparently the FBI suspected Protocol was involved with some sort of smuggling operation, so he was put on the case. They've put a clamp on this so tight it would be a waste of time to dig deeper. As far as the FBI is concerned, Klenz was a bad apple and the matter is closed."

Grinning, Stacy said, "How goddamned convenient, eh? Did any one of your contacts review his file?"

Woollam shook his head. "What file? It disappeared along with the file on one of the FBI types that asked Chief Couling to fire you and Pete. That's something else we weren't made aware of. Agent Alex Cornwell, the eldest of the two in the chief's boardroom was found dead in his sailboat. He died of asphyxiation after starting a small bilge pump motor in the cabin. The other guy's been posted elsewhere. I contacted him, but he's as thick as a fucking dodo bird. In my opinion, he's clean."

Listening to George raised the hair on the back of Joe's head. These Nazi bastards that wormed themselves into the FBI were slamming those doors as well.

George continued. "Joe are you ready for this? In the past eight months, sixty-three kids, ranging in age from four to fourteen have gone missing in the western states. Three quarters of them came from California. Of the sixty-three, nine were Jewish, twelve were Muslim, seven were Sikhs, twenty were black, and fifteen were Latinos. Over the years, loads of kids have gone missing, but it appears to me a religious and racial pattern is forming. Lord knows what's happening in the rest of the country. I've checked with Interpol and the same racial, religious disappearance model exists in most Western counties. Also, since the wall came down, kidnapping kids has started topping the charts in Eastern countries. The world is aware authorities have got their hands full in Belgium right now, and Belgian authorities are still digging deeper. South America is another story. Kids are missing by the thousands. I haven't bothered checking into the Far East, but the figures are mind-boggling in India, Pakistan and Bangladesh."

Joe Stacy ran a hand through his hair after standing up and walking to the window again. "It all fits," he said. "These bastards have been at it all along. Right now we're only concerned about this portion of the globe."

"Have the, er, local disappearances stopped or slowed down since we've entered the picture?" Barker asked pouring a coffee.

A damned good question, Joe thought, re-fixing his eyes on Woollam.

"You bet! The odd one has gone missing, but that's also part of the pattern. It's almost as if it's on hold or been stopped entirely."

"What else?" Stacy asked, finding it difficult to suppress his frustration.

George Woollam examined his co-workers' faces. "I don't know if you want to hear this? Our Bellingham skinheads are out on bail. Three-hundred thousand dollars each was paid without a whimper."

Rage filled Joe's face as he returned to his chair. "You've got to be goddamned joking? Who paid it?"

"Their lawyers, who else? Can you believe it?"

Stacy had asked Barker to check on the legal firms, so Dave accepted a piece of paper off Gebara and flipped through a few pages in his own notebook.

"Yeah, I checked on those legal beagles, and with Sam's help the picture's getting brighter. They work for reputable law firms representing seventeen companies that donated charitable money to the Dreischners'. Let's start with Protocol, Systems, Rhine Shipping, The Germanic Youth Authority, Crux Tools, Axis Surgical Appliances, various others and..."

As usual, Barker hesitated and the others knew the punch line was coming.

"... And let's end with the Kraven Clinic, United Sovereign Farmers of Idaho, and Standen Chemical of Wisconsin."

Dave Barker's triumphant grin had no effect on those around him. The others had turned into analytical clones, wanting to hear more but assessing the information as totally inconceivable.

"All the firms have federal charters and offices throughout the United States," he added. "The lawyers providing bail represent the companies I've mentioned and I'm not finished yet. The majority of shares in each enterprise is owned by a Swiss firm called Wulfe Worldwide Industries Corporation, with its American head office in New York."

Chapter 7

The enamel had rotted or worn away over many years, leaving yellow stained stumps riddled throughout with wide coal black holes three-quarters the size of each tooth in his happy open mouth.

Moments before placing his gun down, semi-drunk, unshaved, unwashed, and dressed only in soiled briefs, Barry Putreds opened the door of his low cost motel room in Spokane to let Hans Krupp walk in followed a few seconds later by Kurt.

"Hey man, what the fuck took you so long?" Putreds asked a disgusted Krupp, almost retching from the stench in the hot room. Even the handkerchief Krupp placed over his mouth and nose didn't help.

Boils, open sores, and deep acne scars covered Putred's body, and his feet were almost black from fungal infection. He had scratched them so often, puss and blood oozed from the open scabs between his toes.

"Wowee, lookee here," Putreds declared, slipping his squalid nicotine-stained left hand down the front of his filthy briefs and stroking his penis and testicles. "Hans, you lucky prick - where did you pick up this fuckin' beauty?"

Completely nauseated from the smell and the look of the *rat* standing in front of him, Hans didn't answer as Kurt shut the door.

The room was a pigsty filled with whiskey bottles and half-filled drinking glasses stuffed with the remains of chicken bones, chips, and floating cigarette butts. Mouldy pieces of chewed pizza and week-old cartons of Chinese food containers crawling with maggots littered the room. Any space void of mouldy food and spilled sticky liquid lay cluttered with child sex magazines and pictures of naked boys and girls with cigarette holes burned through their private parts.

"Kurt, wait in the car!" Krupp ordered, viewing the absolute loathing building up on the young man's frozen face. "I said wait in the car!"

Kurt did not have to be told again, and when he closed the door, Krupp's right foot connected with Putreds' sweating kisser - the force hurtling the man over a chair covered with empty sardine tins.

When Putreds tried to stand, the same foot kicked him in the crotch forcing him to fold over and vault forward leaving an imprint where his head hit the wall.

Squealing madly, retching, and moaning for mercy, Putreds tried to curl up in the foetal position before Hans kicked him hard on the right side of his head. Another swift strike to the man's stomach compelled Putreds to cough up phlegm, blood, and pieces of undigested sardines.

"You despicable bastard! I feel like cutting your fucking balls off!" Krupp bellowed, grabbing and hauling the skinhead up by the throat and ripping off his underwear. Seconds later he pushed the whimpering semi-conscious Putreds' into the bathroom at which point the injured man's face slammed hard against the shower-wall tiles before his body crumpled and hit the floor.

As Putreds writhed in agony, Krupp turned on the scalding water diluting the skinhead's blood swirling towards the drain.

"This is probably the first fucking shower you've had in your life. Get cleaned up or in thirty minutes I'll break off those decaying teeth one tooth at a time."

Once outside, Krupp motioned Kurt out of the car. "Come with me. We'll each have a coffee while that asshole in there cleans himself up."

"Who is he?" Kurt asked, grimacing.

Hans gently placed the palm of his right hand over the back of Kurt's head. Stroking the *boy's* hair, he replied, "It's none of your business, and if he or anyone else ever lays a finger on you, I'll cut their fucking balls off. Yours too if you let them. Do you understand me, Gorgeous?"

Upon feeling Krupp's powerful right arm around his shoulders, Kurt's tense but compliant behaviour assured his mentor of his submission. "Yes, Hans."

When the duo returned to the filthy room, Putreds sat in a chair nursing his swollen face. Physically clean, but wearing clothes that had not been washed in months, the man gave Krupp a grovelling glance before getting up and limping to the door. "I've got my motorcycle, so I'll follow you to Kravenhall."

"Have you taken care of the bill?" Hans asked, still exhibiting utter loathing of being near the man.

"Yeah, let's fuck off."

The ride to the Kraven Clinic took one-and-a-half hours on secondary roads cutting through fog covered Prairie wheat fields stretching in every direction to the horizon and beyond. Most of the way, Kurt played with the car's radio, attempting to find a station not playing country music. Finally turning it off, he asked, "Aren't you going to tell me where we're going, Hans?"

Krupp ran his right hand back and forth between Kurt's crotch and knee. "Does it matter? You're a nosy little fucker, aren't you? What's your last name?"

"Buss. I just like to know where I'm going to live, that's all."

Taking his hand off Kurt's leg and putting his arm around the boy's shoulders, Hans changed the subject. "How many men have you had?"

"I told you, only one before you. He gave me a blow job, that's all."

"Have you ever had a woman?"

"No, but I think I want one. I've gone out with a few, but they came on too ... strong."

Krupp smiled. "Do you mean, they were too aggressive for you?"

"Yes."

"You wanted to lead and they wouldn't let you?"

"Yeah, sort of."

Hans stroked Kurt's crotch again. "Well, you don't need any women, Kurt. You'll hate the bitches by the time I've shown you the finer side of life. Uh, what do you know about Heinrich Himmler?"

Kurt thought for a moment. "Not much. Wasn't he the head of Hitler's Gestapo? Didn't his men gas the Jews?"

Proudly, Krupp stated, "You bet they did. Do you like Jews, Darling?"

Buss did not like being referred to as "Darling," but he accepted the term of endearment. "I've never given the matter much thought. Why?"

Every vein in Krupp's neck and face enlarged when he bellowed, "Why? You ask me why? Because you're a German, that's why! You have to ask me 'why?'"

Kurt cowered a little and moved closer to his door in the car. "Perhaps I'm not as well versed in history as you."

Krupp was not repentant. "Then you need to be educated, and I'm going to discipline you like never before. SS Reichsfuehrer Heinrich Himmler was our master. Next to the Fuehrer, he was the greatest man that ever lived. To this day, his foresight and vision guide us to cleanse the world of impure blood. Aryan blood must rule this world; not the rank inferior blood running through the arteries of low-grade sub-human monkeys. Yes, the other tainted species in this world referring to themselves as humans are animals, just fucking animals. You and I are the master race, and those unworthy subhuman bastards will grovel before us as lowly workers must." His voice rose again. "Do you understand me now, Kurt Buss?"

Kurt didn't answer as Krupp babbled on, and the car's wipers worked to clear a cloudburst of icy rain.

The dark, narrow, underground tunnel built at the turn of century connected four Chinese restaurants and various stores. Far East immigrants arriving in Seattle's early years were uncertain of their safety because their customs were ridiculed and not accepted. Asian ways presented an uncommon mystery to European settlers, so Chinese pioneers kept to themselves, progressing well through all man-made adversity.

Joe Stacy and Pete Durnell were last to enter a room that sixty years earlier held bunk beds for weary illegal restaurant workers. It wasn't a large room and straw mats covered the uneven dirt floor.

Over the decades, electric wires had been installed to provide heat and light for countless Chinese sitting around a crude wooden table, eating, resting their heads on their hands, or playing Mahjong and other games they learned in China. Today would be the first time non-Asians had used the table.

Detectives, Green, Mathieson, Barker, Woollam, Gebara, and Captain Glover already sat in the room before a fellow called Mah brought Joe and Pete in through a small side tunnel. The other police officers had entered individually through several Chinese shops and restaurants linked by a maze of tunnels under a square city block.

It took a moment for Joe and Pete's eyes to become accustomed to the light before their guide departed and the pair sat down to face their concerned co-workers.

Massaging the back of his neck from stooping so low in the tunnel, Glover said, "It's Christmas Eve tomorrow, and we've all got things to do. What's this all about, Joe?"

The others didn't say anything. Instead, they waited for their boss's answer.

Joe was going to light up a smoke but he placed his cigarettes back in his pocket. "I'm sorry I had to put you through this, but I've got the feeling our Nazi adversaries are watching us. Now, whether we want to believe it or not, all of our lives are in danger, and that goes for our loved ones. These people will stop at nothing to shut us down, and they've demonstrated their *determination* by knocking off many of their own. Their next targets will be our families then us. To stay alive, we've got to end this whole thing now."

Looks of utter disbelief filled the faces around the table, and Glover revealed his weariness when he spoke. Trying to ease the pain in his ankles, he said, "Joe, we've been through this sort of thing with gangs before, and we've never let them get the better of us. Why do you think these people are so different?"

"Ray, certain information came to us today that made my skin crawl. We're not up against gangs, or the Mafia. If we were, it would be a piece of cake. We're up against hundreds of cells in an organization that once again has started its move for world domination. And guess what ... they've got billions of dollars to play with this time. Not millions, billions, and that kind of money doesn't just talk and ask, it yells and dictates. At this point, I don't believe anything can stop the dough from screaming, never mind yelling. We stumbled on this thing by accident, but these bastards have been operating for a long time, and until now, not one law enforcement agency had a clue as to what was going on."

"Can't we just take them out one by one?" Glover asked.

"It's international, Ray. In my opinion, they're operating in all the goddamned countries in the world. They're involved in every low down scheme and they've got legitimate fronts. If we shut down their US operation, it will only be a matter of time before they start it up again. These bastards have infiltrated most financial institutions, politics, large businesses, and law enforcement agencies."

Glover shifted to lease his stiff back. "So we just call it quits? I can't go along with that, Joe. I know I'm close to retirement, but I'm still a cop and you know I don't give up."

Joe finally pushed his resistance aside and lit up a smoke. After taking a full drag on the cigarette, he said, "Yeah, and I'm with you a hundred percent. When I said we should stop, I didn't mean totally. I mean we've got to give these pricks the impression we've wrapped it up."

"How?" Glover asked, wincing again from his gout.

Let's give them the impression we think it's just a local scheme. We clean up our area's obligation and pass our information and intelligence on to the feds. We can't operate out of our own jurisdiction anyway. Even the Bellingham Police didn't like our interference. From their most recent actions, these Nazis believe they've convinced us the whole thing is regional. Pete, you take it from here."

While picking up his briefcase, Durnell cleared his throat. He didn't like was he was about to reveal, and it showed.

"This afternoon I had a good talk with Terry Sawasy. The contents of Dreischner's safe were intact after the explosion. Let me read you a notation in Dreischner's so-called diary, which by the way is typed on individual pages fitted into this binder. Christ, these assholes must really think we've got shit for brains.

'I ended Erik Roltz's life today, as I have a few others in the recent past. Erik had gotten greedy. Initially when we came up with the idea and started abducting children, it was mostly for our own pleasure. After awhile we found there was a large amount of money to be made sharing our spoils and we hired our own kind to market the *booty*. Then Roltz got selfish and went into business for himself. Erik Roltz jeopardized our actions by sharing certain children and adults with his occult friends, and I didn't like that. Also, I would not go along with his demand to start kidnapping older children. Maryann likes them under eight, and I agree with her. I now have to find another transportation company, and I have one in mind.'"

Pete paused after reading the journal entry. Taking in the sick expressions around him, he continued. "It goes on. The whole diary's nauseous. Along with the book, Sawasy found the weapon that killed Roltz, forty-two thousand dollars, and two CDs loaded with numbers and letters that we can't decipher. Dreischner's diary tells us how he met Roltz. It also gives dates and statistics, but it doesn't tell us what happened to the children after the bastards finished with them. Also, there were no fingerprints on the gun. How convenient, eh?"

Ray Glover sat shaking his head. As a cop, he thought he had seen and heard it all, but now he knew he obviously hadn't. There were some sick sons-of-bitches out there - really sick sons-of-bitches, and he wanted them. "Do we know who blew up the Dreischner's house?" he asked.

Joe took over again. "Thanks, Pete. Not entirely, Ray. Or let me say we have no proof the explosion was set up. The fire people tell us it was caused by a faulty furnace, but I think that's another insult to our intelligence."

"Nice job, though. A fitting end to those *man* and *wife* assholes," Glover mouthed before Joe continued.

"Our person in Spokane informed us today that Putreds was visited by a tall, well dressed blond guy about 30 years old. The guy's driving a new rented Buick Regal and after checking the licence number with the car company, we've come up with the name Hans Krupp, from Germany. His travelling companion is a blond young man about eighteen or nineteen, and in good shape. Krupp's listed his local address as the Sheraton here in Seattle and we had the room dusted for prints. George forwarded them to Interpol and this afternoon they sent us this photo and profile on Krupp. I know this sounds stupid, but I've got the feeling I've seen or met this man before."

Stacy gave the photo to Glover who passed it around.

"Krupp's never been arrested, but the amazing part is when this guy visits a city anywhere in the world, someone or a group of people end up dead. There's no doubt he's one of their hit men and he was obviously sent here to sort this mess out. I'm certain others will follow. Right now, though, they know more about us than we know about ourselves. And if you think I'm joking ... don't. I've received personal information and I've promised not to reveal the source. These pricks are involved in everything from dope production to race riots, blackmail, prostitution, paedophilia, body parts, kidnapping, and robbery. If it makes money, they're in it. The mafia is like a kindergarten compared to these bastards."

Perusing Krupp's picture before passing it along, Gwen asked, "So we look after our end and pass it on. But to whom? You said they've infiltrated most law enforcement agencies, so who can we trust?"

Shrugging, Joe took another deep drag on his smoke. "I don't know. For Christ's sake, they've even invaded the Governor's office. If Schrems worked there, who else has turned? Maybe the governor is one of them. I want all of you to think who we should pass this on to. In the meantime, Ray, I suggest you tell the chief what he wants to hear."

"What's that?"

"That we're finished with it. That Dreischner and Roltz were the kingpins and that's that. Pete, give the captain the details we worked out; the whole story's there. Ray, Chief Couling will think you're the Second Coming when you hand it to him."

"He thinks that anyway, Glover said, his eyes sparkling while reading the document. Moments later he declared, "Shit, this stuff will make headlines around the world."

"That's what it's supposed to do," Pete declared. "We think the pricks will fall for it and pull off their dogs. Nice Christmas present, eh, Captain?"

Joe took over again. "Okay, now I want you to listen to a taped telephone conversation. The call was made from our cafeteria. Play it Pete."

Durnell placed a small tape recorder on the table and pressed the play button.

"Yo, who wants me?"

"It's me. Are you drinkin' again?"

"Yeah, I am. How are ya, ya old fucker? What have ya got to report?"

"Nothin'. They've been given their own office. I can't get near 'em, so I just placed a bug in there."

"How much do they know?"

"Not much, Barry. What did you find in Stacy's joint?"

"Not a fuckin' thing except the Paris Match."

"And Durnell's?"

"Fuck all. Are you stayin' on top o' things?"

"That's what I'm fuckin' paid for, isn't it? I can't befriend the prick ... he doesn't like me. I've even asked Glover, and that fat fucker's lips are sealed as well."

"Oh yeah? Well I gotta go. I met a kid in the mall and he's comin' over in a few minutes. Fuckin' nice, too. Cheap at fifty."

"Ya got one for me? I ain't had a young set of lips around this thick one in three weeks."

"Get your own for a change, ya cheap asshole. Hey, they're a dime a dozen here. I'm fuckin' myself silly."

"You're making me drool. If they get past eight, it's too late."

"I agree, but who gives a fuck? What are a few extra years? I picked up a fourteen year old today."

"Nice. Er, when's the man arriving?"

"Who knows? Too soon for me. When he gets here, I've gotta go to Kravenhall with him."

"Why haven't you gone before now?"

"They've got *guests*. We can only enter when the guests leave."

"Well, fuck yourself silly while you can."

"Hey, this town's fuckin' smorgasbord, Smitty. Keep in touch."

"Yeah, you know it."

After Pete turned off the machine, Mathieson added a little levity to the voiceless room. "Captain, I believe he wants you to go on a diet."

It took three seconds of total silence for the captain to grin, and when he did, he had nothing to say.

"Who would have suspected it?" Stacy asked, watching Glover's hatred form. "There are more tapes but they're filled with the same trash. He planted the bug after we decided to move down here. I just want you to know these animals are everywhere. If they're in our small police force, can you imagine how many there must be in the larger cities. Well, we all learned something today ... our friend Schmidt likes little kids and I've got something planned for him."

Encouraged looks filled the faces of those present before Joe continued. Those around him all wanted to share in Schmidt's punishment that Joe would brief them on later.

"Now, before we wrap this up, are we all clear? We'll meet here every three days starting at 1300 hours on the December 27th. We'll move each meeting up an hour, therefore our meeting on the 30th will be at 1200 hours, and so on. Under no conditions will you mention this arrangement to anyone. Even family members can't know. When you leave this room, buy a cheap item before you leave the store or restaurant you exit from, or ask for a bag. That way if you're being watched, the assholes will just think you're shopping. I don't believe we'll have any problems after tomorrow. Do you agree, Ray?"

Glover indicated he was still upset. "Yeah, I think you're right; count me in. So that bastard called me a 'fat fucker,' did he?"

The group of them chuckled looking at the incensed expression now fixed on Glover's face.

Joe found it funny as well. "He did, but don't worry, Captain, we'll get him. Now, there's something I told Ray and Pete, but not the rest of you. I'm due for a little rest and recuperation, so I'm booked into the Kraven Retreat for a week, starting January second."

Barker sat straight up in his chair. "Christ, Joe, with all the press you're getting, they'll recognize you. Also, who's paying for it?"

Glover grinned. "Not us. Joe's sold some of his Microsoft shares."

"They won't identify me, Dave. I've bought a few longish grey wigs, and thick horn-rimmed glasses with normal glass. When I wear them with a phoney waterproof moustache, I can't even recognize myself."

"Why are you doing this?" Gwen asked.

"I've got to look around that joint. Maybe the answer to this whole thing lies in Spokane."

Concerned for Joe's life, Mathieson asked, "What about back up?"
"Not necessary. I've got a cellular and that should be enough."

Light snowflakes covered the car when Hans Krupp read the large wooden sign, *Kraven Retreat, Members Only*.

With Putreds following, Krupp turned north off the highway heading up a winding snow-packed road passing another sign that read: *Trespassers will be prosecuted to the fullest extent of the law*.

After driving through thick trees and dense brush, a guarded gatehouse appeared next to high solid steel barrier gates completely blocking the road. The gates opened in the middle, swinging inwardly onto the property. Broad spiked razor wire originating at the gates continued outwards on the property lines.

The instant Krupp stopped his car, two tall heavy-set men armed with holstered pistols and wearing brown uniforms, brown berets, black ties and highly polished black jackboots, stepped from the guardhouse.

"Yes, what do you want?" the one nearest the driver asked, forcefully, looking in, studying Krupp, and glancing around the interior of the automobile. The second walked to the opposite side of the car, keeping one hand on his holster and glaring at Kurt.

Krupp didn't say anything as he handed the guard a sealed envelope.

Seconds later, the heels of both pairs of shiny military boots clicked together and the sentries assumed the position of attention. Upon returning the envelope, the guard closest to Krupp raised his right hand firmly upward to his front, presenting Krupp with the Nazi salute. "Welcome to Kravenhall, Herr Krupp! Please proceed."

As the gates slowly opened, the guard staring at Kurt smiled and presented a normal salute.

Another barrier blocked the road up ahead, and the same procedure took place. "You are expected, Herr Krupp!" one of the four saluting sentries voiced reviewing the contents of the now open envelope, and directing Putreds to take a different road. The skinhead now drove his motorcycle north passing a thirty-foot high silo a hundred yards away just east of the main road.

A few minutes later, the forest came to an end, and Krupp turned right on a circular crushed quartz driveway leading to an immense two story red brick building 500 yards away. A labyrinth of five-foot-high finely trimmed hedges covered with patches of snow occupied the abundant grounds inside the orbicular driveway.

The elegant design markedly impressed wide-eyed Kurt Buss who took in everything. He thought the snow covered entrance was what wonderland must look life if there were such a place. "Hans, this is awesome. Who lives here?"

Hans Krupp arrogantly smiled while pulling up under an imposing entranceway at the foot of seven gleaming white marble stairs leading up to two giant oak doors. "You do, my boy."

A *man* resembling one of the guards at the original gatehouse stood at the bottom of the stairs and opened Hans' door. "Herr Krupp, I have been asked to show you to your suite. May I take your luggage, please?"

Krupp stepped out and opened the trunk of the Buick, allowing the man to pick up everything except a briefcase that Krupp now tightly held. When the guard closed the trunk, another uniformed man appeared and drove the car away to a vehicle car park situated one hundred yards right of the building.

Kurt could not believe the opulence. On the drive in, he had noticed a large service transportation lot and garage with gasoline and diesel fuel storage tanks up a small hill a brief distance beyond the silo. Huge steel pipes originating at the fuel storage area led north, disappearing behind a vast copse of trees.

The man with the luggage said, "Please follow me, Herr Krupp. Herr Kraven will receive you in one hour."

Buss was not prepared for the elegance as he followed the luggage carrier and Krupp up the spotless granite stairs through the majestic doors.

Inside, two circular staircases wound their way up from the enormous marble-floored grand hall. A massive crystal chandelier hung from a painted glass dome interrupting the second floor and above. A thick eight-foot wide blood-red carpet ran from the entranceway, forming a 'V' as it separated, parading up each staircase. Patterned gold trimmed egg-blue ceilings faded into towering cream coloured walls adorned with exquisite hand-carved frames protecting landscapes and portraits painted by European masters eons ago.

Throughout the vastness, stations of stately brown-leathered chairs surrounded polished oak tables holding silver ashtrays reflecting a prism of colours radiating from a superbly decorated Christmas tree at the room's centre.

Both men trailed the uniformed porter up the west side staircase, turning left at the top. Again, blood-red running carpets covered spotless white marble floors as they passed numerous doorways, elegant tables, vases, flowers, and more priceless paintings.

"This is your suite, Herr Krupp," the man said, opening the door to a four-room apartment fit for an emperor.

When they entered, a warm fire crackled under a large mantelpiece decked with shiny wartime relics of engraved steins, small cannons, shell-casings, and crystal chalices. Above the mantelpiece, an enormous portrait of Adolf Hitler stared down on everyone entering - his burning eyes following the room's occupants.

The porter clicked his heels while bowing his head before handing Krupp a key. "May I say I've heard about you, and it is my honour to serve you Herr Krupp."

Hans' chin rose. Unsmiling, he replied, "Thank you - you may go."

The doors of two large bedrooms with ensuite bathrooms stood off to one side of the living room. On the other side, another door opened into a regal study containing a billiards table and floor to ceiling bookshelves filled with leather-bound books.

Krupp picked up his two suitcases and took the larger of the two bedrooms. Before leaving Spokane, he had bought Kurt some appropriate clothes and a satchel. "I'm going to unpack and shower, and I recommend you do the same," he told Buss. "I have a two-hour meeting to attend, and then we'll dine here." Firmly he added, "Do not leave this these quarters, do you understand?"

Although Kurt wanted to go exploring, Krupp's admonition suggested otherwise. "I'm in no hurry to go anywhere, Hans. This place is unbelievable."

The elder of the two did not answer. Instead, he entered his bedroom and shut the door. When he re-emerged fifty minutes later, Hans Krupp's skin shone, and every blond hair in his head was in place. His starched white shirt, yellow tie, and crisp navy-blue suit complimented the lustre of his black quarter-Wellingtons. Picking up his briefcase, he opened Kurt's bedroom door.

"I'm going now," he said, both amused and aroused viewing the well-toned, squeaky clean young man with a towel around his waist, lying on his bed. "What book are you reading?"

Buss glanced over the top. "*Mein Kampf.* I've heard of it, but never read it. When did Hitler write this?"

Krupp felt pleased Kurt was already taking an interest. "When he was imprisoned for trying to help his people. You're learning quickly, Kurt. Read and heed our Fuehrer's words. His struggle lives on, and such knowledge will always benefit you. I'll be back in two hours."

Moments later, Hans Krupp paused at the bottom of the giant staircases and checked his watch. He knew of Kraven's resolute decree for punctuality, and he was right. The sounds of heavy footsteps walking in his direction from a side corridor filled the main hall before Xavier Kraven appeared.

Aged sixty, tall and thickset with a full head of wavy grey hair, the square-jawed, blue-eyed doctor was dressed immaculately.

"Hans, dear Hans, how are you?" Kraven asked, approaching elegantly with his right hand extended. The doctor's left hand held his swaying glasses extending from a cord around his neck.

Krupp clicked his heels and bowed his head before feeling Kraven's firm handclasp. "Much better now that we meet again, sir. You're looking well."

Kraven never withheld his exhibit of vanity. "Thank you, thank you, young man. I always feel and look this good. Come, let's go into my office."

Gently placing his right hand around the back of Krupp's upper left arm, Kravenhall's master guided his guest down a hallway and through a door into a huge luxuriously furnished office with a roaring fire. As the two entered, a good-looking crimson haired woman in her middle forties was just leaving.

"Have you met my devoted wife, Inga?" Kraven asked, as the woman held out her right hand.

Krupp bowed his head and gently kissed the back of the offered hand. "No, I have not had the privilege. An extreme pleasure, Frau Kraven."

Inga Kraven smiled demurely. A lifetime of entertaining dignitaries induced the somewhat younger woman to be meticulous, courteous, exacting, and impeccably dressed. "An honour, Herr Krupp," she said, before letting her husband get on with his work.

Instead of sitting behind the immense highly polished desk holding a white telephone on one side and a red telephone on the other, Kraven asked Hans to join him in two of four impressive soft leather-covered chairs placed around a gleaming circular teak coffee table.

"How was your flight, my dear boy?" Kraven asked. "Would you like a light refreshment?"

"No thank you, Doctor Kraven. My flight was fine. It feels good being in the United States again."

"Yes, it is a wonderful country that will be much better when we set its proper course. I, er, congratulate you on your recent achievements, Hans. It's most unfortunate such drastic measures were necessary. As you know, we were not prepared for such a degree of, should I say, inappropriate *intrusion* in our affairs."

Krupp nodded briskly, and his whole being expressed intense bitterness. "What surprises me is how it happened, Doctor Kraven. We must never let our guard down, and those responsible should pay dearly."

Kraven's twisted smile augmented Krupp's hatred of those who had softened within the movement. "They have, Hans, and it will not happen again. This Lieutenant Stacy is indeed a devil to say the least. Such intelligence is wasted on this decadent American system of government, but people of his kind do exist ... for now, that is. Tell me, how is our leader? Is he well?"

"Herr Schtaff's health is excellent and he sends his respects, sir."

"So he thinks of me? Wonderful. What about Herr Kruger?" Kraven asked inquisitively, trying not to miss the slightest hint of duplicity while turning his head slightly but not his eyes.

"I believe Herr Schtaff relies on you considerably. I have not been informed of his present opinion of Herr Krueger."

Kraven's eyes lit up intrusively. "Of course you wouldn't, but er, I feel certain you've interpreted some understanding as to Herr Schtaff's patience with, should I say … Herr Krueger's blunders?"

Krupp felt uncomfortable with this line of questioning. He knew nothing of Schtaff's plans for Krueger, but he did know Kraven was close to the leader in New York. If Kraven fostered aspirations for Krueger's position, it was between Kraven and Schtaff.

"My loyalty to our cause precludes me from speculating, Doctor Kraven."

"Yes, of course my boy, and rightfully so," Kraven replied, leaning back in his chair, seemingly let down and not about to push the matter further. "Now, let us discuss this Lieutenant Stacy. Do you think eliminating Dreischner and Roltz will finally end this quandary?"

Krupp's eyes narrowed. "If it doesn't, the Elite Team will be sent to assist in the extermination of all who step in our way."

Just the mention of the Elite Team compelled Kraven to sit up. He had not heard mention of the group of ten professional killers in many years. Not since they were unleashed in South America in the 70s. Over a period of eight months, hundreds of people were annihilated by various means. Absolutely no one escaped when Gustaf Schtaff issued orders to these death squad members.

"Wouldn't that be a little suspect here in the United States?" Kraven asked.

Once again, Krupp knew he had to watch his words. Although Krueger had the list of insurgents operating in the US, perhaps Kraven did also; particularly those in the media who would play such action down, or place the blame elsewhere. "I don't think so, sir. Like you, I believe we have the appropriate people in place to suppress any national *anxiety*."

Kraven stared blankly through the strong-faced man next to him. He knew Krupp was undoubtedly one of the most vicious killers in the world. He was also cunning and kept all information to himself. "Of course … Herr Schtaff has implemented Reichsfuehrer Himmler's project most perfectly. Er, tell me, Hans, who is this good-looking boy with you?"

Krupp was not prepared for the question. "His name is Kurt Buss, and he's one of us who needs training. With your permission I thought perhaps we could include him in your indoctrination program?"

After offering Krupp a sceptical glance, Kraven pushed a white button on the front of his desk. "Have you completed a background check?"

Cordell Cross

Hans considered the question, and deciding Kurt could not possibly be a threat, he lied. "Thoroughly, sir, and I would also ask that he be left *untouched*, if that is all right?"

Licking his lips, a peculiar lustful grin Krupp had not seen before stretched Xavier Kraven's lips. Almost immediately, the look changed to a sincere smile, but Kraven's lustrous eyes revealed his true feelings. "Untouched? Hmm, difficult, but not impossible. Kurt? Such a good German name. I saw him coming in with you, Hans. Why don't you wish to share him?"

"With who?"

Clearly indicating he did not like the question, Kraven pounded a knee with his right hand and shot back, "Us of course. Who else?" His face becoming more austere, he added, "My wife and I."

Krupp had to think fast. Sitting stiffly he said, "Herr Kraven, before leaving Switzerland, I was informed your visitors are considered out of bounds. Sir, if you believe it is inappropriate for me to request the same courtesy, I will contact Switzerland and..."

Doctor Kraven did not appreciate being collared, but Krupp was right. As much as Kraven and his wife desired to *sample* Kurt's charms, Hans Krupp was Switzerland's man, and as such Switzerland would want him treated with the pomp and deference his rank merited.

"Certainly. You must know I was simply jesting, Hans, dear friend. But let me commend you on your excellent taste." Changing the subject, he asked, "Did Putreds drive here with you?"

Krupp winced. "I wouldn't allow that filthy animal within two feet my car. He rode his motorcycle. I think he's with your people right now."

"Hans, don't underestimate Barry Putreds. If you look beyond his personal habits, he is a talented individual. I knew his father well. Heinz Putreds served with Reichsfuehrer Himmler in the early days, you know?"

A light tap came to the door before it opened. "You called, sir?"

Kraven glanced at the small white-uniformed man entering. "Yes, we'll have coffee and sandwiches, Gerhardt."

"At once, sir," the old orderly replied, gently closing the door.

Stretching before strolling over to one of six lofty windows, Kraven asked, "How do you find the Adolf Hitler suite?"

"Perfect, Herr Doctor."

"Did you sign the guest book?"

"Not yet, but I will. I must be moving up in the world. The last time I visited, you placed me in one of the dormitories."

"A simple error of judgement my dear friend. You will be surprised to learn who has stayed with us, Hans ... really surprised. The clinic is quiet right now because guests are only allowed here two weeks of every month. Some sixty guests will be arriving on 2 January. How long will you be remaining with us?"

Krupp watched the doctor return to the chair. "Just until this Stacy matter is over with, that's all. I also have to look after a certain thing in Ottawa, Canada."

"And you have the updates?"

"Yes, but Herr Krueger must be with you when we transfer them."

A sinister smile preceded, "Yes, I know. Herr Krueger will be here shortly."

"So, you're off to Canada? And if Stacy doesn't ease off?"

"Then I will slaughter the ones he loves before the Elite Team arrives. They'll take care of him and the rest."

"Excellent," Kraven said, slapping and rubbing his hands together as the servant entered and departed. Quickly selecting a sandwich and chewing rapidly he added, "Help yourself, Hans, then we'll get down to business. Are you assisting with the upcoming Rhine Shipping robbery?"

Krupp's meeting took three hours, not two. When he entered his suite, Kurt had fallen asleep reading Mein Kampf, and his towel had parted, stirring Hans' desire.

Quickly stripping off his clothes, Krupp calmly lay down next to Kurt. Tenderly stroking the boy's forehead, he amorously whispered, "I'm sorry I took so long, Kurt."

Buss lay on his back and a bashful grin appeared. "That's Okay, I needed some sleep. Hans, this will be the first Yuletide I've been away from home. When can I telephone my parents and wish them a merry Christmas?"

Krupp slipped his left arm under Kurt's head, bringing their faces together. Wrapping his right hand around the young man's waist and gently moving his body towards him, he softy replied, "Whenever you want, my love. My world is yours."

The headline read: *LOCAL PAEDOPHILE RING BUSTED!* Copies of the newspaper covered every desk in the squad room Stacy and Durnell had worked out of for so many years.

Earlier that Christmas Eve morning, Stacy, Durnell and their team had received applause and congratulations from all their co-workers as the duo reclaimed their old desks after closing the upstairs office. Even Captain Glover made a big point of coming over and shaking their hands. Another press conference was planned later that day with the chief of police, mayor, and the governor in attendance.

"You're after my job, aren't you, Stacy?" Captain Glover asked, patting the backs of the lieutenant and sergeant and making certain everyone in the office heard his voice. "Well done, guys, now get busy on some of the other cases poor old Schmidt here has been carrying. Isn't that right, Sergeant Schmidt?"

Schmidt beamed. "You've got that right, Captain! Congratulations fellas. When they sick you two bulldogs on to someone, your teeth-marks are big and deep. Welcome back to the real world."

As usual, Joe ignored Schmidt's comments. Pete, however, played his part well. "Thanks Smitty. It was tough, but they put the right cops on the job. What cases have you got for us?"

Schmidt selected three file-folders on his desk and handed them to Durnell.

"I'll start you with the easy ones. Over the past week, three car lots have been robbed on Aurora and…"

Later as the two detectives familiarized themselves with their new caseloads, Joe leaned over his desk. Whispering to Pete, he said, "It should be happening right about now."

Durnell found it hard to control his exuberance. "A little morning surprise never hurt anyone."

Both detectives were referring to the fact that after a good grilling by Mathieson, the two hoods that robbed the convenience store had confessed and co-operated with the police. Although they had spent the money, they told Mathieson where they had dumped the wallets taken from the couple that supposedly had gone into the store to make a phone call. Mathieson not only found the wallets, he also visited a nearby pawnshop and located the woman's wedding rings along with two other rings, each marked with the SS insignia.

After speaking with Mathieson, Captain Glover had disguised his voice and made a telephone call to the federal government's Alcohol, Tobacco, and Firearms people.

At exactly the same time as Schmidt passed over the new caseloads, four federal ATF agents surrounded an affluent-looking house in the Queen Anne Hill area of Seattle. Not only did the fancy hand-carved sign above the front door contain the street numbers of the house, it also included the last name of the occupants, 'The Grunds'.

"Nice joint, eh?" asked one of the two men with pistols drawn, standing off to one side of the front door. His partner had already rung the doorbell and stood off to the other side. Two other agents covered the back door and garage side door.

"Their bootlegging operation probably paid for it," the second man replied.

Moments later when a smiling Mrs. Grunds wearing an apron over her neat blouse and slacks opened her front door, her face changed to the colour of the bread she was baking.

"Mrs. Grunds? Mrs. Ernst Grunds?"

"Yes?"

"We have a warrant to arrest you and your husband, and a search warrant for this house," the officer told Mrs. Grunds while handcuffing her and reading off her rights.

"What's going on here?" Mr. Grunds asked before being handcuffed after coming out of the bedroom.

Subsequent to reading Mr. Grunds his rights, three officers searched the house looking for stolen alcohol and cigarettes. Within minutes, they found a case of *knocked-off* bourbon and two large cartons of stolen cigarettes that *just happened* to be in the garage.

Impounding the spoils did not disturb the agents. What made them furious was finding mounds of photographs of naked children and young adults participating in sex acts. Shortly afterwards, they also discovered a secret photographic studio in the basement with similar pictures, negatives, and videos.

While packing the illicit material in boxes, one agent said, "My God, Charlie, listen to these titles: *Tender Toddlers, Masked Marvin, Smooth Inexperience, Age Six and Willing, Little Boy Blew, The Farmer in the Doll, Our First Day at Penetration School,* and *Young and Juicy.* These two bastards are perverts to the umpteenth degree."

When the paddy wagon hauled the Grunds' away, the couple emphatically denied any knowledge of having illicit tobacco and alcohol in their house. Regardless, still looking ill, one of the ATF agents yelled, "They should throw away the key when they book you sick bastards! I hope you'll never get out! Merry Christmas!"

Within minutes, and in accordance with Stacy's *plan*, Sergeant Schmidt and his partner Victorson arrived to witness the agents taking inventory. Initially, when the ATF deputies telephoned Seattle Police, Schmidt had opposed being assigned this case, however, Captain Glover had played his role skilfully.

"Schmidt and Victorson, I want to see you."

Schmidt had entered Glover's office first. "Yeah, Captain?"

"Alcohol, Tobacco and Firearms have arrested two people for selling stolen booze and cigarettes. I want you and Victorson to get on it right away. Find out what the charges are, and whether or not we'll be involved? Okay, Schmidt?"

"You got it, Captain. What's the address?"

"It's 6453 Laidlaw Street. The agents have arrested a Mr. and Mrs. Grunds, the owners of the house."

Schmidt swallowed deeply as he expressed total shock. "Uh ... Laidlaw Street? Grunds? Er, you know, Captain, we're busy as hell. Can't you assign another team?"

"First you want it, and then you don't. What is the matter with you, Schmidt? I've got no one else. Get on it!"

"What about Stacy and Durnell, Captain?"

"For Christ's sake, Sergeant, those two have earned a rest. Get on it; that's an order!"

"Yes, sir."

Slowly strolling into the house, Schmidt displayed his badge and said, "I'm Sergeant Schmidt and this is Detective Victorson from Seattle Police. What have you got?"

The agent who had yelled at the Grunds met the sergeant in the hallway.

"Adams, ATF. It looks like serious paedophilia to us. We've booked Mr. and Mrs. Grunds. There are enough smutty photographs and videos here to fill a normal sized room from floor to ceiling. Jesus, there are some sick bastards in this world. I hope they get the book thrown at 'em."

Schmidt curiously asked, "What, er ... brought ATF to *this* house?"

"The Grunds have been selling illegal bourbon and cigarettes. We've confiscated what's left as evidence. We want you to charge them right away with producing child pornography. We've gone over every square foot of the house, including the attic and garage. It's clean now."

Schmidt indicated his displeasure. "What do you plan on doing with the photographic evidence?"

"We're leaving that in your hands. Is that all right with you?"

That was all Schmidt wanted to hear. It would give him the chance to destroy it. "Yeah, that's absolutely great. Wonderful, we'll take it from here. Thanks a lot."

"Good, sign here," Adams declared, presenting the inventory list with two carbon copies to Schmidt.

"What's this?" asked Schmidt.

"Hey, Mac, we know what's here, and we're covering our asses. A copy will be sent to the FBI and your chief. Sign here, please."

Hesitating, Schmidt had no choice but to sign. Now he had to ensure he questioned the Grunds, alone.

"Lieutenant Stacy, how did you determine both Dreischners and Erik Roltz were running the ring?" a female reporter asked, squeezing in closer at the end of the governor's press conference, and knowing her camera crew was sending this live signal to all network affiliates.

"Let's just say we have absolute proof."

"Could others be involved?"

"No, we don't believe so. We've arrested those who are left. If by chance there are a few others, the FBI will be on their case."

"Who killed Erik Roltz?"

"I can't answer that at this time. We're awaiting the autopsy report, but it looks like a leadership battle."

"Were the Dreischners murdered by Roltz?"

"No, fire investigators tell us the gas explosion was an accident."

"How long do you think this has been going on?"

Joe backed away slowly. "Years. Listen, that's about all I can tell you. The chief and the mayor have answered most of your questions. Thank you."

The second Stacy and Durnell turned to leave, they heard the reporter announce, "We are now going to take you live to 6453 Laidlaw Street here in Seattle. Our reporter John Oxham is on the scene with Sergeant Schmidt of the Seattle Police Department. Take it away, John."

Joe grabbed Pete's arm, and asked a technician, "Do you mind if we watch this on your monitor?"

"Not at all."

The reporter at the Laidlaw Street address appeared. "Thanks Cindy. I'm standing next to Sergeant Schmidt of the Seattle Police Department. Sergeant, neighbours have told us a couple with the name of Grunds lives here. Since you're the lead investigator, can you tell us if these people were involved in the paedophile ring squashed by Lieutenant Stacy and Sergeant Durnell?"

Schmidt looked like he did not wish to be there at all, and he wondered how he got into this mess. "I have no idea. We'll just have to wait and see, but I doubt it."

"It's people like you our citizens are grateful to, Sergeant Schmidt. How long did it take you to crack this case?"

"Er, well, we all do our bit. I can't tell you much until we review the evidence. We don't know if the Grunds were set up or not, do we? It is alleged they were selling illegal liquor and Lucky Strike cigarettes."

"Set up? Sergeant Schmidt, what about the pictures you have of Sarah Goldfarb, the little girl who was kidnapped, sitting naked on Mr. Grunds' knee?"

"What? Who said that? Schmidt snapped back, angrily. I haven't seen..."

"Your assistant, Detective Victorson told us. He said five pictures were found in Mr. Grunds' bedroom?"

Turning his back to the reporters, Schmidt heavily marched back to the house, yelling, "I won't answer any more of your foolish questions."

Stacy and Durnell did not wait around. Both were dying to shake each other's hands and have a good laugh, but they kept their composure while sauntering away.

Sitting in Choy's, Joe said, "I feel light headed. That's a hell of a weight off our shoulders, old buddy."

Pete agreed. For the first time in weeks, he had noticed a spring in Joe's step. He always knew when his partner neared the finish line. "Now the real work begins, eh?"

"You bet. Have you got all your Christmas shopping done?" Joe asked, changing the subject while loosening his tie.

"Joe, I'm married. Women are organized. Linda has been buying presents all year. She picked the last of 'em up last week, thank God. That's it! No more! Finished! What about you?"

"None. I'm going shopping tonight."

"On Christmas Eve? Jesus, you don't believe in waiting till the final bell, do you? I thought you and Gail went shopping the other night?"

"Nah, Gail picked up a few things, I didn't. I'm going over there tonight. What the hell should I buy her? I don't even know what she likes."

"Perfume. Women always like perfume. Ask someone who works with her what she wears. If not perfume, buy her a pair of..."

Pete didn't finish his suggestion because Choy came over. "Joe, Captain Grubber want you on phone."

Stacy thanked his friend before heading over to the area of the cash register. "Yeah Ray?"

"Are you sitting down?" Glover asked.

Joe moved the phone and sat down on the first stool. "I am now, Ray. Why, what's up?"

The captain hesitated knowing the delay would tease Stacy.

"Go on, Ray, I'm listening?"

"Joe, you've won one of the NICER Prizes. You're due in New York on the 11th of January."

Stacy was lost for words. Finally an incredulous look of suspicion came over him and he smacked his own face. "Ray, you're putting me on. Say you're putting me on. Please say you're putting me on. You're not putting me on, are you?"

Chuckling, the captain repeated, "No I'm not, Joe. You have actually won a NICER Prize. Congratulations, and don't forget we've got witnesses."

"What witnesses?"

"The witnesses who heard you say you'd split it."

"Screw them. I never split anything."

"What?"

"On second thought, I'll split it."

"That's our Joe. I knew you would."

"With Pete."

"What?"

Joe couldn't maintain his straight-toned voice any longer. "Just joking. I didn't want the thing in the first place. Of course, I'll split it. My name's not Schmidt, you know?"

Glover's manner turned serious. "Don't mention that fat fucker, you'll ruin my day."

Chuckling while hanging up the phone, Joe said, "C'mon Pete, I'll buy you a Christmas drink. Choy, here's twenty, keep the change."

Choy bared his gold tooth while using Pete's line: "It not my birthday, so it must be Chlistmas."

"What a fabulous night," Gail announced lifting her head from Joe's shoulder as they softly shuffled to the music of the Mellowtunes in the slow turning Space Needle's romantically-lit restaurant.

While shopping earlier, Joe had phoned Gail and she had invited him over. The children were going to the movies with a married couple she knew with kids, so she suggested she'd light the fire and a few candles and prepare a meal just for two. Joe liked the idea, but thought she also needed a break. For some reason, he suggested they go out dancing at the Space Needle, and Gail pleasantly accepted.

With the fairyland lights of Seattle laid out below them like a wavering sea of diamonds, the smooth voice of Thedda Marie, a beautiful small black singer accompanied the Mellowtunes providing entertainment. *"...A line a day, when you're far away, little things mean a lot..."*

"Joe Stacy, you've brought something back into my life I'd totally forgotten about," Gail said, examining his eyes.

"Oh yeah, what's that?" he asked delicately humming along with Thedda Marie and the band.

"The tingle of nearness," Gail whispered, snuggling her head into his shoulder once more. "Raising the children as a single mother doesn't give me the opportunity to go out very much. Until we met, my life was the hospital, housework, Susan, and Gordon. I never realized something was missing. People get set in their ways believing romance is reserved for the young. It's a wonderful lost feeling that comes along only when you're young and you don't give a hoot about the real world."

Joe smiled, tenderly kissing Gail on the side of her forehead. "It is darling, but some of us are lucky enough to find it again. That's if we foolishly thought we'd discovered it in the first place. I didn't until I met you. Gail for the first time in my life I recognize what love really is. When you say it's the tingle of nearness, I want to be with you every second. It doesn't matter what we're doing, I just want to be close to you."

Two affectionate grins joined two sets of sparkling eyes exploring each other's faces, firmly fixing a bestowal of attachment usually only secured for the rhapsodic few.

"Are you saying you're in love like I'm in love, Lieutenant Stacy?"

The two stopped dancing for a moment, enchantingly savouring each other's closeness. "No, I'm saying much more than that, Nurse Manning. The word *love* is just a common man made creation. My feelings for you far surpass anything synthetic. The authentic word to account for the way I feel is known only by God, and by not telling us, he's doing us a favour and helping us with our destiny."

Minutes later, Joe clasped his hands together in the middle of their table, and Gail curled hers around them. "It's funny, isn't it, Joe ... you say *our destiny* like it's always been here?"

"Darling it has always been here. There appears to be a hidden blueprint for a love like ours; and I've got to tell you I'm glad we found it."

Both lovers fell silent for a moment until Joe softly whispered, "Gail, I have to go away for a few days after Christmas. I'm only going to Spokane, but I want you to know it will tear me apart being away from you."

A lost look took over Gail's eyes. "Is it ... business, sweetheart? Will it be dangerous?"

Stacy changed the position of his hands and wrapped them around hers. "Nah, it's routine. I don't want to go, but it's really necessary.”

“Okay, Joe, but...”

A lump appeared in his throat. "Gail, I know this is a difficult question, and I have no right to ask it, but if it became essential for me to leave Seattle, I mean for good ... would you come with me?"

Gail's distant look disappeared, replaced by a small loving smile and almost a tear. "Joe Stacy, if you tackled Mount Everest, I'd be buying mountaineering gear. I love you so much."

The noise of a plate dropped by a nearby waiter didn't disturb the couple sitting at table thirty-seven. At this moment in time, nothing could. Although the restaurant was full, Joe and Gail were in that special land they had spoken about. A barrier was not required to lock out the world because their newly discovered love had done it for them. Even when Thedda Marie began singing Doris Day's old hit, *Secret Love,* words were not necessary to guide them back to the dance floor. Gail thought Thedda Marie was magically shepherding them as well, because the singer followed the song up with, *Hey There,* and *The Treasure of Your Love.*

It started snowing as Joe and Gail drove home at nine-thirty after Gail telephoned to check on the kids. Both youngsters said they had thoroughly enjoyed the movie and Suzie asked if she and her brother could stay with their playmates until eleven to watch a video of Charlie Brown's Christmas. Gail agreed and thanked her friends when they said they would drop the children off at eleven-fifteen or thereabouts.

As Gail mixed two drinks, Joe stoked up the fire, turned on the Christmas tree lights, and turned off all the others lights.

"Do you mean to tell me we're going to be *alone* for over an hour?" he asked, grinning mischievously and accepting a scotch and water when Gail joined him on the couch. "Just the two of us, *alone,* here on the couch? Such a great big comfortable couch, in front of a fantastic fire, when it's snowing and cold outside? And we're together on this wonderful couch, alone, on Christmas Eve? Is that what you're telling me, Gail Manning?"

When Joe wrapped his right arm around Gail's shoulders, she beamed answering, "Yup, we've only got 360 seconds, alone, here on this couch, *alone.* Nice, eh, being *alone*? I kind of like that word, how about you?"

"Alone?"

"You bet, *alone!*"

Words were not necessary when Joe gently took the drink out of Gail's hand. Placing it down with his, he passionately wrapped her into his arms and their lips discovered the *tingle of nearness.*

"Merry Christmas, sweetheart," he whispered, tenderly picking her up and carrying her into the bedroom.

Each little girl dreams of a chivalrous knight defending her honour and carrying her away on a snow-white charger. For Gail, that dazzling fantasy had finally come true. Her noble cavalier, Joe Stacy, had captured her heart while whisking it away to an enchanted castle created only for two.

Later, when the children came home, they found the two star-struck lovers sitting in front of the fire listening to an old *Jack Benny* radio play.

"Are you coming over tomorrow, Uncle Joe?" Gordie asked, picking up comics, a toy slide-rule, and plastic truck off the floor in the hallway.

Joe stood, lifting Gordie up and transferring him over his shoulders and back and bringing him through his legs before standing him upright. "I wouldn't miss it for the world, Gord. Did you have fun tonight?"

"You bet!" Susan said, sitting next to her mom. "Are you coming over for breakfast, Uncle Joe?"

"You'd better believe it, Suzie! I'm looking forward to more of your mom's fabulous home cooking. What time are you kids getting up?"

"Six o'clock," Gordie replied, yawning.

Gail smiled sympathetically examining her children's faces. "They'll be attacking the presents around that time, but breakfast won't be ready until nine. That's when the lady of the house gets up on holidays. C'mon you guys, it's bed time."

A sleeping pill, a cup of cocoa, counting sheep, and listening to the radio didn't work. Joe just could not get to sleep. Sure he knew Gail was constantly on his mind, but so was something else and he couldn't figure out what it was.

From the time he had left Gail's and driven home, something bothered him and he did not know what it was. He had felt tired and had gone to bed, but everything changed when his head touched the pillow. Damn, he hated tossing and turning. It was two-thirty, and he had been in bed for two hours and he still couldn't sleep.

"What the hell's the matter with me?" he mumbled, reluctantly tossing back the covers and getting up to plug in the kettle. "Could it be my upcoming trip to the Kraven Clinic?" He had booked telling them he was a retired math professor needing a rest. No, that wasn't it. Maybe it was the coffee I had at Gail's? No, that was not it either. Coffee doesn't keep me awake.

"Oh well, another cup of the stuff won't bother me," he muttered, placing a teaspoonful of Maxwell House in his mug marked 'Sonics.'

As Joe waited for the water to boil, he went into the living room, parted the drapes, and gazed at the road below. Snow had finally stopped falling and now the night looked damp and cold. A serene halo of mist surrounded the street lamp outside and the light's brilliance glistened on the snow's crust further padding the quiet of the night. Only one car had left tire-prints in the middle of the street and that was his when he had parked it hours earlier.

Walking back to the kitchen and preparing his coffee, Joe perused the stack of Paris Match magazines, two computer disks, and the little black book sitting in the middle of the table. He had been through the book at least ten times since Harvey had passed it to him, but nothing in it made sense. As well, the disks drew a blank. Like the book, they just contained rows and rows of numbers.

Joe sat at the table, sipped his coffee, and picked up the November issue; the same edition found in the van but without the folded pages. He had questioned Sawasy about those pages but the crime lab professional couldn't be certain of the page numbers. "Joe, I think they were five and seven," he had said. "But I could be wrong. I know you think I'm perfect, but I'm just another normal, humble, human being."

Joe grinned thinking of Sawasy's remark. That phrase seemed to be catching on with everyone, even Pete. "Who says you're normal?" he'd replied. Then he asked himself why would the tips of two pages be turned? Had Kroll turned them as markers? Probably, but why? As well, all articles except for a few English ads were in the French language and Joe had only retained a bit of his high school French. Did every one of these assholes speak French? Probably not, so what is the link between the disks and the magazines? There must be a link - but what is it? Is there one?

Joe finished his coffee, muttering, "There's got to be otherwise they wouldn't have stolen the copy I had."

Picking up the tiny black book, Stacy turned the pages one at a time noticing there were only twelve pages. Each page had two numbers at the top, then a space before two other numbers, then another space before rows and rows of other numbers and letters. The first two sets of numbers separated by a space on the second last page were 43-32. On the next page, they were 57-45. For fifteen minutes, Joe stared at the numbers before quickly standing up to get a pencil. He then wrote down 43 and subtracted 32. The answer was 11. Writing 57 and subtracting 45 left 12. His pencil moved quicker as he added four plus three, three plus two, five plus seven, and four plus five.

The smile that had disappeared earlier reappeared as everything became clearer. It made sense. Subtracting the numbers gave the month of the edition, and adding them separately gave the page numbers. Adding four plus three equalled seven, and three plus two equalled five.

"The corners of pages five and seven were turned over," he declared. "Sawasy you genius, you were right, and if Kroll had had the December edition, he would have turned over the corners of pages nine and twelve."

Stacy rushed to the phone and punched some numbers "Pete, it's me Joe! Joe ... Joe Stacy, your partner! Stacy, your partner with the brains. Are you awake? Pete, I said are you awake? Yeah, I know it's three o'clock. Are you awake? Give her a kiss and then maybe she'll stop cussing. What, she won't? Then tell her I'll give her a kiss when I get over there. What did she call me? Hey, tell Linda my parents *were* married. Yes, I'm coming over. Yes, now! Do you have some coffee on? What do you mean, no? Good, see you in half-an-hour!"

Rushing into the bedroom to get dressed, Joe yelled, "That's why I couldn't sleep. They're using a form of Slidex code the military uses. We've got ya, ya Nazi bastards, and a little boy's toy slide-rule subconsciously tipped me off."

Chapter 8

"Didn't you enjoy your breakfast?" Hans Krupp asked, noticing Kurt had been quiet all Christmas morning. "Surely you can't say there was something wrong with it. You can order whatever you want. You know that, don't you?"

Kurt sat in front of the fireplace reading *Mein Kampf.* He'd been up since eight o'clock, even before Hans. "Yes, I enjoyed it," he answered, sighing. "It's being locked up in this place that's getting to me. Hans, how about showing me around the grounds? This suite is fantastic but I'm climbing the walls. I'd like to work out or have a swim. Is there a swimming pool here?"

Normally resolutely opposed to expressing any sort of benevolence, Krupp countermanded his personal creed and after approaching Kurt, ran a hand through the young man's hair. "I'm sorry. I guess I have been a little selfish, haven't I? Yes, there's a pool and a weight room, but if I show you them, you must close your eyes to anything else you see. Do you understand?

Standing and stretching, Kurt put a marker in the book before closing it. Sitting down again, he asked, "Why? What do you mean?"

"I said do you understand me?"

"Yes, Hans, I understand you, but what's the big deal about a work out and a swim?"

Hans had perceived Kurt's restlessness. He knew it was bound to happen but he had not expected it so soon. Sitting opposite him, he indirectly answered the young man's question. "Are you familiar with the Aryan Nations, Kurt?"

"I think I've read a few things about them. Isn't the federal government always trying to infiltrate them?"

"Yes, they are, but it's all show. Federal officials usually do what we tell them, but once in a while even they have to bow to pressure placed on them by nigger groups, or kikes."

Kurt strummed his fingers in his eagerness to get out of the suite. "What's that got to do with me having a swim?"

"Kurt, you're reading *Mein Kampf,* surely by now you understand the gist of what our Fuehrer was saying. You and I are pure white. Pedigreed Aryan blood runs through our veins, not the desecrated fluid of ever-breeding sub-humans. We, the white, blond, blue-eyed people are the masters of this world, Kurt, don't ever forget that."

As Krupp's voice rose, his eyes widened to insanity's limit, and perspiration formed on his forehead and upper lip. "We must always be on guard to protect our race before it becomes contaminated. We can impregnate them for our pleasure only, but if any loathsome piece of shit forces themselves on one of us, his or her throat must be cut from ear to ear. Do you understand me, Kurt?

And remember, if we do impregnate them, at the very least their offspring must die or be segregated."

Spittle shot from Hans' mouth and his cruel bombarding eyes resembled the demoniac stare of the maniac in the painting staring down from above the mantelpiece.

"Yes Hans, I do. The Fuehrer spells it out perfectly. We of the white race are the bastions of purity."

Krupp mellowed and held out his arms. "I feel so proud to hear you say that, Kurt my love. Come, mein schotz, sit on my knee."

Kurt knew he had said the right words. He was starting to learn what buttons to push because instantly this tyrant had turned into a kitten. "Can we do that later, Hans? Will you show me around now?"

"Show you around? I'll give you the place," Krupp said, hastily standing to get his overcoat from his closet. "Dress warmly Kurt - it's cold out there."

A north-heading gravel road originating at the centre rear of the building branched into two roads after 100 yards. Along this short stretch, Kurt noticed four large greenhouses containing thousands of beautiful flowering plants. Workers inside appeared to be moving like robots or zombies exactly like the individuals attending the grounds. All these men wore dirty-white coveralls with the words 'Kraven Clinic' visible on the back of each garment.

After passing the conservatories, the duo took the winding northeast fork passing soccer fields, tennis courts, the remains of summer gardens, and a massive outdoor swimming pool with its steam rising in the cold air. To the east, Kurt could see an unused par-three, golf course with more workers manicuring its fine lawns and shovelling up the remains of the last snowfall. Suddenly, the road ended at two giant steel doors built into an east-west twelve-foot high brick wall resembling the Great Wall of China.

"Wow, what's the length of this thing?" Kurt asked, amazed at its size.

Krupp took an electronically coded card out of his wallet and inserted it into a computerized slit. "Miles. It cuts the property totally in half."

Instantly the doors started opening slowly and Kurt's inquisitive eyes widened. On the other side, two brown-uniformed guards carrying sub-machine guns at the ready closely observed the two of them.

As the doors closed, Hans' authoritarian temperament returned. Keeping his chin up, he resolutely stated, "My name is Krupp, and he is my guest!"

Both guards placed the slings of their weapons over their shoulders and one moved closer. "Welcome, Herr Krupp! We are honoured that you visit us!"

Krupp didn't acknowledge the greeting. Instead, he continued guiding Kurt up the road past rows and rows of half-moon Quonset huts. Activities of sorts took place in some of the buildings, but others remained silent.

"These are where the *troops* live," Hans said proudly. "Would you like to step inside a barracks? Not much training is taking place today, it's Christmas."

Kurt couldn't contain his enthusiasm. "You bet - I'd really like that."

Krupp directed Kurt towards to the nearest Quonset hut. When they entered, the young man saw two giant flags on flagpoles at the other end of the empty building. The first was the Nazi swastika, and the other the death's head and lightning bolts of the SS.

The barracks held two individual rows of twenty steel-framed single beds separated by an eight-foot wide aisle. All the beds were faultlessly made and aligned. Steel wardrobe-lockers and writing desks stood between each bed and even these were perfectly in line. The highly waxed stone floor shone as did the windows and shelving. To their left, halfway up the aisle, a double doorway led to a large square ablution room. One wall contained showers without partitions, with the wall opposite retaining toilets without partitions. Sinks covered the third wall, and across from the sinks stood washing and drying machines.

Kurt couldn't believe the cleanliness and neatness of the place. "Hans, where is everyone?" he asked.

A conceited grin curled Krupp's lips. He enjoyed showing newcomers around. It would have been better on a training day, but he thought Kurt would get the idea.

"They're celebrating Christmas in their club. Come, we'll join them?"

After walking two hundred yards past dining huts, the hospital, a stores building, and an athletic centre, Kurt could hear the excitement and singing coming from a large swastika-shaped structure with a sign out front that read, *Canteen.*

When Hans opened the door, the huge long wing was in chaos. A cloud of foul-smelling cigarette and cigar smoke engulfed them along with the stale stench of beer. At least four-hundred skinheads in various styles of dress and undress sang along with German war recordings, played cards, arm-wrestled, leg-wrestled, argued, threw knives into fire logs, and fought, paying no attention whatsoever to the two newcomers.

Prestige furniture and carpets that had seen much better days were strewn everywhere. Amidst wall flags, hundreds of WW2 German navy, army and air force training pictures surrounded photographs of Adolf Hitler, Heinrich Himmler, Joseph Goebbels, and other Nazi leaders dressed in full Third Reich regalia.

The younger of the two hesitated and instantly wanted to leave. The noise was ear shattering and the room reeked of spoiled cabbages and unclean bodies.

"Cheer up. This is *their* room," Krupp yelled, smirking devotedly. "Anything and everything goes on in here!"

"Is it always like this?" Kurt bellowed in Krupp's ear, noticing many were just wearing underwear and sitting on each other's knees, kissing and groping.

"Only on holidays."

"Where are the women?"

"Our females aren't trained at Kravenhall. Every type of male Aryan sexual persuasion is in this room and I would imagine someone's going to notice you pretty damned quick."

"What do you mean?" Kurt asked. No sooner had the words left his mouth, four strong raging young drunks forced him to the floor and started undressing him. Hans stood laughing excitedly, watching Kurt frantically trying to get free. Finally when Kurt was naked except for his shorts that were about to be ripped off, Hans acted.

Viciously, with the speed of a thunderbolt, and thoroughly enjoying himself, Krupp's right foot nearly took the head off one of the skinheads, sending him sharing what was left of his nose, teeth, and cheeks with a wall. A fraction of a second later, he lifted up the head of another *kneeler*, generously extending the full force of his right knee under the young man's chin. It didn't matter if the person bit off half his tongue, or lost all his front teeth, to Krupp, it was fun. The other two were easy. He picked one up by his waist sending him flying head first into the lit fireplace, and the last one got a boot in his testicles and another size eleven in the right side of his head - the force ripping the man's right ear in half.

Appearing shaken and half-frightened to death, Kurt quickly retrieved his clothes and rushed to a corner of the room. Swiftly getting dressed, he noticed the assault had not created the slightest interest from those in the immediate area; songs and merriment continued. The *fellow* with a burnt face, hands, arms, and upper body had been pulled from the fire, but the other three remained untouched, bleeding and moaning where they fell. Kurt also saw Krupp's crazed excited look. Hans wanted to inflict more pain, but the other *troops* weren't paying attention.

"I'm sorry about that, but it happens," Krupp eventually said loudly, guiding Kurt to the door, then to the road. "Let's continue with our tour, shall we?"

The main road turned northwest at its end, and 200 yards later it curved again heading southwest back to the wall. Close by, a giant blacktop parade square occupied an area close to an airport control tower. Kurt could see a landing strip through the bush at the end of the parade square, and its length was sufficient to land jets.

On the way back, Buss also noticed a large physical obstacle course next to a medium-sized red brick building with a huge smokestack. The building had no windows, and Kurt had only seen that size of chimney near hospitals.

"Hans, what's, er ... what's that building used for?"

Krupp didn't respond right away and Kurt got the impression the man didn't want to answer. When he did, his face became firm again. "This is ... let's call it, the crematorium and furnace room. Doctor Kraven performs operations in his clinic, and there are certain items that must be burned afterwards." Conveniently changing the subject, he added, "Come, we'll go back and have a swim in the indoor pool."

Before reaching another area of the wall where further armed sentries guarded two similar giant gates, the pair walked by an enormous vehicle car park loaded with aged military-style trucks, jeeps and earth-moving equipment. Kurt's eyes caught everything. The transportation appeared to be well looked after and in good running condition.

"Did you enjoy your tour, Herr Krupp?" an unsmiling guard asked, pushing an electrical apparatus that opened the solid barriers.

"It was sufficient, but it's none of your business," Krupp replied, paying no attention to the man.

On their way back to the greenhouses, a small picturesque lake occupied the western side of the property. Fat ducks and geese that hadn't flown south for the winter surrounded eight rowboats and four canoes tied to a dock. One of the weird looking men Kurt had seen earlier in a greenhouse stood on the wharf, feeding the birds. "How come that lake hasn't frozen over?" he asked.

"Because it's heated to forty degrees. Certain patients of Doctor Kraven enjoy rowing. All the property's water is heated in the crematorium."

It was near lunchtime when Krupp and Buss entered the main building from a rear entrance in the basement. Kurt could smell the chlorine emanating from the indoor swimming pool along with the sweet fragrance of body-rub gels.

The odours became stronger as Kurt followed Hans down a well-lit corridor leading to an impressive blue and white tiled Olympic-sized swimming pool brightly lit by five huge triangular roof lights. There were no windows. At the deep end, a high diving board was separated to the right of its lower cousin by twenty feet, and a tall water slide entered the sparkling liquid halfway down the pool's length. At the shallow end, two-inch ceiling to floor heavy plastic strips covered the entrance to a fair-sized professional steam room adjacent to a foaming Roman-style Jacuzzi and the door to a Finnish-designed sauna.

After uttering, "Let's go undress," Hans led Kurt to the lone changing room on the other side of the pool where neatly piled stacks of dazzling white towels lay next to cupboards laden with individual containers of expensive gels, creams, razors, and aftershave lotions. A doorway led to a body massage room where two husky white-uniformed attendants sat reading magazines. Two other doors, one marked Men, and the other, Women, led to various showers, sinks, and floor-to-ceiling tiled toilet cubicles.

"Take off your clothes!" Hans ordered, stepping out of his pants and shorts. "After you have a swim, Gretta will give you a rubdown."

Kurt glanced around. "Gretta? Er, where are the bathing suits?"

"They're not necessary here at Kravenhall. I said get your clothes off!"

Kurt didn't waste any time undressing, but he felt embarrassed when the female orderly entered to hang up both sets of clothes. She also handed each of them white bathrobes and towels.

The water was warm, beautifully warm as Kurt swam length after length like a torpedo. He knew he was fast, but surprisingly he wasn't as speedy as Hans. When Krupp accelerated, he left Kurt in his wake.

"How do you like it?" Hans asked, passing him on his fifth length.

"Fantastic. This is what I needed. Can we use this any time we want?"

"Yes, but only for a few days. I've made arrangements for you to enter training with the troops."

Buss stopped at the end of the pool and a concerned look came over him. He wanted no part of that mob on the other side of the wall. Holding on to the edge of the pool under the diving boards, he asked, "What do you mean, Hans? Are you proposing that I live with that load of thugs? I'll never get out alive!"

"I'm not proposing anything; you're going to be trained. Don't worry, Kurt, they won't bother you. I'll guarantee your safety."

Troubled, Buss did not respond so Krupp swam over and extended his arms around Kurt. Grabbing the edge of the pool-deck, he corralled his young *ward*.

"Listen, my sweet, I want you to take three weeks of training, that's all. After that, you'll be able to take care of yourself when you're in a fight. I promise you it will only be three weeks."

"Where will you be?" Kurt asked, turning his head to one side so Hans' kiss of affection touched his cheek instead of his lips.

"That's none of your business! Just be assured you'll be looked after. All right?"

Kurt didn't respond, and his attitude tested Krupp's patience. "I said is that all right? Is it possible you can't hear as well as you look?"

The young man studied the fire building up in Krupp's eyes. He'd seen it before and he indicated it terrified him. "Yes, that's fine."

A satisfied smile gradually appeared on Hans' face, and this time Kurt's lips could not escape his *guardian's* display of fondness.

After a further fifteen minutes of swimming lengths, both men were using the slide and diving boards when Xavier and Inga Kraven entered with another man and woman. All wore sparkling white bathrobes and held towels. The women also wore bathing caps.

"We've been watching you from below and you've simply got to introduce us to this beautiful young man," Kraven announced, keeping his calculated attention on Kurt. "Hans, have you met Heinz and Marlene Krause?"

Kurt dipped below the water. Sure enough, the one-way glass mirror ran the full width of the deep end under the pool's diving boards.

Hans instantly climbed out of the pool offering his hand to the couple. "Yes, we've met. Good to see you again Herr Doctor … Frau Krause."

Krause also had difficulty taking his eyes off Kurt, but he did for a moment. "It's wonderful seeing you again, Herr Krupp. Aren't you going to introduce us?"

"Certainly," Hans reluctantly replied. "Kurt, come up here and meet Herr Doctor and Frau Kraven, and Herr Doctor and Frau Krause."

The young man hesitated, not knowing what to do. Standing naked in front of women had not happened before today.

Both Krauses' seemed fascinated with Kurt, especially the beaming host. "You don't have to be shy, my dear, dear boy. We've been watching you since you started swimming. Come up and say hello. I ... we, won't bite you."

Thoroughly self-conscious, Kurt slowly swam over to the ladder, stepped up, and cautiously joined the group. The young man absolutely hated being exposed in front of them, and after introductions were made, he quickly jumped back in the pool and clung to the side.

Kraven's eyes narrowed suspiciously. "Why were you circumcised, Kurt? It's a Jewish trait."

Kurt didn't know what to say as Krupp laughed, offering, "His mother probably had a Jewish doctor. Turning towards Kurt, he mouthed, "You must have a stupid mother, trusting herself to a Jew."

"What a charming young man," Marlene said before dropping her robe and joining Kurt. Moments later, there were six unclothed people in the pool, and Kurt remained the quiet centrepiece. Even keeping his distance, he could do no wrong; he also wondered what the letters, numbers, and symbols meant tattooed on Xavier Kraven's inner left wrist.

Half an hour later when the two senior couples left, Hans ensured Kurt became acquainted with heavy set forty-five year old Gretta. Here, Kurt allowed his naked body to be pressed and kneaded by the non English-speaking female with Herculean strength and braided blonde hair. At first, he felt uncomfortable, but the biting, sweet smelling body rub felt marvellous and if this was his new life, the young man indicated to Hans he wanted more.

The toy car Gordie gently ran over Joe Stacy's arm hanging loosely over the edge of the couch woke up the detective. Either that or Joe might have woken himself up with a light snore. Smiling while opening one eye followed by the other, Joe stretched, asking, "Is that the kind of car you're going to drive when you get older?"

"You bet, Uncle Joe," the excited boy replied, before his mother came out of the kitchen.

"Gordon, I thought I told you to let Uncle Joe sleep? He's been up all night."

Joe sat up wiping his eyes and stretched again. "That's all right, Gail. What time is it?"

"Two-thirty. At least you've had a few hours rest. I'm just cooking the turkey. Would you like a coffee, Joe?"

"Don't go to any trouble, sweetheart, I'll make it."

Gail laughed heading back into the kitchen. "It's no trouble at all. When you've got two kids, nothing is trouble."

Stacy still wasn't quite awake, but the coffee got him on track. He and Pete had worked until eight o'clock on Pete's computer partially cracking the code that had stymied Dave Barker's knowledgeable associates. Joe couldn't blame them though - they had not known the book and disks were connected to particular Paris Match magazines.

Similar to the military's old Slidex code, the first two numbers delineated the month and the pages to be used. The next two numbers represented the number of lines down the page, and the number of letters counted to the right from the beginning of the line. Whatever letter it was became 'A' and all other letter after that ran in alphabetically numbered sequence.

At times, he and Pete had been baffled, because periodically the letters on the computer disk replaced the letters in the black book. It was Linda who eventually figured out that although 'A' was the primary letter, if a letter appeared in the book next to the two numbers, 'A' became 'Z'. Counting the number of letters backwards from 'Z' to the book's letter, whatever it was, became 'A' again.

Originally, the search was difficult, but at seven o'clock, Pete discovered the numbers and letters in the book could be programmed on the second disk, meaning they didn't have to count any numbers or letters. After a key letter was entered, messages shot right out at them until the book's letters and numbers changed. At that point, the programming had to be repeated using a new key letter.

On the way home, Stacy stopped at a pay phone and phoned someone he was getting used to calling, usually from pay phones.

"Hi Harv, we've cracked their code. It'll be a freeway robbery."

Stacy stayed on the phone for a good half-hour. Since the meeting at Bea's, Joe had called his new friend daily, passing along all information gained. Under Cohen's guidance, the Israelis had moved fast and now Harvey was in the position to provide assistance piecing the puzzles together.

"I don't think so, Joe. They're not going to wait until the truck gets on the highway. It's not their style. They'll knock it off in the dockyard area. Whereabouts though, we don't know. So it's coming in on the LaHoncha is it? Well, here's what I suggest you do."

At eight-thirty in the morning when Joe had arrived at Gail's, the living room was filled with wrapping paper, toys, games, and new clothes. The kids had gotten up early and the presents he had bought them along with Gail's perfume present were well received and most appreciated by hugs and kisses. In turn, he had received a scarf, a pocket calculator, and a Canadian book Gordie had picked out entitled, '*Stand By Your Beds*!'. The novel was a funny and heart-warming book about young army cadets leaving home for the first time to attend six weeks at summer military camp. Joe had started reading it before falling asleep, and Gail must have lifted his feet up and covered him with a blanket.

After Joe got up and washed, Gail approached him wearing a foxy smile. "Well, it's that time. Are you ready, Joe Stacy?"

Joe swallowed and an apprehensive grin appeared. "Are you sure about this? All I'm going to do is drag you guys down with me?"

While the children got warmly dressed, the lady of the house had already put on her coat, scarf, and earmuffs. "Nonsense, it's never too late to learn," she replied, chuckling. C'mon, you'll enjoy yourself."

"But Gail, I've never been on ice-skates in my life?"

"So, there's a first time for everything? You're a dancer, so skating should come natural."

"What if I break my leg?" he jokingly asked, standing up and grabbing his coat.

Zipping up Gordie's heavy windbreaker, Gail gleefully replied, "Then that will come natural as well. I'm sorry I'm laughing Joe. I just find it funny. Relax - you'll have a grand time."

"Yeah, that's what worries me."

Gail was partially right; Joe did have a terrific time, but being a dancer didn't mean skating came naturally. The arena was packed, and Joe had the beginner's experience of being blitzed by young skaters whizzing by at speeds only known to the National Hockey League. Throughout though, Gail loyally stayed by his side as he reached for anyone nearby and took them and her down with him as he had forewarned. Eventually with her coaching and a bit of help from the rink's wall, Joe cautiously made it around the ice on his own.

Before heading home for dinner, Stacy was able to confidently skate to the music as long as he held on to Gail, Susan, Gordie's arm or anybody else's hand, arm or body in his immediate area.

"How did ya like that, Uncle Joe?" Gordie asked on the way home.

"You were great," Susan offered. "Even with a sore bum, you hung in there, Uncle Joe."

Stacy checked his rear-view mirror noticing the cheerful faces of the two children. Gail expressed her exhilaration as well.

"I'm proud of you," she said. "So are the children. Just think, this morning you couldn't skate, and now..."

"...I can, and I've got the lumps and scars to prove it," Joe said, laughing with them. "I'll tell you one thing, when those skates came off, I couldn't feel my feet, but I sure appreciated my shoes."

When they arrived back at the apartment, the aroma of roast turkey met them at the door. Gail prepared a delightful Christmas dinner, and with children's laughter, pull-crackers, paper hats, and playing Suzie's new Monopoly game, Joe Stacy appreciated Christmas more than ever. When it came time to leave, even the few skating aches had disappeared, cured by wine, wrestling, and rolling on the floor with the kids.

Gail held him tightly as they kissed goodbye. "I love you, Joe. Thanks for making it a great Christmas."

Before wrapping Gail in his arms, Joe tenderly moved a few strands of hair away from her eyes. "Darling, if love is a magnet, my electrons couldn't get more excited. Gail, I want to be with you every living minute and afterwards too."

Gail found herself wrapped in the warm strong arms of his affection, never wanting them to unwind. "Joe, must you go tonight?"

"I'd give the world not to, but..." His voice trailed off and he swallowed to clear the lump from his throat.

"It's this case, isn't it?" she asked, searchingly.

"Yes ... yes it is. But it'll be over soon, don't worry."

"Please be careful, Joe."

"I will, sweetheart. Thanks for a wonderful Christmas. A Christmas I'll never forget. Uh ... you're working tomorrow, aren't you?" he asked, changing the subject.

"Unfortunately, yes."

"Then I'll call you at the hospital," he said, kissing her and cherishing the smoothness of her cheeks.

Both knew of the danger ahead, and as they held each other tightly, their throbbing hearts tricked their minds, hiding anxiety screaming to be extinguished.

"Damn it, I'll get this case thing out of way," Joe said, heading out the door. "Goodnight, darling?"

"Goodnight, Joe. I love you."

Halfway down the outer hallway he stopped and turned. "Does that mean you'll go skating with me again?"

A sentimental smile accompanied the dimple Joe treasured. "Anytime. I'll skate with you to the end of the world, Lieutenant Stacy."

"Even when I fall off?" he asked.

The sight of Gail's melancholy smile and welled up eyes would remain in Joe's mind forever. "Especially when you fall off," she whispered.

"That's the woman, mummy. Her hair is different, but that's her," little Sarah Goldfarb stated after number four was asked to step forward in the police line-up. Mrs. Ernst Grunds could change her hairstyle, but she could not hide her guilt-ridden face. Moreover, half-an-hour earlier, Sarah had also picked out Ernst Grunds as the man who drove the truck, and she had pointed out his hairstyle had also been changed.

"Sarah, I'm so proud of you," Mrs. Goldfarb said, hugging her daughter, before leaving to return home.

Sergeant Schmidt indicated he did not want to be anywhere near the line-up, but earlier Captain Glover had insisted he be present, saying, "Schmidt, we'll interview Mr. Grunds first. I've got a lot of questions I want to ask that bastard."

"You must be busy, I can handle it, Captain," Schmidt declared, fidgeting and exhibiting a deceitful smile.

"No, I'm not that busy. As a matter of fact, I'm looking forward to it. Get the son-of-a-bitch brought down!"

"But Captain, their lawyer is here," Schmidt said, trying anything to delay the proceedings. "They've hired the best from New York. A Mr. Karl Truppe."

Glover enjoyed toying with Schmidt. "A French lawyer, eh?"

"Er, no, he's not French! Truppe is an old German name.

Glover rubbed his hands together. "Excellent. Tell the affluent kraut prick he can talk to them when I'm finished."

Only a few people remaining on the force knew Captain Ray Glover to be an interrogator, but at one time, it was Glover's preeminent field of interest. As a detective and a detective sergeant he had been known as, "Get 'em Glover," the best damned examiner in the business. Now he was out from behind his desk and he looked forward to showing the Grunds' how to play football. They would be the ball, and Glover the kicker.

Stacy and Durnell were not at work that day. Knowing they were working on the code with Sawasy at Pete's home, the captain had told everyone he had given them a few days off. The head crime-lab technician had also been informed to tell everyone he had a cold, and was staying home. Sawasy had been briefed on the magnitude of secrecy required.

When Sawasy had first arrived, he'd suggested taking the disks over to Microsoft, but Joe wouldn't stand for it.

"This has got to remain on the inside, Terry. Right now, I'm suspecting everyone from my cleaner to the grocer. I think my cleaning lady's all right, but I'm not too certain about the grocer."

With tongue in cheek, Sawasy had replied, "Yeah, we've got to watch out for those supermarkets. All the soups and cereal have secret alphabets."

The painstaking job took eight hours before the group fully understood what the disks contained. Finally, when they did learn the complete story, the three police officers appeared most apprehensive. The disks were named Genesis because every letter and number was counted from the start of a sentence or paragraph. At times, the codes 'C2' or 'BC3' did not fit the structure of various sentences, but once again, Linda had come to their rescue. She'd heard their frustration while she baked cookies. Wiping the flour off her hands on her apron and joining the *intelligentsia*, she said, "'C2' probably means the start of the second line on the front cover of the magazine. ' BC3' means the third line on the back cover."

When Sawasy offered her a job at his laboratory, Linda just snickered, replying, "I'm just an uncomplicated and unpretentious housewife. Why would you need little ol' me?"

"Christ, from the look of it, we need a bunch of simple, modest, and humble housewives," Terry answered. "We could crack all the NSA, CIA, and FBI codes."

The next day at 1300 hours when Stacy's team met in the Chinese room off the main tunnel, Captain Glover felt particularly happy. After questioning Mr. and Mrs. Grunds for six solid hours, the couple had finally cracked, and fancy lawyer or not, bail had been denied.

"They've named four other couples who are involved, and we've picked them up. You're right, Joe, this thing does operate in cells. The only reason they knew the other names is because when air transport was delayed, their house got full and they had to find room elsewhere for the kids. At that point, a telephone voice told them where to take the youngsters. They used an old garage to transfer the children, and they have no idea who picked up the *packages* as they call them. We've checked the phone numbers and they're pay phones.

"But how did they know when kids were required?" Pete asked.

Glover threw a newspaper on the table. "Newspaper ads. That's how the Grunds knew to kidnap Sarah. I'll read this to you: *'Lost paws. A female German shepherd, aged six, answers to the name of Sarah. Call Mr. Widmann, 865-3467 at 9am only.'* That's the number of a pay phone, and when they called, they were given all the instructions needed. We have no idea who placed the ad. Whoever it was paid cash and left phoney names. I have a feeling it was either the Dreischners or Roltz. There's also no doubt these bastards have contacts working in the Social Services Family Matters Agency. All ads start with the words *lost paws*, and the contact person is either Mr. Widmann, or Mrs. Schauugh."

"More German names," Gebara offered.

Glover nodded. "Yeah, and obviously bogus. Believe me, these conniving pricks are smart. Before calling the Grunds or the others, they had already selected and studied their victims."

After picking up the paper and reading the circled ad, Joe asked, "Ray, what action have you personally taken on this?"

"Nothing yet. They've obviously shut their operation down here, but it would be interesting to see if the same type of ad is appearing in other cities. I'm just not certain how to tackle it."

"Why don't I subscribe to all newspapers in major cities with a population of two million or more?" Barker asked, reviewing the ad. "It would be a start. They all have overnight courier services."

Joe liked the idea. "Good, do that, but don't subscribe to them in your own name. Get Mah to give us the names of each store and restaurant owner above us, and let them subscribe. Have them sent to these business addresses and they can pass 'em to us here. Anything else, Ray?"

Glover's face imitated the brightness of the sun. "Yeah, two things," he said, throwing another newspaper on the table. "Have you read this headline in the noon edition?"

The print was large enough for all to read: *Sergeant Nabs Child Kidnappers! Seattle - Allied Press. Sergeant Nebe Schmidt of the Seattle Police Department has cracked a child-kidnapping ring. Apparently, the sergeant has been working on the case for six months, and through his leadership, ten people have been charged. While the unassuming sergeant refuses to talk about his amazing accomplishment, he did say, "We all do out bit, and sometimes we get a lucky strike."*

The article took up the whole front page and half of the second page, and as chuckles expanded around the table, Earl Mathieson said, "That son-of-a-bitch Schmidt is probably gonna get promoted if he keeps this up."

After the laughter died, Joe got down to business. "What's the other point, Ray?"

"I've moved Victorson away from Schmidt. The kid's clean and I don't want him being tarnished. The Grunds knew Schmidt; he'd *sampled* various kids they had held."

"They told you that?"

"They spilled their guts, so did the other two pairs. Are you ready for this? Bradford, from Internal Affairs also *savoured* various kids picked up by one of the other couples."

Joe cringed. "Christ, Bradford's involved? Who would have ever thought? He has a wife and three children. Does this change our plans for Schmidt?"

"Hell no," Glover said, smiling confidently. "I've put the two together."

All faces appeared amazed at the decision, including Stacy's. "What?"

"Schmidt's got a new partner, that's all. I figure since we're setting Schmidt up, we may as well look after Bradford at the same time."

When Green voiced, "Two blind mice," the rest chuckled quietly.

"I've got to hand it to you, Ray," Stacy declared, lighting up a smoke, "You're definitely not just another pretty face."

"Tell me about it," Mathieson quipped, his eyes glistening, but turning away from Glover's instant *inquisitive* look.

Joe switched his attention to Green. "Gwen, with a lot of help from the fairer sex, we've managed to crack their code."

"Who was she?" Gwen asked curiously.

"My wife, Linda," Pete answered proudly. "In some ways she's like you, Gwen. She says one day this country will have a female president."

Green snickered. "There's no doubt about it. Hey, maybe I should run?"

Mathieson intervened. "This country can never have a president that's barefoot, pregnant and in the kitchen?"

If looks could kill, Earl had met his end until Joe carried on and got the meeting on track. "We now know everything these bastards have done over the past year. They've robbed 21 banks, and kidnapped 112 adults and 52 kids. That, plus they've started five race riots and defaced Jewish synagogues and cemeteries from here to Mexico. They've moved 150 million dollars worth of heroin, 100 million dollars worth of cocaine, 42 million dollars worth of marijuana, and taken in 87 million in diamond heists. They also grabbed the reward from that 250 million rare coin heist, and they're making millions from prostitution."

Joe stopped for a moment running the fingers of his right hand back and forth across his forehead. "Also, they've made untold millions in ... the shipment of *body parts*."

Only faint haunting sounds from the tunnels entered the room for the next few seconds as nauseous expressions appeared on every face, except Pete's. The rest knew Joe had mentioned body parts at the last meeting, but did he mean these Nazis were conducting a human butcher shop operation?

Stacy didn't have to be asked - his facial cast said it all. "The parts are kept on ice and shipped by jet out of the Kraven Retreat. Doctors Kraven and Krause probably conduct the surgery, and when I visit, I'm going to find out."

Gwen looked like she wanted to throw up. "My God, are these people born or hatched?"

Indignation made Woollam share a disgusting look with the group. "They're not people, Gwen. They're the devil's offspring, and the sooner we *take care* of them, the better."

Stacy wasn't finished. "There's more. In the past year, they've recruited another 200 weirdoes to their cause. Now that's just in the West, God knows how many more they've enrolled in the rest of the country. Last night, the CBS Evening News reported on skinheads in our armed forces. In addition, the RCMP in Canada thought they had closed down two camps in the provinces of Alberta and Manitoba, and to their surprise, the camps started operating again in other regions of Canada. The Canadian Armed Forces have disbanded their Airborne Regiment because of certain *occurrences*, and..." Joe's voice rose. "...from reviewing the disks, we've discerned these local madmen are going to pull a major job in our area on 30 December, three days from now."

"What kind of a job?" Glover asked, shifting a foot. "Don't tell me they're going to be abducting more kids?"

"No, thank God," Joe said, expressing the same sadness etched on Glover's face. "A freighter called LaHoncha is arriving here on 30 December. Its main cargo is television sets but four-hundred-million dollars worth of foreign exchange bank notes from American banks in the Far East is in two half containers. It's not even guarded. The money is being transported this way to cloak the significance of the shipment. The minute the vessel arrives, the currency will be unloaded and conveyed to the mint in Denver. The Captain of the vessel doesn't even know he's carrying the cargo. He just thinks he has television sets and VCRs. No guards, nothin'."

Gwen whistled. "Four hundred million and no guards? Is Rhine Shipping involved?"

"You bet it is. Mrs. Dreischner did her job well. Dave, you take it from here."

As usual, Barker reviewed his notes. "From what I've learned, the two half containers carrying the money are on deck. The ship arrives sometime around 1700 hours. Normally, it wouldn't be unloaded until the following day, but in this case, Amalgamated Television Stores in Denver have asked that the two containers be shipped that same night. We don't know what time, but we do know the method of transportation. Without escorts of any kind, the containers will be moved directly to Denver by a single truck. As far as the driver is concerned, the containers are loaded with televisions and VCRs. Somewhere between here and Denver, the fiends are going to help themselves."

"You mean they think they are?" Mathieson voiced. "How are we going to handle this one? Do you have a plan, Joe?"

"Yeah, a simple idea we should discuss. They're going to make the grab in the area of the dockyard, not on the highway."

"How the hell did you find that out so soon?" Barker asked, scratching out information on his notepad.

"A little bird told me."

"Love those birds," Dave said, adding new notes.

The room emptied two hours later, after the group had decided on a plan of action.

Heavy rain bounced off the Kenworth truck's low profile conventional cab coupled to a special trailer the licensed operator positioned underneath Rhine Shipping's container crane at the dark waterfront.

The docks were quiet except for a crane operating in the area where the steamship LaHoncha lay berthed. Up top on the large freighter, the ship's officer-of-the-watch impatiently awaited the two crates being unloaded.

A deluge had been pounding the docks all evening, but at eleven-thirty that night, clouds delivered twice the punch.

The Kenworth's driver felt relaxed because he had arrived the previous day from Denver and for the first time in a month, he had stayed in a motel rather than sleep in the back of his cab. His stomach was full and at this time of night, he would travel above the speed limit. He was impatient to get home because every mile would take him closer to his loving wife and kids. The day after arriving back, he and his family would board a flight to Disneyland.

"You're lucky you dressed for this weather," the ship's officer yelled down as the driver snapped the two containers in place. "It's a hell of a lot warmer where we've just come from."

"I'll be heading to Disneyland soon, so this doesn't bother me!" the waving truck driver yelled, stepping into his warm cab out of the sheets of wind-blown driving rain.

Placing his 350 horsepower Cummins diesel engine in gear and turning up his favourite country music disk, the operator started slowly moving his cargo out of the dockyard, and was on his way.

I should apply for these special jobs more often, the driver thought, winding the rig further down the dock road. Jesus I was lucky to get this trip. A few more like this and I can buy Sally that new washing machine she wants. Oh well, at least I'm number two on the seniority list. I hope Josh's feeling better though. He'd looked forward to visiting the Pacific Northwest. How could our number one driver get a hernia when he doesn't lift anything? Only wrestlers get hernias. I wonder what kind of clothes Sally bought the kids. They're really going to enjoy Disneyland ... I did when my mom and dad took me. Was it really that long ago? Let me see, it was in...?

The driver's attention became sidetracked when a freight train started crossing in front of him, forcing him to stop.

"Jeez, just my luck," he murmured. Ten minutes earlier and I would have missed this train. Look at the size of the thing; I'll be here for half-an-hour. Why is it when I drive at this time of night, I always get the goddamned trains? Josh doesn't get 'em; it just seems to be me that ... What the hell ... where did this pickup come from? Christ, he's close; why isn't he behind me? If he thinks he's gonna beat me across the tracks when the arm lifts up he'd better think again.

After rolling his window down, the Kenworth's driver bellowed, "Hey, fella, what the hell do you think you're...?"

The two men in the pickup did not intend to beat the rig across the tracks, and the upset truck-driver never saw the silenced pistol or felt the two slugs punching holes in his face.

Before he proceeded to smash the large vehicle's electronic satellite tracking system, the killer jerked open the Kenworth's door, grabbed the driver's body and dumped it the back of the pickup below. The second man covered the dead driver with a large tarpaulin before climbing up into the Kenworth's cab.

It took fifteen minutes for the slow-moving train to clear the railway crossing. When it did, the semi still could not move because the traffic arms stayed down and four police cars with their lights on high beam blocked the route. Two other police cars screeched to a halt behind the pickup truck.

Sergeant Schmidt's voice blared loudly. "Get out of the trucks with your hands up!"

As the Kenworth's new driver disembarked, the operator of the pickup ground it into reverse gear and floored the vehicle attempting to ram it through the police cars behind. One blast from a shotgun smashed the pickup's rear window, splattering the driver's brains through the windshield. With its wheels still spinning recklessly, the truck turned ninety degrees to its right, almost turning over before slamming into a telephone pole.

Schmidt yelled, "Lie down! I said lie down on your stomach," but the man standing beside the rig wasn't listening. Pulling a silenced pistol from his belt, he fired two shots at the blinding police headlights before running up a nearby embankment. The killer's brief escape ended when a rifle bullet ripped out the back of his skull.

This time Sergeant Nebe Schmidt was far more cordial when the media arrived and ambulances appeared.

A reporter recognizing Schmidt rushed up to him, asking, "What's happened here, Sergeant?"

"Just a drug-dealer's nightmare!" Schmidt mouthed, grinning while walking toward the cameras. "We received a tip from the Hong Kong police, and we've just cleaned it up, that's all. These containers will remain locked until the feds arrive."

"Sergeant, whose body is that in the back of the pickup?"

Schmidt opened up his umbrella. "Unfortunately, the drug-runners killed the legitimate driver of the semi. We tried to take his killers into custody but they fired at us!"

"If you had this staked out, why didn't you stop them from killing him?" a reporter asked, shoving a microphone in front of Schmidt's kisser.

"It happened too fast! We were going to follow the rig to see where it led us, but these two came out of nowhere. I can't tell you anything else at this time, except your viewers can sleep easier, their Seattle Police Department is on the job. Right now, I'm heading over to the ship to await customs personnel. We'll be going over that vessel from bow to stern. This is my assistant, Detective Gary Bradford. He's the one who took out the pickup driver. I got the other guy."

As more police-cars pulled up, Schmidt and Bradford went over to take a closer look at the man who had jumped down from the Kenworth.

"Good shot, Smitty – right through the *pump*," Bradford said.

The guy lay on his stomach, but when the ambulance personnel placed him in a body bag, Schmidt turned white - he knew Albert Frick from Kravenhall very well.

What the hell have I done? Schmidt asked himself, trying to hide his panic from Bradford, who also turned pale and was sick to his stomach after recognizing Frick.

Glover limped over, furious at the fact that the two dead Nazis had killed the trucking firm's driver.

"Schmidt, this looks like a fucking blood bath! What the hell's been going on here?"

"Uh, we ... they fired at us, so we took them out. It happened so fast, I don't really know what happened. Captain, did you say the Hong Kong police tipped you off on this? Who ... who invited the media?"

"What media?" Glover asked, looking around. The television truck had disappeared just after Schmidt gave his statement.

"They were here a minute ago. Maybe I said too much?"

Glover remained in Schmidt's face. "Who the hell gave you permission to speak to the media, Sergeant? Did you call the fucking media again?"

Schmidt's coat absorbed the mixed perspiration and rain running down his cheeks. "No, no, I didn't. They, they, er, just showed up. What, what do you mean, *again*?"

"We've been told you called them to the Dreischners' house when it blew up. You weren't in charge of this operation, Schmidt, Sergeant Rumberg was. You and Bradford were supposed to wait in the rear as backup?"

Schmidt could not stop stuttering. "Captain, for ... for some reason, our ... our car ended up in the front."

Glover called Rumberg over. "Matt, you were in charge, why the hell did you allow Schmidt to speak to the media?"

Rumberg didn't have a raincoat and was soaked. Also, he wasn't in the mood for Glover's anger. "What did you want me to do, put a goddamned muzzle on him. It's a wonder the guy didn't open with a song and dance routine. He loves cameras."

"All right, all right. What happened?" Glover asked.

"I told Bradford to stay back, but the next minute their vehicle cut my guys off and Bradford was blasting away with a shotgun at the pickup. I wanted to take both of those bastards alive, but Rambo Schmidt here wasted the other guy."

A sad expression took over Glover's face. "That innocent driver paid with his life. Didn't you know the pickup was around?"

"No," Rumberg said, sadly shaking his head before glancing down at the ground and allowing his right shoe to scratch out a small six-inch trough between two puddles. "The assholes hid on the other side of that abandoned building over there. We got here before the ship docked, so they must have arrived ahead of us. I saw the half-ton at the last moment, but there was nothing we could do, Captain. They came out of there like a cat after a bird ... pulled up next to him and shot him in the head. These druggies don't fuck around, do they? All they had to do was tell the guy to get out."

Glover placed his hands in his raincoat's pockets and lowered his head. Sauntering away, he muttered, "No, unfortunately they certainly don't. I wonder if he had a family?"

At five-thirty that same morning, Sergeant Nebe Schmidt lay on his back snoring. During his drive home at three o'clock that morning, he'd angrily tuned in every radio station in town reporting the facts of his latest *accomplishment.* Callers to the number one all-night talk show had been heaping praise on him since midnight, and when Schmidt checked his telephone answering machine, seven talk-show hosts from across the nation had left urgent messages asking him to call.

After finishing off a half bottle of vodka, Schmidt's mind was in a state of total confusion when he finally went to bed. This was the second time he'd been caught in the middle. He wondered how it all happened. It wasn't a set up because Glover had given him shit. Also, who the hell had informed the media? They appeared out of nowhere, and had disappeared just as quickly.

A moment later Schmidt sat up straight. Even in his drunken state things were becoming much clearer. When the order to move in was first given, another car had held up Rumberg's boys. He and Bradford were there first because the rest had not moved right away. Who the hell was driving that other car?

Schmidt's memory raced and he soon had the answer. It was Glover, that's who it was, he thought. That fat fucker set me up. He also set me up at the Dreischners'. "This thing isn't over; Stacy's still pulling the strings," he mumbled. "Goddamnit, how could I be so fucking dumb?"

Briskly reaching for the phone by his bed, Schmidt suddenly had second thoughts and checked his watch while muttering, "I can't call Kravenhall at this hour ... it's too fucking late. I'll phone them in the morning at seven."

Sergeant Nebe Schmidt never had the chance to contact Doctor Kraven. The pounding rain outside his bedroom window drowned out the sounds of two intruders entering his house.

Sleeping soundly, Schmidt woke up for a split second to feel his shoulders being held down, and he probably observed a smiling mouthful of rotten teeth as his left arm was being raised. The sergeant also may have felt the jab of a needle puncturing his left armpit, and heard the words, "Fucking traitor," but nothing else.

The flag atop Seattle Police Department's building flew at half-mast when Chief Couling faced the army of reporters. Using one hand to hold the microphone while reading his notes, the chief sincerely expressed the sadness of all members on his force.

"Sergeant Schmidt was special and he'll be sorely missed," Couling stated. "He was a dedicated police officer, and a good friend to all who served with him.

"Nebe wasn't married; his family was here in this building. For over twenty-five years, he accepted the huge responsibilities I placed on him, and he diligently carried out those orders. Sadly, the pressure of last night's drug bust must have brought on the heart attack. All of us, along with the citizens of our fine city will grieve for a long time to come.

"Many will say we don't turn out police officers like Nebe Schmidt anymore, and perhaps that's true. We were fortunate to have a man like him serving with us. I know thousands of you will be joining us at his funeral. Thank you all for coming."

Chief Couling's assistant was waiting when the headman left the stage and returned to his office. "Chief, we've got a problem."

"What is it now?"

"Schmidt's house was loaded with pictures of naked little boys and girls. He also had over 400 videos of kids performing sexual acts. The guy was a raving paedophile."

Sighing in utter disbelief, the chief crossed his arms on his desk and laid his head on them. Looking up after a few seconds, he asked, "Who knows about this?"

"Just Captain Glover and Sergeant Rumberg. They discovered the room where Schmidt hid the stuff."

Couling picked up his phone and pushed a few buttons. "Ray, I've just heard about Schmidt's *secret* habits. We can't have that getting out. This guy was a hero in the minds of our citizens and civic officials. Is there any way we can...?" A smile appeared. "What's that? Great, thank you, I owe you one. Okay, okay, I owe you about twenty. Where will you burn the stuff? Wonderful, thanks a lot, Ray. Oh, and er, Ray ... what about Rumberg? Can you keep him quiet? Good, that lifts a load off my shoulders."

After hanging up the phone, Couling turned to his assistant. "Your lips are sealed. The material is being burned. Put Schmidt's picture up, but cancel the plaque I ordered for the hallway."

"You're a genius. How did you get these?" Joe asked Harvey in the room below the Chinese restaurant that same afternoon.

Harvey hesitated, showing no appreciation for Joe's praise of certain drawings laid out on the table.

"They're not complete, but they'll give you an idea of the layout of Kraven's Clinic. I was going to ask my contact in Israel for a satellite photo, but the wrong people in this country would probably learn about it. Let's just say we sketched these from a photo taken from a high flying plane. Are you certain you want to go in that place?"

"Yeah. There's no doubt it's the local headquarters for these monsters. Do I have a choice? If we want to get to the bottom of this thing, it's all I can do."

"It's going to be dangerous, Joe."

"I know, but I was lucky to get on their list. They limit their guests at this time of the year. Being a retired math professor with a German name may have helped. I've registered as Dr. Helmut Schumann, a nephew of Dr. Horst Schumann."

Harvey knew the name and he hated mention of it. "Horst Schumann? He was one of the butchers at Auschwitz?"

Joe became sombre. "I know, Harv. I've been reading up on that son-of-a-bitch Himmler ever since I read those Bellingham excerpts. Dr. Horst Schumann worked at Auschwitz experimenting on males. He figured subjecting human genital glands to x-rays, worked better than castration. His boss, Dr. Blankenburg didn't agree, suggesting instead that a six-minute surgical castration operation would be more reliable."

Stacy watched Cohen's face tighten. "Harv, I'm certain it was the only way I could get in. Schumann's nephew, Helmut, teaches mathematics at UCLA, and right now he's on a three month holiday in South America."

"What if they check you out? They'll want to see your university identification cards. What will you show them?"

Joe took an ID card out of his wallet. "A Chinese friend of mine has provided me with all the identification I'll need, as well as credit cards, etc. I don't think they'll check with UCLA."

Cohen took the card and made notes. "Don't be a fool, Joe. If there's the slightest suspicion, they'll check everything out. They'll do it anyway. I'll orchestrate that end of things and get all the details to you tomorrow. Memorize everything you can about your new identity and your profession. If you don't, you could end up with a bullet in your head and we'll never see you again. They're also going to check your fingerprints, so I've brought this little kit with me. Give me your right hand."

As Joe offered his fingers, he grinned saying, "Don't tell me you can also arrange my new name to go with my prints? My prints are already registered on the national file."

Cohen's seriousness didn't change. "It's my profession - leave it to me. I kind of like you the way you are ... out of the morgue."

Harvey's pleading look brought home the intense gravity of the situation and got Joe whispering, "Yeah, I guess you're right. Thanks."

After handing the cards back along with some alcohol and a paper towel so Stacy could clean off his fingers, Harvey changed the subject. "I see you've taken care of Schmidt. Nice fella, wasn't he?"

"Salt of the earth. We didn't do the deed, his so-called friends did. When the chief said his kind doesn't come along too often, I thought to myself, thank Christ."

"What plans have you got for Bradford?" Cohen asked, his smile widening.

"We thought they'd look after him as well, but two would be a little questionable. We'll take care of Detective Bradford, but you know Harv, there are probably a lot more in the system. God willing, that's what I hope to find out at Kraven's Retreat. There has to be a list of some sort."

Harvey extended his right hand. "I wish I was going with you."

Joe accepted the handshake. "So do I, buddy. Thanks for everything."

Chapter 9

The man in front of Joe complained he would have preferred to take his own car to the Kraven Retreat, and the young blond and impeccably dressed woman holding a clipboard was most sympathetic. "You're not alone, Mr. Brack," she said, showing the whitest of teeth with her beautiful smile. "Many of our patients have shared the same concern, and Doctor Kraven is reviewing the clinic's policy. Until he makes changes, everyone must travel by bus. I think you'll enjoy the ride. We've got sandwiches and refreshments on board."

Brack nodded, accepting her explanation. "Thank you. Dr. Kraven's a wonderful man."

"So true, Mr. Brack. Here's your Kravenhall Identification. Just wear it around your neck. Please board the first bus, and have a wonderful time."

Joe was next in line. "Helmut Schumann," he said to the *receptionist*.

"Thank you," the pretty woman replied, checking her list. "Ah yes, Dr. Schumann. This is your first visit to Kravenhall, isn't it?"

"Yes. It was highly recommended," Joe said, noticing her *ring*.

While the attendant made further notes on her clipboard, the detective casually glanced at his travelling companions. All of them wore similar rings - a wolf with the SS bars.

"Is your luggage on board?" the smiling representative asked, after finding Joe's nametag.

"Yes, it is.”

"Good, then you can board. Here's your Kravenhall identification. Just wear it around your neck at all times. Have a wonderful stay at Kravenhall."

About twenty casually dressed men had already boarded the bus before Joe climbed the vehicle's steps. Most were middle aged or beyond, and he found it odd there were no women. Some passengers knew each other, and the ones that didn't soon came around and introduced themselves.

After a few people asked who he was, Joe selected a window seat halfway up the aisle of the chartered motor coach. He wasn't alone long. A fat, bald-headed man about fifty, wearing a loud pink and yellow sports shirt sat next to him. Waving his identification tag in Stacy's face, the man said, "I'm Rodney Friesen, from the legal firm of Friesen and Friesen."

Joe smiled and nodded before returning his eyes to the window.

Friesen's fat fingers fumbled around in his shirt pocket. "You must have heard of our legal firm - the vice-president is a client. Here, take my card."

Stacy accepted the business card but didn't respond as the man leaned forward straining to read Joe's tag. "You're ... Dr. Schumann, from Los Angeles.

Are you a surgeon, Dr. Schumann? I've got this back problem; had if for twenty years, and…"

Smiling, Joe interrupted the sweating man. "No, I specialize in mathematics. Uh, the vice-president of what firm?"

The man appeared puzzled at first. "What? What firm? Why the Vice-President of the United States, of course. Oh, that was probably a joke, right Schumann? Ha, ha, good, very good indeed. I'll mention that to the vice-president when I see him. He visits me often. What firm? Ha, ha. You're a riot, Schumann. I'm going to remember that one."

Joe faced the window and raised his eyes to the ceiling for a moment, thinking, Christ, why is it when I travel, all the assholes in the world join me? This braggart's thunderous laugh probably collected the attention of half the passengers. That, plus the fact spittle from the *jerk's* guffaw nailed my face and upper body.

"How come all you academics have hair down to your shoulders?" Friesen asked, chewing a salmon sandwich and bringing his perspiring face inches from Joe's.

"A good question. We're probably all holdovers from the hippie era. Why are you going to the Kraven Clinic, Mr. Friesen?" Joe asked, changing the subject after noticing the man's vile breath.

Once again, Friesen appeared puzzled. Winking, he replied, "For a rest, Schumann, for a rest, if you know what I mean?" Then the man grabbed Joe's left arm and whispered, "Does your wife know you're going to Kravenhall? Mine doesn't, she thinks I'm in Dallas on business. Ha, ha. I'll be in Dallas, all right. Dallas is quite the broad."

"Er, I'm not married," Joe murmured, wanting to grin and hammer his stout travelling companion's nose.

Friesen nudged Joe's arm. "Oh, you're one of those. Well, you'll still have a great time, all your kind does. You'll also have a fine selection to choose from at Kravenhall, won't you, Schumann?"

"My kind?" Stacy asked, trying hard to keep the man's sweating bulk with its gnawing mouth in its own seat-space.

Friesen winked and nudged Joe again. "I wouldn't mind switching myself once in a while, but it's not good for our company's image. Know what I mean, Schumann? I'm more open-minded than a lot of people though. What goes on between two people in private is between them and them alone. Right Schumann?"

Nodding without reason, Joe couldn't believe this individual. It was time to put Mr. *Halitosis* in his place. "Now you're getting it, Friesen. I like hearing that. Not just two people, four or even six. I might just knock on your bedroom door when we need a seventh. It's rare when *my kind* meet tolerant people like you. Such understanding is hard to come by these days."

The fright on Friesen's face brought a grain of satisfaction to Joe as he turned his head to gaze out the window. Friesen never said another word to Joe during the trip. Even when the girl who welcomed them came around offering refreshments and more sandwiches, Friesen kept his distance. Squeezing into the aisle arm of his sear, the man whispered his order.

Stacy found the trip long and tedious. Twice during the journey, he had to push Friesen's sweating snoring head away from his shoulder. To occupy himself, when he asked the girl to bring him an interesting magazine, she brought him a copy of *North-Western Geology.*

As the buses turned off the main highway, those sleeping woke up to the driver's announcement. "Gentlemen, we'll be arriving at Kravenhall in a few minutes. Thank you for allowing Custom Road Services this opportunity to be of service. As soon as we stop at Kravenhall, I'll unload your luggage, and it will be taken to your room or suite while you're attending the reception."

Joe's seat *buddy* came to life after the announcement. Squirting a breath spray into his mouth and talking to an older man across the aisle, he said, "I hope Dallas is still here. What a broad. Man oh man, what a great broad."

Guards weren't present at the two checkpoints, but Joe wouldn't have noticed the difference. Instead, four gorgeous smiling girls in their middle twenties formed the welcoming committee. Wearing tight tennis outfits, the giggling young ladies jumped and yelled, allowing their bouncing breasts to convey their message. "Welcome to Kravenhall!" they yelled excitedly.

Some of the men on the bus made appreciative comments, particularly Friesen as he continued his conversation with the man across the aisle. After standing up and fluttering his arms out the opposite window, he nudged his new *sucker.* "There's Dallas! There she is. Oh, this is going to be a wonderful time - right Leska? In the summer they wear bikinis, but not for long. Ha, haaa! I'll be in Dallas all right."

At the entranceway to the grand hall, the same stunning young woman that accompanied them now stood ticking off names and presenting each disembarking passenger with an envelope.

Upon receiving his envelope, Stacy viewed the thick black gothic letters forming the name Dr. Helmut Schumann - Room 23. Scanning the area, he also noticed another doorway down on ground level to the left of impressive main doors. A sign above it read: Sanatorium Admission Room.

"This envelope contains your room key and your program. Welcome to Kravenhall, Dr. Schumann. Enjoy, enjoy. Next, please."

The detective couldn't believe the opulence of the place. A sixteen-piece string orchestra played softy as servants in starched white uniforms walked around serving refreshments and food from sparkling sterling silver trays. Upon receiving orders, the domestics presented their instructions to any one of six immaculately attired bartenders attending two large portable bars straddling the space between two massive staircases. The bars dispensed every brand of liquor available, including the finest champagnes.

The delectable selection of food spread out on highly polished mahogany tables was beyond Joe's imagination. He was so hungry he didn't know where to start.

Two expensively dressed couples formed a receiving line to the right of the main doors, and cheerfully introduced themselves when Joe shook their offered hands.

"Welcome Doctor Schumann. I'm Dr. Kraven and this is my wife, Inga. So nice of you to join us. This is your first stay here, isn't it?"

"It certainly is, sir, and I'm immensely looking forward to a good rest. What a beautiful building."

His hosts smiled proudly before Inga Kraven replied, "Thank you, we love it too. Our life's work has gone into building Kravenhall. I feel certain you'll have a wonderful relaxing time here, Dr. Schumann. Enjoy your stay. If there's anything we can do to make your visit with us more comfortable, please let us know."

Just before Joe moved on, Dr. Kraven said, "We normally don't allow first-time guests here at this time of year, but your name intrigued us. I've read that you are related to the late Dr. Horst Schumann?"

Stacy was uncertain what to reply. "Yes, although I'm not familiar with my uncle's side of the family."

Kraven's eyes remained smiling but turned cold. "What? Are you saying you haven't acquainted yourself with the brilliance of your late uncle's work? He was a genius, Schumann."

Joe smiled knowingly, thinking, I know what the bastard did in the concentration camps. His work probably qualified him for a job with the devil.

"Not exactly, Dr. Kraven. I am thoroughly familiar with that period of his life. Aren't we all? I meant I'm not well versed with his complete family tree. When it comes to his accomplishments, he was indeed an ingenious man."

Kraven didn't say anything else, but Joe saw the doctor's astute wink. His host's eyes suddenly gleamed and a small refined smile graced his pompously nodding face.

Moments later, Joe shook the extended hands of Dr. Heinz Krause and his wife, Marlene.

Krause peered inquisitively at Joe's nametag. "Ah, another fellow of the college. What do you specialize in, Schumann?"

Humbly, Joe replied, "No, sir, I'm simply a retired math professor, here for a much needed rest. It is an honour meeting you and Dr. Kraven and your lovely ladies. I've read much about your fine achievements, Dr. Krause, and now that I've actually met you, I feel exhilarated."

Joe speculated he had said the right words, but he wasn't certain until he felt Krause place a hand on his left shoulder. "Thank you my accomplished friend. While you're here, I'll personally give you a tour of our surgical facilities. A worthy colleague, Chris Berndt in South Africa influenced Dr. Kraven and I. We are modestly overjoyed that we have the opportunity to broaden his magnificent pioneering work in heart research. Where were you born here or in Germany?"

"In the United States."

Krause's eyes smothered Stacy. "Obviously from excellent stock. Helmut, if I may, I'd like to share with you my views on racial unrest in this country. Would you find that particular subject of any interest?"

"Definitely, Dr. Krause. Other than having a good rest, that's why I'm here."

"Superb, Schumann. We'll meet in a day or so. No, we'll talk tomorrow."

Mrs. Krause smiled kindly. "If you require anything, absolutely anything, just make your needs known. How nice it is to meet you, Dr. Schumann."

As Joe moved away, forty guests remained in the receiving line that now extended through the giant doors.

Although Stacy's thick eyeglasses were just normal glass, he would have dearly loved to take them off as he wandered through the swelling affluent fraternity of lunatic Nazis.

"I'm in a room full of them," he murmured. "Where's a hand grenade when I need one?"

"What would you like to drink, sir?" a servant asked.

"Er, do you have any single malt scotch?"

"Yes, sir, we have seven of them. From which area of the highlands do you favour your scotch?"

"Seven? Er, any one will do. On the rocks, please."

When he received his scotch, Joe helped himself to food from the magnificent spread that was replenished as soon as it *disappeared.*

A fellow filling his plate next to Joe, said, "Delightful, isn't it? How long have you been a member?"

Although Stacy was well prepared for this trip, he had to control himself from not acting too surprised. There, standing in the flesh next to him was

Senator Robert Eugene Millington the Third, Chairman of the Defence Spending Committee. Joe wondered what this chubby asshole with the grey John F. Kennedy haircut was asking him. Member? A member of what?

"I'm Gene Millington," the man said, holding out his free hand."

"I recognize you, Senator," Stacy said, accepting the handshake. "Helmut Schumann, from Los Angeles. No, this is my first visit, but I'm certain it's not going to be my last. Have you been here many times before?"

The senator acknowledged a passing acquaintance before returning his attention to Joe. "I come here often when my batteries need recharging. You know what I mean, don't you, Schumann?" Not waiting for a response, he added, "Are you taking in Dr. Krause's address tomorrow?"

"I haven't had a chance to review my program yet. What's his topic?"

Still stuffing his face, Millington held the china plate a few inches under his chin. "Something that should interest you. The genetic differences between the various races. I feel certain you and your medical colleagues have considered the theoretical proposition that abnormalities of some sort do exist in, shall we say, non-whites?"

What a pompous prick, Joe thought. Here we have a United States senator filling his stomach, unemotionally condemning human beings not of the Nordic race.

"Theoretical? I believe we've far surpassed that stage, senator. I'm a mathematician, not a medical doctor, but the differences incomparably exceed the hypothetical level, don't you agree?"

Millington's eyes widened and he stopped chewing. He obviously liked what he heard. After swallowing, he said, "Yes, quite right, Dr. Schumann. You must pardon me, I assumed you were a member of the medical profession. It is our duty to convince the world that this appalling dilemma exists. The *Himmler Stratagem* spells out the answers for us, and, er, we must proceed with it, mustn't we?"

"The Himmler Stratagem?" Joe asked.

"Oh, I forgot, you're new, aren't you? I propose you sit down with Dr. Krause after he speaks. We've waited long enough for the right moment, Schumann. We must do something about this quandary before it gets out of hand again. And it is getting out of hand."

"I agree. Thank you for mentioning it, Senator, I'll make certain I attend."

Millington turned to *work* the crowd, but he stopped, returning his attention to Joe for a moment. "I'm in suite thirty six. Our organization needs people like you, Schumann. Nice talking to you."

I'll bet you bastards do, Joe thought, grinning knowingly. Himmler Stratagem, eh? What the hell is that all about? I wonder if it's got something to do with those Bellingham excerpts about Himmler

"I'm certain we'll meet up again, Senator. It has indeed been an honour meeting you."

Just as Millington strolled away to pump more hands, every nerve in Joe's body came alive. There was something familiar with the man coming down the stairs. Christ, it's Krupp, Joe thought. What if he sees me? This guy's more observant than Kraven or Krause - he's bound to recognize me. Look at the way he struts. Jesus, what cold eyes. Stay away from him Stacy. Just keep your back to him and all will be fine.

Dressed impeccably and not wearing identification, Hans Krupp stood out as an icon of arrogance and stayed to himself in the throng. Keeping his hands behind his back and maintaining a chin-up stance, Krupp stood at the edge of discussions, listening, not missing a thing, but at the same time appearing totally unconcerned. These were his kind of people so why would he be on his guard, Joe thought, watching Krupp now talking with Senator Millington. Moving away, he knew Krupp was the kind who never let his guard down.

Over the next hour, additional beautiful girls entered the room. All wore tight tennis outfits that displayed their gorgeous figures for everyone to see. There appeared to be a steady influx of well-built shaven headed young men as well, wearing tight-fitting white pants, tight white shirts and dazzling white tennis shoes. The girls paid no attention to the young men, and for that matter, nor did the young men to the girls. Rather, the women attached themselves to certain guests, as did the men. He saw his old travelling *companion* Friesen with a girl on each arm, and even Senator Millington had two beauties. Fascinating, Stacy thought, watching Friesen out of the corners of his eyes. The man was pointing him out to a skinhead, who instantly came over.

"Dr. Schumann, I'm Franz, and I'm here to serve your needs."

"I'll have a single-malt scotch, Franz. Thank you."

The young man smiled. "No, I think you misunderstood me, Doctor. Do you find me attractive?"

Every muscle in Joe's body tightened and he wanted to slam the guy. This immaculate young body builder was putting the make on him. "Uh, Franz, did Mr. Friesen send you over to me?"

"Yes, sir."

"How did you find his breath?"

Franz looked a little puzzled. He wasn't here to pass judgement on the guests, and Joe noticed his confusion.

"Franz, I travelled with him on the bus. He kept breathing on me, so I fed him the wrong facts. You understand what I mean, don't you?"

The young man knew exactly what Joe meant. Shyly grinning, he said, "I understand completely, sir. Should I send over...?"

"No, not today, I'm far too tired for female companionship tonight. Thank you for your consideration though, most appreciated. Is one of those girls with Friesen, named Dallas?"

"Yes, sir."

"I figured as much. Thank you, Franz."

As a disheartened Franz strolled away looking for a *partner*, the orchestra stopped playing and Stacy heard the sounds of a glockenspiel. Immediately, the guests formed a large circle around Dr. Xavier Kraven, and Joe Stacy found himself facing inwards from the outside of that loop.

"Good friends, my wife and I have already welcomed you to Kravenhall; let me welcome you again. I feel certain all of you are a little weary from your trip and you wish to freshen up. As you know, the indoor and outdoor pools are available, as are all amenities here at Kravenhall.

"Dinner tonight will be served at 1900 hours in the President Lincoln Dining Room. Those of you wishing to dine with us this evening will inform the headwaiter by 1700 hours. If you desire to eat in your suites or rooms, simply pick up your telephones. Naturally, this lower bar will remain open until midnight.

"We have some excellent after dinner entertainment planned for you in the President Jefferson Theatre. But why am I telling you this? Please read your programs.

"I must give you the normal precaution. The wall is to protect you from stepping out onto our airport. If you walk the grounds, please do not go near it.

"We are expecting some special guests for dinner, and if they're up to it, they'll be joining us later. Also, we are absolutely thrilled that Senators Millington, Strobe, Garner, Smith, and Bouhler are here with us today."

Applause filled the room but Joe didn't join in.

"We also welcome Congressmen George Miller and Steven Gilbert. All of you know our most noted southern governor, Governor George Walters, and his friend Reverend Jerry Frolich. Did I miss someone? Oh, yes, welcome Matt Robinson. Matthew, we appreciate your television addresses on behalf of our movement. Well done, Matt!"

Once again, praise swept the room and even Krupp clapped, reluctantly.

"So, my friends, if you hear the sounds of jets, you'll know our distinguished dinner guests are arriving. Relax and enjoy yourselves here at

Kravenhall. If you need anything, and you know I mean *anything*, just mention it to a member of our staff. Thank you and relish the luxury of Kravenhall."

During the final round of approval, Joe asked himself who the distinguished guests must be. With five senators, two congressmen and a governor around, who else was more important?

Just as the circle broke up and Stacy turned to get another drink, his heart stopped, his eyes widened, and for a brief moment, his mouth remained open. Standing directly in front of him inches away was an unsmiling Hans Krupp - his wild eyes curiously scanning Stacy's face.

"I'm terribly sorry," Joe said, apologetically. "I must watch where I'm going."

"It was my fault ... Dr. Schumann," Krupp replied, maintaining an inquiring look while reading Joe's nametag. "Dr. Schumann? You're not one of us. Have we met before?"

Stacy had to think fast. He had let his guard down and he knew one could not afford to do that with these *people*, particularly Krupp. Looking unconcerned, he said, "And you are...?"

A hand shot forward as heels clicked together. "Forgive me, I'm Hans Krupp."

"Where is your identification, Krupp?"

Robotically, Krupp placed his right hand on the left side of his chest. "I must have left it in my suite. I have the feeling we've met before, Dr. Schumann. Is that possible?"

Joe ensured his eyes never left Krupp's as he thought, not before now, you prick, but I remember seeing you in the hotel's restaurant. "I'm a retired mathematician, Mr. Krupp. Perhaps you've seen me on The Learning Channel defining my theory."

Krupp relaxed slightly. "Theory? What theory is that, Doctor?"

Christ, that's all I need, Joe thought. "That light does not travel in a straight line."

Krupp appeared brazenly puzzled. "That's common knowledge, Doctor. Everyone knows it curves. Surely, you don't think...?"

It was time to try the bullshit baffles brains part. "No, Krupp, I mean light oscillates. You've heard of the unified field theory of E equals MC squared. Well, I believe it to be wrong. You see we measure light particles in rectilinear proportions that Einstein recommended. We should measure its mass, not its length. Don't you agree? I believe objects in space are much closer than we think."

Krupp grinned slyly. "Interesting. So, Schumann, you believe the Jew Einstein was overrated?"

"Perhaps, I haven't made up my mind."

"Are you aware that Professor Wilhelm Mueller of the Technical College of Aschen wrote in his book, *Jewry and Science* that Einstein was part of a world-wide Jewish plot to pollute science and destroy civilization?"

"Yes, I've read it. I'm pleased you show an interest in mathematics. Would you like me to explain my...?

Krupp indicated he was not in the mood for Joe's hypothesis. "No, Doctor, my interests lie elsewhere. How long are you staying?"

"A week. Listen, what was your name again?"

Krupp's heels came together again. "Hans Krupp."

"Hans, if you will give me five hours of your time, I'll take you through a guided tour of the mathematically unique universe. You won't believe the wonders we are..."

Krupp abruptly clicked his heels and began turning away. "Impossible, Herr Doctor, I'm leaving tomorrow. Perhaps we'll talk about it at dinner. It was nice meeting you, Dr. Schumann."

Joe's eyes followed the man's back walking away to join Senator Millington. "A pleasure, Mr. Krupp. I'll look forward to our chat."

For the first time since putting it on, Stacy thought well of his wig. While talking with the Nazi, it had soaked it up all the perspiration.

Proud of himself for playing the part well, Joe asked the same waiter for another scotch.

As the crowd thinned, the detective found himself climbing the imposing red-carpeted staircase. On the upstairs landing, a numbered sign read: *1-38 left, 39-64 right.* Joe turned left heading along the hallway until he found his room.

After closing the door behind him, Joe could not believe the luxury of his lodgings. He had entered a beautifully furnished spacious room with a king-size bed. The person who had lit the small fireplace had also placed four presto logs in a brass bucket lying to the right side of the hearth. Above the fire, a highlight had been turned on divulging the superb artistry of a painting of President John F. Kennedy.

Sitting in one of two velvet-covered chairs in front of the fire, Stacy turned his neck and reviewed his room. The paintings on the walls were originals, as were the various ornaments sitting on the mantelpiece, polished tables and television set.

Getting up to gaze out the large window, he found his room overlooked the estate's greenhouses at the back of the building, and in the distance, he could see a small lake. His locked briefcase had been placed next to a writing desk, and he knew it had not been opened. The writing paper on the desk read: John

F. Kennedy Room - Kravenhall. Even the letter opener was inscribed with the late president's name.

Stacy shook his head thinking these bastards actually convince their members that this is an honourable American organization. All the goddamned suites and rooms are named after American presidents and heroes.

The objects Joe could not see were his bags. Walking into a huge closet, he found they had been unpacked. His clothes had been neatly hung up on hangers, with his ties uniformly suspending from a tie-rack. His spare shoes stood on shoe stands at the bottom right side of the clothes room.

Opening three drawers of the dresser, he noticed all his sweaters, shirts, socks, and underwear had been tidily arranged. Other drawers contained formal, lounging and tennis clothes of his size, provided by Kravenhall.

Notably impressed, but suspicious, Joe asked himself what they would place in here that he wouldn't appreciate. Microphones? Definitely, along with cameras. Yeah, the sneaky bastards have probably planted a few of them. Should he search for them? Nah, they weren't worth the bother, but he must remember they were here, somewhere.

The bathroom was also large, with an oval shaped bathtub built into the floor. Shelving forming part of the walls contained four swim suits, sparkling white towels, bathrobes, paper throwaway slippers, gels, shampoos, aftershaves, razors, and various sweet-smelling soaps. Stacy knew one thing; the mirror in the bathroom faced his bedroom wall so there were no cameras behind that. A further thorough inspection of the bathroom revealed nothing.

Upon checking his pocket watch, which read five o'clock, Joe wondered if he should have dinner in his room, or attend the meal with the bigwigs. He decided to attend dinner. It would be interesting to see the special guests. Uncertain of what he should do in the interim, he decided go for a swim. But what about his wig? They said it was waterproof, but would it stay on? Grinning, he thought, I'll tell them my eyes can't take chlorine and ask for a pair of goggles. At least the moustache is waterproof. "Stacy, you're absolutely brilliant," he murmured, before he checked the map enclosed with his key and itinerary. "I hope you don't get your throat cut."

Dressed in a swimsuit, a bathrobe, and wearing a pair of brown paper slippers, Joe finally found the busy pool, and upon entering, he had to do a double take. Most guests using the pool wore bathing suits, but not their escorts. The young women and skinheads he had seen earlier in the grand hall frolicked naked with the newly arrived guests. Friesen from the bus had taken off his swimming trunks, and Dallas sat on his shoulders, while another girl rested in his arms.

Immediately, Friesen noticed him. "Ah, Schumann, do you see what your kind misses?"

"It certainly beats the City of Dallas, doesn't it Friesen?" Joe replied, taking off his glasses after obtaining a pair of goggles from a nearby attendant. Placing them over his *hairpiece* like a headband, Joe entered the water and started swimming. The warm water felt wonderful and the subsurface view was just as fascinating as that above the surface.

It was after his third length that Joe noticed the momentary flicker of light originating from behind the mirrored wall below the diving board. Well, well, well, we're being viewed and someone has just lit up a smoke. So, the dirty bastards are voyeurs as well. Who would have guessed it?

In the well-furnished suite below, Inga Kraven poured herself a drink and after passing one to her husband, asked, "Isn't that the new fellow, Dr. Schumann?"

Both sat on comfy soft leather chairs at eye-level to the lower torsos of the swimmers, while another man with a camera sat filming the fun *next door.*

Kraven seemed far more interested watching his staff cavorting than exchanging small talk with his wife. "Yes, you met him when he entered. Seems like a good fellow."

"Xavier, aren't you taking a bit of a chance allowing him here? You've never done that before at this time of year. Why now?"

"His name intrigued me, my dear. If he is a relative of Dr. Horst Schumann, it is indeed our honour. If he isn't, he won't leave here alive. We're checking up on him now."

When Inga smiled, her eyes and lips revealed her excitement with the nearby bareness of the young male and female swimmers.

The goggles allowed Joe to enjoy the sights as well. Senator Millington's frolicking head might have been above water, but his hands weren't. In the corner of the pool by the deep end ladder, Millington's right hand gyrated between the thighs of a beautiful girl in her twenties, while his left hand massaged the genitals of a squirming skinhead who in turn massaged the senator's penis and rubbed the girl's breasts. Above the water, all three expressed their gleeful gratitude to each other.

Below, Kraven calmly turned to the cameraman. "Are you getting all of this?"

"Yes, Herr Doctor, everything," the man replied, not missing a beat when the senator brought his head below water, placing his face between the girl's legs.

Half an hour later, Joe found the masseurs and allowed his body to receive an excellent rubdown by Gretta. Twice he attempted to converse with the burly blonde woman, but she made it plain she only spoke German, as did her male companion.

Joe Stacy thought the Queen of England could not have arranged a finer dinner than the one served in the President Lincoln dining room that evening; nor could her attendants have designed the superlative layout of the table setting.

As all guests stood behind their chairs waiting for Kraven, Krause and other head-table guests to arrive, Stacy noticed not one piece of solid sterling silver cutlery, or gold, silver and crystal tableware service was out of line. Even the napkins, flower holders, and bouquets were pointed in one direction on the dazzling white tablecloths. Whoever had set the tables formed in the letter 'E' had even measured the space between chairs, and their distance from each table. Impeccably dressed shaven-headed stewards wearing white clothing, and white cotton gloves, stood slightly behind and in the middle of every two guests. As well, similarly dressed stewards stood stiffly behind every chair at the head table.

At exactly 1900 hours, members of the head table arrived and after Reverend Frolich offered a short prayer, they took their seats, followed by everyone else.

Straining his eyes while looking through his coke-bottle glasses, Joe Stacy's throat dried up. Three guests had flown in all right and they joined the five senators, two congressmen, Governor Walters, Reverend Frolich, and Matt Robinson at the head table. The distinguished looking man sitting between Dr. and Mrs. Kraven was none other than the Vice-President of the United States.

Joe didn't recognize the second person, an affluent-looking man sitting between Mrs. Kraven and Governor Walters, but he did recognize the Chief Justice of the Supreme Court sitting between Dr. and Mrs. Krause. Not surprisingly, all three *guests* wore rings.

Perhaps Stacy stared a little longer than he should have, he didn't know. He wondered just who the hell was not on their payroll? If the vice-president was one of them, what about President Aird?

For some reason Krupp did not attend the dinner, and during the delicious six-course meal served with four delightful wines, Joe listened with interest to those around him. All were wealthy and the men appeared to come from every state in the union.

"This country cannot prevail until we send all Africans, Asians and non-whites back where they belong," a middle-aged, balding, flabby man declared, forcing an overloaded fork into his mouth.

"What if they won't go?" an affluent-looking man asked, running his right hand through his full head of white hair.

"Then we must dispatch them. You know what I mean? Then they will go!"

"And the Jews?"

"Back to Israel naturally. We can isolate them there until another solution is found. We require that total area for its mineral wealth. We must do the same with the other countries. Look at what our glorious leader did in Poland. If we arrange individual homelands as airtight ghettos, afterwards we can clean them up. Disease will complete half the job for us."

"The United States forms the fortification for the white race. Our white citizens are the majority and they will be with us one hundred percent."

"Is our timetable being met?"

"Slowly, but more gun legislation and other laws in our favour are required. We must eliminate armed resistance. And I mean completely. I hear rumours we have one thousand training camps, and as you know we've fully infiltrated the armed forces."

"But Jewish legislators and bleeding-heart Liberals are forcing racial integration in our armed forces. Such action must be restrained."

"It is. As we speak, it's being curtailed. Don't forget we're keeping the niggers in their place. Niggers are like children - they're so easy to control. Even the few educated ones continue to speak southern jive talk, er, slave talk. Can you believe that? We've actually got them believing it's their God-given right to communicate like fucking idiots. Furthermore, if we sustain the race riots, the pure blooded people of our country will eventually get fed up and demand action."

"We're on the right track, and this time we have the money, and lots of it!"

"Isn't it humorous? The money we're using is really Jewish money, taken from them during the war. And we're going to use it to *accommodate* them again. How absolutely ingenuous."

"Ha, it's ironic. The kikes think they're going to get their money back from the Swiss bankers. They'll only get a pittance because we *are* the bankers."

"It'll be returned to them all right ... one percent in cash, and ninety-nine percent in *other* ways. Gentlemen, it's thoroughly remarkable that Jewish money will be used to rid the world of the undesired."

Joe Stacy could not listen to anymore, but he couldn't leave the table. These individuals, or whatever they were, were walking talking pieces of maggot shit, he thought. They're not human beings. Every one of them is insane.

For the next hour or so, Joe kept a low profile and although he clapped with the rest, inwardly, he wanted to *harm* each of them.

After the two women retired, Cuban cigars and fine liquors were served, and Kraven stood, tapping a glass with one of his sterling silver spoons.

"My friends, I promised you special guests, and once again I've delivered. You all know Vice-President MacPherson, and Chief Justice Bell."

Both men stood to tumultuous applause, and then sat down again.

"And of course, no introduction is necessary for our glorious leader in the United States, Mr. Dieter Krueger."

Joe strained his eyes to get a good look at Krueger. As a standing ovation rose from the guests, the heavy-set, elderly, grey-haired man remained standing, waiting for it to die down before he gave his speech.

"Doctor Kraven, Mr. Vice-President, honoured guests. Thank you, gentlemen, for your most gracious welcome. It warms my heart to be here with you tonight."

What fucking heart do you have? Joe asked himself. Like the rest of these bastards, iced sewer water runs through your veins, mister.

"Before getting down to business, I want all of you to remember the term, *Plan-Z*. I feel certain you have heard the expression before, a long time ago perhaps, and you've probably forgotten what it means. Plan-Z was the codeword our glorious leader Adolf Hitler used to rearm Germany under the world's ever-watchful eyes after the Treaty of Versailles was signed. Well, that term is also our organization's battle cry in this impure world. It is the order for our cells to emerge, unite, and begin the revolution so long overdue. Please remember the term, gentlemen. When you hear a national figure demanding the implementation of Plan-Z, it means our time has finally come."

Joe joined in the thunderous applause and stood for a standing toast to Plan-Z before Krueger's hands asked for quiet. "Thank you my friends ... thank you. Now, I understand we have a relative of Dr. Horst Schumann here with us. Would you please stand up, Helmut, so everyone can see you?"

This is all I need, Stacy thought, smiling, standing, and looking eager to please.

Krueger walked over from the head table, looked Joe admiringly in the eyes, shook his right hand, and hugged him. After Krueger returned to his position and the hand clapping subsided, Joe sat down again, saying, "Thank you, thank you very much."

"I had the opportunity of meeting your uncle several times. He was a medical genius. Reichsfuehrer Himmler also thought well of him. To this day, your uncle's medical experiments are acclaimed around the world. Many still say he was a cruel man, but we know that to be entirely false. He once told me about an eight year old Jew boy he was *working on*. During the 'experiment,' the boy asked if his cat, Liebling, which he had left behind would be all right. So you see the Jew wasn't suffering. If he could think of his cat during the operation, the research must have been painless. In this case, I can assure you, the cat outlived the boy."

Krueger beamed to whistles and applause.

"It amazes me that mankind's knowledge of medicine is held back due to the vacillating rationalization of today's medical doctors. Conducting research on rats, rabbits, mice and dogs is a slow process, and your uncle brought this to Reichsfuehrer Himmler's attention. If we are to solve humanity's medical problems then we must conduct research on living beings. It's common sense, and when I say living beings, I'm referring to those sub humans who are not of the Aryan race ... the niggers, coloureds, Jews, and *those* of the eastern persuasions. Now remember, I'm not talking about the ape family. Rather, I point to a specific anomaly breeding in imposing numbers. An aberration that won't be missed ... the non-whites."

If Dieter Krueger thought he was ringing the right bells, he was correct. Half the guests jumped to their feet cheering and whistling. The rest applauded loudly.

"Thank you. You know, we are a special group of caring people. All we seek is a beautiful world with beautiful inhabitants; intelligent inhabitants that will guide our decreed destiny. In short, our people will accomplish the impossible. Did you hear me? I said we will accomplish the impossible. Jews conjured up the word 'impossible.' How foolish that word really is. The end of disease is not impossible. The end of an uncontrolled population is not impossible. Only people like us can accomplish these goals. We must reduce the ever-breeding non-white vermin by the billions. And how should we do it? With clean minds, caring hearts, pure blood, absolute determination, and proper leadership."

Krueger knew he had the whole room in his hands and once again, he relished the rousing standing ovation. Joe stood and applauded with the rest of them, but his mind aimed an invisible gun sight between Krueger's eyes.

"Let me tell you a quick story about a brilliant pragmatist who remained loyal to Germany when so many of that country's citizens were demanding a soviet style revolution leading to government. This proud, much decorated man still serving in Germany's army after the Great War, was ordered three times to investigate a small political party primarily referred to as the German Workers Party. His military bosses knew undesirables with very little use for Germany's proud veterans controlled most of Germany's political parties and they wanted to do something about it. Well, that realist attended all right, and the rest is history. That man, gentlemen, was our great leader Adolf Hitler, a hero that stood for law and..."

As Krueger rambled on, wide-eyed dinner guests doted on every lie that came out of his mouth. One hour later when he sat down, three-quarters of the crowd including everyone at the head table offered the Nazi salute along with a resounding ovation.

Following dinner, some guests departed for the *ecstasy* waiting for them in their rooms, but most attended the President Jefferson Theatre. The entertainment consisted of a string orchestra joining brass musicians playing all the German wartime songs. Beautiful girls moved throughout offering fine cigarettes, cigars, liquors, and *promises*.

At midnight, when Joe climbed the grand staircase, he felt tired and his mind reeled from the detestable five-hour experience. When he entered his room, something wasn't right. He could sense it, but he couldn't see it.

Knowing he was being watched, Joe casually undressed throwing his clothes over a chair before going into the bathroom to brush his teeth. Reaching behind the heat radiator, his briefcase remained untouched where it was hidden.

The police officer's suspicions were confirmed when he re-entered the main room. A beautiful naked young woman with her eyes closed lay on top of his bed. She had obviously been hiding in the closet.

Joe's eyes travelled her perfect body from the lustrous strands of her whitish-blond hair to her firm well-developed breasts, flat stomach, curvaceously shaved pubis, and long legs.

"I didn't ask for you. What are you doing here?" he asked, grabbing her soft hand and helping her up.

When the girl smiled flipping her head back, her angelic hair fell behind her body. Purring softly, she said, "Dr. Kraven sent me. If you turn me away, the doctor will think you're one of those."

Curious, Stacy asked, "What does one of *those* mean?"

"One of those. You know what I'm referring to, Dr. Schumann. Are you one of those?" she asked, her voice almost softly singing. Lying down again, she patted his side of the bed. "Helmut, you're not are you?"

Joe found his eyes smiling along with his small grin. Turning out the light and joining her, he thought, Kraven you demented son of a bitch, you may have me in mate, but not checkmate.

Chapter 10

The barracks to which Kurt Buss was assigned lay unlit and silent. Kurt had put in a gruelling day and as he stretched out on top of his bunk he recalled his activities since getting involved with the, "mob out back," as the skinheads referred to themselves.

Kurt's shower before going to bed had felt invigorating but he'd seen the naked body of a depressed red-eyed eighteen-year-old recruit in the end shower. The boy had cuts and bruises all over his body as if he had been in a fight of some sort. Kurt had met the young man the night before when entering the camp and had spent the day with him. The kid had introduced himself as Rudy Reickhardt, and that morning when the camp barbers had lopped off Reickhardt's hair, they hadn't touched Kurt's head. He was the only one in the camp with a full head of hair. No one had ordered him to report to the barbers with Rudy, also the senior skinheads had not laid a hand on him. Strangely enough, he appeared to be receiving special treatment and he knew Krupp had arranged it.

This was Kurt's second night in the camp, and from the moment someone had stormed into the barracks at 0600 hours this day, every minute except for meals had been taken up with training. Lying back reminiscing, he recalled all the day's events since the initial *wake-up* call, and thought the experience must be similar to that in the army.

"You bastards, get you're fucking asses out of bed, and get in the showers," an immaculately uniformed skinhead had bellowed upon entering the Quonset hut. "When you're properly dressed, get your asses over to breakfast."

As bedclothes were thrown off or ripped off, World War Two German military music blared over the loudspeakers in each hut, continuing for half-an-hour as the *robots* shaved, showered, dressed, and cleaned their quarters.

Little was said as the private army of soldiers went about their morning routine in the ablution room. Kurt found the room *layout* uncomfortable. While people showered, others sat relieving themselves or stood washing and ironing clothes. To his surprise, his injured young friend whispered, "Kurt, have you showered yet?"

"Yes I have, Rudy, and you look horrible. What happened to you?"

"A group of sergeants woke me up last night suggesting I was going to be shared. They wanted to pass me around. "

Kurt saw the pain in the young man's face. "What do you mean *shared?*"

"You know? They said it was time for my initiation ... that all recruits get it their first night. I told them to fuck off so they punched and kicked me for an hour. I want out of this joint now!"

"What are you doing here in the first place?"

"My mom and dad sent me. My dad teaches explosive techniques at the Reichsland Camp in Montana. I always thought he sold insurance until he levelled with me about what he did for a living and told me I must be trained."

Kurt smiled sympathetically. "I wonder if your dad knows gang rape is part of the training process. Have you told him?"

"Hell, you know there's no way of getting messages out. Last night when I told those assholes I wasn't gay, the leader punched me saying, 'Neither are we you son-of-a-bitch, but since there are no women in camp you're going to take their place! If we don't get you tonight, we'll get you another night.' Kurt, I don't know if I could take that punishment again."

Combing his hair, Kurt thought of the damage to Reickhardt's body. The boy's wrists and ankles were red raw from rope marks and someone had used a whip on his back. His buttocks, penis, testicles, and lower stomach displayed large welts as well.

"I've got to get out of here. Kurt, what am I going to do?"

Buss didn't know what to say and he knew he had to choose his words carefully. There were too many people around and a closed circuit video camera high above the door swivelled regularly.

Keeping his voice low, and placing his back to the camera, Kurt asked, "Surely there must be a way of phoning your parents?"

"We can't use the phones for the first three months. If my dad knew this was going on he'd be here in a second. Can you help me get out?"

"Rudy, there are guards everywhere, even along the full length of the wall. The only way out would be to cross over the airfield and try to get out the back route. Remember they've got dogs so they'll come after you. Where would you go if you did get out?"

"Spokane. I could phone home from there. Help me, Kurt, please?"

Kurt thought for a moment, asking himself if this was a set-up. No, it couldn't be, Rudy's body was black and blue.

"We'll talk about it on the way to breakfast."

As the hut emptied, Kurt helped Rudy make his bed and the two of them walked the 100 yards to the kitchen.

"Rudy, the only way I can see you escaping from here is at night. That way, they won't notice you're missing until the next morning. I'll help because I want to check out this place. We'll leave after midnight, around one."

"Why one o'clock? How will you get back in?"

"Don't worry about me - I'll be okay. Last night I noticed the sentry on the road in front of our hut left at 0100 and his substitute didn't arrive until ten minutes later. They replace each other every three hours, but four o'clock would be too late. If you want to leave, we'll have to make our move at one."

Entering the mess hall, Reickhardt whispered, "Thanks, Kurt. I don't know how I can pay you back."

Kurt was touched to see the pleading look in Rudy's eyes. Offering a sympathetic glance, he said, "I have a suggestion but I don't think you'd go along with it. Then slightly shaking his head and clearing his sensual thoughts, he added, "Anyway, you're not out yet. Thank me if you make it to the perimeter."

Following breakfast, Kurt's troop was marched to the rifle range for three hours. At noon, lunch was served in the field, and then they received instruction on throwing grenades, firing rocket launchers, and using fertilizer as an explosive device. Throughout, skinhead instructors yelled at them, kicking and punching the trainees.

After supper that evening when everyone had showered and dressed in casual clothes, two hours of *brainwashing* indoctrination took place in a lecture hut. As the instructor started speaking, Rudy whispered to Kurt, "He's the leader of the group that tried to nail me."

The instructor's face became vicious as he stopped lecturing and strolled over. "I didn't give you permission to speak! Stand up!"

Rudy quickly stood to attention, the way he had been taught earlier.

Towering over the boy, the brawny educator bellowed, "What did you say to him?"

Kurt also stood to attention. "He was telling me how much he enjoyed your instruction and..."

The instructor's muscles flexed and he slammed his wooden pointer on Kurt and Rudy's table. "Did I ask you? Sit down, you fuckhead!"

Buss didn't sit down. As the skinhead grabbed Reickhardt's ear to yank him over, Kurt firmly seized the man's wrist and mildly said, "Take your hand off him, now, and back away!"

A vicious grin mixed with the instructor's cruel eyes as he slowly released Rudy. "Or you'll what?"

Kurt's eyes narrowed and bored into the instructor. "Or I'll propel your nose into your brain and when they take you out of here in a box, I'll inform Herr Krupp and Herr Doctor Kraven that you were disloyal to our cause. My name is Buss, and I want you to remember it. If you refer to me as fuckhead again, it will be the last word you speak. Do you understand me, or is that matter between your ears as thick as I think it is?"

Swallowing and licking his twitching dry lips, an expression of fear mingled with the cowardly pout on the beefy instructor's face. "I, uh, apologize for my behaviour, Herr Buss. It will not happen again."

"See that it doesn't," Buss said, sitting, and totally ignoring the astonished stares of those around him.

Kurt chuckled to himself lying on his bed recalling the day's activities. These bastards only understand the same treatment they pass out, he thought. The instructor had guardedly continued with his lecture, ensuring his eyes never met Kurt's eyes.

At 12:45pm, Kurt Buss silently placed his feet on the floor and put on his dark uniform. Within minutes, he put a hand over Rudy's mouth and woke him up. Reickhardt was already dressed in civilian clothes and had been dozing on top of his blankets. Although the camera at the flags end of the hut still swivelled quietly, the barracks was dark and all other occupants either snored or slept quietly.

Keeping his voice low, Kurt said, "It's time to go. Are you taking any other clothes with you?"

Rudy shook his head and whispered, "No. I just want out of here. I'm leaving everything else."

For the next ten minutes, the duo peered through a window above the sinks in the ablution room. Normally the sentry moved around, but this time he needed a smoke and he stayed in one spot. At five after one, he threw his cigarette on the ground, stomped on it, picked up the butt, and moved away a few minutes before his replacement arrived.

As the pair quietly closed the hut door behind them, their hot breath shot out in the cold night air. The previous day's light snowfall had melted so they knew there would not be tracks as they ran in between the huts on the other side of the road.

"Stay close to me," Kurt murmured, spreading a substance on the ground as he moved. "We'll head through the vehicle compound, then through the rifle range and over the airport tarmac."

Rudy was too nervous to reply. Breathing heavily, he just nodded, kept low, and stayed behind Kurt.

Laughter ruptured the quiet of the night as they stopped behind a shed near the vehicle car park. The guards inside were playing cards and drinking while listening to a local radio station.

Just as Kurt started to make his move through the vehicles, he heard the door open and quickly pulled Rudy back. The two stayed hidden behind a three-ton truck waiting for the man at the top of the three steps to finish urinating.

"Fuck it's cold our here," the sentry complained, zipping up his fly before going back inside. "Okay, it's my deal!" he said, slamming the door shut.

Rudy was so frightened he wanted to throw up, so Kurt grabbed the boy's arm and lightly shook it. "C'mon, the worst is over. You're going to be all right."

Twenty minutes later, when they lay breathless on their stomachs at the edge of the runway, Kurt wasn't prepared for the illumination. "Shit, the landing lights are on - breathe towards the ground. There are two private jets with guards standing around them, so we'll have to move about 500 metres along this side before we cross. This brush is thick, so pull the back of your jacket up over your forehead and the front up over your nose. Try to stay a foot behind me, got it?"

A reply wasn't necessary. Kurt's accomplice wasn't about to get lost.

It took an hour of hard slogging though trees and heavy brush to reach the first razor-wire fence. Rudy could not believe the ease in which Kurt cut some strands before picking up two large dead tree branches and throwing them across the section of wire to hold it down.

"You're wondering where I got the wire cutters, aren't you?" Buss whispered, grinning and training his eyes in all directions.

Rudy appeared more relaxed. "Yeah. Didn't they search you when you came in?"

"They frisked me, but not the guy I was with. I planted them on him and got them later without him being any the wiser. It's better if you don't ask how. Okay, once we get past the next barrier, we've got another four hundred metres before we reach the road. Are you ready?"

Displaying a weak smile, Rudy swallowed and nodded.

Kurt smacked him on the back. "Good, let's go."

Half an hour later, both men crawled through the third barbed wire barrier strung along the side of the asphalt road off base. There, Kurt gently grabbed the back of Reickhardt's neck. "Well, you're out. Now listen to me, there are four farms straight ahead across this road. On the other side of the last farm is the main highway. Go through those farms and stay hidden in the last farm until the start of daybreak. There's a small country school a quarter mile to your right. Parents will be dropping their kids off, and there'll be school buses. Do not phone home. Just ask someone for a ride into town. When you arrive, find a phone book, and look up Rosenbloom's Boarding House. Make certain you walk there, and mention my name to Mrs. Rosenbloom. Got it?"

Rudy's quizzed expression expanded. "Yeah, but how do you know all this? Why shouldn't I phone home from the boarding house?"

Buss didn't answer the lad's first question. Shaking Rudy's hand, he said, "I've told you, don't phone home at all. Mr. Rosenbloom will take you elsewhere to catch a bus, not in Spokane. One other thing ... I didn't help you, and what I've told you is strictly between us. When you get home, tell your parents nothing. Nothing, do you understand me? As far as they're concerned, you just walked out. Do we have a deal?"

Gratitude filled Reickhardt's face. "How do I thank you?"

"You can thank me by staying out of this organization. I'll tell you something else. You probably can't trust your mom and dad, or anyone in your family. That's why I don't want you to phone home. They're brainwashed, Rudy, and they'll send you back. If there's the slightest hint of that, get out of your house. Look in their eyes when you tell them what happened to you here. That will tip you off as to their sincerity."

Turning to head back, Kurt said, "Good luck. I don't want to see you again. Check and make certain there are no headlights before you cross."

Rudy looked both ways prior to opening his mouth to say something else, but he was alone.

"Ah, Dr. Schumann, you're up early this morning," Kraven said walking into the President Lincoln dining room at 8am. All the tables from the previous night had been dispersed individually throughout the room.

Even at this time of the day, the head of the establishment was impeccably dressed in white slacks, white shoes, a starched white shirt, red tie, and navy-blue blazer.

"How did you sleep, my friend?" Kraven asked approaching Joe's table.

Trimming some bacon, Stacy looked up, smiling. "Much better after receiving your *prescription*, thank you, doctor."

Kraven grinned conceitedly as he continued walking towards Senator Millington's table. "I believe she is one of our finest sleeping powders, and I knew you would enjoy the experience. Just ask if you require her again."

"Thank you, I will."

Kraven suddenly stopped and spun around. "Will you be attending Dr. Krause's talk today?"

Still grinning cordially, Joe replied, "I wouldn't miss it for the world. He's giving me a personal tour afterward."

"Splendid, Dr. Schumann, absolutely splendid. We'll talk as the week progresses. Enjoy your breakfast and the tour."

"Thank you, sir."

Stacy could not hear the conversation at Millington's table and he noticed the vice-president was not seated. Perhaps he was aboard the jet that took off at four in the morning, two hours before the sirens blared. Nah, he probably left here after getting laid, he thought. But what the hell were the sirens for at that ungodly hour. Did they use them to wake people up, or had someone escaped.

When he had breakfast, Joe reached into his pocket and brought out his schedule. Since Krause's conference wasn't until eleven, he had time to look around. After wiping his mouth with his napkin, he stood, pushed his chair forward, and left the table.

Returning to his room to collect his sweater, Joe noticed the maid's cart outside Senator Millington's President Richard M. Nixon suite. For some reason, his eyes centred on the letter opener inscribed with the suite's name. It was probably a spare one. These letter openers were like knives, he thought. If he had to use one, it had better come from someone else's room. Quickly palming it and placing the object up his sleeve, he continued on his way, whistling.

For a winter's day, Stacy thought the weather wasn't too bad. Clouds still filled the sky, but every so often the sun's rays shone through evaporating the ground mist. Other people were also out strolling, talking in muffled tones to each other, and Joe found himself laughing inwardly at the sight of them staring at the ground and mumbling. As he walked past, he received nods, but nothing else. Every one of these pricks is so damned secretive, he thought. What a way to live. Also, they're so goddamned cocksure of themselves.

In the distance, Joe could hear organized gunfire starting and stopping. From time to time, he heard periodic explosions coming from the same region beyond the wall. The detective did not have to be told what was occurring; he had served his stint in the Marines and had thrown hand grenades many times. The loud reverberating explosions tweaked his curiosity. What the hell were they? He wasn't hearing tank or bazooka fire; these detonations ripped the air and were powerful, very powerful. When they exploded, the land shook and in some locations, he heard rumbling sounds underneath his feet. Wondering why this was happening only in certain spots, he finally concluded there were tunnels below. "Sure, how stupid of me not thinking about that possibility before," he murmured. The whole place was probably spider-webbed with underground passages. The explosions were taking place above ground, but the sound resonated throughout the tunnels.

Joe picked up a rock and while pretending to study it listened to the noise below. His suspicions were confirmed. When explosions took place on the other side of the wall, reverberation noise was limited only to certain areas of the ground beneath and around him.

Sensing someone could be watching, when Joe straightened up, he examined the rock before tossing it away.

A voice crackled. "Does geology interest you, Dr. Schumann?"

Stacy feigned looking around for the source of Kraven's voice, knowing it came from a small loud speaker situated next to a video camera on a nearby pole.

"I'm not near you, Schumann, I'm inside Kravenhall. Just speak into the camera to your right. Do you normally walk around examining ordinary rocks?"

Joe had to think fast, and he felt perspiration building up under his wig. Don't these bastards ever relax? he asked himself, visibly smiling at the lens.

"Ingenious, Dr. Kraven. Yes, in fact I am fascinated with geology. It's a hobby of mine. Some of these rocks indicate this area conforms to models of the Cretaceous Age. That last rock had pyroclastic tuffs and breccias interbedded with thin beds of brittle shale and siltstone."

Kraven didn't respond right away. "Which means?"

"At one time, this area was part of a huge volcano," Joe answered, still smiling. "It appears that deformation has been largely concentrated in narrow north-west tending zones, leaving the intervening areas with well preserved original textures. If you have time, Dr. Kraven, I'd be only too pleased to explain the ground formation to you."

There was another pause before Kraven gracefully declined Joe's offer. "Fascinating, Dr. Schumann. Let me know if you find any gold on our property, will you?"

"Certainly, sir. It's possible … even some silver."

"See you at dinner, Schumann."

Inwardly chuckling, Joe moved on examining a few more rocks before taking a deep breath. Had that asshole been on the bus, he might have read the same boring geological article I read. Then he wouldn't have to ask, would he? One of these days I should find out what *pyroclastic* and the rest of those other words mean.

Stacy's tour took him an hour. He'd seen the golf course, tennis courts, lake and sports fields, and he'd paid particular attention to the tip of the large smokestack across the wall. By the time he started walking back to the main building, he had made mental notes of the whereabouts of exposed and hidden video cameras placed on or near the tall brick barrier; a barrier with broken glass cemented into the top and upper sides, and with doors so thick, a tank would have difficulty breaking through.

"Winston Churchill's book, A History of the English Speaking Peoples, was written by one who held onto a purely absurd perspective. That it was the largest empire, and so forth and so on and so forth. However, the man deceitfully omitted the importance of the Germanic race and our empire.

"Certainly he referred to Martin Luther and the Reformation, and he made mention of the Restoration, but to what extent? My friends, the Reformation of the whole known world was German inspired. A purity so wonderful it was as if God had come to earth and made it himself. We must remember that at the time of Henry VIII, the Holy Roman Empire was Germany.

"The whole of Europe except Germany and England was sullied with Mongolian blood. Certainly, some Germanic people died on Mongolian swords near Breslau, but German and Austrian blood was not tainted. It remains pure today, but just look at what those Jew-loving political bastards are doing to our beloved country. Germany is up to its ears in Jewish, Slav, Turkish, and every other type of shit possible.

"Today, we Germans are blamed for banishing the Jews. Can you believe that? Did you know England banished them for four hundred years? Why? You know why! I shouldn't have to tell you ... our beloved Fuehrer, Adolf Hitler, told you why. Today, do we hear about what England did? Not on your life! My friends, I tell you..."

As Krause rambled on and on, Joe Stacy thought the man must have spent years reviewing all the film-clips of Adolf Hitler's speeches. The doctor's eyes and arm movements imitated every movement of the maniac who had ruled Germany during the 1930s and 1940s. Even his voice sounded similar.

When the hateful dictatorial speech ended, followed by boisterous applause, Doctor Krause didn't bow or smile. Instead, he nodded tenaciously keeping his tempestuous eyes scanning the motivated faces in front of him.

Once again, Joe could not believe what he was witnessing. These people were not Germans; they were American businessmen with trustful wives and with kids in school. They ate apple pie, lined up at McDonald's, and went on Sunday drives. They attended church, took their children out on Halloween, bowled, placed hands over their hearts when they sang the national anthem, and many had served in Vietnam.

Although Stacy could not let his true feelings show, he wanted to stand up and punch Krause when he heard the final part of his speech. Near the end, someone asked the doctor what he would do if he was dying and only Black, Asian, or Jewish doctors were present to help him.

"I would use whoever was available," Krause bellowed. "I would allow them to attend me and make me well, before I had them shot. Don't get soft hearted; we must never lose sight of our purpose. Our will must remain steadfast. The preservation of the white race should always be foremost in our minds and hearts."

Joe had seen and heard enough. He wanted to get out of the room as quickly as possible, but Krause saw him and came over.

"Well, Schumann, did my speech invigorate you? Are you ready to carry the banner of our mission?"

"I only wish I had four hands, Dr. Krause."

Krause's chest stuck out and he raised his chin. "Wonderful, that's what I like to hear. Don't forget you can always assist us with a donation. We have a large *organization* to support and we are always seeking funds."

And I know where you're getting them from, you wretch, Joe thought, before saying, "I'm going to rearrange my finances and make certain I donate. What is the usual donation?"

"Whatever you can spare, Schumann. That's exactly what our glorious leader Adolf Hitler said when gaining prestige within our party. Of course, we appreciate those who give a little more. Do you know what I mean, Schumann? I believe Xavier demonstrated that to you last night when he sent you a certain *present*, did he not?"

Modestly smiling, Joe replied, "He certainly did, Dr. Krause. I understand precisely what you mean."

Krause placed his right arm lightly around Joe's shoulders then released it.

"Excellent. Come, Schumann, join me at my table for lunch, then afterwards I'll give you a tour."

Joe followed dutifully. "I'd like to hear about The Himmler Stratagem, Dr. Krause."

The orator paused thinking for a fraction of a second before he relaxed again. Mentally eliminating any cause for suspicion, he replied, "Ah, yes, The Himmler Stratagem. All in good time, Schumann … all in good time."

Senator Millington also joined Krause for lunch, as did three other heads of industry. Throughout the meal, Krause heaped praise on Vice-President MacPherson, saying, "It took us twelve long years to plant him in that position. He'll be running for the presidency in three years, and he'll get elected, we'll make certain of it. It's difficult for MacPherson to speak up now, so our plan is to have him gradually change the way our nation thinks. We feel it will take four years. Then after he seeks re-election and wins, we'll make our move and change the constitution. Gentlemen, the world will be ours. With our military might, no country will dare stand in our way. Not that they'll want to, because we have leaders in place the world over. Money talks, gentlemen," Krause said, laughing loudly. "In this case, Jewish money talks. Finally, world domination is within our grasp. How very phenomenal and exhilarating."

They've checked me out, Joe thought while dining. That must be why Krupp isn't around. Whatever Harvey Cohen did, he pulled it off well.

Following lunch, Krause brought Millington along on the tour. The senator had seen it all before but changes had been made and Krause insisted he join them. The tour started one floor below the indoor pool deck, but did not include the room with the special pool *window.*

"This floor is our operations floor," Krause said, guiding both men into an enormous room filled with large printing presses and computers. "We produce our posters and brochures here, also all printed material for our world operations. It's idle now due to the Christmas break. We have additional presses in Detroit however they'll only be required when we run MacPherson for President."

"Is Carl MacPherson his real name?" Joe subconsciously asked, marvelling at the number of solid Heidelberg presses.

The question brought on a hostile response. "Naturally not! He's not a fucking heathen Scot ... he's German. He was born in this country, but his grandparents came from the Fatherland. They changed their name from Schuetz to MacPherson for social acceptance sake. Karl Schuetz will be the next president, just wait and see."

Millington didn't utter a word during the first part of the tour, and at one point Joe grinned thinking the senator would be absolutely furious if he knew he'd been filmed in the pool.

When the trio entered the next giant room full of radio equipment, nine uniformed skinheads wearing radio headsets jumped to attention before Krause told them to continue working.

"This is our communications room. It's here that we maintain contact with our people in all states, most civilized countries, and our ships at sea. Similar to what the Soviet Union did, we utilize our fishing trawlers to monitor world communications. The FBI and CIA codes are not a problem for us, but sometimes we do have difficulty with the National Security Agency's transmissions. Our people in that facility are gradually supplying us with, shall I say, *updated material.* Schumann, you're probably asking yourself if we own a satellite.

"I was thinking of that possibility, sir."

"Naturally we do. We also own 400 radio stations and 37 television stations. It stands to reason we require satellites doesn't it?"

Joe didn't just look interested - he was astonished. He also thought it was *kind* of Dr. Krause to supply all this information. "What about the Internet?" he asked.

The surgeon guilefully grinned. "Most definitely. Our material is available to all children and adults throughout the world. Obviously, we must tone it down until we take power, however, the meaning is there. Israel continues lobbying to close down some of our Internet Information Centres, but we open more than we close. You'll find it astonishing what we do, Schumann. We turn the Arabs against the Jews and vice-versa. We turn the Japs against their old Korean and Chinese enemies, and we turn blacks everywhere against the whites. Everyone is working for us, but they just don't know it."

Not for long, Joe thought, before mouthing, "Remarkable, Dr. Krause. Most ingenious."

Krause nodded in a calculated way, guiding the men to a small elevator at the back of the communications room. When the doors closed, the doctor continued. "You're a mathematician Schumann, so you're already aware how our philosophies work. We simply divide and conquer. It's easy to overthrow governments when the people are divided. If the blacks of this world ever figured out that a good number of their leaders are on our payroll, we'd have problems. Now let me show you our hospital below. It can also be accessed by an elevator up top in the sanatorium admission room next to the main entrance."

If Joe Stacy was overwhelmed with the facilities on the floor above, he went into shock when he stepped out of the elevator in the hospital. The infirmary covered twice the space of the building above. It also appeared like a regular hospital, with nursing staff and doctors moving about, but something was different. The doors to each room were closed and locked. When staff members entered or departed rooms, they used keys. Zombie-like men with scars on their scalps stumbled around as if they were in a trance of some sort. The same men he'd seen attending the grounds and pottering in the hothouses.

"Our hospital is split into three wings. One wing is for the health of our members, one is for *misfits*, and the last small wing is used for supplying our..." Krause paused, finding it difficult to select his words. "... *organ donations.*"

"Did you say *misfits*?" Joe asked, wondering to what Krause was referring.

Unemotionally Krause voiced, "Yes, this is the area where we prepare them for surgery. They're mentally retarded, Schumann. We try to assist these people by operating on their cerebrums ... brains, and our ministration helps them to fulfil certain roles. Kravenhall's gardeners and labourers come from this sector of the hospital. They can't talk or think well, but considering their *disabilities*, they work diligently."

Christ he's operating on the brains of these poor bastards and producing human zombies, Stacy thought, trying to act as indifferently as his host and Millington.

"But where do they come from?"

"From the streets of course, where else? Specific states do us a favour by opening up their asylums and letting these people out. It's called individual rights, or some sort of silly democratic thing. Well, we just do our part and try to make them useful. Some would call it kidnapping, but I don't."

Millington finally added his spontaneous judgment and laughed. "How can it be called kidnapping when we provide each of them with a roof over his heads, a meal a day, and warm clothing. Right Heinz? And when they get sick, they're *utilized*."

"Utilized?" Joe's mouth remained open after repeating the word and he found himself letting his guard down.

Both the doctor and the senator noticed Joe's intrusive look.

"Yes, utilized for their organs," Millington added, his face questioning Joe's astonishment. "Do you have a problem with that, Schumann?"

Quickly recovering, Joe thought he'd better put the senator in his place. "No, I don't have a problem, Millington. I think it's an absolute innovation. Christ, I've seen these homeless simpletons on the streets; they need all the help they can get. But it obviously upsets you, Senator? What do *you* have against the practice?"

As Krause frowned, Millington squirmed a little. "No, it er ... I didn't mean that. I just thought you didn't approve. I was obviously wrong."

The medical doctor moved them along. "My friends, I'm not going to show you the other wing. Millington, you've already seen it. Let me just say, the *vermin* are still in there and they are strictly used for experiments and transplants. They're of inferior races and they come in all ages and sexes. Rest assured that not one of them is white, nor do we offer their *donations* to our kind. We treat them humanely as possible and instead of being a burden to the world, they serve it."

Millington laughed again. "Heinz, tell Schumann what you call that place."

Passing the steel door leading to the mysterious annex, Krause did not just have to act proud, he was exceedingly proud. "Xavier and I refer to it as Auschwitz III. Now, let me show you our heating plant."

The doctor's unemotional disposition nearly made Joe trip over his own feet. "Uh, what about your operating room?" he asked, trying to act rational but finding it almost impossible.

Krause continued strolling down the well-lit corridor. Turning right at the end, he replied, "We'll be coming to that after we ride through this tunnel. There are many underground passages at Kravenhall, but this is the primary tunnel. It connects the mansion with the heating plant on the other side of the wall. The various doors you see off to the left and right here all lead to different holding cells, but that particular door there..." Krause pointed to a larger door. "... leads to a specific area outside the main gates."

A double electric cable track built into the right and left sides of the cemented oval tunnel's floor provided steel rail for open fibreglass vehicles that could hold ten people. The seats were made from the same material and certain seats could be removed allowing the car to hold two stretchers. As well, thick canvass restraining straps with tough plastic fasteners were attached to the sides of all seats. Joe thought these were probably used to strap in victims on their last ride to *donation-land or misfit haven.* Those walking the route would use the six-foot space in between the tracks.

When the three sat in a car, Krause pushed a button and the near-quiet conveyance lit up and steered itself through the passageway. Like mountain cable cars, at the halfway point, a head-lighted empty vehicle passed them on the other track.

"There is always a car at each end," Krause pointed out. The second we departed, that car left the other end."

Five minutes later when the car entered a lit holding bay and stopped, a large hospital-style elevator with three buttons singly marked A, B, and C, would take them higher. Krause pushed B, and after disembarking at the next level, the three stood behind a thick glass partition facing a modern operating room with three tables. Scrub sinks, showers, and a changing room stood to their right, and Stacy noticed the operating room could only be entered from the scrub room.

"There's our operating theatre, Dr. Schumann, the surgeon smugly declared. It's far better equipped than most hospitals and we're proud of it."

Joe noticed a stainless steel dumbwaiter off to one side of the room behind the glass, and its doors were open. "What's that used for?"

Krause nudged Joe to a door on his left. "I'll get to that in a minute. This is our morgue," he said, pushing the door open. We can hold thirty cadavers here. Right now we only have five."

The smell reminded Joe of the Seattle morgue and he hated it. Built with stainless steel lockers, the room was almost identical, with the same odours.

"So you're low on...?" Stacy almost nearly used the word *stiffs.* "... bodies, are you, Dr. Krause?"

Krause appeared pensive for a moment before discerning again that his guest was new on the scene. "Xavier and I aren't getting any younger, Dr. Schumann. At one time we ensured it remained full, but not anymore."

Joe opened a locker and thanked God it was empty. "How do you... er...?"

"He wants to know how you kill them?" Millington mouthed, gleefully.

"I must be coming down with a cold," Krause said, taking out his handkerchief and blowing his nose. "Usually by injection, unless we don't want a chemical imbalance," he offered before putting his hankie back in its pocket. "If we have a substance difference then it's necessary to have certain misfits take care of them. Strangulation or smothering is quite quick. I can assure you they don't suffer, Dr. Schumann. We have thought of gassing them, but for this small surgery, our present method is quite suitable. Let's move along shall we?"

Even experienced police officers feel a strange uncomfortable tightening in their testicles when they see open gashes or horrible wounds. In this instance Joe Stacy did not need to see anything of the kind; he felt the extreme discomfort just listening to Krause. Joe didn't want to see or hear anymore. He had had enough. Here he was standing in the middle of a slaughterhouse trying to smile and act intelligent while a couple of maniacs ranted on about slaughtering innocent human beings. He couldn't take it any longer. No rational person could. But how the hell could he get out of this? He wanted to breathe some fresh air and destroy the place.

Krause noticed it right away. "You look a little pallid, Schumann. Are you feeling all right?"

"I'm fine doctor, just a little tired from last night."

"You deserve to be tired, my boy. Healthy sexual encounters nearly always wear me out as well. We're nearly finished, so let's go up one floor."

"How do you like them?" Krause asked, as the trio exited the elevator and stood in front of two oval ovens identical to the ones used in concentration camps during the war. The devices looked so *authentic,* Joe thought they could have been dismantled in Europe and reassembled here. The rest of the room was filled with giant hot water tanks, massive pipes, and two huge softly humming furnaces.

Krause opened up an oven door. Rails for stretchers of some sort lined the sides. "We don't use coal or heating oil any longer," he said, glancing at Millington. "They're fired by natural gas. Senator, these are the new additions I wanted to show you - what do you think? An improvement on the old ones, eh?"

"Absolute perfection, Heinz! Brilliant! How much quicker are they?"

The doctor welcomed Millington's approval. "Gene my friend, it only takes minutes. Helmut, there's that dumbwaiter you questioned me about. When we're through down below, we send what's left up here to be disposed of. The ashes are spread on our gardens. Our misfits handle that end of the business, and guess what?"

Joe didn't need anymore information; he just wanted out. "What?"

"We're planning on building thousands of these throughout the country."

Chapter 11

The hot lecture rooms and lack of sleep took their toll on Kurt Buss as a uniformed hardnosed skinhead instructor rambled on and on about the benefits of National Socialism. Buss could barely keep his eyes open but did not let his predicament show.

After guiding Rudy to the camp's perimeter, he had not returned until five o'clock and reveille had sounded at six. At six-fifteen, the sirens blared and all *troops* had been rounded up and marched to the parade square in various types of dress. Some were fully dressed, or had towels wrapped around them or were in their underwear or pyjamas.

For twenty minutes while dog squads searched the entire camp looking for Rudy, the skinhead commander of the establishment had ranted on informing the assemblage what the consequences were for helping trainees escape.

The black pepper Kurt had spread had made the dogs sneeze, heading in all directions except the correct route. Since the search was unsuccessful, after breakfast Kurt had been called into the office because he'd stuck up for Rudy the day before. They had questioned him delicately knowing he was a friend of Krupp.

"I didn't know him at all," Kurt had said convincingly to the mean-looking pimply-faced officer. "But he did tell me what some of your senior people did to him."

"Oh, and what was that?"

"They wanted to sexually assault him and when he declined, they beat him up. The kid was hurt. If this is the way you treat recruits, you're not going to keep them long."

"Don't tell me how to run this camp!" the commander had yelled, his face turning red as he pounded his right fist on his desk.

"Fine, then I'll tell you nothing."

Stern faced and trying to maintain control, the commander stood up from his desk. Walking behind Kurt and running the tip of his swagger stick up and down the back of Kurt's neck, he said, "Buss, you may be Herr Krupp's friend, but that doesn't give you the right to withhold information. We can deal with you in other ways, do you understand me?"

"Right now, I'm telling you what you want to know," Buss said, turning to face the commandant. Let me tell you something else. Are you aware his father is a high-ranking officer in the *system*?"

Kurt's statement surprised the headman. Quickly returning to his desk to review Reickhardt's file again," he asked, "He is? Er, in which camp?"

"At the Reichsland Camp in Montana."

The officer's face became confused and he rubbed his chin indicating to Kurt that someone had really screwed up. "That's our top secret camp. Do you know what his father does there?"

"No, he didn't tell me."

"Anything else, Herr Buss?" the commandant had asked, making a note of Rudy's home telephone number.

"No, I've told you all I know. The kid's probably heading home."

When Buss had left the office, he heard the commander shouting for certain people to be brought to him.

The rest of Kurt's day had consisted of physical training, and the proper way to make bombs out of fertilizer and diesel oil. After supper, he had nearly fallen asleep twice, and now this idiot in front of him still rambled on about Hitler's achievements.

When the lecture finished at nine o'clock, Kurt showered and went to bed totally oblivious to the noise in the barracks. At one o'clock though, someone stroking his hair awakened him. After throwing the intruder's hand off and sitting up ready to throw a punch, he noticed Krupp's sensual smile.

Looking surprised, Kurt shoved the covers down and sat on the side of his bunk. Allowing Krupp to gently caress the side of his face, he whispered, "Hans, I missed you, how did your trip go?"

Passion gripped Krupp's wild eyes as he placed his hands on Kurt's knees. "I also missed you my sweet - really missed you. You smell nice. I'm going to take my clothes off and join you."

"Uh, no, that wouldn't be wise in here, Hans. How did you get past the wall sentries? Visitors are not allowed in camp after midnight?"

"I didn't come in through the wall, I used the Kravenhall tunnel."

A fraction of a second after asking, "Through the heating plant?" Kurt knew he'd made a mistake. Krupp's arm left his shoulders and his firm fingers firmly grabbed the young man's chin.

"How did you know about that? Who told you about it?"

Kurt had to think fast. "The commandant did when the dogs couldn't track someone's exit route out of the camp today. Did I say something wrong? The commanding officer knows I'm a friend of yours?"

Krupp's eyes studied Kurt's face looking for a sign of betrayal, but only innocence showed. "You keep that information to yourself ... have you got that?"

Kurt thought his chin was about to be ripped off. "Hans you're hurting me. Why would I talk about it, it means nothing to me?"

The killer released his grip. "Of course, how silly of me? How have you enjoyed the training so far?"

"It's been interesting, but I don't believe it's for me," Buss said, rubbing his painful chin. "Hans, how long do you want me to stay on this side of the wall anyway? I want to be with you."

Krupp began caressing Kurt's face again until the young man backed his head away.

"I thought I'd be gone longer, but you're right, Kurt, it isn't for you. When you're on this side, I can't have you with me. I've got something to take care of then I'll get you out of here. After we visit Paraguay, you can come with me to Switzerland. Would you like that?"

Wriggling while trying to evade Krupp's groping hands, Kurt finally stood up by the side of his bed.

"Paraguay? Switzerland? Wow, that's unbelievable! What do you have to take care of before we leave?"

Krupp wrapped the same hands around the back of the young man's neck, bringing him closer. "Someone escaped from here last night."

"I know. That's what they were questioning me about today."

"Why were they questioning you? You don't know anyone here?"

"This guy, er, Rudy Reickhardt, complained to me about a group trying to gang rape him, and they thought I knew him. Is that what you have to do? Are you going to find him and bring him back?"

The maniac's voice became agreeable again. "No, I'm going to execute the person that probably helped him get away. Would you like to see how it's done?"

Kurt managed to back away for a second but Krupp's right hand caught the back of the young man's neck again. Swallowing, Kurt asked, "You mean you know who helped him escape and you want me to see how you're going to kill him?"

Even in the darkness, Buss could see the coldness in Krupp's cruel eyes when his menacing smile reappeared. "Yes, it's an art you should learn, and I'm the best at it. Kurt, my sweet, let's go for a walk outside. We'll go to Kravenhall where I can enjoy the warmth of your body next to me."

The *boy* hesitated before reaching for his clothes and shoes. "Hans, you ... you don't think I helped him escape, do you? I didn't even know him."

Krupp remained silent until they were outside in the cold air, and Kurt felt an arm placed around his waist. Ignoring the salute of the lone sentry, Krupp replied, "Naturally not. I found out today that we've got an infiltrator staying at Kravenhall. An impudent fellow impersonating the good name of Dr. Schumann. He probably assisted the escapee."

Kurt found himself being slowly guided towards the heating plant. "Hans, in my opinion it wouldn't be possible for anyone to infiltrate this place? Who told you, Dr. Kraven?"

"No, I discovered it today and haven't had time to inform the doctor. I phoned Kraven yesterday informing him Schumann was legit, but I was wrong. The Dr. Schumann staying at Kravenhall is not who he says he is."

"How did you find out?"

"The fingerprints I took in his room matched Dr. Schumann's prints on the FBI file, that's why I told Kraven he was genuine. Then I decided to check with our people in the academic world. The man's ID picture matches, but his prints don't. I have no idea who this person is, but it doesn't matter anyway because he won't be leaving here alive."

Krupp lingered for a moment, his eyes getting excited at the thought of a kill. Allowing an evil laugh, he added, "Even after he's dead he won't be leaving here. He'll be a part of our garden."

When the pair entered the brick heating plant, two strange-looking men dressed in coveralls stood slowly but meticulously washing the floor in front of the two ovens. The *cleaners* didn't look up or pay any attention. Each had their hair shaved off the front of their heads and their scalps revealed surgical scars.

"What's wrong with these people?" Kurt asked.

"These aren't people. We refer to them as misfits," Krupp replied, quite nonchalantly. "The doctors have operated on their brains. Misfits do all the physical labour at Kravenhall. We work them sixteen hours a day and when they get worn out, we utilize their parts. Don't concern yourself with them, my sweet ... they're harmless. When we want them to do chores, we simply show them and they take it from there and stay on the job. These two would be washing the floors all night and tomorrow as well, if they weren't redirected later. Sometimes when we want them to wear themselves out we let them do that. Want to see something funny?"

Before Kurt had the chance to reply, Krupp kicked the buttocks of one of the men so hard the individual went head first into a concrete wall. The impact knocked the man out for a few seconds. Paying no attention to his cuts and bruises, he slowly got up, picked up the mop and began working again.

Krupp's intense eyes never noticed Kurt's look of disgust; he was too busy laughing, pointing, and making fun of the man.

As quickly as Hans started laughing, he stopped and aimed a hand at the ovens. "That's were you and I are going to place our Dr. Schumann. I'm going over to get him and I want you to wait here. When we're finished, I'll take you through the tunnel to Kravenhall. Will you feel at ease being left with these two?" he asked, grinning at the now disappointed boy. "They won't bother you."

Kurt swallowed. "I, er … I suppose so. How long will you be?"

Krupp chuckled wickedly while stepping into the elevator. "Don't fret, my pet, I shouldn't be long. Then, Kurt, I'll show you the proper way to cut a throat."

Kurt showed some apprehension. "Please hurry back, Hans."

Hans Krupp was more than prepared for the task, and he knew the layout of Kravenhall well, but there are times when all the planning in the world goes for naught. The railcar he sat in only hummed along for ninety seconds before all lights went out and it stopped. Cursing to himself in the blackness of the tunnel, Krupp disembarked and started walking back towards the heating plant.

A moment later he stopped, as did the echo of his footsteps. Krupp, however, was certain he'd heard something else; perhaps other footsteps and the rustling of clothing. Straining his ears to listen, the man knew he wasn't alone. He had heard something out of place and all of his senses told him danger was imminent. Normally the quiet whine of the cable motor dampened the tunnel's reverberations but even then he could still recognize the origin of sounds, but not this time.

"Is that you, Kurt?" he yelled, hearing his voice resonating throughout the tunnel. There wasn't a reply, and he thought he heard the rustle of moving clothing again. "Could a misfit be in here?" he mumbled, taking out his stiletto and flicking it open. No, that wouldn't be possible; those imbeciles couldn't walk two feet in the dark without falling. What the hell is it? Did I imagine the sounds? No, someone's in here with me. Who could it be? "Who's there?" he yelled again. There was no answer.

After quietly taking off his shoes, Krupp continued walking slowly back towards his starting point. When he heard the noise again, cold sweat formed on his forehead and he nervously moved to one side of the underground passage. Someone or something was coming towards him, or perhaps approaching him from behind, he couldn't tell. He stopped and spun around but could hear nothing.

Turning back, Krupp wasn't ready for the object smashing into his face, breaking his nose, splitting his teeth, and nearly taking off his head. Groaning loudly, he reeled back and fell, hitting his head hard against a rail track. Getting up and wildly slicing at the air around him didn't help either because the second whack of the object smashed the upper part of his back, cracking four vertebrae as it pushed him downward and forward, his face slamming hard onto the concrete floor.

Panic set in as Krupp yelped loudly. Slowly turning over and lying on his back, he could hear his own heavy wet breathing and a gurgling sound originating from his larynx. As hard as he tried, his throat could not keep swallowing the flow of blood filling his nose and mouth. Crawling up the wall to get on his feet, he didn't feel his legs getting forced out from under him before another blow broke both his kneecaps and a second blow pulverized his testicles. In excruciating pain, he tried to yell, "Who, who ... are you? Why are you doing...?"

It was no use, Krupp couldn't speak, he had lost half his face, and what pieces of teeth he had left were partially stuck in his tongue and lips.

When the beating stopped, a light flashed in his one eye that was still half-open. When the light slowly moved to the side, Krupp saw his opponent and gasped heavier. "You ... why...?" were the only words he could utter before coughing up mouthfuls of blood and bits of his gums and teeth.

"You know why, *Sweetie*," the man replied, his face determined. "My real name isn't Kurt Buss, you horrid fucking psychopath. It's Moshe Goldberg, and yes, I'm part of what you refer to as the 'Israeli Set.' You didn't select me, you depraved wretch; I was ordered to entice you to pick me. Well, you're going to hell now where you belong. I'm not going to cut your throat because I'm too civilized. Oh, I've been trained to do it, but I don't have a blade dull enough for you. Just before you go to hell, *Sweetie*, it might piss you off knowing there will be no more holocausts. Did you hear me? I said no more holocausts. Tell that to Hitler, and don't give him my regards."

Seconds later, Krupp didn't feel the large furnace wrench splitting his skull open and crushing his brain.

Still holding the blood soaked wrench, Moshe thoroughly cleaned out Krupp's pockets, and pocketed the man's ring. Afterward, he picked up Krupp's knife and shoes and returned to the furnace room. The two misfits followed his instructions as he gently removed the mops from their hands and compassionately directed them to join him in the elevator.

It took both men fifteen minutes to lug Krupp's body back, and another minute to place it in the left side oven. After Moshe threw in the pipe wrench and Krupp's shoes, he closed the door and pushed the oven's red starting button.

"Dear God, understand and forgive me for my actions," he prayed. "And please concur with my judgement."

Later as the misfits spread Krupp's ashes over the garden, Moshe removed the wrench from the oven, placed it in its rightful spot, and turned the tunnel lights back on. The only evidence Krupp had been there was the immense amount of blood on the tunnel floor and walls. Presently, the pair of *labourers* stood swabbing it away.

Goldberg knew he had problems because the guard on the road outside the barracks had seen him leave with Krupp. Also, closed-circuit cameras in Kravenhall would have caught Krupp heading to the lower level. He asked himself what he should do. Should he kill the sentry? Probably, but then he would be behaving like these bastards. "No, I think it's time for me to leave," he muttered before hearing a noise. Quickly turning his head, he observed the elevator's door closing, and the whine of the motor taking the conveyance down. He knew the misfits' wouldn't know how to run it, so he must be getting *visited*.

Opening up Krupp's flick knife, Moshe hid behind a large hot water tank and waited. He didn't have to wait long. When the door opened again and four armed shaven-headed orderlies stepped out, Moshe held his breath and clutched the knife tightly.

"I'm tellin' ya I heard someone yellin'," one of the four said getting out of the elevator. "It happened just after the lights went out. It couldn't have been the misfits' - they can't speak. Who the fuck moved them here anyway? They're not supposed to be moppin' the floors in here."

Another orderly placed his hands on the oven doors. "This furnace is still hot. Something's not right. Let's separate and look around."

The Israeli agent knew the muzzle velocity of the Luger pistols each of the four carried. When a Luger was fired at close range, it made a real mess of anyone on the receiving end. He also knew he would be a sitting duck if he stayed, but it was impossible for him to cover all directions at once. The only thing he could do was even up the odds.

With two skinheads outside, and one down in the operating room, only one remained cautiously moving around the furnace room. Although he held his pistol at the ready, when the man walked in between the two large hot water tanks, Goldberg confidently grabbed him around his mouth. The orderly dropped his cocked pistol and struggled violently, but his life was over in a fraction of a second. Moshe's other hand had come around delivering two lightning knife jabs to the man's heart.

Goldberg picked up the firearm and dragged the dead man into a corner, shoving the body under four large asbestos-covered pipes that entered the floor.

With his heart pounding heavily and every nerve on edge, Moshe stayed to one side as he silently descended the dimly lit staircase to the morgue below. Before reaching the bottom, he took off his jacket and wrapped it around the Luger.

The open morgue door allowed Moshe to view one of the operating tables through the Plexiglas, but he couldn't see the other orderly? Suddenly, when he saw an enlarging silhouette on the open door, he quickly moved to the side of the room. He figured if he could take this guy out now, it would only leave two, and the odds would be better. It didn't happen. The shadow got smaller as the person headed towards the elevator.

Damn it, the bastard's moving away from me, he thought, trying to collect moisture to lick his lips. Why doesn't he join the others?

Moshe knew he only had one chance to get out and was just about ready to make his move when the shadow returned, growing larger. The orderly was definitely heading his way again, and the silhouette revealed an extended arm with a gun.

Silently pushing every ounce of his body against the wall, Moshe hid while the orderly turned on the lights and stood quietly at the entrance, listening for a sound. When he heard nothing, the skinhead stepped in and only his footsteps gave away his position in the room.

Knowing the element of surprise was on his side, Moshe knew he had to make his move, and it had to be now. Quickly falling forward and down, Goldberg released two shots hitting the man in the chest and forehead and sending him flying against a row of *lockers*.

Although the noise of his smoking German automatic was muffled, the action of the orderly's body hitting the lockers wasn't. Similarly, when the bullets had struck home, the man had released one wild round, and the sound reverberated around the room and down to the tunnel.

Goldberg could not take the time to pick up the spare Luger as he rushed back up the stairs. His plan was to catch the other two as they entered, but it was too late. He never felt the pain of a pistol butt handle clubbing the back of his head, but he did see thousands of stars.

When his eyes tried to focus, Moshe knew his nose was broken but he had no idea how long he had been out. He also knew he was naked and lying soaking wet on the furnace room floor, but nothing else. His throbbing head made it difficult for him to view two grinning orderlies, one holding an empty water bucket.

"Well, what do we have here?" the larger of the two asked, kicking Goldberg hard in the right side of his ribs. "Who are you, you son-of-a-bitch? Speak up!"

Moshe didn't respond and he found himself being yanked to his feet and hammered against a wall. The person behind entwined his arms under Goldberg's arms locking his fingers around the back of his neck. Moshe knew if he moved, his neck would be broken.

While one man held him, the other kept smacking Goldberg's face, saying, "You're a good-looking fucker, aren't you? Have you escaped? No, you're not one of us. You probably helped the other little fucker escape, didn't you?"

Goldberg recognized the man's crazed look. He'd seen the same expression many times since arriving at Kravenhall, and he knew what was coming next. As the orderly facing him took out a stiletto, Moshe felt his legs being spread.

"You know what we do with the likes of you, don't you? After you finish telling us what we want to know, we're going to cut off your nuts and let Dr. Kraven complete the job. By the time he's through with you, you'll wish the earth was never..."

The familiar smell of gunpowder instantly joined the resonance of the two muffled shots Goldberg heard along with the rustle of falling bodies, including his own.

Only slightly conscious, Moshe knew he was bent over a large pipe, but other than the humming furnaces, the only other noticeable noise in the room was the sound of footsteps coming towards him.

A moment later, he felt himself being helped up and slowly turned around so he could sit down. The person also helped him get his arms into his wet shirt.

Once more, Moshe had to concentrate to focus his eyes. As two images of a longhaired man dressed in a tracksuit came together, he heard, "I don't know who you are, son, but I've seen you before and I'm certain those two weren't friends of yours."

Finding it difficult to speak, Goldberg recognized his liberator. Before passing out again, he managed to say, "Thanks, Joe. We've both ... helped each other tonight."

When Moshe woke up next to a warm boiler, he was dressed and he felt a soft cloth cleansing the blood off his neck and head.

"That's a hell of a lump you've got. How do you feel?" Joe asked.

Goldberg's face brightened as Joe helped him stagger to his feet. Lightly touching the back of his head he replied, "I'm all right. Where ... where did you come from?"

"I was in the operating theatre when you took one of them out," Stacy said, holding Moshe's arm and guiding him to sit down again. "As a matter of fact, I used his weapon to finish off these two. I was about to walk in that room before your other *friend* entered, but I'm glad I didn't. How do you know my name?"

Gently trying to straighten his nose, and feeling the back of his head, Moshe replied, "Then you were the first shadow I saw. Uh ... I'm Moshe

Goldberg, an associate of Harvey Cohen. He sent me here to keep an eye on you and check the place out."

Joe's look of incredibility even started Moshe grinning.

"Well, Moshe, you've done one hell of a good job. The last time I saw you, you were having breakfast with Hans Krupp. So we're even - it's two each."

Wincing while feeling the back of his head again, Cohen's associate also managed a grin while correcting the lieutenant. "Not really, Joe, it's four to two. Krupp's not with us anymore, and I took out the guy in the alley outside the Cat's Meow."

"Krupp's dead?"

"Yeah, his ashes are spread over the grass outside. Benevolent guy wasn't he? Krupp was going to kill you tonight. Originally, he'd phoned Kraven telling him you were genuine, and then he checked with someone at the school and never got the chance to correct his mistake."

Joe sat next to the young man. "So my cover was blown?"

"That's right. I know Harvey swapped your prints with Schumann's at the FBI, but he forgot to change the professor's prints at the university. He altered the identification picture, but not Schumann's prints. Harvey probably wasn't aware UCLA performs staff fingerprinting."

Joe whistled. "Too close for comfort. Jesus, they're going to miss that son of a bitch, and we can't stay here, too many of their people are absent."

"How did you get out without being noticed?" Goldberg asked, improving minute by minute.

"Out a window and down a drainage pipe. Then I took the sanatorium's elevator. I was lucky no one noticed me coming through the hospital. I must have got in a railcar just as Krupp did. When the tunnel lights went out and my car stopped, I walked the rest of the way. Did anyone see Krupp once he returned to Kravenhall?"

"Yeah, a guard outside my barracks and probably some of the hospital's staff. He entered the camp through the tunnel."

"Barracks?" asked Stacy. "You mean you've been staying behind the wall? How the hell did you arrange that?"

"It's a long story, Joe," Goldberg said, his mouth widening. "When we meet after I leave here, I'll fill you in."

"You mean, if you leave here."

"Well, uh, yeah, that too."

Both men knew the problem. Moshe had to get out, but Joe could probably finish his *holiday*. When Stacy suggested that the orderlies could also end up as grass fertilizer, Goldberg wouldn't have any part in it.

"Joe, I felt ashamed placing Krupp in one of those ovens. I don't want to be involved in burning any more of them. That's their fucking game. The bastards invented it."

Stacy understood. The next half-hour was spent dragging and concealing the orderlies' bodies and weapons behind some nearby bushes and sheds. Moshe kept hold of one Luger and two loaded magazines.

While the misfits mopped up, Stacy asked Moshe to join him in investigating the remaining tunnels and holding cells. He had felt drafts in certain places during his tour with Krause and Millington, and now he could smell the cold night air.

To the surprise of both men, one underground passage ended in an abandoned farmer's shack on the other side of the road outside the main entrance to the estate. This was the only escape tunnel they could find. Krause had mentioned others, but the two couldn't locate them.

The additional routes were not as pleasant. It was impossible for them to explore the misfit wing of the hospital, but after sliding open heavy steel bolts, they managed to enter the *donation* passageway located through a side door off the main tunnel.

The squalid six-foot-wide passageway measuring about twenty yards long contained eight other doors located left and right. When Moshe turned on the dim row of lights, the two men found the first six cells empty. The seventh and eighth proved otherwise and the stench emanating from the two open doors forced the duo to retch, cough, and cover their noses and mouths.

The packed rooms contained a mixture of toddlers, pre-teens, teenagers, and young adults. All were of the supposed non-white race, including Blacks, East Indians, Chinese, Japanese, and Latinos.

The chambers were barren of lights and running water, and there were no toilets, chairs, bunks, or even blankets. When the occupants relieved themselves, they used single buckets that had spilled over onto the much used clay floors.

Joe and Moshe counted forty-two silent, frightened inhabitants crouching together and gawking anywhere but at them. In each cell, terrified wide-eyed children kept their mouths shut by pressing their faces into the bodies of caring adults. Like everyone else, these youngsters had learned to understand if someone other than a misfit entered, it was selection time, and their cell's number would be reduced again.

"Christ, they've been slaughtering these people and selling their organs," Joe declared, speaking into his handkerchief. "We can't just leave them here, what the hell are we going to do?"

Moshe had already made his decision. "I'm taking them out through that farmer's tunnel."

"But some of them are probably too weak to walk. How far will you get?"

"We've got to do something." Moshe said, still wanting to throw up.

Joe perceived the compassionate look in Goldberg's eyes. Allied troops entering concentration camps during the war revealed the same sentiment.

"Okay, okay, let's do it."

As Goldberg brought the cells' occupants together in the passageway, the young man's gentle professionalism impressed Joe Stacy. Soon, expressions of elation joined smiles, hand kisses, and gestures of immeasurable gratitude.

For the next ten minutes, Moshe informed the prisoners of their delicate and dangerous situation. Some interpreted to those who couldn't understand. Moshe told them to be quiet, and to keep up as best they could. He also mentioned they needed a lot of luck to get away from Kravenhall, but he would do his utmost to ensure their safety. Finally, he stated daylight was only two hours away, and the dogs would be set loose.

"Joe, I need a truck. It doesn't matter what size. Do you know how to hot-wire a vehicle?"

Stacy picked up one of the trembling kids. "Sure, but where the hell will I find one?"

"Before visiting this madhouse, I did my homework. You should have done the same. There's an old barn a quarter of a mile straight ahead from where we'll come out. I know you've got to get back before dawn, but there's an ancient truck in that barn and it's got current plates. It looks in good shape."

Placing the child in a woman's arms, Joe got ready to leave. "Moshe, when you get to the field, take them a quarter of a mile east before you come out on the highway, not before. I'll get you that truck, son, but where will you go from there?"

"Rosenbloom's Boarding House in Spokane. If we make it, we'll be all right. Joe, this hellhole on earth has got to be destroyed. Whether or not you'll want to participate is up to you."

Stacy didn't have to think about it. There was no way Kravenhall could remain. "That's out of my field ... have you got a plan?"

When Cohen's associate nodded, he also became defiant. "Yeah, and I'll be discussing it with Harvey at Rosenbloom's."

"Harvey's in Spokane?" Joe asked, enjoying the good news.

"Yeah. He's been there since I entered with Krupp. Some of our friends are with him."

Joe didn't ask who the *friends* were.

"Joe, we've also got to try and get these misfits out. Meet me outside the tunnel at eight tonight. Also, there's a fire hose curled up by the hydrant on the right side of the mansion. It'll be heavy, but drag it to the diesel tanks?"

Joe now knew part of the plan. "Okay. I'll see you at eight."

Goldberg picked up two children. "You know, Stacy, for a cop, you're all right. Best of luck."

"You'll need all the luck, not me," Joe replied, patting his new buddy on the back. "Ever think about becoming a cop yourself?"

"A cop? The job wouldn't be exciting enough."

As Moshe formed up his *followers*, Joe plodded through the wet farmer's field in the cold night air. The rain had held off, but the heavy dew soaking Stacy's running shoes and socks created a blister that started to bleed by the time he reached the barn's open doors. There it was - a 1953 International three-ton truck.

Quietly opening the driver's door and climbing in, Joe asked himself how Moshe knew about it. To his delight, he found a single key in the ignition, and when he turned it, the tank showed half-full. Now what was he going to do? Starting the truck would definitely wake the people in the nearby farmhouse. He knew farms always had dogs and he was surprised they hadn't started barking. His route out would take him next to the house, and he would have to keep moving, crashing through the main gate. But what if the farmer followed him, or called the police?

Stacy knew he had a good sense of direction. If he could get the truck out he would unite with Goldberg, but how long would it take Moshe to travel the distance? Probably not too long, but then again the people were half-starved and frightened - they couldn't move swiftly.

Joe thought about waking the farmer and explaining the situation, but the idea didn't sit right. Living this close to Kravenhall probably had its perks. Kraven was no dummy - the bastard most likely held parties for his neighbours.

"Damn it," he murmured. "What should I do? If I blow my cover, what will happen? They'll go after everyone, that's what. How much time have I got? About half-an-hour. Christ, it's freezing and I'm sweating."

With his eyes accustomed to the dark, Joe got out of the truck and searched the barn. Moments later, he found what he was looking for. A pair of wire cutters and a spiked tool sat on the workbench. He also found the *guard* dogs. Turning around, he nearly tripped on two tail-wagging bassets standing next to him and wanting to play.

After releasing a sigh of relief, Stacy stroked their heads, whispering, "What are your names? Mr. and Mrs. Friendly, I hope?"

The phone wire leaving the barn led Joe to the connection box on the side of the house. After cutting the wires, he silently moved over to an old jeep parked next to a new Ford Explorer. The spike did its job, and after flattening two tires on each vehicle, he returned to the International. "It's time, Stacy," he muttered, grabbing and twisting the key. "Let's get it over with."

The first time the engine turned, a light went on in the upstairs of the farmhouse, and a heavy throated dog barked. The second time the machine moaned without starting, more lights came on and an old guy dressed in longjons came out onto the back porch before heading back inside.

The large Rottweiler didn't join its owner. The massive dog came towards the truck with the speed of a jaguar, jumping, frothing, and clawing at the closed window. This action started the Bassets' barking and the uproar sounded like what would be expected on opening day at Coney Island. Still, Stacy kept the starter churning. "He's probably gone for a shotgun," he mumbled, flinching his head away from the charging canine.

"Come on, you bastard, start," Joe found himself shouting, trying the third time, keeping his foot on the clutch and ferociously pumping the gas pedal.

When Stacy yelled, "Where the hell is the choke?" more lights appeared and an elderly woman joined the farmer aiming his gun. "Don't worry dear," she yelled, excitedly. "Big Butch will get him!"

All of a sudden the old engine caught. It ran rough at first, but that didn't stop Joe from accelerating past the house and crashing through the large wooden gate. The last thing he saw in his rear-view mirror was the farmer in standing twenty yards behind the vehicle and firing both barrels. When the weapon erupted, most buckshot scattered in the air, but some pellets shattered the truck's passenger side mirror.

"Not a bad shot," Stacy said, under his breath. "He's better than me."

The three-ton's engine ran smoothly and the cab had warmed before Joe found Moshe standing alone on the road.

After receiving the proper signal, the group rushed forward climbing up as fast as they could. The strongest men also helped to assist the weak, and soon, Moshe, and Joe closed the vehicle's tailgates.

When Moshe drove away with Joe standing on the driver's running board, little was said. The sky was brightening in the east, which meant time was running against them. Five minutes later Stacy jumped off across from the estate's boundary. Knowing daybreak was only minutes away, he said, "I've got to hurry. See you tonight."

Joe was not too certain what he should do at this point. He had to enter through the same tunnel. It was the only entrance other than going past two sets of sentries. He knew he had not been seen earlier when he had cut through the hospital, but could he do it again. Probably not, he thought. The sun's coming up and the shifts were going to change.

Running as fast as he could through the underground passage, he started muttering to himself. "There must be another tunnel leading to the grounds, but where the hell is it? Did that crazy doctor mention it? Moshe and I checked all the doors. It must be off the hall leading past the misfit annex."

Joe slowed his pace nearing the main tunnel where Moshe had killed Krupp. While catching his breath he wondered what he was going to do. He knew he didn't have a choice; he had to get into that misfit hallway.

Other than the normal cavern buzz, the main tunnel remained quiet and uninhabited as Joe slowly stuck his head out the door and entered the passageway. Closing the barrier before turning left, he moved silently past a railcar, and then turned right into the misfits' annex hallway. Ten closed doors lined each side of the hallway before he spotted the steel door at the end.

"That's got to be it," he murmured, hurrying and knowing his heart was about to jump out of his chest at any moment.

Just as the detective reached his objective, the tenth door opened and Joe found himself nose to nose with a muscular shaven-headed orderly being followed by a misfit.

Swallowing and trying to control his fright, Stacy smiled while attempting to walk past the man. "Good morning. Looks like another fine day, doesn't it?"

Weather was the last thing on the huge orderly's mind. Grabbing Stacy by the throat, the man flung him against a wall before knocking him down. "Who are you, and what the fuck are you doing here?"

When Joe jumped to his feet and rapidly punched the skinhead twice in the stomach, it was like hitting a cement block. This orderly had a lead belly and the lieutenant's blows had little effect.

Briskly responding, the orderly instantly pinned Stacy up against the same wall and Joe felt two giant hands squeezing his throat. Close to losing consciousness, Stacy abruptly brought his arms up between his attacker's arms forcing the orderly to release his grip. After grabbing the front of the man's coat, Joe immediately slammed his forehead into the attendant's face, but once again, he couldn't stop this giant.

A split second later, the man had Joe in a bear hug. Stacy's arms were free but his back was about to be broken and he couldn't breathe. Using every ounce of his strength, Joe pressed his left thumb into the giant's left eye. Screaming wildly, the man still didn't let go, but he relaxed his hold for a moment, allowing Joe to reach for Millington's letter opener. With a quick thrust, Stacy drove the sharp instrument up under the skinhead's jaw, turning it as he pressed it deeper. As it entered the huge man's brain, the attendant collapsed convulsing and was dead before he hit the ground

The expired hospital attendant had not had time to lock the door he had exited, so Joe directed a robotically grinning misfit to help him drag the man's heavy body back inside. The room's interior was nearly identical to the cells Joe had seen earlier. Although it had lights, there were no toilet facilities except for the usual buckets, and the place reeked of faeces and urine.

While the detective searched the orderly's uniform looking for passkeys, twenty misfits arose from their bare mattresses and walked aimlessly past him towards the door. As they dispersed in the hallway, Joe knew this was the diversion he needed. If he could open all the doors, these people would end up in every room and area in the estate, causing panic and complete disorder.

Moving as fast as possible, Joe released the misfits from every room, and a few minutes later watched pathetically as scores of them wandered through the tunnels and hospital's hallways.

Fortunately, a key from the dead orderly opened the door at the end of the hallway, and the underground passage came out inside a gardening tool shack fifty feet from the greenhouses. Stacy purposefully left the lower tunnel door open and now he could hear misfits shuffling along behind him.

Stripping off his bloodied track jacket only left a t-shirt and track pants to fend off the cold. Once out, though, the detective welcomed the wintry morning air accompanied by the start of daybreak. His predicament still wasn't over. What should he do? Misfits were coming up behind him and he had to make a decision. Should he run up the front stairs yelling the misfits are loose? No, that wasn't natural enough. He had to let Kravenhall's authorities and guests confront the reality themselves. He would jog, that's what he'd do.

"Screw the blister," he mumbled. "Stacy, get jogging around that soccer field."

Jogging, Joe found other guests had the same thing in mind. Governor Walters and three other heavily breathing men welcomed him.

"Morning, Schumann?" Walters offered, jumping on the spot while clearing his throat and spitting. "You like burning off the calories too, eh?"

Knowing his blister had burst and feeling a heel bone wearing away, Joe still managed a pleasant smile and joined in. "Good morning, Governor. It's the food here at Kravenhall. I've never eaten like this in my life. I put weight on quickly and if I don't run, it stays on. How about you?"

Moving his arms like a boxer and punching the air, Walters replied, "I'm the same, if..."

The governor stopped running in his tracks, as did Joe. Twenty misfits appeared out of nowhere, and some had taken direction jogging or slowly walking. One randomly punched the air by imitating Walters while others spontaneously ambled across the field, sauntered in circles, or mimicked guests doing push-ups.

"What the...? Who the fuck are these people?" the governor yelled, feeling fearful, and taking partial cover behind Joe.

Joe found the scene terribly pitiful, and he couldn't control the sadness slowly taking over his face.

At the other end of the field, one of the governor's pals stood trying to inform a misfit that this area was for guests only. The happy man in front of him copied every move the guest made, while more headed his way.

Unlike Millington, it was obvious Walters had not seen these people before.

"Governor, this is the first morning I've jogged here," Joe said. "Is it possible Dr. Kraven allows members of his staff to use the facilities during the early hours?"

"Well, if he does, it's fucking outrageous. What the hell is wrong with these people? Come with me, Schumann! Kraven's going to hear about this nonsense. This could start a panic!"

The governor couldn't have been more correct. As the two of them approached the mansion, guests screamed as misfits washed and opened windows, climbed ladders, mowed lawns, and painted anything they had painted previously.

Joe found the turmoil inside could not be described. While bed sheets were being pulled out from under people and folded, other guests who had been taking showers were *moved out* as misfits took their towels and bathrobes, cleaned, exchanged portraits, polished, rolled up rugs, and did everything they'd been shown beforehand.

When Kraven and Krause appeared in their bathrobes, they turned pale. Misfits were everywhere, even in their offices. People eating breakfast had their utensils snatched out of their hands, tables were moved, and chairs stacked. Soon, that same cutlery was being washed along with the floors and tables.

At the same time as sirens erupted behind the wall, loud horns blared throughout Kravenhall. A few minutes later, trucks carrying brown-uniformed skinheads turned up, and the jackbooted *soldiers* streamed into the mansion, attempting to secure control.

While misfits were being hauled out the main, back, and side doors, Kraven and Krause stood apologizing profusely to incensed guests and their *partners* scurrying everywhere in various stages of dress and undress.

It took nearly an hour to clear Kravenhall, so Stacy knew it would take hours to clear the grounds, golf course, lake, and the various field-training areas on the other side of the wall.

Joe stood with Walters when Kraven eventually used the estate's loudspeakers.

"My good friends please accept our heartfelt apologies for this unfortunate inconvenience. As you know, this is a clinic, and while we do our utmost to care for and control our patients, there are times when, er ... little things go wrong. Please return to your apartments and prepare for another splendid day at Kravenhall. Breakfast will continue in half-an-hour. Thank you."

"Where were you gentlemen when this happened?" Kraven asked when he came out of his office and approached Joe and the governor.

Still visibly upset, Walters shot back, "Schumann and I were jogging with some friends. What's going on here, Kraven? Who the hell are these madmen roaming around?"

The doctor chose his words carefully. "They're, er, patients of ours, Governor Walters. My colleague, Dr. Krause and I are helping them get their lives back together. I'm terribly sorry this happened. We'll make it up to you somehow - you can be assured. In the meantime..."

Kraven stopped apologizing when Dr. Krause quickly appeared and pulled him aside to whisper in his ear.

"Excuse me for a moment, gentlemen," Kraven said, becoming more alarmed as seconds ticked away. "What? Are you certain? My God, when did this happen?"

Krause's excited eyes scanned the room while he further explained certain other matters to Kraven. After he finished, both of them rapidly walked away.

Walters yelled, "Dr. Kraven, I'm not through with you yet!"

Kraven didn't turn when he bellowed, "Don't bother me now, Walters!"

"What are you still doing here?" Moshe Goldberg asked recognizing someone he knew after joining Mr. and Mrs. Rosenbloom, five of Harvey's *associates*, and local Jewish doctors assisting the passengers he unloaded at Rosenbloom's Boarding House.

Goldberg's trip from Kravenhall had been uneventful and when he had driven the three-ton into Rosenbloom's backyard, tall bushy trees encircling the old four-story rooming house had shielded the off-loading procedure from prying eyes. Ten minutes later, the truck was parked at the Spokane train station and an accompanying car drove the driver back to the boarding house.

While Moshe spoke with Rudy Reickhardt, few regular residents of Spokane noticed the influx of curious muscular young men frantically milling around the streets, bus terminal, and railway station. All wore civilian clothes with various types of sports caps, and the absence of any cavorting was evident as they searched.

"My parents weren't home when I phoned from the bus depot," Rudy explained. "Cathy said they're in Iowa and won't be returning until three o'clock this afternoon."

"Cathy? Who's Cathy?" Moshe asked conscious of Harvey's icy stare. Moshe knew he had broken the rules, and although Cohen had accepted his reasoning, the regional director of the Israeli Set was still highly upset.

"Cathy's our maid. She said they had been away for three days. I'm sorry if my presence endangers you. I'll leave now and..."

Harvey stood to pour a coffee. "You stay where you are. What's done is done. Are you thoroughly aware what Kraven and his ilk are doing?"

"Yeah, it's all new to me, but I now know my parents are part of it."

"Are you trying to tell us you had no idea whatsoever of your father and mother's involvement?"

"Yes, sir, not until I was sent here. My dad's golfing club meets at our house once a month, but it's held behind locked doors in his office in our basement. I've asked my mom and dad why they lock the door, but they've never answered me."

Harvey didn't let up. "So your mother also attends the meetings?"

Rudy shrugged. "Yes sir, so do other wives. When my dad told me he teaches explosive techniques at the Reichsland Camp, I thought it had something to do with his gun club. Then when they said it was time for me to be trained, I thought I was going to be taught how to shoot."

Harvey's eyes thoroughly searched every part of Rudy's face. "Are you a racist, Rudy?"

"No sir. In the past, I've been given shit for hanging around with some Chinese friends of mine, but I still hang around with them."

"Who was against it?"

"My mom and dad. I didn't understand their gibberish about my friends being unclean. They're cleaner than me."

"Did your mother and father ever discuss ... Judaism?"

"Yes, sir. When I was twelve, they told me Jews belong to a closed clique of anti-religious money lenders that don't believe in Christ."

Harvey's eyes lit up and he could not help grinning. "Did you believe them, Rudy?"

A guilty look appeared but only for a moment. "I did before I met my best friend, Lew Groberman. I spend more time at his house than mine. His folks run a delicatessen and Mr. and Mrs. Groberman set me straight."

"What did they tell you?"

"They told me about the world's different religions. That Jesus was a Jew and while the high priests thought he was special, they didn't believe he was the

Son of God. They said their religion is still waiting for the chosen one. They also showed me the Old Testament in our bible. Mr. and Mrs. Groberman are closer to me than my parents are. Whenever I have problems, I talk them over with Lew's family. My mom and dad have always been distant - they've never had time for me."

Harvey nodded compassionately. "Then you're your own man, Rudy? You seem to make up you're own mind?"

"Yes, sir, and I always have," Rudy said, smiling and accepting Harvey and Moshe's hands and shaking them. A moment later when five other men offered their hands, Rudy Reickhardt was pleased with himself.

At three-thirty that afternoon, Rudy was not prepared for the attitude of his enraged father. Although the call was made from the Rosenbloom house, Harvey *utilized* a special telephone scrambling device ensuring the call could not be traced. The boy's father in Montana would be unable to know the whereabouts of his son. Also, Mr. Reickhardt did not know the call was being taped.

"Hi dad, it's me, Rudy."

"Where the hell are you?"

"I can't tell you, dad. I ran away from that madhouse you sent me to."

"You had no right doing that. I want you to get back there now, Rudy!"

"I'm not going back, dad. It's a racist organization and they tried raping me."

"Rudy, that racist organization you refer to is my bread and butter. It's the preservation of our kind. Do you hear me? It's not racist. The people are our kind."

"But dad, they're all lunatics and they were going to rape me."

"I don't care if they were going to pass you around the whole fucking complex; everyone who's a man goes through it. It's called initiation. If you think you're untouchable, Rudy, you're wrong! You're of my Aryan blood. Goddamnit. No son of mine is going to be a chicken-shit! Do you understand me ... you're going back!"

"You've never talked to me this way before, dad. Count me out!"

"That's because you've embarrassed your mother and me. Both Dr. Kraven and Dr. Krause have been on the phone to us at Reichsland and our Fatherland Camp in Iowa. Those two fucking turncoats did this to you, didn't they?"

"Who do you mean?"

"You know who I'm referring to ... Hans Krupp and Kurt Buss! Listen Rudy, they're as good as dead. They don't know it, but both of them are dead. The Elite Team has been called in. Get away from them, Rudy, or you'll go down with them."

"What's the Elite Team?"

"It's none of your business. Where are those two mother fuckers now?"

"With me, and they want to come and speak with you. Dad, you don't know what's going on in places like Kravenhall. I'm taking the bus home with them. The least you can do is listen to them. Come on, dad: I think you and mom are in over your heads and..."

In a flash, Rudy's father became amiable. "Okay, son, sure, sure I'll listen to them, but only for your sake. Rudy, you know your mother and I love you. Er, when are you travelling with them?"

As Rudy spoke, the eyes of those around him bore into his person.

"We'll be arriving in Billings tomorrow night. There's only one bus."

"Tomorrow night? Good, good, that will give me a little time to collect my thoughts so I can understand their rationale in getting you out. Rudy, I was only joking about the Elite Team. If you mention it to Krupp, he won't come with you, and I really do want you to understand what takes place at Kravenhall. Don't mention the team to him, Rudy. Promise me ... all right, son?"

"Sure dad, I promise. Can you hold on a sec?"

"You bet, son."

"Dad, they're doing me a favour and they want to know if they can trust you. Hans Krupp also says he knows you."

"Rudy, would I endanger the life of my only son?"

"No."

"Well, you tell them that. Certainly, I know Hans. He's a fine fellow. Listen, Rudy, perhaps I was a little brusque with you. You're eighteen now, and your mother and I can't always be guiding you all of your life. You live it your way. I want to hear what those bastards did to you at Kravenhall. All right, son, I'll straighten Kraven out, you know I will!"

"Thanks, dad, I knew you'd understand. Give my love to mom."

"I will, Rudy, God bless."

Rudy's eyes stared blankly after he had slowly hung up the phone and the tape was played back.

Harvey put his arm around the boy's shoulders. "It's tough when you have to learn the hard way, isn't it Rudy?"

The same blank eyes started welling up, and the young man did not know what to say. He more than understood what his father's plans were for Krupp and Buss. He also knew if he were in the way, he'd be disposed of with them. "I ... I didn't think my mother would..."

After guiding Rudy to a chair, Cohen sat next to him. With all the sincerity in the world, he said, "The problem is you don't know if she's been brainwashed to the same degree as your dad. Your dad is beyond help, Rudy. It was the same in pre-war and wartime Germany. Kids from the Hitler Youth turned in their parents, brothers, sisters, best friends, and anyone else who stood up for freedom and went against Hitler and his Nazis. Those youngsters were so indoctrinated, they couldn't think properly. As far as they were concerned, Adolf Hitler was their new father. That's what your dad had intended for you at Kravenhall. Now, let's you and I discuss my plans for this so-called Elite Team. We've been looking for them for a long time, Rudy, and through a stroke of luck you're going to help us catch them."

Harvey spoke to Rudy for another hour before leaving the house with Moshe. After they left, Rudy assisted the Rosenblooms who had their hands full cooking meals and making certain their houseguests were comfortable. Two of Harvey's five associates also relieved Mr. and Mrs. Rosenbloom periodically, but the remaining three stayed outside, keeping their eyes peeled.

Chapter 12

When all the misfits were accounted for, Dr. Kraven sat at his desk and telephoned Dieter Krueger in New York to explain the various problems at Kravenhall. Krueger didn't hold back his rage because he had already learned of Rudy's escape, Krupp's supposed betrayal, the killing of orderlies, and the misfit problem.

"What are you talking about, Kraven? I was just there and everything was fine. This news has spread to our offices throughout the world. How the hell could you be so careless? I've just heard from Schtaff, and the Elite Team is already in the air."

Utter terror shot through Kraven as he stood and nearly pulled the telephone off his desk. "What?"

"Schtaff tells me Krupp has got to be eliminated because he knows far too much. Kraven, why did you allow Switzerland's top *messenger* to fall in love with some young pup?"

"Herr Krueger, I had no involvement in that affair. It was a fait accompli before he arrived here."

"But you allowed this Kurt Buss access to Kravenhall without investigating him. You broke the cardinal rule you son-of-a-bitch! Between you and Schmidt, I'm looking like an incompetent fool!"

Kraven sat down again, straightening anything within reach and trying to keep his trembling free hand occupied. Swallowing, and feeling sweat forming all over his body, he replied, "I … I asked Krupp if he'd cleared Buss and he told me he had. Look, Dieter, I..."

"Don't Dieter me, you brainless idiot! You and Krause have jeopardized our whole American operation. If Krupp isn't found, both of you will pay dearly. Fortunately, we know where Krupp is, and that might be your passport to go on living. He and his lover will be dealt with tomorrow. Get everyone out of that unorganized kindergarten, right now, until we sort this matter out. Do you understand me, Kraven?"

"Yes, Herr Krueger, at once. Now, will you let me explain about...? Hello, hello, hello. Are you there, Herr Krueger…?"

Krause entered the room as Kraven hung up the phone. Just one look at his colleague told Krause there were going to be repercussions.

"What's wrong, Xavier?"

Doctor Kraven stood nervously pacing the floor behind his desk. He knew the deadly reputation of the Elite Team. Each one of them would think nothing of slicing open babies' throats without feeling shame.

"Krueger informed me the Elite Team is on its way."

Krause's eyes began blinking rapidly. "Good God! Surely not for us? Krupp is *their* man, not ours. How can they blame us for his desertion?"

Pouring a stiff drink, Kraven looked like a defeated man. "I don't know why, but they are. We've been ordered to ask our guests to leave. I think we'd better protect ourselves, Heinz. We'll hold a special black tie dinner for everyone tonight and you and I will fly out with the VIPs first thing in the morning. The Elite Team won't touch us if we're with five senators, two congressional representatives and Governors' Walters, Frolich and Robinson. Do you want a drink?"

Krause nodded, saying, "You mean four senators, don't you?"

"Four? We've got five?" declared Kraven, passing a scotch to Krause.

"Aren't you forgetting that Putreds found Millington's letter opener stuck in an orderly's head? It's up to you, Xavier, but I personally don't think we can take a chance with Millington. He was also friendly with Krupp. It's possible he assisted releasing the misfits."

"What do you propose, Heinz?"

"I think we should have Putreds take care of him, and burn him. We'll simply say he left early, and…"

To stop his associate from speaking, Kraven held the open palm of his right hand in front of Krause's face. "Too messy, old friend. We'll get him drunk at dinner and when he's put to bed, I'll give him a shot of Iodzathene. Not a full shot because I want him conscious when the ambulance arrives. He'll be taken to Spokane General where he'll die of cardiac arrest."

Krause breathed easier. "Yes, that's better. You know, Xavier, I kind of liked Gene Millington. I really find it hard to believe he's turned against us."

Kraven shook his head. "I agree, Heinz, but can we take that chance?"

As Krause refreshed Kraven's drink and poured himself another scotch, he said, "Of course not, dear friend. With your permission, I'll make the announcements informing our guests we will prorate their refunds, and buses will arrive here after breakfast tomorrow. Also, I'll tell them tonight's meal will be superb and we'll arrange suitable *entertainment* for them when they retire."

Krause paused for a moment. "What excuse should I use? They're going to want an explanation?"

Kraven thought for a moment. "Tell them Krueger's returning to hold a special meeting with our international departmental heads. That should be sufficient."

"What time is dinner?" Krause asked.

"We'll need an early night, so make it seven o'clock. You know, Heinz, something is puzzling me. Why would Krupp leave his rented car here?"

"Xavier, I think he did it to throw us off track. With his car parked here, we'd believe he was still on the premises."

Nodding and refilling his glass, Kraven replied, "Yes of course, you're probably right."

After putting on his jacket, Joe Stacy checked himself in the full mirror. Kravenhall's tuxedo and black patent leather shoes fit fairly well.

You look great now, he thought, standing just inside his open door. In a few hours you won't.

The lieutenant had his plan worked out and had left his room door open. When he heard Senator Millington's voice, he would join him going down the stairs. As it happened, he didn't have to wait long. Other guests leaving their rooms and apartments offered their comments to Millington as the man came out of his suite, and that was Joe's cue. After closing his door, he approached the senator in the hallway. "Excuse me, Gene. Do you have a minute?"

The senator turned and waited. "Certainly, Helmut, what can I do for you?"

When Joe caught up to the government official, the two men walked along the hallway and down the stairs together. "Er, how does one go about making a donation to Kravenhall? Also, is it tax deductible?"

Millington appeared pleased to answer. "Make your cheque out to the Xavier Kraven Heart Foundation, that's all. Yes you can deduct it, and I'm sure Dr. Kraven will appreciate your contribution."

Just as the pair approached the last two steps at the bottom of the stairs, Joe feigned a tripping action causing him to fall sideways on the floor. Sprawled face down on the plush carpet, he moaned slightly as Millington and two other guests assisted him to his feet.

"What the hell did I trip on?" Stacy asked, reviewing the last rung.

The senator still held on to him. "I have no idea, and I'm glad you didn't take me down with you. How do you feel, Schumann?"

Grimacing, Joe started hobbling towards the dining room, but had to stop.

"Gene, I think I've twisted my ankle. Please carry on without me; I'll soak it and join you as soon as I can. Will you tell Dr. Kraven that I'll be...?"

"Yes, don't worry, I'll inform Xavier. Do you need any help getting back to your room?"

"No, thank you - I'll be all right. Damn it! Why do these things always happen at inopportune moments? I was looking forward to the same wonderful dinner and comradeship we enjoyed last night."

Millington helped Joe to the top of the staircase. "It never fails, does it? Your foot will feel better after you soak and wrap it. They place first aid kits in the bathrooms, so use the elastic bandage. See you soon."

Aware of the fact that cameras were watching his every movement, Stacy limped along to his room. Double locking the door and purposely leaving the lights off, he climbed down the drainage pipe and went and unhooked the hose from the fire hydrant. Straining from the weight, when he dropped it next to the fuel tanks, he had to sit down and rest for a few minutes. Five minutes later, he entered the sanatorium's entrance at the front of the mansion.

Unfortunately, Stacy's second jaunt through Kravenhall's hospital wasn't as uneventful as his first visit. As soon as the elevator doors opened, a nurse appeared; the same girl he'd spent the night with. The beautiful young woman appeared more surprised than he did. Smiling bashfully, she asked, "Helmut, what are you doing here? Look at you you're all dirty. What happened?"

Joe felt perspiration building up under his wig. Gently taking her arm and guiding her towards the railcar, he said, "I've, twisted my ankle, but I also wanted to see you again. If I promise to keep it to myself, will you tell me why you work here?"

The young woman squirmed a little. "Where are you taking me?"

Joe tightened his grip and they kept moving. "You haven't answered my question. Surely you don't like what they make you do?"

An orderly appeared and quickly approached them, asking, "What the fuck is he doing down here?"

The girl anxiously glanced at Joe before answering, "Dr. Schumann has tripped and sprained his ankle. Dr. Kraven sent him here to have me look at it."

The orderly's suspicion disappeared, and he grunted turning away towards the misfit section. "Well, hurry it up then, and get back to your ward."

A moment later when they arrived at the tunnel entrance, Joe held her against the wall. "Thanks, I owe you one. Now are you going to answer me?"

"My parents are cleaners at the Fatherland Camp," she said. "They'll be killed if I don't co-operate. I can be executed simply for telling you this, and I shouldn't be talking to you. Let me go."

"I can't let you go. Come with me, and I'll get you out of this madhouse."

The girl struggled violently. "I'm not going anywhere with you, Dr. Schumann. Get your hands off me ... my parents will be..."

Joe's consolation of, "Sorry, honey," went unheard as he slugged her and threw her over his right shoulder. Swiftly moving through the tunnel, he knew the girl would be out for half-an-hour, and when she came to, she wouldn't be in the slaughterhouse any longer. "Sweetheart, you can thank me later."

The quiet shack was just as dark as the tunnel, and Joe Stacy's heart was not prepared for the unseen voice that welcomed him when he laid the nurse down.

"Jesus, Stacy, trust you to bring a broad out with you. When the hell are you going to get your priorities right?"

"I think he's got his priorities right, Captain," Pete's voice said. "Not bad, Joe. Not bad at all."

Joe's delight at seeing them joined the white teeth smiles on the two dark figures sitting in a corner waiting for him. Amidst pats and handshakes, he still could not believe Glover and Durnell were here with him.

"How...? Jesus it's good to see you guys. How long have you been here?"

"An hour," Glover replied, adding, "From what we've heard, you've seen Satan, and he's human."

Stacy's facial expression said it all. "He sure is. Do you really want to be here? You know what's going to happen don't you?"

Glover buttoned up his coat to keep out the damp. "We're not here, Joe, and neither are you, remember? Yeah, we know what's goin' down, and we wouldn't miss it for the world. Harvey's briefed us."

"So he finally introduced himself, did he?"

"He had to. He also drove us here. Our vehicles are in Seattle. When he told Pete what your plans were, your partner explained that a team's a team, and we had every right to be here."

"Damned right," Durnell said. "Joe, life hasn't been the same without you."

"Or you guys," Stacy shot back. "Where's Harvey now?"

Glancing at the nurse, Glover said, "Who knows? He just said to wait for him. Who's the broad?"

Joe's pocket-watch read seven-thirty. Over the next half-hour, he explained everything to shaking heads exhibiting expressions of utter disgust. Even the nurse who had regained consciousness displayed revulsion as she listened with interest and exhibited admiration for Stacy. She introduced herself as Mildred, regretfully telling them that most of Kraven's activities were not known to her because she had only been employed a month. As far as the misfits were concerned, Krause had told her they were brain tumour patients and if operations had not been performed, they would have died. "Better to be in this condition than dead, eh, young lady," Krause had said. "If you try to leave us, we'll catch you and pass you around our storm troopers on the other side of the wall. Also, your parents will be shot."

"Your parents will be fine, Mildred," Joe said, checking his watch again. "I've got things to do, and I want you to stay here. Is that all right?"

Tears ran down Mildred's cheeks. "Thank you for getting me out. I never want to go in there again. Thank you, Dr. Schumann, er ... Joe."

At five after eight, Harvey Cohen appeared. When he saw Joe, he let out a low whistle. "Do you always wear a tux when the party's going to be lively? Good to see you again, Joe. Moshe told me about his adventure."

Stacy shook Cohen's offered hand. "You're an amazing man, Harvey. Thanks for tipping these guys off ... I missed 'em. Well, are you ready?"

"Ready as we'll ever be. Who's she?" Harvey asked, pointing at Mildred.

After Joe explained, Cohen stepped outside and appointed a female assistant to stay with the young lady. Returning, he inquired, "What's happening at Kravenhall?"

"Kraven's obviously been ordered to clear the place, so he's throwing a final dinner party. It started at seven, and knowing the length of his speeches, it should last two-and-a-half hours. Where are the buses for moving the misfits?"

"We're not using buses, Joe. We've brought one tractor-trailer and we're going to squeeze them in. It's parked two-hundred metres down the road. We don't wish to attract any attention. When we're finished, it'll be parked at the emergency door at Spokane's hospital."

Glover chuckled but winced from the pain of his gout. "Shit, that'll make the World News. Who owns the truck?"

"Don't know. It's stolen, and it won't be missed until the police are called by the hospital's staff." Glancing at Joe, he added, "Did you have problems moving the hose?"

"Yeah, it weighed a ton. Say, how did you know I moved it?"

"Let's just say there's diesel fuel flowing through it right now."

Joe grinned and cocked his head in a manner indicating he was thoroughly amazed at the professionalism of Harvey's crew. "You guys don't screw around, do you? What about the guards at the two checkpoints?"

A hard expression Joe had not seen before came over Cohen. It was as if the job had to be done at all costs and absolutely nobody could get in the way.

"They're dead, Joe. Our people are wearing their uniforms."

Stacy didn't know if he liked the sudden reality of what he had heard, or not. "You've killed them? Why?"

"Joe, it was either us or them. It's better that it's them. These bastards are sneaky. They had radio devices on them that would have given the game away in seconds. They were even wearing SS belt-buckle guns. Look, a lot more of them are going to die tonight, you know that. You also know what they do to innocent people, so don't get soft on me, okay?"

Stacy knew Harvey was right, but it was hard for him to accept this new *process* of settling the score. The action went against everything he had been taught about ethics.

"Sorry, Harv. I wasn't thinking. But I don't know if we should be acting like them."

Glover growled, saying, "I just wish I could have had the chance to do it. Not one of these monsters deserves to live. Joe, Harvey's right, they aren't worthy of breaks. "

"Okay, let's get to it," Harvey said, opening the door, and then closing it again. "Listen, I just want you people to help with the misfits. What we do later might bother you, and I don't want you to get involved. Do we agree on that point?"

After glancing at one another, two of the three police officers nodded. Joe, however, still had a gnawing uncertain feeling in his stomach, and Harvey sensed it.

"Hear me, Joe. We're no different than you. We believe in law and order, but these animals don't. If they get their way, democracy will be outdated, and the world will slowly sink in a sea of blood, as it did before. Totalitarianism has always been humankind's enemy. If you're naive enough to believe this detestable organization can be stopped using the judicial process, you're out of your mind. Remember Hitler was appointed democratically. Need I remind you of the judges he appointed? Those *people*, if they can be called that, spit on everything democratic."

Stacy slowly shook his head. "Yeah, I know. It's just that I..."

"I know what you're going through. You're a decent person, but you don't make the laws, you enforce them. Well, think of that when Vice-President MacPherson becomes President, and every official and judge in the country is a Nazi. You'll have some aberrant laws to impose by force then. Chief Justice Bell will make certain of that."

Harvey opened the door again and looked back. "I've got no time to play games - are you with us or not?"

Several long seconds passed. "Okay, but ... Yeah, let's get it over with."

Cohen remained staring at the detective for a few more seconds, his inflexible face indicating he was thinking of the smallest of details. "Moshe and two of us will lead the group of you into the building. Do you have a key to the misfits' rooms?"

Joe took it out of his pocket. "Right here."

"Good, give it to Moshe," he said, preparing to leave.

When Moshe and Joe's eyes met after Harvey's main assistant entered with two *friends* holding curled-up ropes, both he and Joe indicated a bond had been set after their previous *adventures*. Moshe then took hold of Stacy's offered hand, yanked him close, and gave him a pat on his back. "Joe, did I ever thank you for saving my life?"

Joe handed him the key. "Yeah you did. And thanks for saving mine."

Harvey glanced at his watch. "We've allowed forty-five minutes for everything. The time is now eight-fifteen. At nine o'clock, the truck will be here along with our own transportation. Moshe, away you go."

Moshe took out a small pistol and screwed a silencer onto it before motioning the police officers to follow him into the tunnel. Harvey departed through the shed's door.

A few minutes earlier when Joe had said, "You guys don't screw around," he never realized just how right he was. Obviously, Moshe and his two assistants had done their homework. Goldberg asked the police officers to stay in the tunnel until he returned. When the Goldberg trio left the tunnel, two headed for the guest hospital and Moshe directed himself towards the misfit section. Ten minutes later after Moshe and one assistant returned, the five intruders started opening doors after stepping over three dead orderlies lying sprawled in the hall of the misfit area. All had been shot twice in their hearts. Joe didn't bother asking what would happen if more appeared; he knew the rest had been killed. He also had a gut feeling the communications room staff had been *silenced* in addition to all staff members in the guest hospital. He learned later that six other nurses had already returned to their quarters behind the wall.

Glover and the group recoiled from the smell as they opened the first door and turned on the lights. Methodically, Moshe and his friend got the misfits up and showed each of them how to hold on to a rope. Goldberg then passed the end of the rope to Glover and told him to tie it around his waist and start moving out. It worked. Each misfit gripped the rope tightly and obediently hobbled after the captain. With Joe and Pete pitching in and controlling the ropes, misfits in the other rooms were treated exactly the same way.

While the misfits were being moved, Harvey Cohen remained outside watching two of his team stick large amounts of plastic explosive with small electrical devices underneath the support struts on either side of the huge storage tank. From the look of the hose, the diesel fuel was flowing well, mixing thoroughly with the silo's fertilizer, known to the group as ammonium nitrate.

Cohen moved next to one of his men. "Simon, we're out of here in twenty minutes, how much fuel has gone through?"

The bushy-eyed and moustached bodybuilder rubbed his chin. "The way it's gushing, I'd say the tank will be empty by the time we leave. This is going to be one massive blast, Harvey."

"The bigger, the better," Cohen replied, before repeating himself. "The bigger the better."

Moshe's method of moving the misfits exceeded his best expectations. At times, various men let go of the rope and started walking back towards the hospital, but were turned around by *conformists* dutifully shuffling along.

Half the misfits were outside when the truck arrived at the tunnel's end and the loading procedure took place with little difficulty. When all the misfits were aboard, the doors were closed and locked.

Joe had led the last group out, and now he waited for Moshe to follow, but his friend didn't show. In a moment, he knew why. Goldberg, without being noticed from the mansion, had managed to move Krupp's rented vehicle out of the compound and down the driveway. Once parked on the main road outside the tunnel shack, the driver got out smiling. "I knew Krupp left his briefcase in the trunk. Should be some interesting reading the material inside."

Good thinking, Joe thought. "I hope you share it, Moshe?"

"Joe, you'll be with us when we open it," his friend replied, before adding, "Harvey and the others will be here soon, I passed them on the driveway."

A minute later, Moshe ordered two of his people to get moving with the rig. A black car driven by a single driver would follow it all the way into town. "Remember now," he said, "Back it up to the hospital's emergency entrance. Don't waste any time opening the doors, and then guide the first few in. The rest will follow. Away you go."

As the semi and its support car headed towards Spokane, Durnell came over and stood by Joe. "When they arrive at this time of night, the shit's going to hit the fan. I hope the hospital can handle them?"

"What else could we do with them?" Moshe asked, spotting Harvey and his crew walking towards them. "All done, Harv?"

Cohen nodded holding a black transmission apparatus in his hand. "Yeah, let's get the hell out of here. Is that Krupp's car?"

"Yeah," Moshe said. "Joseph's driving it, with Josh following. I'll take Joe, Pete, and Captain Glover with me. The nurse is with Josh."

"Then our people are all loaded?"

"Say the word and we'll be out of here, Harvey."

Harvey nodded, waving his right hand to signal the various cars to move out. "Okay, everyone knows their various routes to Rosenbloom's. Moshe, you leave now before I blow this thing. Joe, this detonation will be heard in Seattle."

A solitary look came over Stacy as his car drove away. "It should go well with the popping of champagne corks inside Kravenhall," he said. "Will there be much left of the building?"

A familiar but much more resolute expression appeared on Moshe's face. "When that 200 ton baby blows, I don't believe any part of Kraven's empire will remain. And that goes for most of the camp. Keep in mind, Joe, this is their way, not ours. These people live for the death of everyone except their own depraved breed."

Regretful expressions may have been evident, but the minds and hearts of the four men understood the truth. Those within the Aryan movement adhered to a policy of absolute hate and total abhorrence for anyone not of their so-called *pure* blood. A loathing so strong it eliminated any semblance of humankind's sanity. Kraven and his species cherished a hunger so incomprehensibly hideous, the devil himself would be hard pushed to surmount it.

As sleet started to fall, Moshe didn't stop at the high point of a bridge a mile away from Kravenhall, but Harvey did. Walking around the front of his van and examining the darkness of the night for at least a minute, he uttered, "May God forgive me," and pushed a button on the device he held.

Harvey Cohen's hands shook as he drove away. In the never-ending second when the sky had lit up, the rumble following the terrifying blast shook the earth, the moon, the stars, and the universe. Hell on earth seemed to turn itself inside out, and Harvey knew the wrath he had unleashed should have been rendered and witnessed only by the Creator and the devil.

The driving sleet had turned to a heavy rain when the rig operator backed the semi up against Spokane's General Hospital's emergency doors and got out to unload his *passengers*.

Moments later, one of four nurses in the near empty emergency ward noticed five soaking-wet but smiling men ambling past her desk. Each was dressed in coveralls and running shoes, and paid no attention to her when she cleared her throat indicating they should stop.

"Can I help you gentlemen?" she yelled, before her mouth locked in the open position. Twenty identically dressed males followed and when she glanced at the automatic doors, over a hundred more stood shuffling and pushing each other trying to enter.

The nurse's scream attracted the attention of the other three nurses and two doctors on duty, and when they rushed to the scene, a misfit had the listening end of a stethoscope on a frozen nurse's forehead. By the time the police arrived, and local radio stations pleaded for citizen assistance, misfits *owned* the hospital.

The Rosenbloom house was near empty when Harvey arrived and quickly got down to business."Captain Glover, I suggest you, Joe, and Pete, leave immediately. Within the hour, this area will be overflowing with state troopers and the National Guard. Simon, get the van ready and take our friends home. Moshe, open Krupp's briefcase."

Three Seattle police officers and Harvey Cohen gathered around while Moshe picked the lock on the expensive attaché case. When he opened it, the contents consisted of a five-foot nylon rope, an inch-thick file, a computer disk, a pistol, a silencer, three full magazines, two stilettos, and a set of small tools.

Perusing the items, Cohen still bore the distaste of his experience an hour before. He was in no mood for explanations or talk of any kind and it showed. Reading the file while leaving the room, he said, "It's going to take me awhile to study this file, Joe. Give me a few days - agreed?"

Stacy really didn't have any choice. As Harvey left the room, Glover motioned it was time to move on.

"Moshe, how are you releasing the escapees?" the captain asked. "They're going to talk."

"We've given them money and we want them to talk, but they won't discuss the Rosenbloom house. They don't know us, and the Rosenblooms are following the routine we've set up. We've been moving people out every half-hour after obtaining signed affidavits and taping their statements. Seven who are ill have been moved to a small hospital in Colorado. Tomorrow, the world will know about Dr. Kraven and his clinic. Right now, we've got other matters to take care of. Switzerland has dispatched a highly trained group of killers whose sole purpose is assassination. These thugs are good ... really good."

"Can you handle them?" Joe asked, heading towards the door.

Moshe poured a coffee and after exhibiting his usual self-satisfied grin, he said, "Normally I would have said no, but this time we've got the element of surprise on our side for a change. We've been waiting to meet these bastards for a long time. Anyway, thanks Joe. See you in a few days, I hope."

Joe was the last police officer to leave, and after saying, "Good luck," he suddenly thought of something and turned around. "Oh, I almost forgot. Moshe, I need a copy of that disk."

"When?"

"Right now. Copy it for me, will ya?"

Appearing indecisive, Goldberg took the disk out of the briefcase. Pausing for a moment while fingering it, he said, "I'll have to ask Harvey."

Determined, Joe replied, "Go ahead, and if he says no, tell him the *property* is jointly owned."

"I see a cop's look in your eyes, Joe."

"Yeah, you will until I'm off this case. I'll wait."

Harvey agreed and after a copy was made, the three left the Rosenbloom house for good.

During the drive out of Spokane, their vehicle passed scores of police cars with red lights flashing and sirens blaring. Half an hour later, a convoy of at least twenty army trucks loaded with troops joined another thirty police cars' heading towards Spokane, and what was left of Kravenhall.

"Let's hear what the radio has to say about it?" Glover asked Simon, the driver, who tuned in to a local station. A female reporter was questioning the farmer with the Rottweiler and the missing three-ton truck.

"... Yes, every goddamned window in my house. The wife and I thought an atom bomb had gone off. Even my pacemaker skipped."

"Then what happened?" the reporter asked.

"Well, I rushed up here with my Rottweiler, Big Butch, and shit... sorry, I... are we on the radio?"

"Yes, please go on."

"Sorry. Well, the place was like a war zone. When I passed the dead guys on the road, they were only wearin' their underwear, and three quarters of the clinic was gone. There were fires and rubble everywhere."

"Dead people dressed in underwear? Where?"

"At the barrier gates. They'd been shot in their heads and hearts. There was blood all over 'em."

"Did you see anyone alive?"

"Yeah, comin' out from behind the brick wall ... lots of 'em, all injured and bleedin', limpin', and crawlin' around. I had to get the hell outta there because ammo started goin' off. Rockets shot up in the air, and there was more explosions than Independence Day."

"What was the site used for? We have information it was a rest home?"

"The wife and me have only been invited twice. Dr. Xavier Kraven runs the place, and he's a real nice guy. He put on a few shindigs in the joint just for us. I guess it was a gas leak that caused the explosion."

"Then you think it *was* a gas blast?"

"Shit, lady, what else could cause this?"

The announcer took over. "There you are, Andy. We'll try and question some of the other locals milling around, but in the meantime, police and troops have cordoned off the whole area."

"Thanks Carol, we'll check back with you shortly. If you've just tuned in, a major blast rocked the Kraven Clinic tonight, and it is believed casualties are high. Police, fire, and the army are having difficulty wading through the rubble. Now, let's go over to Max Arden with another strange story breaking at Spokane's General Hospital. Hello, Max, what's going on over there?"

"It's mayhem here, Andy. What with troops and police trying to round up a hundred or more escaped mental patients, and ambulances and trucks bringing in the injured from the explosion, the scene here is chaotic. All these male mental patients apparently came here from the clinic after it exploded."

"How did they get there?"

"In a semi-trailer, Andy. Two have just been taken out of the front seat. These people are like zombies. They can't talk or move properly, yet they actually drove here themselves. Police have searched for the keys to the vehicle without luck, and it's being towed away now."

"You mean not one of them can talk?"

"You got it, Andy! They've all got scars on their heads, indicating they've been operated on. Not only that, they stink to high heaven. Andy, I can't describe the action. Doctors and nurses are being rushed here from every hospital within a hundred miles. Hold on a sec ... we've just received word the governor is on his way here in a helicopter. There's nothing else I can report until I can get close to the police or a staff member. Whatever happened..."

"That's enough," Glover said, requesting the radio be turned off. "At least those poor bastards will be looked after. Simon, what's been done with Krupp's car?"

"It's been wiped clean and it's at the bottom of a lake."

"Why didn't you just put it in the middle of some railway tracks? Pete asked."

The bluntness of Simon's voice matched the look on his face. "We want them to think the son-of-a-bitch is alive."

Not much was said after that. Glover snored quietly, Pete rested his eyes, and Joe silently stared out the window at the night's darkness.

Joe's head still reeled after Simon dropped him off at home. The Lieutenant's mind couldn't sort out the judgement battle that two wrongs make a right. They shouldn't, he thought. Later, after soaking in the bath, he settled his conflict of conscience before going to sleep. The weight was off his shoulders now. As far as he was concerned, Harvey Cohen's decision was right!

Before two Greyhound buses left Coeur d'Alene, Idaho, for Billings, Montana, the union driver of the first bus had questioned the need for two buses. He was told the company expected full loads due to a winter national map and compass orienteering practice taking place along the route. It sounded logical so he did not question the matter any further. He also didn't inquire why the second bus stayed close to him. At various stops, the other bus driver remained on board, but that was okay because he didn't know him anyway. He was probably an East Coast driver catching up on some hours, he thought.

He was wrong. Harvey Cohen had leased the second bus, and all male and female passengers, plus the driver, were his agents.

Harvey's seventh and eighth senses told him the Elite Team would not take *Krupp*, Moshe, and Rudy Reickhardt out at Billings, Montana. He knew how they worked, and they didn't operate that way. They were perfectionists; they would complete their dirty work before the bus arrived at its final destination. Rudy had told his father they were coming by bus, therefore what better chance would the killing team have than this. But where would they board the bus? That was the million-dollar question, so Harvey didn't take any chances. If it meant a fourteen-hour trip, so be it.

Instead of getting off the bus each time it stopped between Coeur d'Alene, Idaho, and Missoula Montana, Harvey's passengers assumed various assigned seating positions. As well, in seats halfway through the aisle, a man wearing a short blonde wig and sunglasses put his arm around Moshe and both assumed the sleeping position. Their heads touched, and it was difficult to see their faces.

Making no effort to hide his face, Rudy sat opposite them next to a chubby man snoozing by the window. The seats in front and behind both parties were occupied by a mixture of couples, while the remainder of Harvey's main crew sat at the rear.

Heavy snow swirled as both buses neared Missoula. When the vehicles stopped, most passengers on the first bus got out to stretch their legs or have a coffee. The doors to the second bus remained closed and the operator read a newspaper.

It was here Harvey saw a well-built warmly dressed man wearing earmuffs and carrying a rucksack, step out of the cafe and board the first bus. He appeared like an everyday sort of passenger except for his grey jacket and brown shoes. They appeared European.

Moments later, the same man rushed off the first bus and pounded on the door of the second. While boarding, the man's cold eyes roamed everywhere. "Are you going through to Billings?"

"Yeah, but weren't you on the first bus?" the driver asked, now reviewing the man's ticket.

"Too many kids in there," the man replied, before heading towards the rear. While moving up the aisle, he paid particular attention to the sleeping duo and glanced persistently at Rudy.

Harvey cautiously glimpsed up from his Time magazine when the man passed him. The newcomer spoke perfect English, but couldn't hide his German accent.

Since the game had now started, each of Harvey's people remained seated. Those at the rear of the bus never took their eyes off the new *traveller's* seat.

A minute later, the man got up, stretched, and approached the driver. "How long are we here for?"

The driver continued eating his roast beef sandwich while checking his watch and timetable. "We'll be leaving in about ten minutes."

"Good, I want to buy a book."

A passenger from the first bus followed the man inside. The *tourist* indeed bought a book, but not before making a phone call. Harvey paid particular attention to the slight nod given to him from the male with a coffee in his hand re-boarding the first bus. Shortly, the new *rider* stepped on board again, whistling and not paying any regard to Simon now sitting in the seat behind him.

Darkness closed in as the buses neared Great Falls, Montana. The snow had not eased off and normal low chatter in the second bus was typical. A few times when Rudy stood up to stretch or to allow his seatmate out to visit the washroom, the new man's head came up from his book, but quickly returned when the boy retook his seat.

"Great Falls!" the driver announced. "We've got a twenty minute stop here, so you can grab a coffee or a sandwich. They make good soup, if you're interested."

A *married couple* left Harvey's bus talking to each other about Disneyland, and so did Rudy, followed by the new man. Rudy didn't stray far though, and not surprisingly neither did the man with the book. After stretching and taking a few deep breaths, Rudy stepped back on, and so did his *tail*. Five minutes later, another male passenger joined the bus and sat across the aisle from the first visitor.

Just before it came time for the vehicle to leave, the *Disneyland* couple returned shivering with some sandwiches and thanked the driver for opening the door. The door remained open for a few seconds to allow two other strangers on board, and they *conveniently* sat near the first two *visitors*.

As the bus left Great Falls and entered the highway leading to Butte, Montana, Harvey stood up, walked forward, and spoke softly with the driver. Suddenly, when the bus pulled over and the door opened, Moshe and his friend stretched their arms, sat upright, and quickly exited. Instantly, the four strangers stood to follow, but not for long. Needles were inserted in the arms of the two already in the aisle, and similar needles pierced the necks of the two attempting to enter the aisle. When Goldberg and his buddy stepped back up and the bus proceeded, the four unconscious men were being *fixed*. In addition to their hands and feet being tied, duct tape was fastened over their mouths, eyes, and ears, before black hoods covered their heads. The four were then taken to the rear and pushed below seats.

"Four down, a few more to go," Harvey said, his face still stern, but satisfied. "That was easier than I thought it would be with these pricks. Now, at Butte, the remaining assassins will board our bus. Finding their friends aren't here, they'll head to the first bus. How long will it take us to catch up to that vehicle?"

The driver silently calculated the distance. "About ten minutes, Harv."

Harvey nodded, and after taking a full breath and exhaling, he said, "Good work everyone. Myra, have you ever been to Disneyland?"

"No, not yet," a woman in her middle twenties replied. "I thought talking about Disneyland would be a good topic."

"It's a perfectly natural topic, but it's Mickey Mouse, not Mister Mouse."

Myra turned red as the crew chuckled. "Did I really say, Mister Mouse?"

"You did."

"I must have been more nervous than I thought. This supposed Elite Team has gotten to me a little."

Cohen's face became inflexible again. "Don't let their murderous reputation get to you, Myra. Remember they're not smart - just sly. Like everyone else, they all put their pants on one leg at a time. This time the odds weren't in their favour, that's all."

Harvey then turned his attention to another man. "Harry, what did you find in their luggage?"

Harry had dumped the contents of four bags onto a seat. In addition to clothes, there were handcuffs, rope, plastic bindings, rubber tape, silencer equipped pistols, knives, ice picks and protected needles containing a brown substance.

Rudy looked wide-eyed at the items, saying, "Jesus, to think they were going to..."

"Not just your average tourists, eh, Rudy?" Harvey quipped, mock-punching the boy's right shoulder.

"Yeah, and my dad knew this was meant for me."

"Don't think of him as your dad, Rudy. Parents have to have pride, love, understanding, and respect for their kids. He lost all that when he joined these bastards. In their case, ideology comes before integrity. Remember that. They could never allow flesh and blood to stand in the way of their ultimate goal. You had the common sense to get out before being brainwashed. Somewhere along the line, your parents made a mistake."

"What mistake?"

"They didn't start training you soon enough. Those pricks under the seats back there were indoctrinated by the time they were five years old."

"What are you going to do with them?" Rudy asked.

"I know what I'd like to do with them, but, er... they'll be shipped out of the country. Rudy, they're not tough anymore; they're the weakest of cowards. These bastards are only tough when they've got the edge. When our people get through with them, we'll know more about their training procedures and *other matters* than they do."

"Then what will happen to 'em?"

Harvey didn't answer the young man. He just patted him on his left shoulder and said, "Okay, limber up and let's get ready for the next visit."

To everyone's surprise, no additional *travellers* joined the bus at Butte, and there was only one more stop before Billings.

Harvey's mind raced. He knew the Elite Team would want everything over with before the bus arrived at its final destination. Was he wrong? No, he knew how they worked. The next stop was Bozeman, Montana. These villains intended to get their prizes off the bus and into a waiting car somewhere between Bozeman and Billings. After being questioned, the three would be killed, he was sure of it. The odds had been reduced, so now it was time to proceed with the second part of his plan.

Due to heavy snow near Bozeman, traffic was near non-existent, so Harvey told the bus driver to pull over. The stop was quick as Cohen and three others stepped down and opened the the left side exterior luggage compartments. Before the bus proceeded, Harvey and three associates occupied those storage areas. Both cargo space doors were left unlocked so they could be easily pushed open.

Fifteen minutes into a twenty-minute stop at Bozeman, three burly male passengers presented their tickets to the driver and glanced up and down the bus before questioning each other's faces. One sat down two seats behind the supposedly sleeping duo of Moshe and *Krupp*, but the other two rushed off the bus and entered the vehicle in front. Seconds later, they arrived back and after offering shrugging motions to their lone accomplice, they occupied the seats two rows behind Rudy.

When the bus pulled out, the lone man behind Moshe stood and walked up to the driver, who just happened to be eating a sandwich.

"Have you been driving this bus from Missoula?"

"Yes, sir. I'd appreciate it if you'd please stand back of the line when you talk to me."

The man moved back a step. "I'm looking for four friends of mine that were supposed to be on this bus. Have there been many other passengers?"

"Quite a few. What did they look like?"

After the man described the four, the bus driver offered, "They missed the bus at our last stop, sir."

The man's face hardened. "What the fuck do you mean they missed the bus? What are you telling me, driver?"

Chewing and taking a sip of his coffee lying next to his thermos, the driver sternly said, "Please watch your language, sir. They got off to have a bowl of soup and a sandwich, and never returned. I think two of them said they were going to buy a bottle of liquor."

"Did you see them before you departed?"

"Yeah, I beeped my horn and went in to tell two of them we were leaving in three minutes. They said they were waiting for their two friends with the bottle. They took off to find them, and that was the last I saw of 'em. Ten minutes after I left, I got a radio call stating they were in the depot waiting for the next bus. I couldn't go back, and they're gonna have a long wait, 'cause it ain't due until tomorrow. Not even then if this snow keeps up."

His face full of confusion and not taking his eyes off the sleeping duo, the lone male walked back to his seat in the dimly lit bus. Shortly, he checked his watch before leaning across the aisle and whispering to the other two.

Grinning while glancing at his interior mirror, the bus driver thought all three killers appeared thoroughly pissed off.

Just after the driver announced his bus would be arriving in Billings in half-an-hour, the three made their move. Silently without displaying any alarm, one of the men sitting two seats behind Rudy got up and murmured in the young man's ear.

"Your father sent us. You're going to join us in the car following this bus. Stand up and come with us, and don't create a scene, otherwise you and a few others will be hurt. Do you understand?"

Rudy swallowed, stood, and uttered, "Yes."

While one held a silenced pistol, another yanked *Krupp* and Moshe into the aisle of the darkened bus and quickly searched them. The third who had spoken to the driver minutes before now held a knife to the driver's throat.

"What the…"

The member of the Elite Team spoke softly. "Pull over here and let us out! Quickly, or I'll slit your throat." A second later, he reached over towards the driver's window and yanked out the cord connecting the handset to the two-way radio.

"When we leave, get the fuck out of here, do you understand?"

The driver nodded, pulling over slowly, and bringing the bus to a complete stop. After the five stepped out into the blackness of the night and the carrier pulled away, the gangster behind *Krupp*, pushed him forward and spoke in German.

"I never liked you, you son-of-a-bitch. You think you're so fucking good." He pushed him again. "I'm personally going to cut your nuts off one at a time and then disembowel you. I want to hear you scream, you fuckin' turncoat."

Krupp kept his face to his front and the darkness hid the man's real facial features. In the distance, a car's headlights appeared.

When a large Lincoln limousine pulled up, its headlights changed to parking lights, and two men stepped out, leaving their doors open.

"So, we meet again, Mr. Krupp, you fucking..."

The man speaking spun violently around trying to reach for something on his way down after two muffled pistol shots snuffed out his life and that of his partner. Each had two holes in them, and in a fraction of the same second, so did the other three as similar sounds joined the moan of the wind.

One Elite Team member that had pushed *Krupp* managed to draw his weapon squeezing off one wildly aimed round before his face slammed through the red snow and the gravel below. The projectile fired from the gun grazed Rudy's right arm.

As each of the five heads received another *opening*, Rudy stood dazed and confused with blood streaming down his hand. He couldn't move as he watched the others dragging the five bodies to the car then forcing them into the back seat and trunk.

Harvey unzipped the young man's coat and peeled it off him. After rolling up the lad's sleeve and placing a handkerchief in Rudy's left hand, he brought the boy's arm up so the dressing pressed against the wound.

"Keep pressure on that, Harvey said, sympathetically, as bus taillights appeared a hundred yards away, indicating the vehicle was backing up.

"C'mon, chum, it's all over with. You can get back on the bus now ... we've got a plane to catch. You're a veteran now, Rudy, but don't think that qualifies you for a pension."

In Geneva, Switzerland, Gustaf Schtaff's cold eyes examined the blinking faces of three nervous men standing before his desk. The three could not hear Schtaff's heavy wheezing due to the sounds of their ever-increasing thumping hearts.

With Sigmund, his personal bodyguard behind him, the old man sitting in the fine leather chair prepared a cigar and lit up. "Sit! Not you, Rolf ... you'll stand until I decide what to do with you!"

Twitching nervously, Rolf remained standing as the others sat down.

"After all our setbacks in Seattle, other portions of our American operation are in complete chaos. Kravenhall has gone, Krupp has defected, and the Elite Team has disappeared. We've lost senators Garner, Strobe, Smith, Millington, and Bouhler. Congressmen Miller and Gilbert were also killed along with Governor Walters, Reverend Jerry Frolich, and Matt Robinson. If Vice-President MacPherson and Dieter Krueger had remained, they would have met the same fate. Krueger would have been here today, but he's with MacPherson and the President at Camp David, and I've sent him a note. Federal and state agencies are presently sifting through the Kravenhall wreckage piece by piece and I can't do anything to stop it. Our people have informed me they cannot intervene without putting themselves in jeopardy. What the hell is going on? Let's start with you, Deutsch?"

Gerlund Deutsch thought he should not be at this meeting. Obviously terrified and tensely shifting in his chair, the balding, fiftyish grey-headed man in charge of world finance didn't know what to say.

"Sir ... I ... just don't believe Hans Krupp would betray us. As you know, I'm not involved with active operations, but like yourself, I've known Hans Krupp since he was a boy. I believe he may have died at Kravenhall and..."

"Krupp was seen on the bus with his lover, you drivelling idiot! Also, I've heard from our Reichsland Camp, and this kid, er, Rudy Reickhardt was on the bus with them."

Rolf interjected. "But he never made it home. I think..."

Schtaff stood up quickly. "Silence! Did I ask you to speak?" he bellowed pounding his desk with his left hand.

"No, sir, but..."

"I said, silence, or I'll ... Sigmund, give me your gun," the director yelled, partly swivelling his chair towards his bodyguard.

Schtaff's face muscles tightened, his fiery eyes narrowed, and his lips turned white as he grabbed the offered revolver. Pointing the weapon at Rolf, and tightening his shaking hands finger on the trigger, he yelled, "I trusted you to safeguard our American enterprises, and you allowed this catastrophe to take place."

Rolf's throat went dry and he felt his knees buckling. Fearing the worst and becoming wide-eyed, his left hand took hold of Deutsch's chair. Collecting every ounce of strength, he winced, whimpering, "I ... I apologize, sir. Please, don't shoot me - spare my life, please sir."

The demented look on Schtaff's face indicated he would pull the trigger of the weapon he aimed at Rolf, but he didn't. After a few seconds, he lowered it and placed it on his desk.

"Sit down, Rolf," he said in a subdued voice.

Sobbing, Rolf could not sit down. His knees wouldn't move, and he'd peed himself.

A repulsive sneer formed on Schtaff's lips. "Sigmund, help this snivelling son-of-a-bitch to a chair."

As Sigmund complied, Schtaff pushed an intercom button. "Bring me some brandy!"

"Gentlemen, I was trained by people who practiced our great leader Heinrich Himmler's methods. I'm a Schutzstaffel officer through and through, and if I can resolve this thing, why can't you incompetent idiots? Schumann, whoever he is, did this to us. Dr. Helmut Schumann."

Rolf still could not speak, but one of the other men did. In charge of all doctrines, Albert Strassler had worked his way up in the organization after hiding known Nazi war criminals in South America. He owned one of the largest cattle ranches in Argentina, and as a multi-millionaire, he could spare the time to aid his favourite *cause*.

"That's impossible, sir. Schumann's visiting my family home in Argentina. He's an academic. You may recall his father Horst, who...?"

The brandy arrived and Schtaff held up his right hand to stop Strassler from speaking. Pouring out five glasses and passing one to his bodyguard, his tone mellowed. "Help yourself, gentlemen. Sigmund, give this glass to that incontinent cry-baby. When you've finished, Rolf, go, and clean yourself up. Make it quick!"

Rolf downed the liquid before briskly leaving the room.

"Certainly, I knew his father," Schtaff declared, redirecting his attention to Strassler. "And I *now* know Dr. Helmut Schumann is at your home. Unfortunately, someone impersonating Dr. Helmut Schumann convinced Kraven to let him attend as a guest at Kravenhall. On the evening of the explosion, this impostor apparently sprained his ankle and couldn't attend the dinner. Senator Millington and two others helped the man to his feet when he tripped on the stairs. Walter Reisdorf was one of those men, and he survived the explosion. During the dinner, Reisdorf went out to get some fresh air. His arm's broken, but he's fine."

"I'm glad he survived to tell us," Strassler remarked.

Schtaff poured himself another brandy. "Now we've got to find out about this pretender. He must be well connected, because Krupp informed us by fax the man was indeed Dr. Schumann. He said his fingerprints matched."

"But Krupp's turned on us," Deutsch mouthed, gesturing if he could help himself to the liquor.

Schtaff indicated his approval by waiving his left hand. "I don't think Hans did turn on us. I believe another actor was on that bus. Either Krupp is dead, or he's been captured. The disappearance of the Elite team is puzzling though; I have no idea what's happened, unless..."

Strassler revealed the same questioning look. "The Israeli Set?"

Swirling his brandy around its glass, Schtaff stood and slowly limped to a window. "Exactly, and I've got our people in Israel checking on that now. Maybe this Schumann impostor belongs to them. Up to now, we haven't come up with anything. I'm due in Paraguay shortly and I want answers by then. Strassler, you will take over our American operations. Many changes will have to be made, and a brief is being prepared for you."

Overwhelmed, Strassler said, "I'm honoured, sir, but what about Krueger?"

Returning to his desk, Schtaff sipped his brandy. "He need not concern you," he said unemotionally. "He will be terminated after his visit with President Aird. Krueger has gone soft. The problem facing us now is the disk. Krupp was to deliver something that you aren't familiar with - the most intricate details of The Himmler Stratagem. They're on a disk he was to deliver to Paraguay. He can't access that information because he only has one third of the code. As far as our United States operations are concerned, Krueger and Kraven have the other two-thirds, and Kraven's dead. Goddamnit, I want that disk."

"The Himmler Stratagem? We understand part of it; what other details are there?" Strassler asked, an inquisitive look draining his face.

Returning to his desk, Schtaff's eyes narrowed. "You don't need to know! I want that disk! I cannot produce another until Paraguay's code has been entered. I don't care what you have to do, but get it back. Is that clear?"

Both *gentlemen* smelled the offensive odour of the administrator's breath.

"Quite clear, Herr Schtaff," Strassler replied, trying to control twitching nerves in his left eye and cheek.

Gently knocking on the door and re-entering, Rolf sat down. He had changed his clothes, washed, and combed his hair, but his face still revealed his anxiety. Swallowing heavily, he said, "I'm ... sorry about that, sir."

Grinning openly, the headman poured Rolf another brandy. "Drink it down old friend, you need it. I can't blame you for everything happening in the United States, Rolf, but I did rely on you?"

Rolf smiled gingerly, sipping the alcohol. Certainly, he knew he had made a mistake not watching the American operation properly, but Schtaff still trusted him, and he idolized the man. "I know, sir, and I promise you it won't happen again."

Suddenly, the room erupted and Rolf's liquor glass shattered against a wall. The bullet released by Schtaff had torn through Rolf's left wrist and ripped open his stomach before driving him backwards and sideways off his chair.

Handing the weapon back to Sigmund, Schtaff remarked, "That's right, Rolf, it won't happen again."

Schtaff's sudden action thoroughly stunned Strassler and Deutsch. They both knew Rolf was Schtaff's closest confidant.

The director's demonical eyes narrowed again. Scanning the two men, he bellowed, "Find the impersonator, and get me that disk. Now leave me!"

Chapter 13

When Joe Stacy opened his eyes, his right arm was wrapped around Gail who lay on her right side nestling her head into him. Both were naked and he smiled affectionately watching her sleep.

The evening before was one for books, he thought. Suzie and Gordie were staying with their dad's parents, and when he had arrived, Gail's flew into his arms like there was no tomorrow.

"Oh, Joe, I missed you and worried so much," she said, softly, as he gently caressed her face and their kiss lasted a lifetime before she snuggled her head into his chest.

"I missed you too sweetheart. There was no need to worry," he had said, squeezing her while lifting her up and swirling her around. "Where are the kids?"

When he put her down, Gail took his hand, leading him to the couch in front of the welcoming fire. "They're spending a few days with their grandparents. Well?" she asked, her eyes searching his face. "I've been watching those awful pictures on television about the Kraven Clinic. Did Kraven and that Dr. Krause really do those terrible things?"

"And more," Joe said, placing an arm around her shoulders and staring into the fire. "They're bastards, Gail. What you've seen and heard is only the tip of the iceberg. It's not over yet."

"But Joe, the FBI have arrested another sixteen here in Washington State. All the information is coming out."

"No it's not. I thought it would, but it isn't. Sure, the president's called for an inquiry, but only for this cell. Gail, they've wedged themselves into every segment of our society. They've got governors, senators, justice officials, the CIA, FBI, police, big business, the unions, and ... well, you don't want to know."

Gail got up and walked to the kitchen to pour two drinks. Returning, she sat down again, handing one to Joe. "What is it I don't wish to know?"

"Carl MacPherson is one of them."

A shiver shot through Gail and her face became confused. "What? The Vice-President? God help us. Surely they'll find out about him."

Joe placed an arm around her again, cuddling her. "Oh yes, but that's not up to us. Someone else will blow the whistle on him. Is the president involved? That's what concerns me."

A few seconds of silence ensued before she asked, "How will you find out?"

Sighing and returning his eyes to the fire, Joe took a sip of his drink. "I don't know yet. This whole thing is getting me down. So much is happening, I can't quite grasp it all."

Gail laid her glass down and turned her body in towards him. Placing her right forefinger over his lips for a moment and stroking his hair with her left hand, she kissed him and whispered gently, "Darling, just relax and I'll make dinner. Will you stay with me tonight?"

Nose to nose, Joe's impish smile appeared, and he cocked his head. "Why Mrs. Manning, are you suggesting we...?"

The same smile took hold of Gail's mouth, and her eyes sparkled. "You bet I am, buster. I never want to let you out of my sight again. I've got your favourite wine chilling, and I'm going to make you the best home-cooked meal you've ever had. How does that sound?"

Joe wrapped both arms around her. "Fabulous! And what did you say was for dessert?"

"The third course is for desert," Gail said shyly, kissing him again before getting up.

"What's the second course?"

Heading into the kitchen, she sang, "You, and I, and the music."

For the next two-candlelit hours, the pair of lovers had dined, sipped wine, and danced slowly to the soft sounds from the stereo. Cushions on the floor became box seats to a display of enchanting prancing flames that drew truths and stories from both of them. When rain started pounding the windowpanes, Joe gently took hold of Gail's hand and led her to the bedroom. Sitting on the bed and taking off his shirt, he asked, "Have I ever told you how much I love you?"

Gail stood before him removing her blouse and bra, and what little window light there was magnified the rain's graceful window reflection turning her silhouette into a mottled marble sculpture of an angel.

"Yes, six thousand and two times, and there's an equal love ... my devotion to you, my darling," she whispered, accepting the watery transparent beams drenching her hair, face and firm silken breasts.

Joe Stacy knew this moment's ecstasy was unlike any feeling he had ever had. Fate had preserved its significance, hiding the revelation without the slightest hint of existence. In the thousands of days he'd lived and loved, he had not learned worship came in degrees. All his prior experience was for naught as destiny had finally decided to introduce this fairy-tale encounter, ascending him to the ultimate stage of adoration.

Joe stood and embraced the quivering goddess before him. Tenderly sliding his hands down her delicate back, he gently unfastened her skirt, allowing the garment to fall to the floor. Gail remained standing, her heart pounding, and her hands stroking Joe's face and hair as he sat down again. Moving his hands upward on the outside of her velvet legs, he slowly removed her panties and gently caressed her hips and buttocks before delicately luring her onto him.

But now it was morning. Still reminiscing, Joe edged his arm out from around the sleeping beauty lying next to him. Although he wanted to share every single second of his life with Gail, he had to head home to shower and change his clothes.

Gail didn't wake when he kissed her forehead and whispered, "It's time to continue the *chase*. I love you."

"I arrived at the same conclusion you did, it's blank," Barker stated passing the disk to his boss as the seven detectives sat in the secret room under the Chinese restaurant. Glover wasn't present; his gout bothered him, and he had a doctor's appointment for his blood pressure. "Whoever copied it doesn't want you involved, Joe," Barker added.

Six sets of eyes studied the angry expression on Stacy's face before Pete said, "I think that indicates Harvey's going to handle it from here. And maybe he's right. We've shut the bastards down in this state. All hell's breaking loose with those affidavits and tapes."

Joe didn't respond to his partner's remarks. He had trusted Harvey, and as far as he was concerned, the man had no right to exclude him. This was a joint effort, and if Cohen didn't want him involved, then he should have been up front with him.

"I think you're taking this thing too personally," Pete added. "Joe, we've done our job. The FBI announced this morning that they've uncovered six weapons caches throughout Washington and Oregon. They're arresting people and closing down companies left and right. The RCMP and Canadian Intelligence are clamping down in Canada, and the Brits are doing the same. This is the subject of every television and radio talk show in the country. CNN's Wolf Blitzer, and Anderson Cooper, are scouring Kraven and Krause's past and their list of companies. All national news announcers are ranting about the senators and the other bigwigs killed at Kravenhall. That's all going to come up. Also, don't forget President Aird's called for a federal inquiry, and the IRS is onto these pricks asses as well. The bastards are finished in this country."

Disappointed with Harvey's methods, Stacy lit up a smoke, then butted it. "What about Vice-President MacPherson - he's still around? What about the other camps that haven't been closed down? This thing isn't finished, Pete. It hasn't even begun to finish! I tell you, these monsters are so goddamned entrenched and organized it will take a miracle to sniff them all out."

"But what can *we* do about it?" Barker asked, throwing a newspaper in front of Joe. The headline and subheading read: *KRAVENHALL WAS AN ARYAN*

STRONGHOLD! Nazi Doctors Gave Cloning Secrets to Russians in 1945.

"We're just Seattle cops," Pete persisted. "Listen, Joe, let Harvey get on with it. Give him a call and find out what the hell he's doing. I'm sure he's got plans for the whole rotten lot of 'em. All our information has been surreptitiously passed to the press. This thing is out of our hands now."

"Also, what about your wedding?" Gwen asked, grinning and moving her eyes between Joe and Pete. "Shouldn't we be making plans for it?"

Now Joe tried to look innocent as his eyes moved curiously between Gwen and Pete. "Wedding? What goddamned wedding? How the hell can you make plans for my wedding? Who says I'm getting married?"

Pete's face turned a bright shade of pink. "Well, er I, uh, might have, er."

Joe feigned astonishment. "Christ, my number one buddy informs the world? I haven't even popped the question yet. She might say no."

Gwen stood and stretched. "That's bullshit, Lieutenant Stacy, and you know it. What woman could say no to you?"

"You'd better," Mathieson mouthed, grinning and smacking Gwen's butt.

"Earl, he didn't ask me to marry him," Gwen shot back.

"Yeah, but the way his mind works these days, he just might."

The room erupted in laughter and Joe laughed the loudest. It was just what he needed. Hey maybe they're right, he thought, before mentioning, "I'm off to New York tomorrow. We're all gonna split some money. When you see me on television signing autographs, you can say, 'I know that guy.'"

Gebara rubbed his hands together. "That's right, it's NICER PRIZE time. I'm going to make a down payment on a new car with my share."

Stacy stood up to leave. "Want my autograph?"

"Sure, on a cheque or money order," Sam said, chortling and smacking Joe's back. "I'll take your autograph right to my bank."

When the seat-belt sign came on and the plane's wing tipped slightly to Joe's side, a huge opening in the third cloud layer revealed the studded grey carpet of New York spreading for miles in all directions. Joe knew it was raining hard because pellets of water steamed across and down his window creating patterns resembling shooting stars in a night-time sky.

The trip had been somewhat uneventful and Stacy had managed to read another sixty pages of *Stand By Your Beds*! the novel Gordie had given him for Christmas. He wanted to read more, but identical twin boys about four years old had decided to make Joe their best friend.

When he had left Seattle, Stacy was pleased to find the two seats next to him unoccupied. They weren't empty for long because the *effervescent* youngsters covered them and him with colouring books, crayons, toys, and even wet cookies.

During the trip, the toddlers had owned the aisle, all vacant aisle seats, and most of the flight attendants. The boys' huge mother didn't help matters. This unique respite gave her the opportunity to eat the airline's food, along with the many sandwiches she had brought with her. When Joe felt like having a coffee, the attendants were always busy serving the kids' mother.

After the tires squealed on the runway, and the aircraft stopped, Joe got up, retrieved his jacket and raincoat from the overhead compartment, and found himself wedged in the aisle shuffling between the twins and their heavy mother trying to keep a sandwich in her mouth and retie her nylons above her flabby knees.

"I hope they weren't any bother?" Mrs. Chester asked, adding, "I'm Rhonda L. Chester and these are my two boys."

Joe didn't know if his facial expression betrayed the fact he got hit in the eye with a flying piece of wet cheese that shot from her mouth. "Not at all. How old are they?"

The gap between the huge woman's teeth still bore signs of the partially eaten cucumber and cheese sandwich she kept in her hands. "Four, going on twelve. They're going to see their grandmother in the Bronx. Isn't this exciting? Do you live here?"

The detective cringed in the crowded aisle way when one of the boys went to kick his brother and the hard toe of the kid's shoe connected with Joe's ankle.

"Aggghhh, no, I'm just visiting. What does your middle initial stand for?" he asked referring to her name.

"*Lunchroom*. I always got called 'Lunchroom' in school, but I don't know why. Haaa, it's actually, Lana. Would you like a sandwich?" the woman asked, pushing a bag in his face.

"No, thanks. Is someone meeting you?"

"Yes, my brother is. He's a doctor."

Stacy found himself in the middle of a soccer match and he was the ball.

"That's nice. He'll be able to give these young fellas some sedatives."

"No, he's a carpet doctor."

"A carpet doctor?"

"Yeah, he rips out old carpets and installs new ones. His business is called, Doctor Rugs. Wanna know what his motto is?"

Stacy checked his pocket watch and grinned at the airline's attendant offering adieu at the door. "Sure, why not?"

"*If your rugs ain't great, let me operate.* I thought of that and he hasn't paid me yet. Would you like an apple?"

"Nice slogan," Joe found himself saying while watching three layers of double chin bounce after each apple bite. "No, thanks. Well, er, hope you have a wonderful time Mrs. Chester. Good bye."

After taking a very large bite and sputtering, "Good bye," the woman swallowed quickly, yelling, "Settle down you two, or you won't get a bite."

Consciously listening to the airport's ongoing public announcement system, Joe collected his suitcase and coiled his way through the crowds. He knew someone would page him, or failing that, someone would be there to meet him. As he neared the exit, a short, smiling, dark haired young woman dressed in a chauffeur's uniform held up a sign reading: 'Looking for Lieutenant Stacy.'

"Hi, I'm Joe Stacy," he said, keeping hold of his travel-bag.

The grin never left his *welcomer's* face. With her hair flowing out from under her cap, his driver's broad New York accent took over. "Lieutenant Stacy, I'm Prissy Wallanski. I'll take you to your hotel and pick you up tomorrow for the show."

"Great, thanks."

Attempting to remove the satchel from his hand, she asked, "Is this your only bag?"

"I think I'm a little stronger than you, Prissy. I'll keep it with me. Thanks."

Throughout the limo's rainy fifty-minute ride, Prissy Wallanski described the New York scene, its people, places to dine, and informed him that she and her husband Alek owned the limousine. Her spouse had emigrated from Poland four years back, and she'd met him at a club. They had two kids, and the family had not visited the West Coast, but it was on their "...things to do before we reach the too much older list."

"I hear Seattle's setting is beautiful?" she asked. "Have you always lived there?"

"Yeah, it's totally different, and from what I've been told, more and more of you New Yorkers are packing your bags and moving our way."

"What about the rain? Does is rain a lot?"

"Nah, we call it liquid sunshine. It beats this cold and snow. It's picturesque and there's no humidity. You'd like it."

"Lots of open spaces?"

"You bet. Ten minutes out of town you can be lost in the hills."

"Sounds nice. Here, we're stepping on people from morning to night."

Before dropping him off at the New York Hyatt, Prissy presented Joe with his agenda, two tickets to the musical *Cats*, and an invitation to a late hour cocktail party at the Cabbage Nightclub.

"Just take a cab everywhere and the front desk will reimburse you," she said, before mentioning she would pick him up at eleven o'clock the next morning.

Stacy noticed there wasn't a rehearsal for the awards, and thanked her.

"See you at eleven," she said.

"Eleven it is," he replied, stepping out. "Thanks a lot"

After informing the desk clerk who he was, Joe rode seventeen floors with a bellhop to a well-furnished room with two king-size beds. He liked the large balcony, but the view mainly consisted of other buildings. In the frigid breeze, two seagulls cowering on a nearby window ledge resembled small grey-cloaked monks taking refuge from the cold.

A large basket of fresh fruit containing a note occupied a polished table near two big bay windows. It read, 'Dear Lieutenant Stacy: As chair of NICER, let me welcome you to New York. Whatever you need, just ask. Hope you enjoy the musical and cocktail party. I'd like to be with you, but I'm away until early tomorrow. See you at the studio. Sincerely, Peter Cooper.'

A small fridge containing snacks, tiny bottles of wine and liquor with bottles of mix attracted Joe eyes after he hung up his coats. Using the key the bellboy had handed him, he helped himself to a gin and tonic, selected a bag of cashews, and stepped out on the balcony. The icy rain had not yet washed away the hard-packed snow on the sidewalks below. Joe also noticed the frigid air was different. It was hard and unscented with a hint of exhaust fumes. Furthermore, the wind was sharp, so he went back inside, locking the balcony door.

Joe never liked being alone in strange towns; he felt out of place. And this was New York, a megalopolis of monolithic structures with little green space. Other than snow-covered Central Park, the white congested jungle appeared undisciplined and dispassionate. He had heard if New Yorkers did not know you, their attitudes fit into two categories – "too busy" and "don't give a damn." Even Prissy's welcome had been semi formal and right to the point. People were not like that in Seattle, he thought. They were more laid back, more caring, and friendly. In today's society, inhabitants of all regions were leery of strangers, but those in the Pacific Northwest threw what little remaining caution they held to the wind.

Looking down at the streets, Joe wondered if Seattle folks, or those living in its near sister, Vancouver, British Columbia, could become removed and uninvolved. Yeah, sure, as the population increases, it will have to happen to them as well. Mumbling, "What a shame," he picked up the phone to call Gail.

"Hi, darling, how goes it?"

Gail's voice lit up his face and heart. "Sweetheart, are you in New York?"

"Yeah, I've just checked into the hotel. Christ, it's cold here."

"Then I won't tell you how warm it is in Seattle. The minute you left, the sun came out. Are you the Grinch that kept the sun in his pocket?"

Gail's innocent statement relaxed every muscle in Stacy's body. He longed for her now more than ever before. Damn, why didn't he bring her? He knew why. Gail couldn't get time off, and she wanted to stay close to her children.

"Not me, Kiddo. I have the sun sitting on my right shoulder. God, I love you, Gail. How I lasted this long without you, I'll never know."

"Oh, Joe, now we've got the sun in our pockets *and* sitting on our shoulders. It's in your smile and your eyes. We're both lost in love, darling. A love that only comes once in a lifetime."

Joe discovered his eyes welling up. "Gail, honey, will you marry me? I know this isn't the time or…"

"Oh, my darling, just say when. Yes, I'll marry you, Joe Stacy. I want to be with you until every star goes out."

At that moment, Gail's words meant more to him than anything in his life, and it was wonderful knowing she felt the same. Grinning and taking a deep breath, he said, "How are the kids?"

"They're still with their grandparents for another few days. They get doted on over there. If they want hamburgers or pepperoni pizza for lunch, so be it. They even get driven to school. When they're home, they have to walk all the way."

"I got tired of banana sandwiches when I went to school," Joe said, lighting up a smoke. "When my skin started turning yellow, my mom switched over to salmon. Know what happened?"

A laugh came from the telephone's earpiece. "When you started getting scales on your skin, she switched you back to bananas?"

"Exactly, or cheese," he said. "I felt like changing my name to Kraft."

He could hear Gail chuckling before she mentioned, "Everyone I know, even the hospital staff and patients are waiting to watch you on television. Suzie and Gordie told me on the phone they're excited and counting the hours. Joe, I miss you so much."

"I feel like heading back to the airport right now," Joe said, actually thinking about it, checking his watch, but then weighing the negatives. At this time of the day, there would be no more planes to Seattle.

"Darling, I'd like to say you should," Gail said, desirously, "But it's only for another day and then we'll be together. This morning, I heard from an old school friend of mine, and she told me…"

Ten minutes later when he hung up the phone, Joe felt better, but lonelier than ever. After opening up another small bottle, he sat thinking of Gail's warmth, her dimpled smile, and wonderful understanding. Perhaps he should have asked her to use up some of her holidays to come with him. The kids would have loved it, especially getting off school. "But she's right," he murmured. "Oh, well, one day down, and one more to go."

"Are you coming up to bed, dear," Lois Glover shouted from her bedroom. "Today's news is the same as yesterday's … all bad."

Captain Ray Glover was not really watching the news. The television was on, but his mind was on the group of organized killers operating throughout the world.

"I won't be long," he said, gently stroking his cat *Rookie,* sitting on his knee in the living room of their small two story home in one of Seattle's oldest, well-kept neighbourhoods.

Something still bothered Ray since the Kravenhall blast, and he didn't wish to serve on the police force any longer. If he could get out now, tomorrow, or the next day, he would instantly sign on the dotted line. He wanted his mind to shut out what Harvey's people had done at Kravenhall, but he kept thinking of the carnage. He knew all three detectives had second thoughts at the time of the slaughter, because what was done was wrong. Oh, sure, he had said, *"I just wish I could have had the chance to do it. None of these assholes deserve to live,"* but police officers are not supposed to take matters so personally. Every one of those bastards should have been brought to justice, he thought, before concluding all would have gotten off. Since money was of no concern, each would have hired a top lawyer; even the skinheads, and with inside help, they would have walked away.

Sighing deeply, Glover finally settled the conflicting struggle within him. Harvey had been right when he said, *"Joe, hear me. We're no different than you. We believe in law and order, but these animals don't. If they get their way, democracy will be outdated, and the world will slowly sink in a sea of blood, as it did before. Totalitarianism has always been mankind's enemy, Joe. If you're naive enough to believe this detestable organization can be stopped using the judicial process, you're out of your mind. Remember Hitler was appointed democratically. Need I remind you of the judges he appointed? These people, if they can be called that, spit on anything democratic."*

Displaying a resolute look, Ray concluded there was no other way. He'd had enough. It had become a younger man's game, and he wanted out. It was time for him to take Lois to the lake. "Yeah, Rookie, that's what we'll do," he muttered. "Lois has always wanted to live in a cabin on a small lake up north, so we'll get out of here and buy one. Then again maybe I shouldn't even be thinking about retirement. Lois also loves this place, the home we bought thirty-five years ago?"

A devoted look came over Glover wondering how the two of them managed to raise six children in such limited space. If he had not built the large room in the basement for his youngest boys, the now married twins, all members of the family would have been tripping over each other. As it was, he or Lois could never invite guests for dinner - with eight people sitting around the table, there wasn't room or food left for company.

Ray's grin expanded as he reminisced. One day, years earlier when their parish priest just *happened* by at suppertime, and was asked to dine with them, the religious man would have no part of sitting by himself in the living room. He insisted on sitting with them at the kitchen table. Obviously, he had come from a large family and did not mind being cramped. However, things changed after Lois brought in the food, and the priest said grace. When the *starting bell* sounded, and eight sets of hands began reaching, the cleric realized if he didn't "dig in," he'd be going to another parishioner's house for dinner.

Many times Ray and Lois had howled thinking about that moment, plus the fact the priest never visited at dinnertime again. He came when the kids were at school, usually around lunchtime.

Glover laughed out loud. "Jesus he was fast. He snared the last goddamned roast potato … the one I wanted."

Stretching and receiving a dirty look from Rookie, Captain Glover had made up his mind. He had seen it all, done it all, and he wanted out. Let other people put up with the political bullshit that goes with being a department head, he thought. Whether or not Joe Stacy would *accommodate* the nonsense if he took over would be interesting. Joe was a meat and potatoes kind of guy, and he shot from the hip. Ray knew solving crimes was Joe's priority, not attending fancy dinner parties with the chief or the mayor.

Kravenhall came back to Glover's mind for a moment. He knew Stacy was the only person who could have pulled it off - certainly not any of the others in Homicide and Robbery. At one time, he was like Joe except for one difference. If anyone then had told him he was going to be up to his neck in maggots with Heinrich Himmler attitudes, he would have called them nuts. After all, this was the twenty-first century, Adolf Hitler had been dead since 1945, and as far as he knew, the maniac's ideals had gone to hell with him. Now he knew they hadn't. Still, though, he had looked the other way at Kravenhall, and the action of Harvey's men did not sit easy with him.

"No, I should get out," Ray muttered, standing and walking to the front door to put Rookie outside for five minutes. When the animal wanted to get back in, it would use various railings and trees and would come in through the bedroom window.

Rookie tensed up before the captain opened the front door. The small animal did not normally do this, and had the captain not been tired, he would have suspected something was wrong. No sooner had Glover unlatched and opened the door, it was pushed open with horrendous force, sending the captain flying backwards and landing on his back. Rookie screeched and ran out the open door.

Glover could not rise fast enough to get his automatic off the top of the refrigerator in the kitchen. No one could have been fast enough. After the three men entered, one went upstairs, one travelled into the kitchen, and one with rotten teeth kicked Glover in his left side. Holding a stiletto to the captain's left cheek, he asked, "Where is it?"

The captain moaned. "Where's what?"

The man kicked Glover again. "The fuckin' disk. Tell me where it is or I'll cut ya. You can count on it."

Glover coughed and his face became defiant. "Even if I knew, and there were only two of us left on this good old earth, I'd tell you nothing you filthy prick."

Ray Glover might have felt the sharp instrument slicing in, through, and around his neck. He even might have heard the whoosh of gurgling bloody froth spewing from his open trachea as he struggled for breath, but it would not have mattered - a second later, he was dead.

After forty minutes, when the three intruders left, the house was a shambles. Upstairs in her bedroom, Lois had received two shots in her head, and Rookie, who had come in through the window as he always did, lay next to her, with half his head blown off.

"Midnight, not a sound from the pavement - has the moon lost her memory, she is smiling alone? In the lamplight, the withered leaves collect at my feet, and the wind..."

For the first time in weeks, Joe found himself relaxed with his mind clear of Nazi intrigue. The brilliant costumes, colours, and the wonderful music of *Cats* created an escape from the real world of death and suffering. For the next two hours, he remained immersed in the talented world of stage actors and actresses playing for a packed house of thrilled, hypnotized, patrons, captivated by the marvellous performance.

Although the seat next to Joe was vacant, the seat behind him wasn't, and the firm-faced man in his thirties, wearing a black suit, was not interested in the musical. He had been with Joe since the hotel, sitting in the lobby waiting for Stacy to exit the elevator. After the detective had hailed a cab, a large Chrysler New Yorker had appeared to allow the man to follow him. Even during the intermission, the man remained close, and inconspicuous. After the stage production, the same male would follow Joe to the Cabbage Nightclub.

At first, Stacy didn't realize the party was for guests only, nor did he think he was dressed properly. His itinerary had stated dress was casual, but when his eyes grew accustomed to the room's dim light, he was the only one dressed in a sports jacket and slacks. The fifty or so guests sipping champagne or dancing wore tuxes and evening gowns, and their bodies were adorned with gold watches, gold and diamond earrings, gold cufflinks, and diamond broaches. Joe thought the men looked like penguins, except, that is, for a man sitting at the bar. Dressed in a black suit and a red tie, the guy's eyes met Joe's more than a few times, allowing Stacy to make casual mental notes.

Trying not to be noticeable, but finding it nearly impossible due to the way he was dressed, Stacy accepted a glass of champagne and meandered around picking up bits and pieces of various conversations. All soon-to-be honoured recipients of the National Independent Citizens for Equal and Better Race Relations Prize [NICER] were present with their wives and nominees. As well, the higher echelon of the television production group mingled about the plush mirrored room.

About fifteen minutes later, a tipsy *penguin* and his wife came over and introduced themselves.

"I'm Cornelius Cunningham and this is my gorgeous wife Correlea. I only call her gorgeous when I'm drinking," the fellow said, finding it difficult to stand, and complicated to puff his cigar.

"Which is constantly," Correlea offered, laughing and staggering.

Finding the names intriguing, Joe grinned and cocked his head, asking, "Cornelius and Correlea Cunningham? Do you have any children?"

The woman hiccupped while grabbing champagne from a passing waiter. "Why yes, two girls - Corine and Carrie."

"It figures."

"And who might you be?" the man, about fifty, asked, slurping his champagne and breathing on Stacy, who backed off a little. Joe figured somewhere along the line, the guy had gotten hold of a bucket of blue cheese, and the combination of cheese and wine was staggering. "Joe Stacy, from Seattle."

Cornelius closed the gap again and his blurry eyes narrowed. "Oh, so you're the famous detective. Well, well, well, nice job. Yes, nice job, Lieutenant."

Once again, Joe had to back away. "Thank you. Say Cornelius, why is everyone dressed up here? I was told this gathering was to be casual."

"So were we, until they changed it. Are you staying at the Hyatt like the rest of us?"

"Yes."

"You should have checked with the desk. The Cabbage Nightclub is always formal. By the way, Joe, I've won the prize for Religious Kinship. My new book, *Prayers Aren't Coloured like Skin* is selling big in the south. I'm thinking about writing a new one called, *We're All One Colour in Heaven*. Hey, waiter, let's have another one of those," Cunningham slurred to a passing attendant.

"That's nice. And, er, what's this nomination stuff about?" Joe asked.

As Cornelius *purloined* another glass, and Mrs Cunningham burped, proudly announcing, "You have to be nominated for the prize. Cornelius was nominated by Vice-President MacPherson, himself."

Joe's throat went dry and a cold hair-raising shiver shot through his body. The musical Cats had relaxed him so much he had not noticed the couple's rings. Cunningham and his wife were both Nazis, and as he glanced around, a few other *penguins* wore SS rings.

Without offering a farewell, Stacy quickly headed towards the door, knowing the man in the black suit would follow. When the tail stepped outside and could not see Joe, he ran fifteen yards to the end of the dark street before two hands grabbed him yanking him into a doorway.

Slamming the man against the club's service entrance door, Joe's right hand firmly clenched the centre of the man's throat and his left hand seized the man's testicles.

"Okay, you son-of-a-bitch, speak, or I'm going to rip out your throat, and tear off your balls. Who are you? Tell me, or so help me, I'll..."

Stacy eased his grip on the man's throat but tightened the other hand. His pursuer could talk in pain, but he couldn't move.

Afraid to squirm, he moaned, "…Harvey sent me."

Probingly staring at the man's face, Joe released his grip. "Harvey? Why?"

Coughing and clearing his throat a few times, the man said, "I believe he thinks something is going to happen." Stretching his neck and wriggling his groin a few times, he added, "He phoned me this morning saying I should keep an eye on you. The bastards are searching for something and they're intense about it."

As the man spoke, a Chrysler rolled up. "Joe, I can't talk here. Get in the car and I'll drop you off close to your hotel."

The driver casually grinned as Joe climbed in the back seat with Harvey's associate, who introduced himself as "Manny," and the driver as "Jack."

"Any idiot would understand what they want," Joe offered, paying no attention to the introduction. "They want the disk Harvey's got."

Manny took out a cellular phone, and after pushing a few buttons, handed it to Joe. "Tell *him* that!"

Stacy recognized Cohen's voice. "So, Harvey, you're protecting me here as well, eh?"

"Someone's gotta do it." How ya doin', Joe? Still pissed off at me?"

"I was, but now I don't give a damn. If that's your idea of teamwork, you can stick it. I'm out of it, Harvey. Do what you want with the disk."

"Joe, if you had said that a few days ago, I would have thanked God. There was no reason for you to stay involved – it's too dangerous."

"Who the hell are *you* to tell me that, Harvey? When you were up to your neck in shit trying to solve this puzzle, I was the cat with a live bird in my mouth, and wouldn't let go. You needed the missing pieces and I got them. And now you're telling me to back off? Well, Mr. Cohen, I don't believe it should take foreign agents to sort out this country's problems."

"This so-called American dilemma is the world's quandary, Joe, and you know it! If you think we're only trying to help America, you're out of your mind."

"Like I told you, Harvey, I'm not interested anymore."

Cohen paid no attention. "Anyway, enough of that. This disk isn't in a type of Slidex code like the others. It's totally indecipherable without a series of special codes, and whatever information it contains is dangerous to them, real dangerous."

Still frustrated, Stacy relaxed a bit. Lowering his voice, he said, "Harvey, why are you telling me this? You're the pretentious prick who told Moshe to give me a blank disk."

"Joe, I'm never wrong, but I've been incorrect once in awhile. If you want an apology, okay, I apologize. Will you accept that? By the way, that's the first time I've apologized since I worked in a kibbutz and grabbed the wrong ass by mistake."

Stacy found himself grinning. Harvey was probably upright and he might have his best interest at heart.

"Who's ass did you grab?"

"Not my wife's, that's for sure. She looked like my wife from the rear, but it was my mother-in-law's. To this day, I'm still apologizing, to no avail. Never grab your mother-in-law's ass, Joe. But, enough of that; I put Manny and Jack with you to keep you safe in the big city."

"Then you knew, eh?"

"About what?"

"That I've just attended a cocktail party loaded with wolf rings. NICER's obviously a front. Who the hell nominated me for the prize?"

Cohen didn't answer right away. When he did speak, his voice was abrupt.

"I never knew about that, Joe. Get out of there; it's probably a set up! Get out of there now! The bird in your mouth was a vulture, and it's loose. The pricks nominated you to pay you off in case you got *interested* again."

"The conniving bastards!"

Harvey's voice told Joe something else was wrong.

"Joe, I've got some sad news for you. I thought I could get you mad before I told you this, but Ray Glover's dead, so is his wife, and ... Pete's in hospital."

Joe's right hand reached out rapidly gasping the back of the driver's seat. His eyes became glassy and his heart's energy pounded every vein and artery in his body. "What ... what happened?"

Your apartment's a shambles, so are the rest of your team's residences. Glover was home sick when the fuckers broke in. When Ray tried to stop them, they killed him and Lois. Linda phoned Pete saying a strange car had circled the block three times and had parked out front. He told her to leave through the back door. When he arrived, the pricks were pulling away and they shot him in the leg. He thinks he got one of them. Pete will pull through, Joe, and Linda's fine. I'm sorry, buddy."

Joe's head was nearly in his lap as he rubbed his forehead and ran a hand through his hair not knowing what to think or do.

Ray's original statement about the trip haunted him. *"Listen, if you end up winning and have to fly to New York, look up Malcolm Forbes for me, tell him I really enjoy his magazine, and tell him I think he's honest and he'd make a great president."*

What about Gail? Stacy thought, sitting straight up. They might go after her and the kids. "Harvey can you check on Gail for me?"

"We're watching her place. Gail's fine, Joe, so are the children. She's probably left messages at your hotel. I know what you're going through, and I'm sorry. Are you still there?"

His voice nearly inaudible, Joe said, "Yeah. God, Ray and his wife, and Pete? I can't get out of here until tomorrow at four. What the hell's so important about that disk?"

"I don't know, and we can't crack it. The code is a series of symbols, letters, and numbers. Some symbols and numbers were in Krupp's wallet, but..."

Joe's analytical mind jump-started. "If symbols are involved, Krupp's written them down. Who's got his stuff?"

"We've been over it all, Joe. Moshe should have undressed him. Krupp might have hidden it in his pants or jacket. The volcano's goin' off, and you're standing on the rim. Get back here now before it blows! Screw the NICER prize."

"I'll see if there's an earlier flight. They're not going to get the better of me, Harv. I'm here, and if they want me, they can come and get me."

"Joe, let me speak with Jack."

Half an hour later when Manny and Jack dropped Stacy off at the rear of his hotel, Jack handed him a Beretta, a silencer, a phoney driver's licence, and false identification cards. "Harvey's instructions," Manny said. "We'll be close by."

After Stacy collected his messages from the front desk and arrived at his room, he knew the volcano was erupting. Quickly wading through the shambles of turned over mattresses, stripped sheets and pillowcases, pulled out drawers and strewn clothes, he picked up the phone.

"Gail, sweetheart, are you all right?"

"Oh Joe, a fellow named Moshe was here. I'm frightened, what's going on?"

"Thank God you're safe. Where are the kids?"

"I'm leaving them at their grandparents. If there's a problem, I don't want them involved. But don't worry about us darling, what about you?"

"I'm okay, but Ray and Lois are dead, and Pete's in the hospital. I'm calling Linda now."

"Moshe told me. It's horrible. Will this never end?"

"Yeah, it'll end, don't worry. Gail, I can't get out of New York until tomorrow afternoon; is someone guarding your place?'

"Yes, Moshe and another man. Joe, I'm more concerned about you."

"Don't be, Kid. I'm looking over my shoulders. I'll see you, sweetheart."

"Take care of yourself Joe."

"I will, God bless."

When he hung up, Joe lit up a smoke and called Linda.

"Linda, how's Pete?"

The frailty of Linda's heartrending voice told Joe she had been crying. "Joe, it's good to hear your voice. Thank God you're all right. Pete's getting better, but Ray and Lois are dead."

"Yeah, I've heard. Is someone protecting you?"

"Joe, there are two members of the department inside, and four outside."

"Good, give my best to Pete. Tell him if he thinks this is going to stop him from working, he's got another think coming."

"Joe, if our baby is a boy we're going to call him Glover. If we have a girl, she'll be named Lois. I thought you should know."

A lump formed in Stacy's throat. "That's great, Linda."

Joe knew his call had perked Linda up, and when he placed the telephone down, he read his two messages. One said Rick Appleton, which was the name Harvey usually used in phone messages, and another was from Gail. There was not a notice about a change in dress. The bastards just wanted to take a good look at me, he thought.

After crumpling up the messages, he picked up the phone again.

"Front desk," a sweet-voiced girl answered.

"This is Lieutenant Stacy in 1732. I need a new room."

"What's wrong with your present room?" she asked.

"It's been invaded by rats."

Secret Service personnel always appear to have the knack of behaving like secret service personnel. They're not clones, but they act the same. Maybe it's their training or perhaps those responsible for dressing them get deals on special bolts of dark coloured cloth, and brand name sunglasses. Or maybe the government hires a specific tailor who only likes one colour and can only make one type of suit. Yes, that must be it, Morley Smith thought, enjoying the night time silence and the fresh country air at Camp David.

The presidential retreat was quiet and secure as similarly dressed *robots* walked the manicured grounds and closed-circuit cameras followed the chairman of the Bank of America, out on his nightly walk.

Smith and various leaders of the economy had spent a busy day with President Aird and his advisors, but throughout, it appeared an item weighed heavily on the president's mind. Certainly, the Chief was concerned about interest rates, and America's sprawling trade deficit with China, Japan, and Germany, but Smith had noticed something else. When Vice-President MacPherson was in the same room as the president, Aird was cool towards him. This was not the norm. Smith knew Aird and MacPherson had always been close, extremely close, and the president was the kind of man who delegated authority to his vice-president. No, something was wrong because when the president and vice-president had met alone, they could be heard yelling, and afterwards when group meetings ensued, the two men kept their distance from one another.

Passing several cottages, Smith finally arrived at the conclusion it was none of his business. He'd had severe arguments with his board of directors many times. It's a normal part of business, so it must happen when running a country. After saying good night to a passing secret service agent, Smith entered his assigned bungalow and went to bed.

Most people staying at the retreat had gone to bed early because breakfast was coming up at five-thirty and the length of the meetings had taken its toll on those attending. The lights, however, remained on in a single cottage isolated from the others. The inhabitant had requested this particular cottage because he had stayed there before, enjoying its seclusion. This particular cottage even allowed him to have his own private meetings with a senior member of the Central Intelligence Agency.

"What did you want to see me about?" Dieter Krueger asked.

"We've got a problem, sir. After the Kravenhall affair, President Aird asked the vice-president to come clean."

"How do you know?"

"I was in the next room, and Aird was enraged."

Krueger whistled while pouring out two drinks and passing one to his visitor. "Is that all you're worried about? You don't have to concern yourself with MacPherson; he's one of us - tight-lipped. Don't concern yourself about it."

The man accepted the offered drink, and after downing half of it and clearing his throat, he said, "MacPherson's not in charge of the investigation any longer."

"What? What the fuck are you saying?" Krueger yelled, slamming his glass down and spilling some of the liquid onto his pants. "He has to be in charge! He's been appointed!"

"That was changed today, sir. President Aird has asked for MacPherson's resignation and he wants a full written confession by tomorrow afternoon. If he doesn't get it, he said he would call a joint-session of the house and report the matter to the people. Aird knows the complete picture of MacPherson's involvement. He's given him the opportunity to resign for health reasons, but only if he has the vice-president's confession in his hands by tomorrow afternoon. If he doesn't, MacPherson will be arrested for treason."

"But that's impossible. How did the president learn of all the...?"

"He was informed by the Israeli Prime Minister this morning. I can get you a copy of the coded message if you want?"

The cottage's occupant stood up, placed his right hand on his forehead, and stared blankly at his visitor. After a few moments, he sat down again.

"What information did Aird request?"

"The president demanded names, companies involved, where our bank accounts are, and all locations of our camps."

"And what did MacPherson say?"

"He agreed to provide what information he could."

Thoroughly perplexed, Krueger rested his face in his hands. "That fucking bastard! I haven't even got time to call Switzerland. Will MacPherson be sitting with the president at breakfast tomorrow?"

"No, he's been conveniently placed at the end of your table, sir. The president won't be seen anywhere near him."

Iron-faced, with his mind deep in thought, Dieter Krueger said, "My table? Good, thank you for telling me. Well, I'm going to bed."

The *visitor* walked to the door. "Good night, sir."

Krueger did not reply.

Sitting in the back seat of the limo, Joe thought his suit didn't appear too wrinkled considering the previous night all the pockets and been turned out before his pants and jacket had been thrown on the floor. The hotel had given him a new room on the twentieth floor and had promised to replace anything missing, but nothing had been stolen. As he picked off small pieces of lint off his suit, he wondered why he never asked them to press it.

His driver, Prissy, remained quiet this morning, allowing Stacy to concentrate on the kaleidoscope of New York streets rolling by. It wasn't snowing or raining, but Joe had felt snow in the air when he stepped out on his balcony at seven-thirty and breathed in the fumes. After eating breakfast in his room, he had called Gail before she went to work. She was fine, and pleased that another pair of Harvey's crew was on the job watching her.

Joe had checked out of the hotel before Prissy arrived at exactly eleven o'clock. He had not slept well but he felt good, considering Ray and Lois' deaths still weighed heavily on his mind.

Watching New York go by, he thought of the disk. What the hell could be on it? Harvey and the FBI already know the companies involved; at least they thought they did. Maybe it isn't about companies.

"Did you read the paper or watch television this morning?" Prissy asked, driving around a rack of dresses left in the middle of the road. Two more heavy frames of garments had already been moved off the road to the sidewalk.

"No, why?" Joe asked.

"Then you haven't heard of the vice-president's death?"

The chauffeur's words shot through Joe like bullets rupturing targets at the police handgun range - loud, fiery, and deadly. "What? MacPherson's dead?"

"Yes, he died of a heart attack in his helicopter just before arriving back in Washington this morning. Such a nice, knowledgeable man; he would have been our next president. I would have voted for him."

"Where was he coming from?"

"Camp David," Prissy replied, leaning on her horn to get a truck moving.

"Same to you, you asshole!" she yelled, before saying, "He was there with the president and some of our country's biggest bankers and businessmen. The conference was about interest rates or something like that."

Christ, they've bumped him off as well, Joe thought, his mind racing. Why the hell would they take out MacPherson? To them, he was America's great white *hope*. MacPherson was the *patriot* that would try to change the constitution, allowing these bastards to do their dirty work.

Before Prissy turned a corner and stopped her vehicle, Joe was still attempting to figure it all out.

"Here we are, sir, 333 West 24th Street ... ABT. Just show your ticket to someone at the information desk. I've been told you'll be ready to leave at one on the dot, so I'll be back for you."

"Suits me, Prissy," Joe said, getting out and cautiously glancing around at a never-ending stream of fast shuffling sharply dressed business people sharing what appeared to be a nonexistent moving sidewalk.

With Joe outside, Prissy leaned over and opened the passenger's window. "This gives me a chance to grab a bite to eat. I'll meet you right on this spot. Don't stray now, or you'll get lost in New York. Got it?"

"Yeah, sure, thanks!"

When the circular doors pushed Stacy into the crowded lobby of a well-kept building built in the forties, he headed to the desk where one of three young ladies wrote his name on an ABT identification tag. He also noticed he was being scrutinized by a couple of the building's security guards. When he smiled, they didn't smile back.

"Attach this to your lapel," the woman said. You need Studio 401B. Take any one of the two end elevators to the fortieth floor, and then turn right to the studio. Ask for Mr. Jacque Russell-Wigglen."

While Joe waited for an elevator, a good-looking blonde girl about nineteen stood arguing with another receptionist. "What do you mean there's no pass for me. He's my agent and he said he'd tell you. I'm here auditioning for the Buffet's Baby Food spot."

The more the girl disputed the misplaced pass, the more the receptionist tuned her out. "I suggest you telephone Mr. Hagopian and straighten it out yourself. Thank you. May I help the next person, please?"

Disappointed and swearing under her breath, the girl picked up her grip and stormed out.

At the fortieth floor, Joe dutifully turned right and found studio 401B. After entering and trying to find Jacque Russell-Wigglen, a pleasant woman intercepted him first, and guided him to a relatively small room with a stage, cameras, and seating for about fifty people. Technicians of all kinds worked away with camera and boom operators, various directors, and control room personnel. It felt weird being there, and although he wanted out, he knew he had to follow this through.

When a bustling, short, boyish looking man with tinted bright orange and green hair and wearing a large brass earring appeared, Joe said, "Hi, I'm..."

The coordinator, Russell-Wigglen didn't let him finish. Looking at Joe's nametag, he said, "You're ... Lieutenant Stacy. Well, then, follow me and I'll take you to make-up. Come, come, come, there's no time to dilly-dally. Walk this way. Remember, there's to be no smoking and after makeup, please keep your hands away from your face."

"If I walked that way, Kraven would have enrolled me behind the wall," Joe muttered," permitting his grin to grow, stretching his neck, and allowing his eyes to check out the ceiling.

"What was that?" Russell-Wigglen asked, turning his head.

"Nothing, Jack, er, Jacque, er, Mr. Russell-Wigglen, please lead on."

In the makeup room, Joe had a black plastic cape placed around him from his neck down before a woman brushed rouge and powder on his face and combed his hair.

Smalltalk in the room centred on the death of Vice-President MacPherson, and Joe discovered his *buddy,* Cornelius Cunningham from the night before, sitting two chairs away. It wasn't hard discerning the man was suffering with a hangover. Expensive eyewash could not have helped what remained of Cunningham's eyes.

"I never liked MacPherson anyway," Cunningham sputtered to the girl applying his makeup. "The idiot was too vacillating for me. He couldn't make a decision if his life depended on it. Say, have you got something for a headache? If not, get me a bourbon. You're workin' on the author who wrote, *Prayers Aren't Coloured like Skin*. Shouldn't that qualify me for a bourbon?"

"Hey, Cornelius, where's your gorgeous wife?" Joe asked, grinning sarcastically.

Cornelius' bloodshot corneas found their way to Joe. "Ah, you know my name, so you must have read my book? How did you like it?"

The guy must have been so pissed he's forgotten me already, Joe thought. "No, Cunningham, I haven't read your book. Have you read mine?"

"Ah, another author. We breed don't we? What's *your* book called?"

Joe accepted a piece of gum offered by his attendant. Chewing and turning his head slightly so his eyes could pierce Cunningham's, he replied, "*Aryan Stands For Asshole!* It's selling big in the south, and I'm writing another entitled, "*Syphilis and Hitler Go Hand in Hand."*

Cunningham slowly pushed his make-up cape down but remained seated, his knuckles and fingers turning white grabbing the ends of the chair's arms.

As the two men *studied* each other's faces, Joe's grinning fierce, unyielding eyes cut through Cunningham's hostile shifting gaze. All chatting stopped around them as revulsion met hate head on in a merciless collision of ferocious disdain.

"Your fate's sealed, Stacy," Cunningham mouthed, casually arising from his chair and taking his coat of the coat-rack. "It's over, cop - you're dead."

"I'm glad that pickled heap of brown matter between your ears remembered my name, Cunningham, you phoney sanctimonious bullying piece of maggot shit! You're right - it is over for your kind, and this time for good. Get out of my sight or you'll need more than makeup."

The studio's bright lights prevented Stacy from reviewing the audience as he stepped on stage with nine others. Soon, he was guided to his *spot*. He was number four in line and Cunningham was number seven.

"Okay, ladies and gentlemen retain your positions, please" a man wearing earphones told them. "As I speak, we're running the tape on NICER achievements throughout the United States. Mr. Peter Cooper only has few minutes to make the presentations before he leaves. Remember, when your name is called, step up to Mr. Cooper and stay close to the mike. When you receive your certificate and prize money, accept it with your left hand and shake Mr. Cooper's hand with your right. Each of you has up to ten seconds to offer your statement of gratitude. Don't turn around from whence you came; just walk off stage through the other exit. Right ... are there any questions? No? Perfect! Smile please and look happy. A hundred million Americans want to thank you for your marvellous diverse achievements."

Minutes later when a well dressed, hair-slicked announcer appeared, a drum roll accompanied by brass music blared, and applause spewed from the speakers.

"Yes it is wonderful ... thank you, Robert," the announcer said. "Live from New York City, the National Independent Citizens For Equal And Better Race Relations, and the ABT Television Network are indeed most proud to honour America's ordinary citizens who have done so much to help eradicate bigotry in our fine country. These wonderful unselfish people standing behind me are just everyday folks like you and I, who care about their fellow countrymen. On their own, they stepped to the forefront helping their neighbours regardless of race, colour, or religion. The KINDER awards are presented every two years, and this year's chairman of KINDER is no stranger to philanthropy. Thousands of Americans are leading better lives due to his steadfast belief in equality. You may not recognize him, but you've most definitely heard of him. Let's bring him out and salute ... Mr. Peter Cooper. Welcome, sir, to your awards."

As the ovation tape rolled for five seconds, Joe could not see Peter Cooper's smiling face when the old man shook hands with the announcer, but he knew he had heard his voice before. Where the hell had he heard it? Especially the words, "Thank you, ladies and gentlemen for your most gracious welcome. Thank you America, and thank you honoured guests. It warms my heart to be here with you today."

While Peter Cooper continued his short speech, Joe searched his mind trying to identify the voice. Was it during the last awards? No, Cooper is this year's chairman. Was it...?

As recognition dawned on Joe, he felt his stomach tighten, his heart race, the skin on his face became tight and damp, and he had difficulty swallowing. Joe gasped and tried to lick his lips, but all moisture had left his mouth and his legs were becoming lead weights. Cold sweat formed on his forehead and he wanted to vomit as he strained his eyes and neck trying to focus on the man in front of the microphone. Joe's methodical police officer's mind had solved the problem, but now what was he going to do? Peter Cooper, one of the most important men in the United States was none other than Dieter Krueger.

When Krueger completed his brief dialogue, the award winners obediently shook the man's hand before thanking their co-workers, mothers, fathers, children, and God for allowing them to participate.

Pages in the book of time stop turning as Joe's mind accelerated lost in a chapter of inquisition that made no sense at all. Had the bastards gained complete control already? Krueger had probably just returned from Camp David, but something didn't make sense. Why was the vice-president dead? These ultra-organized fiends had nurtured MacPherson for their final conquest. Was the president involved? God help us if he is, Joe thought.

The *book* remained on the same page as Stacy dimly heard his name being called. At least he thought he heard his name, the announcer's voice sounded cavernous and penetrating.

Stiffly shifting his legs and approaching the smiling Krueger, Joe knew what he had to do. He also perceived Krueger's *interest* because the beast he approached was even more curious – but did not know he was about to meet the policeman who had cracked his egg, eaten the omelette, and shattered his world.

When Joe closed the gap, Krueger's joyful eyes and mouth metamorphosed and became hateful. The man was no fool. Krueger's lifetime of training disallowed hallucination. He had been taught to keep his composure. At the worst possible moment, Dieter Krueger had found the bogus *Dr. Schumann*. It was Joe Stacy. This hated cop had not backed off after all, and Krueger wondered how he could have been so gullible. Then Krueger made another mistake - he hesitated.

Stacy did not make a mistake. He quickly decided on a plan of action and grabbed the microphone. His mouth was moist now and as spittle sprayed, he yelled, "This animal isn't Peter Cooper! He's Dieter Krueger, once a member of

Hitler's SS. This fiend is responsible for all white supremacist atrocities in this country. Under his barbarian's instructions, children and adults have been kidnapped, raped, and killed. His camps and ovens fill the United States, and his money comes from murders, drugs, body parts, robberies, and any other reprehensible thing imaginable, including Swiss bank accounts owned by people slaughtered by Himmler's SS."

As the announcer and a rabid Krueger called for security guards, the director in the control booth yelled frantically at his distraught technicians, "Let it run, don't cut him off, let it run! Stay with him."

Krueger firmly grabbed Joe's left arm, only to have Stacy's right fist come up smashing and breaking the Nazi's nose and left cheek and propelling the man backwards.

"Don't touch me, you filthy degenerate lunatic," Joe yelled, getting ready to hit him again. "You work for someone in Switzerland who controls banks and big business throughout the world. The money you plundered from the Jews and others in Europe amounts to billions and you're using it for world conquest, you monster."

As stagehands assisted Krueger, three security guards grabbed Joe, attempting to haul him away. With the force of desperation and anger raging within, Stacy kicked one in the testicles before dispatching the other two with fists that knew no control. Quickly grabbing the microphone again, he bellowed, "This son-of-a-bitch has senators, justices, and people from every law agency in his pockets. It's happening throughout the world. Vice-President MacPherson was one of his *boys*, and I'm not sure if..."

Upset as he was, Joe remained in control of his senses. After seeing two armed police officers rush into the studio, he ran towards the stage exit. The door was blocked by Krueger sitting on the floor and nursing his face; the same face that now received the full force of Joe's right foot, nearly taking Krueger's head off, and catapulting him out of the way.

Stacy ran around the back of the stage, through the makeup room, changing room, and two empty offices before finding the outside hallway. Although forty stories up, he could hear sirens echoing below as he ran down the fire stairs three at a time.

With his heart nearly in his mouth, he opened the door on the 36th floor to find two painters about to enter the freight elevator.

"Where does this go?" he asked, abruptly pushing both of them in and pressing the lowest button.

The men turned apprehensive and wide-eyed, before one said, "To the basement. Er ... what's going on?"

Joe quickly flashed his badge. "Don't ask! Listen, I'm a police officer and some insane bastard's running around in this building. He's armed, so when we reach the bottom, find a safe place and stay there, do you understand? Or maybe you wanna help me catch him?"

The severity of Stacy's voice carried a message that hit home. As far as the workmen were concerned, the elevator couldn't move fast enough.

"No, no, er, we'll hide in the boiler room."

Joe took a deep breath as he felt the pressure easing. "This lunatic might use the building's service exit. Where is it?" he asked.

The senior of the two said, "Through the boiler room where we're goin'. We'll show ya. It's freezing out there, where's your coat, officer?"

"Up top."

"There're a few old coats in the basement. We'll get ya one."

"Great, any hats?"

"Yeah, some," one of them said.

Stacy smacked the painter's back. "Thanks, much appreciated."

The grey dirt-stained topcoat might have been made in the 60s, but not the New York Islander's cap. The items created a disguise good enough to allow Stacy to walk out of the alley turning the corner into bustling crowds collecting around eight police cars in front of the building. The vehicles blocked the road, and the painter was right, the cold was unmerciful.

Checking his watch, it read fifteen after one. Damn it, he was fifteen minutes late. Would Prissy wait, or would she take off?

Minutes later, an ambulance pulled up and Stacy saw Krueger being taken from the building. The old man might have been on a stretcher, but he still had a cellular phone in his hand, and Joe knew what that meant.

"I've got to find a phone," he murmured, turning his head in all directions, before backing out of the crowd and rushing towards a pay-phone thirty yards away.

"Operator I want to make a collect call to Seattle."

While Joe gave the number of Seattle's Memorial Hospital, he saw Prissy a half-block away, sitting next to her limo. She was held there by a couple of cops stopping traffic. When the hospital operator connected him, Joe yelled and waved wildly, finally catching Prissy's attention. He gave her the sign to wait there for him.

"Hello, Gail... I know, sweetheart, I know. I'm fine. Listen, darling, call Harvey at that number I gave you, and leave work. No, let Harvey's people pick up the kids. No, don't go home. I said, don't go home. I'll be there as soon as I can. When you're talking to Harvey, tell him to telephone Barker and the others, and my brother. I've given him the numbers. You've all got to hide out until this bastard Krueger is taken down. Do it now, Gail. Get going! Love ya!"

Stacy hung up the phone and ran towards Prissy. The driver had now pulled over to the side and was waiting for him. As soon as he climbed in, she asked, "What's going on in that building? Where did you get that coat - it reeks of fuel oil and sweat?"

"Prissy, let's get the hell out of here, and I'll fill you in on the way. Get me to the airport and take any route other than the normal one. Don't take the freeway!"

While speeding to the airport, Joe explained the situation. As he spoke, he could see the anxiety building on her face. The tale made Prissy push her foot down a little harder on the accelerator, and constantly check her mirrors. Her husband was Jewish and she mentioned her mother-in-law had given her factual accounts of Nazi atrocities in Poland, but she couldn't believe it could ever happen in America.

"It's been happening for a while, Prissy. Now it's time to stop the bastards. When we get to the airport, drop me at..."

A bullet striking the hood of their vehicle ricocheted like a rock skimming water. Prissy was doing 60 mph, but the two men in the Jeep Cherokee hogging the next lane weren't concerned about speed or traffic heading their way. When the passenger in the Jeep fired again, he missed entirely.

Pressing Prissy's head down and taking out the Beretta Manny had given him, Joe yelled, "For Christ's sake, duck! If you had good hearing, it's about to change."

"I've got to be able to see the road," Prissy screamed, picking up speed and leaving the other vehicle behind for a few moments."

"How in the hell did they know we were here?" Joe asked, getting ready to return fire.

The limo's driver tried to stay down. "This car's equipped with a satellite positioning system. The company keeps track of me for safety reasons."

"Now you tell me. Jeez, some safety?" Joe said, wincing, getting two rounds off and hitting the passenger in the car trying to ram them. Joe's slug had hit the man's head but it didn't slow the auto. The person in the driver's seat just pushed his co-driver downwards, preparing to come on for another try.

"I think I'm going to be sick," Prissy said, trying to keep the limo on the road after getting rammed the second time.

"Go ahead, what's one more stain on this coat," Joe said, ensuring his angry eyes never lost track of the gun's foresight aimed at the Jeep's driver. When the other vehicle pulled out again, Joe aimed behind Prissy's head, fired, and hit the driver, but not before the man got a round off, grazing Wallanski's forehead before shattering the windshield.

Fully out of control, the Jeep reeled through a farmer's fence before turning over. Now Stacy had other problems on his mind. Prissy was out cold and her foot was locked on the gas pedal. Instantly, he grabbed the steering wheel with his left hand, and after barely missing an oncoming cement truck, he edged over on top of her and quickly yanked her under him to the passenger's seat. After moving her legs across, he took control. Prissy's head wound wasn't life threatening but it bled baldly as she came to, saying, "Jesus I've got a headache. Did we win?"

"We're here aren't we?" he answered decisively while rooting in her purse for a handkerchief. "Hold this against your head. Where's the nearest hospital?"

"Am I gonna live?"

"Yeah, but you'll probably want to take up crocheting instead of driving."

"Then let's keep going, I can knit later. I know a couple of first aid attendants at the airport."

 "Are you sure? What about the pain?"

"This isn't pain. Pain is when you've given birth to two kids refusing to come out peacefully."

Stacey gave Prissy an appreciative glance before pulling the trunk latch and walking to the rear to disconnect the satellite homing device. When he got behind the wheel again his face still illustrated his admiration for his travelling companion. She looked like she had been dragged around the world upside down and inside out.

"I'm glad you didn't throw up and go to pieces on me, Prissy?""

"I had no time to throw up. You're lucky. Now when you sell that coat to a hobo, you'll get more for it. Boy what a story to tell my kids."

"I'm sorry about all this. Are you sure you'll be all right?" Joe said, arriving at the terminal.

The girl chuckled. "I'm fine, but this is the last job I'll take from ABT Television."

"Why? Not enough excitement?" he asked, picking up her newspaper, placing his empty gun in it, and tossing it into a nearby garbage receptacle. "Next time there's a war, I want you with me at the front lines."

Chapter 14

Albert Strassler and Gerlund Deutsch's eyes jerked between Sigmund's cold stare and Gustaf Schtaff's impassive gaze. Both men had been called in early, too early. They knew when Schtaff convened untimely conferences like this, someone usually died, and the well-dressed men could never presume Schtaff's state of mind. Like his mentor, Heinrich Himmler, Schtaff's disposition remained unpredictable. That is how he stayed alive, and on top.

The authoritarian's expression could not be judged this morning. His voice remained calm as if he had prepared himself for the worst-case scenario. He did not appear upset, but Strassler and Deutsch remained on the alert. They had weapons with them, and if the situation worsened, Strassler had agreed to take out Schtaff, and Deutsch would kill Sigmund.

"President Aird has had Krueger arrested, along with the majority of our CIA and FBI operatives. They've been sent to a special holding area, and when they talk, it's only a matter of time before our entire American operation comes crashing down. What do you have to say for yourselves?"

Strassler kept his hand on the small revolver in his right pants pocket.

"Krueger has been ordered to kill himself as you commanded, sir. As far as the others are concerned, only twelve are aware of specific aspects of our network in the United States. They'll be liquidated before they can disclose any information."

Strassler's response had no effect on Gustaf Schtaff as the head man casually lit a cigar and waved the smoke away. Raising his chin, the old man said, "But my dear gentlemen, they've closed down our Fatherland and Reichsland Camps. How long do you think it will it be before the others are discovered?"

"They won't be," Strassler said, squirming slightly because his whole body was sweating and he knew Schtaff took pleasure from such anguish. "We've transported our departmental heads to Paraguay, and nearly completed mothballing all other facilities. Your instructions have also been carried out regarding the internal affairs within our various companies, and everything remains on hold."

Without turning his head, Schtaff leisurely moved his eyes to Deutsch. "And our arms caches?"

"Moved to Alaska," Mr. Chairman. "I would add that we've also finished with Krueger's circle of imbeciles - what remained of them."

The headman's eyes widened angrily, making Strassler tighten his grip on his revolver.

"And the disk?"

Both men swallowed, not saying a word.

Schtaff's voice grew. "And the disk? What about the fucking disk?"

Wiping his forehead with his left hand, and clearing his throat, Strassler could not hide his fear. "We haven't found the disk. If Stacy has it, he's done a good job hiding it."

"Have you found the Elite Team?"

"No."

"Have you found Krupp?"

Strassler's eyes bounced between Schtaff and Sigmund. "Er ... no, not yet, sir."

"Not yet, sir," the madman screamed, standing up and waving his hands in the air. "Not yet, sir! Not yet, sir! How the fuck can one puny American cop do this to me? I must have been out of my mind leaving Krueger in that position! Our total network is on that disk along with *other* matters ... information that will put us out of business for good. Information that will ruin all the preparation our beloved Fuehrer arranged. Intelligence that will send this world shooting out of fucking orbit! The Jews are trying to get their money back. Oh, they'll fucking get it back all right and us along with it!"

Schtaff sighed heavily, gazed at the top of his desk, walked back to his seat, and sat down again. "Where is Lieutenant Stacy, or should I say, *Dr. Helmut Schumann,* now?"

"Montreal," Deutsch nervously replied, still keeping his eyes on both men.

"What the fuck is he doing in Montreal? How do you know he's there?"

Deutsch wanted out of the room instantly and he stood up for a second but Schtaff's eyes ordered him down again. Trying to swallow, he said, "Our sources are following him by his credit card usage. He's bought new clothes and checked into the Queen Elizabeth Hotel."

"Then get him!"

"We can't, sir ... he's no longer there. He checked in, but didn't stay. All means of transportation are covered. We'll find him."

Gustaf Schtaff nodded at Deutsch before pushing an intercom button. "Yes, you certainly will," he declared, prior to ordering in his usual decanter of brandy. When the liquid arrived, two other thugs entered the room. They stood behind Strassler and Deutsch as the attendant left.

Pouring out three glasses, the Nazi master sneered at the duo. "Stand up and gently remove everything from your pockets! Place whatever you have on my desk."

Two pairs of nervous fretful eyes scanned all things before them, especially the cigar smoke gushing from the accordion nostrils of the heavily breathing man in front of them.

Slowly, Strassler and Deutsch took out their firearms and laid them down as ordered. Still standing, their ears and skin observed what their eyes could not - intense inhaling and exhaling, two weapons cocking, and silencers touching each temple.

Schtaff waited at least five seconds before motioning his thugs to leave. Completely calm with the redness leaving his face, he said, "Put your weapons back in your pockets and sit down. Here, have a brandy, my friends. Am I so unpleasant you regale yourself to inappropriate musings of the sort that wish to hurt me? Gentlemen, I am your supporter, not your enemy. Drink up!"

As the two men nervously sipped, Schtaff murmured, "Sigmund, give me your weapon."

Upon placing his glass down, Schtaff accepted his disciple's pistol, waving it at the terrified pair who weren't drinking. The only sounds in the room were two hearts pumping, each aware of the coming end.

"No, I am not that unpleasant," he said, unemotionally passing the gun back to Sigmund. "But I will become that way if this cop Stacy isn't found. Now I want that disk. Do I make myself clear? I said, do I make myself clear?"

Frustrated, Joe searched his mind trying to remember his high school French.

"Er, Ne vous Voyage à Toronto?" he said to a half sleeping cabbie.

The cab driver ignored him and kept on reading a newspaper.

"Shit, what's the word for *take*...?" Joe asked out loud, leaning in the taxi driver's window and displaying some money.

It wasn't necessary for Joe to speak French - the cabby spoke English, and sat up in a hurry.

"T.O.? *Tronna*, Mac," the driver inquired, looking at Joe as if he were insane. "Mac, are you askin' me to drive you from Montreal to Tronna?"

Stacy started flipping through his wad of bills. "Yeah, Toronto! If you don't want to make some big money, there must be other cabbies that do, and..."

"Oui, oui, Tronna, it is! Get in, sir, let's go."

A different looking Joe Stacy climbed in the cab than the Joe Stacy who had arrived in Montreal two hours earlier, booking into the Queen Elizabeth Hotel.

The driver wasn't particularly talkative, and this gave Joe some time to collect his thoughts. Saying good-bye to Prissy and flying to Montreal all came back to him.

The injured limo driver had accompanied Joe to the Air Canada counter before she went to have her wound looked after. "They won't be lookin' for you in this section of the airport," Prissy had said, before giving him a kiss on his cheek. "Don't tell me where you're going ... I don't want to know. I'm in love with my husband, but if I wasn't, you'd have me sitting on your doorstep."

Stacy took his wallet out. He only had two twenty-dollar bills and he gave them to her. "This is all I have - it should be tenfold."

Prissy had snapped them up, and had given him her card. "Thanks. If you're ever in New York again - that's if you survive - give me a call, and I'll arrange some more excitement. Maybe a bank heist or jewellery store robbery. A really big jewellery store robbery."

Joe had laughed aloud while giving her a hug. "I've had enough excitement, Prissy; now it's time to settle down."

The first Air Canada flight out was destined for Montreal, so Joe bought a seat, and thirty minutes later he was in the air.

People in his immediate vicinity did not particularly care for the smell of his coat, but that didn't bother him, he'd gotten used to it. Even if he found himself scratching a lot, at least it kept him warm. He remembered a Marines axiom: *Any fool can be uncomfortable.*

In flight, Joe had time for two complimentary drinks, a small bag of peanuts, an in-flight snack, and a call to Harvey before the plane touched down and Canadian Customs waved him through. He chuckled to himself leaving Customs, thinking they didn't want his coat hanging around.

"Montreal? What are you doin' there?" Harvey had asked.

"Harvey, I'm coming back via the back door. I'm not staying in Montreal, I'm heading to Toronto."

"Yeah, probably a good move."

"How are Gail and the kids?"

"Fine, they're in an apple crate."

"An apple crate? What the hell is that?"

"They're in the country. We don't have to protect your colleagues, Joe. Chief Couling's doing that, and Pete's fine."

"The bastards nearly got me on the road today, Harv. What happened to Jack and Manny?"

"They were watching the ABT building, but you ditched them after your *speech* to the nation. Not bad by the way. All hell's breaking loose and the whole friggin' country wants to congratulate you. Haven't you heard?"

"Heard what?"

"President Aird's been cleaning house. Hundreds of the pricks have been arrested and it's still going on. Oh, yeah, and Krueger's dead."

"Krueger? What happened to him - I only broke his nose and chin?"

"Committed suicide by chewing a cyanide capsule. When they're ordered to end it all, those bastards don't argue. I've got a feeling Switzerland's running the show now, and when *their* backs are against the wall, look out. Their Elite Team may be gone, but there's always more coming up. Listen, Joe, I've got some friends in Toronto. Don't use the customary hotel transportation, take a cab, and see the concierge at the Royal York Hotel. His name's Hymie. I'll tell him you're on your way, and he'll book a prepaid room for you under the name of Rick Appleton. Then I suggest you catch a flight to Sacramento and drive in from there."

"Sounds good, Harv ... thanks."

"There, ya see? I'm not the heartless bastard you think I am, am I?"

"Who says so? See ya soon, buddy."

When Joe Stacy had checked into the Queen Elizabeth, he did not head to his room. Instead, he put the room key in a post-box, bought some clothes on his American Express card, and changed in the men's washroom of a nearby restaurant.

Stacy knew Krueger's mobsters were everywhere, so he played their game of intrigue. He also knew staying one step ahead of them would be tough but necessary if he wanted to survive.

"Why didn't you fly or take the bus?" the taxi driver asked, observing Joe in the rear-view mirror.

"Flying makes me sick, and buses don't run on time. Besides, you looked like you needed a fare. I think I'm going to grab some shuteye. Take me to the Royal York Hotel."

"You got it. Do you want the heat turned up?"

Stacy didn't hear the question - he was beat and he couldn't keep his eyes open.

"Hey, Mac, we're here. Mac, you're at the Royal York."

When Joe woke up, it was evening and he found himself stretched out on the back seat with a blanket covering him.

"You must have been bushed," the driver said, opening the right rear door of the vehicle and folding up the comforter. I covered you three hours ago when I grabbed a hamburger and a coffee."

Stretching after he got out, Joe still felt tired, but there was new life in him.

"Thanks," he said, taking out his wallet. "Are you going back now?"

"You bet. Maybe I'll get a few more trips like this one."

Hymie wasn't on duty when Joe visited the concierge's desk in the grand lobby, but Harvey's friend had left the key with his replacement.

Five minutes later, Joe used the complimentary razor and shaving cream and spent twenty minutes soaking in a hot bath. Afterwards, he knew he could not leave his room, so he relaxed on the bed, asked room service to leave a clubhouse sandwich outside his door, and then turned on the television. Again, Wolf Blitzer from CNN filled the screen.

"... twenty-seven senior members of the CIA, along with sixteen FBI and five Secret Service agents have been arrested. Sources say additional arrests are imminent and the president has ordered all law enforcement agencies to examine their personnel files. Peter Cooper's ... or should I say, Dieter Krueger's death came as a shock to business leaders in the United States and the western world. How this can happen is beyond reason, and in his report to the nation two hours ago, President Aird stated, 'It won't happen again!' He also appealed to the people to give him time to ponder the number of suicides committed by certain state governors and various members of both houses.

"Very little is being said how Lieutenant Joe Stacy infiltrated the Kravenhall estate, or how the Israeli government became involved. It is known that Vice-President MacPherson did not die of a heart attack as previously reported. An unofficial report on the preliminary autopsy revealed he was murdered, but further details have not been released.

"Democrats are also demanding to know why Krueger was invited to Camp David with President Aird and Vice-President MacPherson. The president's press secretary has announced that a statement is forthcoming.

"As far as the stock markets are concerned, the president asks for logic to prevail, saying, 'The economy of our country remains strong, and it will continue that way.'

"In Britain today, under pressure from the conservatives, Prime Minister Norman Aitken called for calm in the House of Commons. The Prime Minister is scheduled to join President Aird in Washington three days from now. British Foreign Secretary, Sir John Gibbons, stated, "If this is a world-wide conspiracy as Lieutenant Stacy believes, President Aird and our counterparts in the European Community will spare no effort to root out those involved."

"In the interim, Seattle's Mayor Lungley and Police Chief Couling have informed CNN they do not know the whereabouts of Lieutenant Stacy, or whether he is still alive. They have confirmed that the lieutenant's team of investigators are in protective custody and will remain there until President Aird's investigation is complete. In other news, an avalanche..."

Joe Stacy never heard the remainder of the news. The hot bath and sandwich had achieved their desired effect. With a look of contentment on his face, he pulled his covers up, rolled on his side, and fell asleep.

While shaking hands and slapping each other on their shoulders, Joe Stacy and Harvey Cohen's happy faces told the story of their accomplishment. Joe had caught an early morning flight out of Toronto, and had called Harvey to arrange a car for him in Sacramento. After a relaxing and uneventful drive to Seattle, when he arrived, he telephoned Harvey and asked him to meet underneath the Chinese restaurant.

"I knew you'd appreciate this," Harvey said, placing a bottle of single malt scotch and a jug of ice on the table. Joe, the whole world is proud of you. The fiends are scrambling to cover their asses. Four of them have even been arrested in Israel - can you imagine that? After the war, a few of these sly maniacs immigrated to Palestine using the identity of gassed concentration camp prisoners. The bastards actually got away with it until now."

Joe poured two drinks and passed one to his friend. He knew the mental anguish Harvey was going through; the man had spilled out his heart's sincerity to him before. Now he did it again. "When Hitler's *game* was over, the key figures did absolutely everything to protect their own skins. They weren't going to get slaughtered. They didn't want to die. They just wanted to escape to carry on with their tasks, ensuring that those of the perfect master race were created superior to all others and were born to dominate the world."

Sadly, Joe said, "Well, I'm glad you got them, buddy, that's the main thing. I can't thank you enough for all your help at this end."

As tough as he was, Harvey's eyes revealed the most heartfelt gaze Joe had ever seen. He even had to clear his throat. "Don't thank me, my friend ... don't even try. What are your plans now?"

Cohen poured two more drinks while Joe said, "I want to see Gail and Pete, and I've got to get collect some clothes and a few things from my apartment."

Cohen's face changed, and a concerned look Joe had seen many times appeared. "I don't know if that's wise, Joe. Our people are watching your place, along with the police, but..."

Joe quaffed his drink and stood. "The pricks won't be there, Harv. That's the last place they'll think of looking for me. I now know how these maniacs think; as far as they're concerned, I'm still in Montreal."

"But it's not necessary, Joe. Wait till things completely settle down."

The detective had made up his mind. "Listen, Harv, I'm not running anymore. All my clothes ... everything I have is in that apartment. I thought about that on the plane and driving here. I've had it up to here with these bastards. They're gone and I'm still around. What am I supposed to do, hide for the rest of my life? I need some money, fresh clothes, and..."

Reluctantly, Harvey acceded. "Okay, where'd you park?"

"Out front."

"Good, leave the car here, I'll drive you home and stay with you. I'll tell my people to distract the cops, and we'll go in the back way."

Sounds good to me," Stacy said, checking his pocket watch. "Then after you drive me back I'll follow you to Gail's."

Rain mixed with hail hammered Cohen's car as he turned into the alley and pulled into the parking lot behind Joe's building. Moments before, Joe had remarked to Harvey that he'd take the rain any day compared to the cold of the East Coast. Perhaps the thought of being home and the warmer weather relaxed Stacy just enough for him not to notice the nose of a Corvette he'd seen before, barely sticking out of adjacent old wooden garage with no doors a few yards up the alley.

Stacy's apartment was a shambles, and Joe quickly filled two suitcases with clothing, underwear, shoes, and some money and valuables he had hidden.

"Harvey, tell me again what you found on Krupp's file?" the detective asked while packing in the bedroom.

Harvey moved from the front door to the kitchen, and opened a cold V-8 juice. "It indicated Krupp visited six world centres passing on Switzerland's instructions which are obviously on that disk. In each country, Krupp's personal code and two other codes are required to furnish specific information. After receiving instructions, the same codes are required to store each country's annual report. Krupp was taking that information somewhere after Kravenhall. Moshe said the monster mentioned something about Paraguay."

When Joe rejoined his friend, Harvey grinned, saying, "A beer would have been better but I know you've been a little busy."

"That stuff's better for you anyway," Joe shot back. "Paraguay? Krupp has a disk and he visits various countries. He gets together in each country with two individuals and they each have codes. When the codes are entered, the disk gives them Switzerland's instructions, and they in turn program their annual report on the same disk?"

Cohen nodded and finished off the juice. "Exactly, but who had or has the American codes? We know Krupp collaborated with Krueger, Kraven, and MacPherson at Kravenhall. We've got Krupp's code, because on one page of the file he'd written four numbers in the corner. On another, he'd written four letters, and on the last page, he'd written four symbols. The way I figure it, his code always changed, therefore, he wrote them down. He wasn't worried ... he knew his code was useless without the other twenty-four numbers, letters, and symbols. Our problem is MacPherson, Krueger, and Kraven are dead, placing us up the perennial creek without a paddle. We know it takes thirty-six representations to read Krueger's annual report."

Carrying a suitcase, Stacy re-entered his bedroom with Harvey following. "Harvey, can you get hold of Krueger's ring?

"Yeah, why?"

"Well, it's possible that's were Krueger's code will be. The rings I've seen all have some sort of scratching inside."

"We'd still be short twelve representations," Harvey said, following Joe to the door.

The detective took one last glance around. "At least it's a start. Christ, I hope my insurance covers this mess. The last time it happened, they..."

Harvey was not at ease and although he moved quickly, he had made a mistake and he knew it. He had stayed behind his friend when they had entered the building, and been in front of him when they went into the apartment. He had not considered the possibility of an attack when they left the apartment.

Harvey was only five feet away when he yelled, "Joe, let me go out first! Joe, don't..."

Harvey's voice couldn't compete with three loud shots sending Stacy hurtling against his neighbour's door across the hall. Harvey's warning also could not rival the guttural moaning sound Joe emitted after grabbing his burning chest when the first discharge opened it up.

Harvey rushed to the door to find Joe's blood-soaked body and left hand smearing the wall with red stains, before sluggishly turning around and sinking.

Before falling to his knees to help his friend, Cohen yelled, "You bastards," and got two rounds off at the running assailant's back.

Joe had not dropped completely. He had turned abruptly and his legs had folded under him partially propping his body up against the wall - his head drooping forwards and to his left side. Throughout the four-second ordeal, Joe's right hand had hung on to his suitcase, and his other hand lay bright red and loose across his left leg.

Harvey heard three more shots as he squat next to his friend and placed his left arm around him. A moment later, he heard footsteps running up the main front stairs, and someone yelling, "We've called for an ambulance!"

Driving cold rain washed some of Joe's blood from Harvey Cohen's hands and face when the ambulance attendants placed Stacy's blanket-covered body in the back of their vehicle. With moist eyes, Harvey rushed forward pushing aside an attendant closing the ambulance's door. "What are you doing, I'm going with him? Let me in there; he's my friend! God damn these bastards - Joe Stacy's my friend."

A sympathetic doctor gently took hold of Harvey's left arm. "It's no use, sir ... he's gone."

One look at Harvey's grieving frenetic face persuaded the doctor otherwise. "I'm sorry, climb in," he said.

Snow doesn't let up for funerals, which must indicate old man winter doesn't give a damn who dies, Pete thought, holding a large black umbrella over Linda and Gail inside a bone chilling cemetery that could not accommodate the massive number of mourners.

Harvey held an umbrella over Gail's children. Earlier, he had been introduced as Mr. Rick Appleton, a friend of Joe's from Bowling Green, Kentucky.

Police officers from every force in the United States, Mexico, Canada, Britain, Australia, and most European countries attended, mourning Joe Stacy's death. They stood at attention as volleys of shots from the honour guard launched pigeons and echoed against the numerous fluffy white gravestones.

When President Aird took the microphone, he said, "I didn't speak in church because I've been told Joe Stacy did everything in the open. That was his way.

"I never had the honour of meeting Lieutenant Stacy, and I'm certain hundreds here, thousands on the roads outside, and millions watching this immensely sad occasion on television share the same grief I hold for this brave American.

"Last night I sat down for three hours trying to find the words to express our nation's gratitude. I wrote down: *Thank you, Joe. Thank you for serving with loyalty, integrity, and bravery. Your sense of justice, your initiative, and your endurance were examples we must all strive to attain if we are to secure our nation's future. The world owes its gratitude to you for your indefatigable courage and tenacity. God bless you Lieutenant Joe Stacy, and God bless freedom.*"

When Joe's coffin was lowered, President Aird followed the minister to be second in line throwing a small handful of soil on top of it.

With tears streaming avenues down her cheeks, Gail threw in a rose, and said, "Good bye, my darling, Joe. I love you so much."

Afterwards, when the crowds dispersed, Harvey took the children to a warm car while Gail remained with Pete and Linda watching large snowflakes caress the coffin and the black tarpaulin covering a mound of dirt. Joe's brother and his family remained with them for a while, and when they left for the wake at Bea Honeywell's, Pete suggested it was too cold for Gail and Linda to stay.

Gail wiped her eyes. "Please, you two, er, don't wait for me. I just want to be alone and remain by Joe's side a little while longer. Thank you."

The couple did as Gail suggested, and Gail stepped closer to the barrier.

"Oh, Joe darling, I … sweetheart, I want you to know..."

Gail couldn't continue. Her mind was numb, cold, and fearful, with a great sense of loss. When her legs started to buckle, two people gently took hold of her arms leading her back to the car. Bea Honeywell and Wilfred Young had been standing under a nearby tree and they too had been weeping.

Thirty minutes later, red-eyed, confused, and wanting to leave, Gail spotted Harvey and struggled through the crowd filling Bea Honeywell's Tavern. "Rick, where are the kids?" she asked, her eyes lost and mournful. Earlier, Harvey had requested she refer to him as Rick in *mixed* company.

Although Joe Stacy's wake was limited to close friends, associates from the Force, and pals that served with him in the Marines, members of the public mixed with government officials, television, and newspaper reporters, out of town police officers, and eager movie producers. The gathering was noisy and hot, and Gail didn't want to be there any longer.

"I took them back to their grandparents," Harvey said sadly, placing his arm around Gail's shoulders. Gail let me take you home to get some rest. This past week has been rough on all of us, you in particular. C'mon, sweetheart, you don't need this. Get your coat while I get the car."

Sombre, with her eyes welling up, Gail slowly nodded as Harvey squeezed her shoulders and left the room. The week had been living hell and most times she did not know up from down or why she was living. A special love that should not have come along at this stage of her life had been snatched away from her as quickly as it had arrived. It wouldn't happen again; she wouldn't let it. Her love had been predestined. From the first time she had seen Joe Stacy she knew she would love him forever. Now she had to get her life back together and hug her children. Suzie and Gordie were just as bewildered. Uncle Joe was the father they never had and they would miss him terribly.

Bea helped Gail into her coat and buttoned it up. Tenderly placing her hands on each of Gail's shoulders, she said, "Gail, we haven't met before today, but I feel like I've always known you. Joe was one of those guys that knew someday the right person would come along. Something told him he'd meet you, and when he did, we were happy because he'd found what he was always searching for. Joe was different; he was the black sheep we all wanted to paint white. We didn't know he kept white wool hung in his closet and only used it when he found you. I know I can't help you in your sorrow, but call me if I can. Promise me you'll do that, Gail?"

Gail kissed Bea's forehead. "Thank you, Bea. You'll always be a friend and I'll..."

The jukebox cut Gail off by playing *Real Love* by the Beatles, and while Gail tried to smile and finish her thoughts, she couldn't. Wiping her eyes, she quickly and quietly walked out.

"It was kind of Bea to offer her tavern for the wake," Harvey said, trying to make conversation while driving Gail to pick up her children. "I wouldn't be surprised if it carries on till morning."

Offering a faint smile, Gail didn't answer. Instead, she kept her eyes on the road, and her mind on memories of Joe.

Ten minutes later when Harvey abruptly changed directions, she asked, "Where are we going, Harvey, this isn't the way?"

Harvey Cohen looked lost, as if he didn't know what to say. Slowly, he pulled the car over and sat there for a few seconds staring at the vehicle's dashboard.

"Harvey, what's wrong?"

When Cohen turned his head and body, every problem in the world appeared to be on his shoulders. Swallowing heavily, he said, "Gail, we're not going to pick up the kids."

Gail's sad face showed even more strain. "Why not? Is something wrong?"

"No, they're fine. Er, I want you to know I'm not the meanest son-of-a-bitch you've ever met. There are times when I can be, but not now. You see, Gail, I..."

"Harvey, get it off your chest. What's wrong?"

Cohen licked his lips, bit his lower lip, released the emergency break, and pulled out in the traffic again. "We're going to a small airfield. Uh, is your heart strong?"

"What? Harvey, I don't need this. Please turn this car around. I'm too worn out for games. Three funerals in two weeks have taken their toll on me."

Harvey's voice almost became inaudible. "Gail, Joe's not dead. He's in a small hospital in Mount Shasta, and I'm taking you there to see him. It's impossible to kill someone like him, er, permanently that is."

When Harvey pulled the car over again, he frowned, mumbling, "Damn it, I knew I should have brought smelling salts."

Chapter 15

"What the hell are you doing out here?" Cohen asked Moshe standing outside Joe's hospital room. "I told you not to leave his side."

Harvey instantly noticed something different about Moshe. The young man appeared uncommonly lively - even whistling at passing nurses.

Since the shooting, smiles had been at the bottom of the barrel, never to surface. Not now, though, because Moshe like Simon was in a much lighter mood.

"Harvey, if you think for a moment that I'm going to sit there watching those two ogle and caress each other, you've got another think coming, *sir*." Still grinning enthusiastically, he added, "I think we'd better order a truck load of Kleenex."

The tough Israeli Set leader's grin copied his associate's mouth. "Heavy on the 'sir,' Moshe my boy. Really mushy, eh?"

"Mushy? If that's love between a man and a woman, I want in. Do you think it's too late for me to switch?"

Cohen chuckled. "Definitely. Er ... do you think this will help Joe recover more quickly?"

"Harvey, I'd be surprised if the tubes are still in him tomorrow. He doesn't need intensive care anymore, he needs a honeymoon suite."

Harvey found himself laughing with his associate, and the more he laughed, Moshe's astonished expression made him laugh even louder. Moshe had rarely seen Harvey grin, never mind laugh, and he said, "I can't believe it - you are human after all?"

Totally exhilarated, Cohen smacked Moshe's back. "Who says so? If word gets out that you saw me laughing, you're back in the army."

Sometime later, when the two men entered Stacy's room, they saw Gail sitting on the side of Joe's bed holding his hand and stroking his hair. Moshe had been right, Harvey thought, and his compassionate face said it all. Gail's visit was just what the doctor ordered. Both lovers had starry-eyed looks on their faces and it was obvious she was here to stay. Now Stacy now had his own private nurse.

With his radiant face full of joy, the *patient* held out his right hand. "Thanks, Harv. Once again, I owe you guys my life."

Harvey didn't let go of Joe's hand. "You'd do the same, pal. But I don't know if I could take three slugs in the chest and survive. When you said you were a cat with a bird in your mouth, you weren't joking. The doc in the ambulance got you goin' again. All I did was tell him to keep at it. I guess Moshe's filled you in on everything else?"

Gail took her eyes off Joe's, but only for an instant. "Harvey, in the plane you never told me who was in the coffin. Was it empty?"

Harvey finally released Joe's hand, and his stretching grin became contagious. "Hell no, Gail, it was occupied. The beast using it had recently received a new set of teeth. Putreds is down below with his friend the devil wondering why he got treated to such a great send off."

"Who got him?" Joe asked.

"Simon did. Not bad, eh, three in the head and neck from fifteen yards? Putreds' body and his Corvette were whisked away in seconds. The police heard the shots, but Simon told them he'd missed. As for the coroner's report and the paperwork, it's amazing what can be done when you know the right people."

"Three in the head and neck? Simon nearly shoots as good as me," Joe said, trying to keep a straight face.

Harvey got the joke. "You're starting to become the old Joe again."

Stacy winced a little after laughing. "I feel it comin' back Harv. Say, did you check out Krueger's ring?"

"Yeah, and as usual you were right. There were twelve characters and symbols. I've been pulling my hair out because we are still short."

Moshe turned to look out the window when Joe replied, "No we're not, Harv. How long have I been lying here with nothing to do?"

Cohen adopted an inquisitive look. "Almost eleven days, but you were out of it for at least a week."

"Well, that gave me plenty of time to talk to our buddy here," Joe said, pointing at Moshe. "While visiting Kravenhall, Moshe apparently decided to have some fun and go skinny-dipping with Kraven. The monster's code formed part of a gothic design tattooed on his left inner wrist."

Moshe cleared his voice twice before gingerly facing his boss. "Yeah, I really had a fun time. Swimming with Krupp could be compared to dancing with the devil. Anyway, those bastards were certainly fond of tattooing, weren't they?"

"Why didn't you tell me?" Harvey asked, flabbergasted that his colleague hadn't mentioned anything about it during debriefing."

Shrugging, Goldberg held out his hands, palms up. "For some reason it slipped my mind. Everything I did with those bastards has slipped my mind. Joe's hounding got me thinking of it, er … 7, 35, 17, 28, F, P, V, Q, a plus sign, a counter-clockwise L, an upside down question-mark, and the symbol for pi."

Harvey felt Joe's eyes on him. "I know, Joe, I know. I promised you we'll look at the information on the disk together and we will."

"It beats looking at a blank disk, Harvey."

"Jesus, are you still on that? Hey, you're looking at a changed man."

A doctor entered the room and departed after saying, "I think it would be wise to let Mr. Benjamin get some rest now."

"Mr. Benjamin?" Gail asked, curiously.

Joe gently squeezed Gail's hand. "Yeah, it has a nice ring to it, eh, kid. Harvey chose the name. How does Mrs. Joe Benjamin sound? Also, do you think the children will like Wyoming after we visit Israel?"

Gail's eyes welled up again and she leaned over and kissed him. "You don't have to ask me that, Mr. Benjamin. Just say when and we'll join you on the moon."

Before Harvey left for the airport, he dropped Gail off at the same adjacent motel housing Moshe and Simon. Both men took shifts watching Joe, so Harvey thought it would be safer if Gail stayed in a room near them.

"Are you sure you don't want to return with me to pick up some clothes."

Snickering, Gail gently straightened Harvey's tie, and said, "I thought he was dead, and now you want me to leave him? I'm staying here and I'll buy some new clothes later"

"What about your job?"

"What job? I'll go back in a few days and tell them I'm quitting. Oh, and by the way, Harv, I've got something to say to you, you louse."

Cohen pretended to wince. "Oh yeah, what's that?"

"Harvey, you *are* the meanest son-of-a-gun I've ever met," Gail said, appreciatively kissing Cohen on his right cheek. "Anyone who would put me through that funeral has got to be. But, you're the nicest, meanest son-of-a-gun in the world, and I think you're the dearest. Thank you."

Two days later, Harvey Cohen telephoned the motel at six o'clock in the morning, and when he did, his voice revealed his excitement. "Who's this, Moshe or Simon?"

"It's Moshe ... I just got off shift."

"Well you're goin' back on shift, and I'll be there in three hours. Rent or borrow the best computer you can find and hook it up in Joe's room. Aaron Vines really outdid himself this time. The disk has been translated, and I've got everything, absolutely everything. Also, buy some blank CDs."

Still lying in bed, Moshe sat up, yawned, wiped his eyes, and stretched. "What do ya mean by everything?"

"Everything, the works... the whole shebang that was going to Paraguay. And tell Joe I've also got The *Himmler Stratagem*."

Four hours later when Harvey, unshaven and with bloodshot eyes came rushing into Stacy's room, he placed a CD in the computer Moshe had set up by the bed. Only Joe, Moshe and Simon were present, Gail had returned to the motel earlier after sitting up all night with Moshe watching the steadily improving *patient*.

"You won't believe this Joe, and don't ask me what our computer expert was talking about when he tried to teach me about arranging variables. I still can't figure it out.

"The three codes got us the American information all right, but by *arranging the variables*, Vines came up with the fourth code, which is Paraguay's key. Apparently every third symbol assigns itself a... oh, who gives a shit. Take a look at this."

Over the next two hours, the information scrolling down the screen strained four sets of eyes glued to the computer. The disk covered past year activities in six districts throughout the world.

"We now know the Heads of State on the payroll, as well as district controllers and staff. We have the handbook of shaping future world leaders, bank dominance, account numbers and balances, as well as percentages of ownership in world financial institutions. The list goes on with loans to countries, establishments and individuals, and all banks holding emergency slush funds. The information reveals recruiting programs together with locations of camps and staff, activities of twelve owned and operated multinational corporations, and details of sixty-five large businesses located in major world cities. We now have maps showing the locations of hidden art treasures, artefacts, gold bullion, and coins. Not bad, eh? Wait until you see the names of all the politicians, judges, law-enforcement officers, and customs officials on the payroll. Hell, they really loved bribe money. These Nazi bastards listed drug production and distribution, kidnapping procedures including dispersal and pricing, body organ sales, slavery, organized robbery and murder, including planned and authorized elimination of those dangerous to the cause. It finishes with propaganda, schemes and insurrection procedures, traitors who had been eliminated, controlled media, friendly media, as well as international entertainers and sports celebrities offering the *right* point of view.

"There's just too much here to grasp," Harvey eventually stated, breaking the stunned silence and wiping the tiredness from his eyes. "But it's their blueprint for world domination at all levels, and we've got it."

Allowing the CD to continue running, Cohen got up and slowly paced the floor. "I know I've said this a million times before, he said, talking to no one in particular. "But how can something like this actually happen?"

At this point Joe would have given everything he owned just to jump out of bed and place an arm around his friend's shoulders. Quietly, he said, "You've also answered your question a million times before, Harv … money and hatred. Other people's money and the indelible hatred these bastards manufacture.

Human culture, if it can be called that, comes in two forms – God and the devil's, and there's no in-between. These are the devil's thugs, and by their actions, each of them sucks on cowards' pacifiers. Those pacifiers emanate the pain, agony, and death the bastards crave. Without them, they're lost. They're all cowards, Harvey, and their hatred is like a rock until someone hammer's them with an iron fist. When that happens, anything can be placed in their spineless mouths, even shit if it means their lives are spared."

Harvey found it difficult to speak and didn't stop pacing. "There's more on that disk, Joe. Something I've always suspected, but a piece of my heart said it couldn't happen. In 1943, Heinrich Himmler wrote a letter to Adolf Hitler. I'm certain Hitler would have wanted the letter destroyed, but the chicken farmer in charge of death was too proud of it. The egotistical son-of-a-bitch wanted his crazed diabolical future of the world imprinted on those who would succeed him."

Cohen returned to the computer and brought up the communication. "It's a copy of the original letter, and it's been translated. Let me read it to you.

"From SS Reichsfuehrer Himmler -- Berlin, 23 August, 1943. Mein Fuehrer, I reaffirm my oath. I swear before God to give my unconditional obedience to you, Adolf Hitler, Fuehrer of the Reich and its people, and Supreme Commander of the German Armed Forces. I pledge my word as a brave soldier to observe this oath always even at the risk of my life. Under the eyes of a loving God who shares His ascendancy with you, I write affirming my obligation of truthfulness and worship for you, my only true and trusted friend, mentor, and Fuehrer. The law and the will of the Fuehrer are one. I assert there is in Germany, only one authority, and that is the authority of its Fuehrer, Adolf Hitler.

"In profound privacy, you have honoured me with your wisdom concerning your foresight for the continuance of our brotherhood in this world. My Fuehrer, as your collaborator and obedient servant, I have initiated the Werwulfe Project based on the identical principles of your prescript embraced by the people of Germany and our conquered lands."

Harvey paused for a moment saying. "Vines told me someone had scratched out Werwulfe Project, and changed it to Himmler Stratagem."

"Let there be no doubt, Mein Fuehrer, I have commenced this plan to ensure your probity will guide the world for a thousand years and more. Yes, there are traitors amongst us - there will always be envious, corrupt beings wishing to eradicate your achievements, but I unmercifully hunt them down. Through your benevolence, I exist to preserve your legacy and your devout ideology for the Third Reich, and eventually, the World Reich.

"Mein Fuehrer, God forbid it is inconceivable that our enemies will gain the upper hand. If they do, it will not happen through my lack of focus, rather, our cowardly generals will let us down. Should they succeed, contingencies (attached in annexes) must be in place to protect you, and if you permit ... myself.

"Hess has delivered the necessary information and funds to allow us to depart Germany if events so decree. You must not die, Mein Fuehrer, and Annex 'A' contains complete details of your double, Herr Frausch's ultimate endowment to Germany.

"After your marriage in the bunker, when you enter your apartment, I will be present with Herr Frausch and Frau Linder. You will depart with Eva, and I will personally dispatch the two substitutes. When I leave through the tunnel and the exit is destroyed, their bodies will be discovered and instantly burned. Transportation has been arranged for the two of you to travel first to Spain aboard the U-boat Nauecilus, which will also pick up gold. You will then change u-boats and travel a chosen but undisclosed route to South America.

"Mein Fuehrer, I won't bore you with my plans for escaping, but be assured I will leave the Fatherland, because you will have announced that I am a traitor. The Allies will proclaim they captured me and I committed suicide. My route takes me through Canada, across the United States to Mexico and by ship to South America, then on to Paraguay. Brodisch, my primary double, that poor simple soul, will die for me because he believes his wife and eight children have been evacuated and set up for life.

"I pray to the God that guides and protects you, Mein Fuehrer, that none of this will be necessary, but it is my duty to keep you safe for the future of our race and a new systematized world. Your obedient servant, Heinrich Himmler. Heil Hitler..."

Harvey Cohen straightened up, staring at the astonished faces of the three men.

"As preposterous as it sounds, the two bastards never died," he said. "They got away with it, and their type is getting ready for the next round."

"What are we going to do about it?" Moshe asked, moving to the computer to read the Annexes.

"Moshe, make me twelve copies to mail out," Harvey said.

"Shouldn't we check with Israel first?" Moshe asked.

Harvey slowly shook his head. "No, I've lost faith in all politicians. Something's amiss here. I'm going to ask my government to demand the Allies release all so-called *delicate* wartime information that's been put on hold for another fifty, to one hundred years."

Joe understood Harvey's well-intentioned meaning, but he also knew the bureaucratic brick wall that would stop his friend. "They'll never release it, Harvey. Even the fact that you're asking for it could be dangerous."

"Did you fathom what I've just read to you? Harvey bellowed. "Those maniacal Nazi bastards bought their way out. Politicians in the United States, Britain, and Canada, have no right to withhold information of any sort. Such insolence is outrageous! Who the hell do they think they are? The truth has got to be told, and by God, I'll..."

Moshe interrupted Harvey's outburst. "This disk is even loaded with information on how to take over countries. Did you know eight million kids joined the Hitler youth? The remaining four million, who had originally declined, joined when their parents were threatened. The bastards were going to take their kids away. Hey, you missed a footnote, listen to this."

"To our District Administrators -- When our beloved Fuehrer, my Godfather, Adolf Hitler died, he did not know my father retained a copy of the Werwulfe Project (The Himmler Stratagem). Read it thoroughly, and learn the shrewdness you must acquire to achieve my father's great plans for our Aryan race.

"If Heinrich Himmler had not planned meticulously, our adored leader would have perished in the bunker, instead of living to plan and map the future of our world. As you all know, my father, Heinrich Himmler, recently died. Let me say to you, even in death he remains with us, and he has carved orders in stone for you to, plot and use The Himmler Stratagem as if the devil himself has hold of your balls.' Adolf Himmler."

"Christ, the two original bastards are dead and a son of Heinrich Himmler is alive and directing the show," Joe said, sitting up. The weasel even named his son, Adolf."

Harvey grinned guilefully. "Did he, now? Well, let's carve this bastard a tombstone. Simon, send a message to Israel. Advise them we're heading to Paraguay. All going well, we'll be back in a week."

Simon instantly took out his notebook and started writing.

Even in great pain, Stacy started getting out of bed. "Now you're talking. Before you carve the bastard's tombstone, let me carve him a new asshole. Moshe, grab my clothes from the closet, and I'll..."

To Joe's chagrin waves of pain proved too much for him, and he sank back on his bed.

Harvey shook his head. "You're not going with us, Joe. All we're going to do is eliminate the son of a bitch and his backers. Ninety percent of their U.S. operation has been closed, so there's not much more to do here."

Stacy couldn't hold back his disappointment. With all that he had been through, surely Harvey wouldn't take him out of the picture at this critical moment. "C'mon, Harv, be a sport. You can't just go without me?"

"But, Joe, how can I take you with us? It's impossible. You don't work for my government, and you can't travel in your condition. No, you just lay back and get well again. Leave this to us."

"Hey, I don't work for anyone; I'm dead and unemployed, remember? C'mon, Harv ... I'm gettin' better."

Joe's earnest appeal made Harvey grin, and the headman's expression transferred itself to three other faces. "Aren't you forgetting there's a farm waiting for you in Wyoming?"

"Yeah, and I'll buy a toothpick, a shovel and a tractor when I get back. C'mon, Harv. It's only for one job?"

Harvey sighed and gazed out the window for the longest moment. "Simon, change that communication. Tell Israel we'll be heading to Paraguay in a month."

Stacy rubbed his hands together. "That's my pal."

When Gail walked in moments later, she kissed Joe, saying, "Wow, do you ever look better. Have I been missing much?"

Placing his hands behind his head, Joe winked when Harvey repeated the question he had asked Gail a few days earlier. "Gail, how's your heart?"

As Gail Manning accepted the reality that Joe *Benjamin* had made up his mind to attend a *brief* meeting in South America, a conference of another kind progressed intimately well in an extremely fortified estate outside a small Paraguayan town.

With their *aides* standing behind them, two men sat comfortably in patio chairs next to a sparkling exterior swimming pool.

"Come, come, Gruppenfuehrer Schtaff, all isn't lost - you did your best. In this business, we have to embrace adversity and carry on. You'll like it here; I've assigned you our beloved Fuehrer's quarters. A good rest will rejuvenate you."

Gustaf Schtaff's despondent face followed his shaky right hand raising a snifter of brandy to his lips. After sipping and placing the glass down, he replied, "Thank you, Herr Himmler. Is there room for Sigmund?"

Adolf Himmler directed his eyes to the iron-faced bodyguard standing behind Schtaff. "Yes, yes, of course there is. Now tell me, Gustaf, what do you know about Senator John Lane?"

"The U.S. Secretary of Defence? Nothing, other than the president thinks highly of him. Why?"

Himmler studied Sigmund's firmly lined face before returning his attention to Schtaff. "President Aird has nominated Senator Lane for vice-president."

Schtaff nodded apathetically. "So, what's the significance?"

After picking up a tiny bell and ringing it, Himmler's arrogance took control of his conduct. "Gustaf, Senator Lane is one of us."

Schtaff's despondency vanished immediately, and he felt lost energy fortifying his body. "What?"

"Of course, Lane's appointment must be approved by the senate, but I see no difficulty there, "Himmler's stated, knowing his confidence intrigued Schtaff.

"Oh, how wonderful. Thank God, Adolf. Then all isn't lost after all?"

Guardedly, Himmler replied, "Did you really think it was?"

A male servant appeared wearing immaculately starched whites. "Yes, Herr Himmler?"

Himmler stood up stretching, and after lighting a cheroot, said, "Show Herr Schtaff to our Fuehrer's apartment and have his luggage taken there." Connecting his eyes with Schtaff's again, he added, "Go, and have a rest, Gustaf, my friend. We'll talk more about Senator Lane in the morning."

Schtaff almost vaulted to his feet. "Adolf, I'm proud of you. Each time we meet, you're more like your father. Come Sigmund."

"Uh, would you mind if Sigmund remains here for a few minutes to allow Jurgen to show him the layout of the estate? He shouldn't be long?"
Schtaff dutifully followed the servant. "Certainly. I'll see you in the morning, then. Thank you, Adolf."

Sitting again, Himmler replied, "It's wonderful having you here with us, Gustaf. Have a good sleep. You'll find the air works miracles."

After Schtaff had left, Himmler motioned Sigmund to come closer and to sit down. "Sigmund, in what year did you swear and sign the oath?"

"In 1966, Herr Himmler."

"What is your rank?"

"SS Hauptscharfuehrer, Herr Himmler."

"Hmm, most impressive. Have you been with Schtaff since then?"

"Constantly, Herr Himmler."

Adolf Himmler became tranquil as he waved his right hand towards the direction of Schtaff's suite. "Good, very good. Go and kill him. Now!"

Six weeks later aboard a cruise ship heading for Israel, the future Mr. and Mrs. Joe *Benjamin* stood holding hands at the stern on the promenade deck. With a billion stars glistening in the black liquid mirror below, the warm air softly jostled Gail's hair as she smiled and gently shook her head while looking at the sling holding up Joe's left arm.

"Joe, you've got more holes in you than a piece of Swiss cheese."

Stacy let go of Gail's left hand and placed his good arm around her waist.

"Yeah, and I'd have a few more if Himmler had not been such a rotten shot. Besides, I got him, didn't I? Although I'm wearing a sling, that bastard is with his dad at the centre of the earth wondering how he got the hole between his eyes and the hole in his throat. My shots saved Harvey's life."

When their eyes met, Gail sensed the excitement of the battle the previous week. "You've changed your mind. We're not going to be farmers, are we, Joe?" she whispered, already aware of his forthcoming response.

"Gail, honey, er … I know I promised you that I'd … er, we'd … but…"

Turning her body inward and continuing to wrap herself in his good arm, Gail enfolded her arms around his neck. "I don't care, Sweetheart, I really don't. I want what's best for you. I want what you really want. Besides, I think you'd make a rotten farmer."

"Why's that?" Joe asked, releasing her and tenderly moving some hair away from her eyes.

"You wouldn't have the patience for it," Gail said, shivering slightly.

"Hey, you're getting cold," he, said. "Let's go get your coat."

Gail kissed him lightly on his lips. "I'll go get it and yours too. Stay right here and keep that romantic mood till I come back. Do you hear me? Don't you move! I want to know you'll be in once piece when I get back. Also, be in the same spot. Have you got that, Joe Benjamin? The captain's marrying us in half-an-hour, and I want you in good shape … tonight."

"Yes, Ma'am," the husband-to-be replied, winking at her before turning his head toward the rolling shimmering molten mass of waves below.

The scent of Gail's clean skin and exquisite perfume remained with Stacy as he leaned slightly over the side watching the ship's wash spread then join together forming a single white thread of foam disappearing into the blackness of the night.

At exactly the same time a week before, twenty of Harvey's personnel and Joe had come together from all directions to attack and enter Adolf Himmler's bastion in Paraguay. The battle had not taken long and when it was over, four of Harvey's associates lay dead amidst thirty of Himmler's henchmen.

During the fray when Joe had entered a bedroom, Harvey was ten feet away and was the centre of attention in the middle of a snarling and maniacal Adolf Himmler's Luger sights. Cohen's pistol had jammed and the Israeli leader knew he was about to die. Himmler, however, instantly turned his attention to Joe and that action saved Harvey's life. The Nazi boss did manage to get two shots off that grazed Joe in his left upper arm and shoulder, but while falling, Stacy released two rounds creating a hole between the maniac's eyes and another at the centre of his neck.

Later as certain Israeli surgeons attended to Joe and some of Harvey's people, the complex was thoroughly searched and then set ablaze. Harvey's group had caught the fanatics by surprise, and the entire action had only taken one hour. The unbelievable shock that the stronghold was not secure and that superior forces had assaulted it had caused panic throughout the Nazi world.

Although a relaxed satisfying feeling crept over Joe, his training more than anything else made him spin around. Joe's peripheral vision had caught something out of the ordinary. He wasn't sure what it was, but he was certain it wasn't Gail. A fraction of a second later, a heavily breathing hulk of a man was almost on top of him.

As Joe instantly turned and ducked, his injured shoulder felt the full force of knuckle-dusters on a black gloved right hand originally meant for his head. The unbearable pain nearly made Stacy black out, and he became aware of Sigmund's same hard right grazing his jaw before joining his other hand and putting Stacy in a bear hug. Sigmund wasn't fighting like the amateur orderly Joe had *dispatched* at Kravenhall. Rather, the man knew his *trade* and there was no way Joe could manage with one hand. Even two hands would find it tough to stop the determined snarling and now frothing burly close-quartered fiend using every ounce of his energy trying to break Stacy's back.

Suddenly the look on Sigmund's face changed from determination to distress. He relaxed his hold while falling gradually to his knees. As he fell, his hands grasped at Joe's body forcing the wounded detective to grab the rail. Sigmund's hands continued clawing down Joe even grabbing the detective's pants and nearly pulling them down. Once in the kneeling position, Sigmund turned to try to reach behind and pull the knife out of his back before the full force of a steel-toed shoe welded his nose lips and teeth with his brain.

The fiery eyes of Moshe Goldberg revealed his loathing as he withdrew his stiletto from the dead bodyguard. Moments later, he wiped the blade off on the SS Hauptscharfuehrer's crisp brown suit before hauling him to his feet and pushing him over the side. "I hate polluting the water with garbage like this, but I think he's the last."

As Joe found his arm gently returned into the sling, his astonished look turned to admiration. "Moshe, what the hell are you doing here?"

"Harvey told me to watch over you," the Israeli agent said self assuredly. "And by the way, I'm two up on you now."

"Thanks pal. I owe you big time."

"You're welcome. Oh, and, er ... how does it feel?"

"How does what feel?" Joe asked, questioning the man's face. "That I owe you two lives?"

"No ... that you're now one of us."

Although he still looked puzzled, Joe's perceptive grin remained fixed, and now Moshe knew Stacy had not been told. "Harvey didn't tell you, did he?"

Immediately, Joe's eyes brightened and his grin widened. "No, and I think I'm going to like what he didn't pass on."

Shaking Joe's good hand, the Israeli said, "Well, Joe, your future's not going to go exactly the way you thought. Uh ... the news is probably better coming from me anyway. You know how Harvey is when he explains things - he includes too many details. Our *head office* has approved your job application, but you're only on loan until the U.S. government needs you."

"They know I'm alive?"

"Only certain trustworthy people. You're now a member of a newly formed intelligence team called the United States Special Services Group. President Aird has stated you can work with us until your country needs you again."

"President Aird?" You mean the president knew all along that I wasn't in that box?"

"He sure did, and he played his part brilliantly. Himmler's remaining criminals still think their people killed you." Moshe then mimed a prize-fighter's stance and took a mock punch at Joe before adding, "That's why you've got to stop getting hurt, Joe."

Joe Stacy liked the fellow standing next to him. Moshe was intelligent, physically fit, loyal, and although he had really seen the darker side, he still maintained a good sense of humour. Then Joe suddenly realized that Moshe wasn't alone in that department – Simon and the rest of Harvey's bunch were all unpretentious. They could roll in blood, but they still found time to have a little fun. Looking at Moshe's smiling eyes, Joe knew why. Many times, he had said the same thing to Pete, "There's humour in this job, Pete. We might have to search for it, but it's there, old buddy. It's the only wall between sanity and the funny farm."

"What's next on our agenda?" Joe asked, looking down and wondering if the sharks got indigestion after eating his attacker.

"In three weeks we'll be heading on a small mission to Russia and Turkey. Joe, something is bothering me."

"What?"

"How did Sigmund know you were on this ship?"

"Sigmund?"

"Yeah, we had him on our list and had photos of him. Information we found in Paraguay said he was Gustaf Schtaff's bodyguard and man servant. Who did you tell you were going to Israel?'

"Absolutely no one, not even Pete."

Now deep in thought, Moshe said, "I thought we got them all, but obviously, we didn't. Someone else is now running the show. Could it be the real top man? I wonder who he is. I'll discuss that with Harvey. Anyway, welcome aboard, and ... oh, oh, I hear female footsteps. Must go. I'm to be incognito on this trip."

The Israeli agent had gone by the time Joe asked, "Can't Gail even know you're here?"

When Gail appeared, she feigned surprise. "What? I must be seeing things. Joe Sta... er, Benjamin, you're still here? A helicopter hasn't swooped down and taken you away, or you're not wearing any additional holes. Wonderful, but I bet you miss the excitement. It's too quiet on this trip, isn't it, darling? Here, let me help you with your coat. Are you ready to say, I do?"

"You bet I am, Babe. Can I say it a hundred times?"

"Sure, I think I'll do the same, and ... Joe, how did your hair get so messed? I can't leave you alone for a minute, can I? Hand me your comb and I'll..."

Moments later as the happy couple walked towards the bridge, the ship's loudspeakers jumped to life. "London calling. This is the BBC Overseas Service. The president of Paraguay has revealed only local Paraguayan forces were involved in attacking and burning a rebel stronghold last week in the Salende District. All the rebels were killed and their cache of arms was destroyed. A United Nations unit is presently sorting through the burned remains.

"In the United States, long time senator, and presidential hopeful, John Lane has been arrested for sedition. Full details are not available but it is now known Senator Lane had strong ties to Nazi groups planning the takeover of that country. Four-hundred-and-seventy-two high profiled United States citizens have also been arrested and thousands more are being hunted down for interrogation.

"Prime Minister Norman Aitken flew to Washington today to confer with President Aird about organized world fascism. The Israelis presented both governments with documents revealing extensive white supremacist activities taking place throughout the world, and Israel is demanding it be allowed to review wartime documents recently classified for another fifty to one-hundred-and-fifty years. Israel's prime minister has made it quite clear if the leading wartime powers are not forthcoming with this information, the State of Israel will release its own testimony forcing the media in democratic countries to form conclusions so damaging, many wartime politicians and world religious leaders could be considered criminals.

"In other world news, The Washington Post has hinted it has received new information about why Germany's Wartime Deputy Fuehrer, Walter Richard Rudolf Hess flew to Britain in May 1941. The newspaper stated it was given a leaked war document alleging certain Western politicians were bought off, allowing thousands of senior Nazis to escape from Germany. The paper also suggests Adolf Hitler and Heinrich Himmler were amongst those thousands.

"A rather odd statement was released today by leaders of thirty-seven member countries of the United Nations. These nations have joined stating world unrest has forced them to begin initiating Plan-Z. Further details are not available at this time. It is known, however, upon hearing the news concerning Plan-Z, President Aird and Prime Minister Aitken made immediate plans to attend an emergency meeting of the Big Eight to be held in Switzerland.

"In sports, Liverpool beat Everton two nil, and…"

Rain has a way of calming anxiety. On a wet Washington, DC afternoon, President Aird and his chief of staff, Hilroy Watkins, appeared fresh in the quiet of the oval office. This had not been the norm. Lately, both men, with the new vice-president, and those forming the president's cabinet had been hard at work calming the American public while keeping in constant touch with world leaders and their appointees.

When the president finished reading a letter, he placed it down, stood, and stared out the centre window. "We cannot afford to let our guard down again, Hilroy. That was close. Very close."

Watkins crossed his left leg over his right knee. Taking off his glasses and rubbing his eyes, he nodded slightly. "Have you given any thought to the Israeli situation?"

"No, not yet. One thing at a time, Hilroy, one thing at a time. Damn! Damn! Damn!"

For some reason Watkins also stood. He knew the president well, and when Aird turned, his intense eyes became fixed on his chief of staff.

Sitting again, the president said, "I'll get to that after I return from Switzerland. You won't have to remind me. How could something like this have happened? It is almost impossible that one man could have brought this to the attention of a sleeping world. Yet he did … he did."

President Aird's eyes became determined and cruel as they remained set on Watkins. "Hilroy, wir können nicht mehr warten. Raten Sie unseren *Freunden*, dass wir bereit sind, und dass Gott ist mit uns. Ausfall ist verboten." ("Hilroy, we can wait no longer. Advise our *friends* that we are ready, and that God is with us. Failure is forbidden.")

Watkins remained standing, and his body stiffened. Loudly, the heels of his highly polished German Salamander shoes smashed together. "Ja, Mein Fuehrer." (Yes, my Leader.)

When he stood again, the president's face became emotionless. Placing his knuckles on his large mahogany desk and leaning over it, he said, "Also, Hilroy, I want you to take care of this criminal, Joe Stacy, and what's left of his Seattle crew. Do it at the same time as you eliminate the Israeli Set. No excuses - Get on with it."

"This time there will be no excuses, my Leader."

OTHER BOOKS BY CORDELL CROSS SOON TO BE AVAILABLE AT
AMAZON.

MANIAC
STAND BY YOUR BEDS!
FORM THREE RANKS ON THE ROAD!
NEXT STOP, VERNON!
RUBBER GEARS NEXT YEAR!
WHERE THE WIND HIDES
RAIN ON MY TONGUE
THE STOPOVER

www.ingramcontent.com/pod-product-compliance
Lightning Source LLC
Chambersburg PA
CBHW071204020726
47502CB00002B/530